UTTERLY

PAULINE MANDERS

Pauline Manders
2017 +

Cover design Rebecca Moss Guyver.

ISBN – 13: 978-1977999962
ISBN – 10: 1977999964

Also by Pauline Manders

Utterly Explosive (2012)

Utterly Fuelled (2013)

Utterly Rafted (2013)

Utterly Reclaimed (2014)

Utterly Knotted (2015)

Utterly Crushed (2016)

To Paul, Fiona, Alastair, Karen, Andrew, Katie and Mathew.

PAULINE MANDERS

Pauline Manders was born in London and trained as a doctor at University College Hospital, London. Having gained her surgical qualifications, she moved with her husband and young family to East Anglia, where she worked in the NHS as an ENT Consultant Surgeon for over 25 years. She used her maiden name throughout her medical career and retired from medicine in 2010.

Retirement has given her time to write crime fiction, become an active member of a local carpentry group, and share her husband's interest in classic cars. She lives deep in the Suffolk countryside.

ACKNOWLEDGMENTS

My thanks to: Beth Wood for her positive advice, support and encouragement; Pat McHugh, my mentor and hardworking editor with a keen sense of humour, mastery of atmosphere and grasp of characters; Rebecca Moss Guyver for her boundless enthusiasm and inspired cover artwork and design; David Withnall for his proof reading skills; John Mischell, Woodland Trust volunteer warden; Tas Ormes, Woodland Trust volunteer; Malcolm Johnson, the inspiration behind the Golf Challenge Trophy repair; Barry Squirrel for his knowledge relating to grain storage and dust clouds; Sue Southey for her cheerful reassurances and advice; the Write Now Bury writers' group for their support; and my husband and family, on both sides of the English Channel & the Atlantic, for their love and support.

CHAPTER 1

'No-o-o!' Chrissie felt the edge of the wardrobe slipping from her hold.

'Whoa, careful now,' Ron Clegg muttered.

She caught the pain in his face as the weight skewed. He moved to steady the wardrobe, but she didn't have enough strength to stop her end gathering momentum. Her grip failed. The polished wood slid away. She crouched as it began to plunge, taking the heavy wood onto her knee.

'Ouch,' she yelped.

The mirrored wardrobe door flipped open.

Boom! The glass splintered. She watched helpless, her hands and knee pinned by the wardrobe as shards flew through the air. Like a spear, one slit the huge wood dust extractor bag supported in its large open wheeled frame. Others shattered on the concrete workshop floor, skittering in all directions.

'Oh no,' she cried as glass scythed around her feet. The wardrobe began to roll off her knee.

'What are you doing?' Ron shouted.

'I can't hold....'

It landed with a *whump*, squashing the edge of the extractor bag, barely thirty centimetres away.

Half a hundredweight of wood dust burst through the gash in the plastic and launched into the air, propelled by the force of the Edwardian satinwood wardrobe coming to rest.

A cloud erupted in front of her, thicker than the densest fog. Millions of tiny particles - the powdered pulverised waste from the band and table saws, router, and

1

sanders threatened to blind and choke. Instinctively she stepped back, her hand to her mouth.

'Mr Clegg? Ron, are you OK?'

Sharply aromatic wood dust caught at her nose. Her eyes watered. She couldn't see him, couldn't hear him. What had she done? She dodged sideways and ran, giving a wide berth to the spreading cloud.

A few more strides and only the workshop door stood between her and clean air.

'Arrgh!' She collided with someone's chest, her face side-on to a breastbone, her shoulder into ribs. 'Ron?' she coughed.

'What the–'

She didn't recognise the man's voice. Where the hell had he come from? Shocked and winded, she focussed on the partly open door. 'We must get out of here. Quick,' she said, driving the stranger before her, hustling him out of the workshop and into the rough courtyard.

'I'm so sorry,' she panted a moment later, drawing in lungfuls of cold November air, 'Are you a customer? Are you OK?' She didn't look at him, her eyes were too busy searching the old doorway, now wide open. The dark weatherboarding might give an impression of indestructibility to the old workshop, but Ron was no youngster. She was pretty certain he wouldn't stand a chance if....

The stranger beside her coughed. 'Yes, I'm all right. What happened in there?'

'What? Sorry, I was looking,' her voice trailed as she dragged her mind back to the man. 'You must have walked in just as the waste bag for the wood dust burst.' Further explanation died on her tongue as a familiar figure appeared around the side of the barn.

'Mr Clegg!' she yelled, as he limped towards them, 'How...? Where...? Are you OK? You disappeared. I couldn't see you.'

'I'm fine, Mrs Jax. I tripped the circuit breaker, and left through the fire exit. That way we get a bit of this wind blowing through.'

'Yes of course, disperse the dust.'

'I didn't know you had a problem with wood dust,' the stranger said. 'Must be a bit awkward if you're a carpenter.'

Chrissie frowned and turned to study the man's face. Had he missed the whole point of what could have just happened? She took in the large nose and heavy brow. It was strangely at odds with his small jaw. Quite distinctive.

'Good morning. You must be James Mawbray,' Ron said, and then to Chrissie, 'James's father and I were at school together. Probably getting on for... almost forty-five years ago.'

'Yes, you said last week when I rang. It was my dad who suggested I ask you to repair the panels in the back of my oak settle. I think I told you I'd be passing this way and I'd drop it in.'

'Ah, right,' Chrissie murmured. 'Well hi, James. I'm Chrissie Jax, Ron's new partner in the firm. I would shake hands, but it seems a bit formal after I've already head butted and manhandled you.'

She watched him smile as Ron said, 'Wood dust is flammable, James.'

'Yes,' she said under her breath, 'we had a lot of it in the air, possibly enough to reach an explosive threshold–'

'Mrs Jax and I were worried because the dust was so dense, like a very thick fog.'

'I'd guess at least 30 grams per cubic metre,' Chrissie added, more to herself than Ron or James.

'That sounds pretty technical,' James muttered.

Professional jargon and a confident air usually impressed. She'd learnt that from her past career as an accountant, especially when delivering unwelcome information. Hopefully this customer would be reassured if she showed her technical knowhow.

'Given the right conditions,' she pressed on, 'a spark, or even static could have ignited the whole thing and there'd have been one hell of a fiery ball of burning wood dust. Quite something, when you consider our workshop is in a wooden barn.' She reckoned she didn't need to spell out the rest of the scenario.

'The circuit breaker, yes I get it now. You didn't want to set fire to the dust. I thought you were worried it might bring on... I don't know, an asthma attack.'

'That as well,' Chrissie murmured.

'Well, James,' Ron said quietly, 'while we're waiting for the dust to clear, let's have a look at your settle. Is it in the Defender over there?' He inclined his head towards a black Land Rover with a metal cab on the back. It was parked next to a green van with *Clegg & Jax. Master Cabinet Makers and Furniture Restorers* printed along a yellow stripe.

Chrissie hung back and let Ron lead the way across the courtyard. He set an unhurried pace, his limp now barely noticeable.

'I didn't see Mrs Jax's name on the notice when I drove in,' she heard James say, as he walked beside Ron. The swagger was obvious.

Her pulse throbbed in her head. Why had she felt the need to embellish the process in a dust explosion? Why use phrases like *one hell of a*, and *great fiery ball*?

A gust of wind cooled her face and swirled around the courtyard. It'll be an easterly picking up from the Suffolk coast, she thought as she stood her ground and let it buffet her body. She counted to five while it pounded the old barn and funnelled past a brick outhouse.

Why, she wondered was she so quick to reach her own dust cloud explosive point? She never used to be so easily riled. Even Clive, her boyfriend of a couple of years, had recently remarked on her growing tetchiness. Moreover, now she came to think about it, the term boyfriend seemed inappropriate and irritating when she pictured him, a detective inspector in his mid-forties. And while on the subject she, virtually on the brink of her mid-forties, didn't particularly relish the label *girlfriend* - although she'd have bitten the head off anyone daring to suggest she was too old for the term. Damn, here she was, working herself into a lather just because she'd got irritated again.

No, she decided, it was best if she left James Mawbray to Ron. She was far too prickly at the moment.

She ran her fingers through her short blonde hair, releasing dust and catching the scent of mahogany, cedar and pine. She turned to focus on the open barn door. The last blast of wind should have cleared the dust cloud, she reckoned.

'Safe to go in,' she muttered and hugged her work sweater tighter around her ribs.

As she walked back to the barn, a rumble separated from the squall of the wind around her and filled the sky above. Instinctively she looked up. A helicopter flew overhead, circuiting from the neighbouring Wattisham Airfield. The noise of the rotary engine and sight of its angular shape jogged her mood.

'Mindfulness,' she murmured, not quite sure if seeing the Apache helicopter fitted the bill for the latest buzzword in coping. 'Or is it more a case of anger management?' Either way it was time to get on with the job of clearing up the dust.

•

Chrissie felt the tension melt away as she drove home. What a day, she thought. It wasn't so much the act of leaving work that made her relax; it was hearing the throaty burble of the Triumph TR7's 2 litre engine. She watched the beam from her headlights cut into the gathering dusk. Gloom encroached from the hedges and verges while the thirty-year old instruments glimmered from the dashboard. This part of mid Suffolk was pretty flat, but it didn't mean the lanes ran straight. They twisted and turned like lazily wrestling eels, following ancient paths, field boundaries, ditches and streams. She kept to the back routes, cutting from the workshop near the Wattisham Airfield and avoiding Stowmarket as she threaded to Woolpit.

By the time she drew up outside her Suffolk brick, end-of-terrace cottage, darkness had well and truly fallen, and her equilibrium had re-established. She switched off the engine and briefly thought back over her day. Now she was able to see that the satinwood wardrobe had been saved by the wood dust bag; the owner had been undecided if she wanted the mirror glass on the doors replaced, but the decision had instantly been made for her; James Mawbray had brought a wonderful 18th century oak settle to be repaired; and the workshop had needed a bit of a spring clean anyway.

'Hmm,' she sighed, remembering the half full bottle of Sauvignon in her fridge, 'Of course a glass of wine could further boost the positive spin.'

The cold air chilled, as she got out of the car and slung her soft leather bag over her shoulder. Just the movement launched more mahogany, cedar and pine. The quiet lane was ill lit, shrouded in shadows. Gripping her keys, she hurried to her front door. It swung open, the lock catch not fully engaged.

She hesitated. Had she been the last to leave that morning? She remembered locking the door, but was it this morning's memory or a vague one, a more general recollection of a repeated act?

She stood on the threshold, reluctant to step inside. She peered into the darkness, straining to see the outlines of her narrow hallway. She recognised the indistinct form of the stairs leading upwards, ahead the shape of a small table against one wall. Beyond, she made out the doorway into the living room, less inky than the surrounding blackness.

'Hi, are you home already?' she called.

She waited, listening for the slightest sound. Were her eyes playing tricks? She detected the hint of a light. It seeped from the living room. It must be coming from the cramped kitchen beyond.

'Clive?'

A shape materialised from the blackness. It rushed at her from the living room doorway.

Wham! It collided with her. Solid. Real. Human.

'Arrgh!' She spun sideways. Her bag flew from her shoulder. She grabbed at the darkness, tried to break her fall. The intruder powered on. She pitched over backwards. Her bottom hit the ground outside the front door, her legs sprawled into the air. The intruder blundered across her, caught a foot and stumbled. Something shot at her, clipped her leg and landed in a bed of late flowering chrysanthemums close to her knee.

He was gone.

'Shit!' she screamed, her voice arcing into the empty night.

•

She sat in her living room, tense, not ready to relax into her sofa. The SOC team had only just left and she reckoned it would take days before the last traces of fingerprint dusting powders disappeared from her coffee table, door frames and kitchen counters. She'd sat and watched while the team took photos, lifted prints, shone LED devices with coloured filters, took more photographs and bagged and removed items. Clive's laptop had been the obvious focus for their attention. He'd left it on the coffee table, so neat and tidy the intruder must have spotted it. The police found it outside where it had landed amongst the chrysanthemums.

'They've pulled out all the stops for you,' she murmured, glancing down and allowing her eyes to be distracted as she followed the geometric designs of burgundies, midnight blues and beige in the rug at her feet. 'I'm sure most house break-ins don't get this kind of attention.'

She nearly added something on the lines - if the police couldn't look after one of their own, who could they look after? And Detective Inspector Clive Merry was definitely one of their own. But even so, all this attention seemed rather excessive.

'Are you sure it was a man?' Clive asked.

'Well no, I just assumed... I mean, he was so solid... and definitely taller than me.'

She waited for Clive to nod, but he didn't. She read the echo of her flawed reasoning in his raised eyebrow. She was forced to picture herself – five foot two, slight build.

'Yes, I see what you mean. Most people are taller than me and....' Her words died as the moment of impact replayed in her mind.

'Now come on Chrissie, try to concentrate,' Clive said quietly beside her. 'One last time - what makes you say it was a man? Did the intruder shout or swear as he tripped over you? Did you notice anything? Footwear, size of feet? There must be something.'

'No, and he didn't have MAN printed on his forehead either. It was dark, Clive. Someone rushed at me, knocked me over. I was too busy landing on the ground to notice much else. I've already told you, I just assumed it was a man.'

'OK, let's leave it.' The weariness in his voice was unmistakable.

'Anyway, what's it matter? You're never going to catch whoever it was. Be realistic.'

'Maybe not, but that's why I called the SOC team in. I've improved the odds.'

'Let's hope so. But at least they didn't get away with your laptop.'

'No, but I'm pretty sure that's exactly what they were after.'

'How can you say that? Now you're the one making assumptions. If mine hadn't been under the heap of dried washing on the kitchen table, it could've been mine as well. They probably wanted easy-to-carry electrical stuff.'

Clive shook his head. 'There's something I haven't told you. I didn't want to worry you, didn't think you needed to know.'

Oh God, she thought. Now what? The bastard took some of my clean washing? Was he a pervert?

'Is there a trail of my bras and panties?' she whispered, her skin feeling creepy.

'What? Are you OK, Chrissie?'

'No... yes, I'm.... Look, I haven't had a proper look around yet. I was scared to go inside by myself and when I rang, you said to wait in the TR7, remember? And then you lot arrived.' She pictured the SOC team, how they'd taken over.

'It's OK.' Clive leaned closer and gave her a hug. She nuzzled into his neck.

'Have you been rolling in pine, or something?' he murmured.

'What? Oh God, the wardrobe.'

'Chrissie?'

'Just a near-disaster at work. We dropped a wardrobe on the wood dust extractor bag. Wood dust everywhere. Enough said. But what were you going to tell me?'

She caught the flash of something in his eyes. Was he phrasing bad news? She braced herself.

'Why didn't you say before about dropping the wardrobe? If you'd mentioned it while the SOC team were here....' He sounded peevish.

She felt irritated. 'But why, Clive?'

'Your sweater. I reckon there'll be wood dust on the intruder. Remember he ran into you? It could be important. Better bag your sweater. I'll hand it in tomorrow.'

'Now this is getting ridiculous,' she muttered, exasperation taking over.

'Please, Chrissie. It's serious. I'm being targeted by someone. I've had threatening emails. And now this. It's too much of a coincidence.'

'Threatening emails?'

This felt altogether more menacing than a thief with a pantie fetish. 'But why didn't you tell me before? Didn't you think I'd want to know?'

'You haven't been exactly yourself these last few weeks. I thought it could wait.'

His words took a moment to sink in. 'So that explains it,' she whispered, struggling with her thoughts. 'But why? And why your laptop?' Reasons floated up from the depths, 'Of course, work related… but it's encrypted isn't it?'

Brrring! Brrring! The ringtone cut through her living room, urgent, demanding.

'Sorry, Chrissie. I have to take this.'

Her mind was numb as he stood up and walked into the kitchen, his mobile to his ear.

CHAPTER 2

'What do you mean Clive is being targeted?' Nick asked, studying Chrissie's face. 'Don't you think you could be reading too much into the break-in?'

They had been friends for several years, right from the moment he joined the Utterly Academy carpentry course in Stowmarket. She was the only female and oldest student on the programme; he was a bruised drop-out from an environmental science degree in Exeter. He'd reckoned she was roughly twice his age when they'd first met, more of an older sister than a dating opportunity. He'd grown used to her conversation darting all over the place when someone or something really upset her, but today he was having trouble following.

'No... before you answer, slow down and make it simple. No better still, let me get in a round. I need another beer, how about you?'

He watched her shake her head. 'Are you sure?'

Now she seemed lost for words.

He made his way to the bar, glad of a moment to make sense of what she was saying.

She'd phoned earlier. He guessed she was in her car, about to drive home from work. He'd been shocked when she told him about the break-in. 'I don't want to get home before Clive,' she'd explained, and it hadn't been difficult to hear the undercurrent in her voice.

He'd held back on the obvious *but you're saying it was a couple of evenings ago, how long were you going to keep it a secret,* response and suggested they meet in the Nags Head. He reckoned he'd rather keep her company in the pub than sit in her cottage waiting for Clive to arrive home. He'd never felt entirely at ease with Clive.

'The same again?' the barman asked, eyeing Nick's empty glass. 'We're coming to the end of the barrel.'

'Yeah, another pint of Land Girl, please.' He waited, the sound of early evening drinkers washing over him.

His gaze drifted along the old floorboards, idly taking in the grubby trainers and jeaned legs of the drinkers standing near the bar. He'd nodded when Chrissie said something about it being impossible to tell if someone was a bloke by looking at their footwear. But Clive had a point. It was pretty obvious which feet belonged to the men, at least in the bar. But then that was Chrissie for you, strong willed and stubborn... and it had been dark when she was burgled. He reckoned she hadn't noticed as much detail as she thought Clive expected her to and didn't want to admit it.

'Thanks,' Nick said as the barman set the brimming glass on the counter. He fumbled in his pocket, and dug out a fistful of loose change. A coin escaped through his fingers and fell to the floor. He cursed under his breath and bobbed down to retrieve it from the beer-stained boards. Shit, he thought, as it rolled past a scruffy pair of trainers now almost at eye level. Maybe Chrissie was right. The size of footwear was a matter of perspective when viewed from the floor.

'You took your time,' Chrissie said when he finally set his beer on the scrubbed pine table and sat down opposite her.

'The barman had to change the barrels.' He caught her questioning look. 'No I waited. I've stuck with Land Girl,' and as if to confirm his choice, he sipped the pale golden ale and let the hoppy citrus flavour embrace him.

'So why did you say the Nags Head, Nick? We could've waited in the White Hart. Now you're renting in Woolpit, it's handy for you too.'

'Come on, Chrissie. The White Hart's your local. If you're seen drinking there, it's obvious you're not at home. If anyone from the village is watching, it's like wearing a notice saying *my house is empty. It's safe for you to break-in.* Anyway, I prefer the Nags Head, it's my regular.' He swept his arm back to encompass the low ceilinged room with its oak beams, tired décor, and beery feel. The fire might be unlit in the old grate, the jukebox silent for the moment, and the flat screen temporarily lifeless by the bar, but the dartboard was already open and in use. Give it another hour and the place would liven up.

'I hadn't thought I might be being watched.' She sipped her ginger beer.

'Well it's a possibility. Now come on, you were saying about Clive. Did he actually tell you he was being targeted, or is it just another one of your hunches?'

'Well, he started to say, and then he got a call from work and clammed up. He'd already let slip something about getting threatening emails. That's why the SOC team came.'

'So it must be pretty serious. Do you reckon it's someone with a grudge? Or a stalker?'

She didn't answer.

'Well I can't believe anyone was out to attack him. I mean the bastard ran away when you disturbed him. You said Clive thinks they were after his laptop. So what the hell's on it?'

'How'd I know? I don't go looking through his stuff.' She appeared to study her glass. 'But if they wanted his laptop, they dropped it. So–'

'You reckon they'll be back.'

He didn't wait for her to nod or say yes. It was clear from her face what she was thinking. He gulped back another mouthful of beer and listened to the pattern of voices ebbing and flowing through the bar. Someone struck a double-sixteen on the dartboard. A throaty *Yes!* A punch in the air.

'Look,' he started. But there was no point in him stating the obvious. Clive was bound to tighten up the security in her cottage and the police were in the best position to track down whoever was sending the emails. Really there was nothing for him to do other than keep her company. Be a shoulder to cry on, distract her.

'Hey, how's this for something a bit different?' he said, opting for the distraction angle. 'I'm doing some work for a golf club. They want another oak board to hang. Running out of space for winners' and captains' names, I guess.'

'What?'

It was obvious she wasn't listening. The distraction line wasn't working. He waited.

'Why did you say it could be a stalker? Is that what you think?' she murmured.

'Ah....' He groped for an answer. 'I didn't mean it had to be a stalker. I was just making suggestions, trying to think of reasons why you'd target someone.'

'Well Clive's a policeman. That'll be a reason.'

'Yes, but that doesn't mean he'll be automatically targeted. There'll be something he's done... as a policeman. Someone he's upset. Something specific.'

'Or not done,' she added.

'Look, we can't possibly–'

'But if it's a stalker... well, I'd notice wouldn't I? They'll go on stalking.'

'But I thought this was about someone stalking Clive. Unless you're with him, how would you notice?' Nick bit his lip. He couldn't see how any of this was going to help. 'Next you'll start thinking everyone in Woolpit's a stalker. Leave it to Clive and the police, Chrissie. It's their job.'

She swigged back the last of her ginger beer and banged her glass down. For a moment they both stared at it, a defiant symbol on the beer ringed table. Across the bar a dart clattered against the dartboard and slammed onto the floorboards.

'Now come on, Chrissie. Don't get–'

'I'm not going to spend my life creeping around, looking over my shoulder. And I'm certainly not going to be ruled by when Clive comes back from work.'

'So?'

She looked at her watch. 'Time to go home.'

He drained his glass. 'Aren't you going to at least ring Clive? Check he's home?'

'No.'

'But?'

'I'm going to drive home. You could follow me and wait outside while I check inside's OK. If it is, I'll text you and you can go. Does that sound good?'

'Sounds like I'm suddenly the stalker.'

•

Nick slept badly. Uneasy and restless, Chrissie's words refused to fade. All their talk of break-ins and stalkers had got to him. It had wormed through his semi-sleeping state, turning over facts, assumptions and generalisations, then heaping up fear and menace. What if someone really had been watching Chrissie's end-terraced cottage? They would have seen him draw up in his Ford Fiesta behind her. He'd tried not to look obvious. But sitting in his car, seemingly studying his mobile and then just driving away? He must have drawn attention.

It was a relief when his morning phone alarm finally burst into life. He threw off his twisted duvet. The small room he rented above a double garage felt cold and damp. There was no point in peering through the narrow end window. It would be another thirty minutes before the sun rose. He hurried into the tiny shower. The water ran icy cold, catching his arm as he reached under the shower head to set the controls.

'Arrgh!' He sucked in his breath, waited a moment and stepped under the stream, now a few more degrees off freezing. He let the water drizzle over him, chilling, then warming as the heater came up to speed. It seemed to both refresh and draw a line between Chrissie's news of the break-in and the start of a new day.

He didn't even bother with a mug of tea. Action, he thought. Get going, throw myself into the day. Distraction might not work for Chrissie, but it certainly works for me.

The drive from Woolpit to Needham Market didn't take him long. At that hour even the A14 was clear. Dawn seeped through the mist-laden air as he turned into the Willows & Son entrance. He drew up alongside the secure parking reserved for the Willows vans, and pulling his bomber jacket close around him, hurried to the workshop side door in the single-storey industrial unit.

He caught the sound of a train powering along the nearby Norwich to London line, disembodied and hidden beyond the buildings and grey morning light. It'll be ten to eight, he thought, turned the handle and slipped into the restroom which doubled as an office.

'Mornin'.,' the elderly foreman grunted. He stood studying a spreadsheet laid out on a table which served as a desk. 'If you get the wood measured and ordered for the Rush Green Golf Club this mornin', then you'll be free to give Dave a hand over in Hadleigh. Might as well make use of you between jobs.'

'I thought the work at Serpells was going well, Mr Walsh,' Nick murmured, his eyes on the kettle near the stainless steel sink. 'Tea?'

'Yes, if you're making, Nick.'

He knew better than to press Mr Walsh for an update on the built-in bookcases at Serpells. He'd find out soon enough, and besides, he liked working with Dave. He reckoned his onetime trainer would let him get on with the job, and if there was any talking, Dave could be relied upon to keep up a running commentary. There'd be no awkward questions.

Feeling more edgy than jaded from his troubled sleep, Nick busied himself with making mugs of tea. He was hardly aware of the background smell of stale sweat and wood dust, or the worn armchair, filing cabinets and plastic stacker chairs crowding the restroom. They were too familiar. He barely even registered the *good mornin's* as the other carpenters arrived. Instead he gulped down his tea, scooped a van key from one of the hooks by the door, and headed into the secure parking area.

A moment later he'd loaded his toolbox into a Willows van, and set off for the golf club. He took the most direct route, following the narrow roads past acres of flatly rolling fields, misty green with the young shoots of winter wheat and barley.

The Rush Green Golf Course lay to the northwest of Stowmarket and the village of Onehouse, close to the A14. The road forked and narrowed, skimming along one edge of the course. Nick glanced at the fairways as he drove, half expecting to see first-light golfers already striding out, but his view was broken by a small copse stretching beside the road. Most of the trees had dropped their leaves, but a few oaks still held on, draped in dying greens and browns while stark branches stretched above the rough.

Something moved at the side of the road.

'What the—'

A woman dashed in front of the van.

'Shit!' He slammed on his brakes.

'Stop!' she shrieked, a hand in the air. She tugged at a bedraggled terrier and flapped her free arm. The dog strained against her, pulling towards the verge and trees.

'Please help!' she wailed, 'Please, Freddie's found something.'

He wound down his window. 'Are you OK? What's happened?'

'Thank God I saw your van. We're miles from the clubhouse. There's... someone's collapsed. I don't carry a....'

Was it a trap? Stalking escalating into abduction? He tried to think, but everything was happening too fast. Surely no one could fake the horror behind those eyes, or the way Freddie pulled and scrabbled against his lead. He guessed middle-aged and read panic; took in her faded anorak, woolly hat and muddy boots. No threat. He flicked on his hazard lights and jumped down from the van.

'What's happened? Are you all right?'

'It's not me. It's Freddie. He's a terrier. You can't stop him, he'll find anything. Now he's found someone. Back along there. This way.' She turned as if expecting him to follow.

'Where? Has someone had an accident?' Nick half leapt onto the rough grassy verge. His work trainers sank into damp rotting leaves and dieback nettles. He picked his way after her.

She didn't turn her head, just raced after the terrier, her voice now excited, stronger. 'It's this way. And I don't know about any accident. It's... I think he's dead. Freddie's found a dead body.'

'A dead body? Are you sure?' he called after her.

'Yes, I think so. I had to drag Freddie away. Hey, don't pull!'

She stopped, and restrained the terrier. Nick caught up with her, not sure of anything. He glanced from Freddie to her excited face.

'Shouldn't we call for help?'

By now trees surrounded them, but were far enough apart to see through to the fairway forty yards ahead.

'Yes, but I haven't got a phone. That's why I waved you down. It's... he's over there.'

Nick looked in the direction she pointed. His stomach lurched.

'OK, OK, but we're wasting time.' He pulled his mobile from his pocket.

'Don't you want to see for yourself?'

'Why? If you're sure of what you've seen, you phone.' He held out his mobile. 'I'll tap in the number, you do the speaking. OK?'

'Right, but you hold Freddie.'

It wasn't an equal swap. Freddie had more strength than Nick expected. The terrier caught him by surprise and darted sideways. Nick pulled back on the lead but staggered off balance. A few wild strides and he saw the body. Nothing too dramatic, just a man sprawled on his back.

'No Freddie!' he yelled, but the scent of blood lured the terrier's nose. 'No!' Nick yanked on the lead as the dog scrabbled towards the man's head.

He tried not to look, turning and pulling Freddie as he stumbled away. But in that first instant he'd seen tar-like blood matting the hair. Dried burgundy rivulets streaked the forehead, the colour strangely stark against the ashen skin. The man was dead all right. There was no mistaking the utter stillness.

'Yes.... Yes that's right. I think he's.... No. He's not breathing.' The woman's voice cut through the cold air.

'Yeah, he's a goner all right,' Nick muttered, so alone in his own bubble he'd forgotten she was using his mobile.

'Freddie.... No, I don't know the man's name. Freddie's my dog. I've just said I was walking my dog.... I've already told you I cut though onto the footpath along the edge of the course.... Yes I....'

His fuddled mind finally clicked into operation. She wasn't talking to him. Her words were meant for the mobile. He stopped listening and sank into his own world,

21

drawn by the image of death. How old, he wondered. Not a young face, but then he'd only really taken in the blood. Wrinkles, care lines, creases? He hadn't noticed any. Had they been smoothed away, relaxed by death? But he'd seen hair on the bloodied head. Real hair, not a shaved scalp. Did that make him young or old? He didn't know.

'Hey, here. Thanks.' The woman jabbed at his arm, breaking into his thoughts and holding out his mobile. 'I'll take Freddie now.'

'Oh, right.' He dragged himself back to the moment, 'Are they coming?'

'Yes, but they said to wait in the road, and then to lead them to the body.'

'OK, so there's no point in hanging around here. Better get back to the van.' Cold was already striking through the soles of his trainers and catching him around his neck.

She hesitated.

'We'll freeze to death. Come on, it's warmer in the van.' He nearly added something about not wanting to mess up the ground, compromising any investigation if they hung around near the body. It was obvious the man hadn't died a natural death.

He led the way. With each step, he tried to distance himself from the horror, determined to ground himself in the day ahead. But determination wasn't always the surest way of driving out an image.

CHAPTER 3

Matt stared at the caller ID. Nick? A call was unusual. Nick normally sent text messages. The last time he'd phoned was to try and sell him a spare ticket to the Aldeburgh Docfest. At first Matt hadn't known what he was talking about. 'Docfest?' If he'd read the word in a text he might have worked out it was a contraction of *documentary festival*. The documentary film festival held annually in Aldeburgh.

'You mean you bought a couple of tickets to impress some bird? What kinda girls you chasing, mate?'

Further probing revealed the girl had stood him up and the documentary in question was *When China Met Africa*. Now if it had been a full length action cartoon on the lines of Demon of the Potteries meets African Spear (superhero), he might have been tempted, but as it was....

Beep-itty-beep! Beep-itty-beep beep! The insistent ringtone pulled him back to the here and now. Time to take the call. He'd made Nick wait long enough.

'Hi, Nick. If it's about that film fest thing, I still aint interested. I told you last week. Right?'

'What? Oh that, yeah well it seemed a pity to waste a ticket. But I'm not calling about that.'

'OK, so?'

'Where are you? Are you able to talk?'

'Course I can talk. I'm talkin' now, aint I?'

'Oh for God's sake Matt, don't be so literal. I meant, are you free to talk.'

'Right.' Matt swallowed the hurt. Nick was a good mate, so why the sharpness? It had to mean he was still annoyed about the Docfest ticket.

'Yeah, sure.' He glanced at the gothic beams spanning the ceiling above. 'I'm in the library. Just me on the computer and,' he cast around, 'hardly anyone's still here. You know what it's like at the Academy by four o'clock, Thursdays.'

He was about to ask if Nick was still annoyed, but thought better of it. 'So what you wanta say?' he muttered, keeping his voice low.

'I've… it's been a bad day. What time do you finish?'

Matt let his eyes drift across the computer monitor in front of him. 'I were just readin' through me *Computer Security and Forensics* course. Why?'

'If you're not at a tutorial or anything, can you just leave the reading bit? Go through it another day?'

'Yeah I s'pose so. But why, what's goin' on?'

'I saw a dead man this morning. I can't get it out of my mind.' Nick's voice faded.

'Phishin' hell! Are you sure, mate? You didn't step on him, or anythin'?'

'God, Matt, you don't half say some weird things.'

'Yeah, but who was this dead guy? And where'd you see him?'

'I don't know his name. I was OK while I was at work, but now, well I don't want to go to the pub. I've got to work tomorrow. Do you want to come round? And bring some beer with you? I could do with some company.'

'Yeah, OK. I knew somethin' were up when you phoned.'

'How?'

'Nothin'. See you in about forty minutes. OK?'

A surge of curiosity engulfed Matt, tinged with feeling just a little stupid. What had he just read on one of the densely worded screen pages? In Computer Security *unusual or unexpected behaviour* was a warning sign, an indication of virus or malware attack. Sure, in computer speak, this might mean a computer's processes unexpectedly trying to make contact with the internet to upload the entire contents of its hard drive. But this had been a mate phoning when usually he texted.

So he'd been right. It had meant something, but he'd got the wrong reason. Not a ticket to a weighty documentary but a dead body. Cool.

Fired with a mix of excitement and dread, he logged onto the Eastern Anglia Daily Tribune site. He reckoned if the discovery of a local dead body hit the news, then the *breaking news* feed would appear in the regional press before the nationals.

'DOS,' he muttered scanning his screen, 'Nothin', just warnin's of *gusty wind* an' *patchy moderate rain across the county.*'

Another headline caught his eye. *Radio Fault at Landmark House in Ipswich.* He read on, impatient to see if it said what he expected. It seemed news had finally surfaced about Suffolk Police having problems with their radio system signal being *variable on the ground floor of the building.* 'Yeah, I bet them *engineers are working on the problem* alright,' he murmured, part reading aloud. But of course he already knew about the glitch. Chrissie had told him weeks ago. It felt good to be one step ahead of the news.

He logged out and shut down.

For a moment his thoughts drifted. If it hadn't been for that fateful carpentry course at Utterly Academy, he'd never have made friends like Chrissie and Nick. That had been several years ago, before he'd discovered his passion for computing and IT. Now the Academy had become his second home and carpentry was just a bad memory.

Old wooden floorboards stretched beneath his feet. Around him bookcases, computer stations, and students had left their footprint - the scent of humanity, paper, dust, and printer ink. It was time to shake off the day's security blanket.

He slipped his mobile into his pocket and slung his backpack over one shoulder. Imitating what he'd seen others do, he let his faded denim jacket hang open, just enough to show the writing across his sweatshirt. COMPUTER SMART. He liked the way the letters were a little haphazard in size and setting. He figured rugged. Anyone reading the words would be automatically drawn closer, and focus above his belly.

'Bye,' he called to Rosie, a favourite library assistant busy loading a paper-feed drawer.

She raised her hand in a half wave and turned her attention back to the photocopier.

Disappointed with Rosie's muted reaction, he shouldered his way out through the library door. A few moments later he slumped down the main staircase and headed for the student car park.

Outside, the gusty wind worried his denim and chilled his hands. With no one else around to impress, he zipped his jacket and unlocked his scooter, the colour of hound dog brown and rapidly blending into the fading light. The Piaggio fired into life, its two-stroke engine whining like a stinging insect as he weaved along the back roads from Stowmarket to Woolpit.

Twenty minutes later, Matt stomped up the outside wooden steps leading to Nick's room above a double garage. Strictly speaking, Nick was the lodger, but being separate from the main house somehow made it feel state-of-the-art, exciting. Already, lights shone through neighbouring windows too early to be hidden by curtains and blinds, only the darkness and moisture-heavy air offered privacy.

'Hi!' Nick's voice sounded outside and above him.

'DOS-in' hell. What you doin' standing up there?' Matt called to staging at the top of the stairs. But his visor muffled his voice and baffled his words.

'Shit, Matt, that helmet makes you look like some kinda ghoul rising from the mist. Aren't you gonna take it off?'

'Yeah... yeah,' he said with each laboured step, his visor now completely steamed up. He held four cans of lager up high, the plastic packaging looped over one finger, like a peace offering. 'A pack of four. I stopped off at Lidl.'

'Then enter, Suffolk Serpent!'

'Are you takin' the piss or somethin'?' Matt pulled off his helmet and stared at Nick. The moods and tones were changing too fast for him to follow. And he didn't recall a comic-strip hero with that name either. A sudden thought struck. 'You've started drinkin' without me.'

'Only a half. Why?'

'Right.' He followed Nick inside. The room was long, squeezed under the garage eaves. A sloping ceiling gave an illusion of height, but there was barely space for more than a bed, dartboard, sink, microwave and instant water heater. The shower was hidden out of sight behind a plastic curtain.

He cut to the chase. 'So tell me, this dead body was today, yeah?'

Nick didn't speak.

'An' the ticket for this Docfest bird? She got a name then?'

Again, Nick didn't answer.

The unease flipped to irritation. 'Look mate, I've ridden all the way out here. You've dragged me from me *Computer Security and Forensics*. You gotta tell me somethin' otherwise I'm off back to Stowmarket. It's a trade-off.'

OK, I'm sorry. It's just I....'

'Yeah, but you can tell me. Maisie said telling me stuff aint like telling most people. I think she meant it's a bit like what you said before. That thing about bein' literal. Ah right, you're smilin' now.'

Matt threw himself down on the bed and propped himself awkwardly against the sloping ceiling. Maisie was his longest running girlfriend; everyone knew, but even so he reckoned mentioning her name counted as trading information, and judging by Nick's smile, he'd got the exchange right.

'Come on Nick. I checked the local news sites before I left. There aint nothin' yet.'

'Really? Nothing? Well maybe it's not going to be anything too nasty, only something like a heart attack or stroke. It's just that I can't face being pulled in for questioning, asked to leave my trainers to eliminate footprints and make a statement - all that kind of thing. But if there's nothing on the news, then maybe....'

'So what happened? Tell me.'

While Nick talked, Matt listened. For once he didn't ask questions or interrupt. Instead he pulled the tab from one of the cans of lager, drank, wiped stray droplets from his scrappy beard and settled back. When Nick finally ran out of words, he let the silence cloak him.

'So aren't you going to say something?' Nick sounded irritated.

'I were thinkin', mate. If the bloke were lyin' on his back with blood across his forehead, he must've walked into somethin'. A low-lying branch. You said it were all trees and stuff where you found him.' He tossed back another mouthful of lager. 'Golf balls. That's the other thing, bein' so close to the course. A golf ball could've done for him.'

'So you think an accident?'

'Yeah, and that terrier woman, well if they've got her statement, why'd they need one from you? I reckon you won't hear any more, mate. You're in the clear.'

'God, I hope you're right.'

'Bet I am. Now, forget the dead bloke and the Docfest. Winter sizzlers - Sausagefests – that's the future, mate.' He shifted his back against the slope of the ceiling. 'Do Jake and Adam bring their guitars here? I mean there aint much room.'

'You mean the band? Nah, there's been a bit of a shake-up. Jake wants to bring in a keyboard. It's up to him, it's his band.'

'A bird?'

'On keyboards? Don't think so. Denton doesn't sound like a girl's name to me.'

The rest of the evening blurred as Matt swigged back cans of lager while Nick sang gloomy riffs. Hungry, they ventured out on foot past ivy and wisteria-clad houses to the centre of Woolpit village, a handkerchief sized cobbled area surrounded by the meeting of three quiet roads. They stumbled towards a porched doorway set on an old brick building painted white and with sash windows, and bought fish and chips. In the near-distance spotlights bathed the church spire.

When Matt woke, it was pitch black. 'Where the?'

Somewhere across the darkness Nick swore at a phone alarm.

'Phishin' hell,' Matt muttered, as memory returned and hard floor pressed against his shoulder. He turned onto his back, his eyes accommodating as he made out the glow of a digital display. 'Microwave?' he murmured, solving the puzzle. He must have crashed out on Nick's floor.

'Sorry, mate, I've got to get up for work.' Nick's voice sounded dry, hoarse.

Something the consistency of a foot stepped on Matt's arm, jabbed against his chest and stumbled away. Sudden light penetrated his eyelids.

'Arrgh,' he groaned and rolled onto his front, one shoulder now tight against the leg of the bed. Then he drifted.

'Hey, Matt! When you leave, make sure you shut the door properly on the catch, OK?'

A shoe prodded his back. Nick's words distanced. The light died.

When Matt next opened his eyes, grey daylight bathed the room. Someone hammered on the door, a key turned in the lock. He moved his head and harsh carpet weave rubbed against his skin.

'DOS-in' hell. Now what?' he groaned.

'Hello? Nick? Anyone here?'

He closed his eyes, held his breath and hoped the familiar voice would go away.

'Matt! It is Matt, isn't it?'

'Yeah, mornin'... Sarah. It is Sarah, aint it?' he said, wary but following her lead.

Sarah was the owner. A friend of Chrissie's from the village. He knew she was the one who'd offered the spare room over her double garage to help Nick out; hardly a professional landlady, but still rather daunting. He'd only met her a few times and cautiously lifted his head and waited for her to either go or say something.

'I-I didn't expect you, I thought Nick had a girl staying over.' Her face reddened. 'Nice to see you again, by the way.'

'Yeah, you too.' He tried to click his brain into gear. Reading nuances wasn't his forte but he sensed another agenda.

'Nick's already left for work if you're wantin' to talk to him,' he mumbled through a yawn.

'Yes, I noticed his car had gone but I forgot you had a scooter. I thought, well you know what I thought.'

'One of his birds? Do he bring many birds back here, cos he don't say?' Matt asked, remembering the unused Docfest ticket, and noticing for the first time that she'd brought clean towels with her.

'I try not to pry but....'

I try not to pry but.... A sudden thought struck Matt. Sarah could be implying something worse. He had a reputation to protect, he was a hot blooded male and she was a landlady-bird with eyeliner and a cool haircut.

'It aint how you think, Sarah. Nick found a dead body yesterday an' he were right upset. We had a few beers and I stopped over. Well I weren't goin' to drive with a skinful.'

'A dead body? Where?'

'You'll have to ask him.'

'I will. No wonder Nick was upset.'

He watched her face, struggled to decipher her reactions and made a decision. 'Yeah, he's right cut up, but don't let on I said.'

'Poor Nick.' She turned to go. 'It's time you got up, Matt. And don't forget to leave the room tidy, OK?'

'You leavin' them towels for me?'

'What these? I only brought them because…. It's OK, I'll pop back with them for Nick, another time.'

Did she just wink at me, Matt wondered. DOS-ing hell. Some birds were weird.

•

He must have fallen asleep again, because the next time he opened his eyes the daylight was stronger. It played off the patch of threadbare carpet near his head. His mouth felt dry and his stomach empty. It was time to get up, and off Nick's floor.

'DOS-in' hell,' he groaned as he checked the time on his phone.

Now Matt was running late and the rest of his day felt like catch-up. There was no time to go home for a change of clothes. Instead he rode directly back to Stowmarket and the Academy for a tutorial on software engineering. Then, with barely time to grab a couple of sausage rolls, he set off to Bury St Edmunds for his late Friday afternoon part-time job at Balcon & Mora, an internet people tracing agency.

A freezing wind channelled around his legs as he hurriedly pushed his scooter onto its parking stand in an alley behind Bury's Buttermarket shopping area. Above him, a stucco-clad building leaned on its ancient wooden frame. He banged his hands together to get the circulation going and tramped up the narrow staircase to an office on the first floor.

The room was dominated by a table desk with hard drives stacked in the trestle legs. Damon Mora sat on a shabby faux leather office chair, his back to the wall, his tawny eyes scanning the computer monitor screen.

'Hi,' Damon murmured, glancing up.

Matt pushed the door closed with a backward jab of his foot and eased his helmet off. 'It's DOS-in' bitter out there,' he muttered by way of a greeting.

'Well what d'you expect for November?'

'Yeah, s'pose so. Hey, you'll never guess,' he said, unable to contain himself, 'a mate of mine found a body yesterday.'

'Really? Where?'

'The Rush Green Golf Course.'

'Well let's see if there's anything.' He turned his attention back to his computer. 'I'm trying out a programme, well more of an app linking news websites. Saves keying each one in and... John Camm!'

'Who's John Camm?'

'Unless I'm mistaken, your Rush Green stiff. Here, come and see for yourself.'

Matt sucked in his breath and squeezed behind Damon's desk. *A man was discovered by a dog walker early yesterday morning*, he read.

'Look, I'll send the link to your computer, it'll be easier,' Damon said, shifting in his chair and indicating a monitor on a narrow table against the opposite wall. 'Has your mate got a dog?' he added.

'I reckon that'll be the terrier lady.'

It didn't take Matt long to unzip his jacket, slump into a plastic chair and log onto the computer facing the wall. He'd got used to working with his back to Damon. It had felt a bit creepy at first, but not as unsettling as knowing every keystroke was being scrutinised. Damon had said it was something to do with security and trust, the business they were in, but Matt reckoned his twenty-eight year old boss didn't want him nicking the clients.

'OK, computer's on. You can send the link,' Matt said without looking back at Damon.

Most of the midday press releases were two-liners, but the Eastern Anglia Daily Tribune site had more. It seemed John Camm wasn't a member of the golf club, but was known to be an early morning walker, apparently often spotted along the footpath skimming the edge of the eleventh tee. 'It don't say why he died,' Matt mumbled, more to himself than Damon.

'Just the usual *waiting for the results of the post mortem* stuff. Yes, and the police are appealing for information from *anybody who saw him or anyone else on the footpath early on Thursday November 15th*. That's yesterday,' Damon said quietly.

'Yeah, and he were a *sixty-six year old man* and *lived near Onehouse. The Northfield Wood area.*'

'Hardly earth-shattering stuff. Now come on, we've wasted enough time. I've a list of names for you to trace for the debt collectors. It's time to get hunting before they become… bodies. I'm sending the names to you now.'

'Bodies?' Matt swung around and stared at Damon. He caught the smile 'You aint bein' serious?'

'No, only joking. Hey, what's that across your front?' He nodded towards Matt's chest.

'What's what?' He followed Damon's gaze and smoothed his sweatshirt over his belly. 'COMPUTER SMART. Why?'

'Not what I'm reading from here.'

Matt looked down and saw the lines of a red indelible marker scoring through the S and M like a spidery T.

'Oh yeah, that'll be…,' memories surfaced, 'a mate. He reckoned I ditch the S and M. He said COMPUTER ART were more stylish, more now.' Matt nearly added something about documentary films. They'd been part of the discussion.

'ART? From here it's a T, Matt. COMPUTER TART. May not be so cool, hmm?'

'Tart?' and then under his breath, 'Nick! Just wait till…. Bloggin' hell, it's tomato sauce. Trojan,' he muttered as he remembered the fish and chips.

CHAPTER 4

Chrissie flipped her laptop closed. It wasn't that she had anything especially personal on her screen, it was just that she'd been surfing the net, finding out more about stalkers. The *who*, *why*, and *how* behind stalking. In itself, her search had been pretty innocent, but it was still a touchy subject with Clive. He clammed up whenever she mentioned it and changed the subject if she persisted. It was a Saturday morning and she wanted to keep things light, and if she was going to have a show-down then she'd prefer to choose her moment.

'Bye, Chrissie. I'm off now,' he said leaning over the narrow kitchen table and kissing her briefly on the lips. He wore his charcoal grey anorak loosely open, the clean lines of his shirt visible at the neck. She couldn't help noticing how the darker tones in his auburn hair were more obvious close-to.

'Oh OK. Will you be long?'

'I don't know. It's the man the walkers found on the Rush Green Golf Course in the rough, Thursday morning. Stickley's just phoned to say the post mortem is through. A few surprises. Thought I'd go in and get a head start.'

Why say walkers, she wondered. He could have said the lady walking her dog and Nick, Nick Cowley, your carpentry friend, the one whose name crops up far too often.

'Your duty weekends seem to come round faster and faster,' she said mildly, while the unspoken simmered, 'Will you be going to Landmark House?'

'Yes. I'll call and let you know if it looks like I'll be late getting back, OK? At least my phone will work from there.' He smiled the smile of the cynical quip, a one-liner for those in the know.

For a moment she felt included in his inner circle again, party to insider information, trusted. And then both the moment and he had gone, the front door swinging closed on the latch and silence filling her small cottage.

'Bye,' she murmured.

She understood confidentiality, knew to keep a secret. It had never proved a problem in the past. Hearing about his cases had always strengthened the bond between them, and she loved it when he felt he could be free with the snippets - never too much, but enough. She wasn't sure she cared for this tighter-lipped detective inspector. What was he hiding from her?

Driven by suspicion and feeling excluded, she opened her laptop and resumed her netsurf. When Clive had said something about threatening emails he'd used the term targeted. It was Nick who'd mentioned stalking, and the article she was reading implied it started as an attraction, commonly unreciprocated, then became controlling, obsessive, and eventually destructive.

Descriptions of: *the rejected*; *the resentful*; *the intimacy-seeking*; *the socially backward*; and finally *the predator* typified the range of stalker profiles, and needless to say, the majority of perpetrators were men.

A headline leapt from her screen. *Digital Stalking Leaves Behind Digital Trail.*

Clive had mentioned the threatening emails. And her reading told her at least 25% of stalking victims reported cyber-stalking. A chilling thought gripped her. Was it conceivable the cyber-stalker was a woman? It would be unusual but not impossible. What may have started as an attraction could have moved on to the controlling, threatening stage. It might explain the threatening emails. And if that was the case, did this theoretical woman set out to steal Clive's laptop as a source of intimacy and control?

Worse still, did the break-in mean the stalker had already progressed to a dangerous and destructive stage? Chrissie would be seen as a love rival. Was her own life at risk?

Everything changed in Chrissie's mind. Anger replaced the hurt and resentment planted by Clive's refusal to talk. She was no longer an incidental, someone on the sidelines who had just happened to disturb a criminal with a grudge against the police.

'How dare he?' she whispered under her breath. If she was to become a target, then she had a right to know. Clive wasn't protecting her by keeping things from her; on the contrary, he was putting her at risk. It was her right to look out for herself.

Now with right and justification on her side, she set about searching for any mention of Clive and past cases reported on the news sites. She reckoned a female stalker might have started from one of his cases. After all, wasn't that how she'd first met him, when he'd interviewed her as a witness a couple of years back?

•

'This is hopeless,' Chrissie groaned an hour later.

She was wasting her Saturday. Her searches were leading nowhere. It was like trying to catch minnows with a colander. The internet search engine parameters were either too broad or too narrow, and there were bucket loads of parish magazines and local monthlies filled with community news to trawl, as well as the regional newspapers. Typing each one into the search box was mind-blowingly tedious. Her neck ached. She needed help - someone who revelled in this kind of thing.

'Matt,' she murmured.

He was the obvious choice, and as long as he stopped short of hacking into Clive's emails, the information she wanted was already out there in the public domain. Clive couldn't complain, nor could he accuse her of acting on privileged information. She, after all, was the one who had disturbed the break-in.

CHAPTER 5

Nick touched the varnished wood lightly.

'Is it dry?' the foreman asked, his weathered face creased in doubt.

'Yes it should be, it's had all Sunday,' Nick said, standing back to admire his work. It was Monday morning and they were in the Willows & Son workshop, the roller shutter doors at one end partially open and an icy breeze biting his ankles.

'Then you'd better get a van reversed up and this loaded, before we all catch our deaths in here.'

'Yeah, sure, Mr Walsh.'

'Rush Green will be impressed you've got it finished so quick.'

'Well Frosticks had the oak veneer multi-ply in stock. I think you were here when they delivered on Friday, and after that it didn't take long to make the oak frame for it. Luckily our mitre saw is an impressive bit of kit.'

'Hmm, you've made mitred corner halving joints, I see. Nice work, Nick.'

'Thanks. But it always seems to be the gluing, finishing and varnishing that takes me the time.'

He rather liked the way the frame was flush with the board, not immediately obvious but at the same time creating a finished edge. He wasn't going to admit it to Mr Walsh but he was pleased with the way it had turned out.

Nick pushed the roller shutter doors upwards and stepped through to the small delivery and loading area outside. He'd been happy to come in on Saturday and make up for time lost because of his disrupted Thursday with its dead body and police. It gave him less empty weekend to brood, and there was an added bonus - noise from the router and sander drowned out any morbid thoughts.

Saturday had been ideal to get on with finishing and varnishing. Few people were around by late afternoon, and there was virtually no dust in the workshop air to settle on the varnish. By chance he'd met Mr Willows senior as he was about to leave, and with a nod and a wink, he'd been given permission to pop in on Sunday to sand back and apply a second coat of varnish.

As Mr Willows had said, 'We wouldn't want the painted letters to be crinkled by the underlying grain in the wood, now would we? When you look up at a board, you can confuse the names if the varnish isn't layered to a smooth finish under the paint.'

So with Mr Willows' endorsement still ringing in his ears, Nick had dropped into the workshop for a couple of hours on Sunday. He figured the quicker he finished the *Winners & Captains* board, then the sooner he'd be free of the golf club and the recent nightmare. He also sensed it was best not to tell the foreman about Sunday. He reckoned he'd probably broken at least half a dozen health and safety rules by working there alone, and he preferred Alfred Walsh to think of him as speedy rather than a reckless rule breaker.

It didn't take Nick long to reverse a Willows van to the open doorway, and by the time he jumped down from the driving seat Alfred had partly draped the board in protective dustsheets.

'This is pretty heavy, Nick. Will you be OK unloadin' it by yourself?'

'Yeah, I reckon so. And if I prop it on the sack carrier....'

'No, no. It's a metre by a metre and a half. It'll tilt and catch on the ground. You'll damage the edge. This veneered multi-ply is heavy stuff. Here, I'll give you a hand.'

Together they lifted the board into the van. By the time Nick strapped it upright against a frame fitted to one side, Alfred had got into the passenger seat. He was like an old goat, Nick thought to himself.

'So are you coming with me to the golf club, Mr Walsh?'

'Yes. I haven't been out Rush Green way in a while and I reckon you'll need a hand with this. Two birds. One stone. Now get a move on, I can only spare an hour.'

Nick felt slightly uncomfortable with the foreman beside him. John Willows was the real boss, but the foreman held enormous sway. It didn't do to upset him.

He drove in silence, a small knot tightening in his stomach as he headed northwest of Stowmarket and out through the village of Onehouse, with its nineteen-seventies houses and ancient woodland, Northfield Wood, dark in the distance. When he reached the fork in the road he kept to the right, tracking north and eventually following the edge of the golf course. Instinctively he slowed as he passed the tyre marks and churned verge where police cars and vans had pulled off the road, but there was no sign of the vehicles now. If it wasn't for the rutted earth no one would have guessed a drama had taken place there. He half expected a terrier to leap into the road, an anoraked walker to.... He forced himself to keep his eyes fixed ahead.

'Not much further now,' he murmured as the road led north towards the A14 and the Rush Green Golf Club entrance.

There was a large gravelled parking area near the clubhouse, and Nick reversed the Willows van into a space close enough to make unloading as easy as possible. If he had been with Dave, his onetime trainer, they would have remarked on the close-cut grass of the nearby eighteenth green, and admired the Suffolk clay bricks and architect designed sweeping roof as they walked into the modern building. However he was with Alfred Walsh and Alfred was economical with words, could only spare an hour, and was effectively his boss.

He busied himself with unstrapping the board while Alfred headed into the clubhouse to talk to whoever was in charge. Nick mentally slipped back into senior apprentice mode. He found it easier that way when they carried the *Winners & Captains* board through the lobby and into a corridor-like room. They lifted it to the correct height alongside an existing board, and balanced it on the adjustable telescopic ladder he'd fetched from the van, and fixed it to the wall.

'Good job!' a man's voice boomed from the lobby, 'Thought I'd wait until you'd finished before I asked. As you've made such a terrific job of this, would you be interested in repairing our Northfield Challenge Trophy?'

Nick turned to see a middle-aged man with thinning hair, smiling and gazing up at the board.

'Why thanks. Did you say repair–'

'Good morning. Alfred Walsh, Willows & Son,' the foreman cut across Nick, before stepping forwards and shaking the man's hand.

'Hello. I'm Paul, Club Secretary. Now it's a wooden trophy board I'm talking about. I wouldn't expect you to repair a silver cup or anything like that.'

'Repair a trophy?' Alfred murmured.

'Well, it's an old hickory golf club with...,' the man hesitated, 'it's difficult to describe. You'd have to see it to understand.'

'I'm sorry but it really doesn't sound the kind of thing Willows do. We're more structural joinery and carpentry than artefact restorers.'

'No problem. I just thought I'd ask. Mind you, I've not heard a golf club described as an artefact before. The captain will be amused when I tell him.' The secretary smiled pleasantly as if the conversation was over.

'You...,' Nick glanced at Alfred before directing his words at the secretary, 'you could try Clegg & Jax. It sounds right up their street. They're cabinet makers and furniture restorers. Their workshop is over Wattisham way.'

'Clegg & Jax, you say? Right, thank you for that.'

The drive back to the Willows workshop seemed less stressful than the outward journey. It was only as they joined the fork in the road beyond the golf course that Nick realised he'd driven past the rutted verge without registering any anxiety or flashbacks. In fact he'd barely noticed the chewed grass and mud. Could he have put his demons to rest, he wondered.

'Do you think the Northfield Challenge Trophy has anything to do with Northfield Wood?' he asked, his thoughts unhampered and relaxed as they drove through Onehouse.

'I wouldn't rightly know,' Alfred murmured, 'but I reckon it was an old coppice and standards woodland for

44

growin' oak and ash. But hickory? Now that aint right for Suffolk.'

'We should've asked about the man found dead near the 11th fairway, while we were up at the clubhouse,' Nick said, emboldened by his restored equilibrium.

'Funny you should mention him, but I'm sure they're sayin' he comes from somewhere near Northfield Wood.'

'Yeah, well I s'pose he was bound to come from somewhere round these parts. You'd think he'd have stuck to walking in the wood. Funny old world,' Nick said, thinking it was anything but funny. 'Do you want me to go over to Hadleigh and give Dave a hand with the built-in bookcases?'

'Might as well. You didn't get to spend much time there on Thursday, if I remember right.'

CHAPTER 6

The Piaggio two-stroke engine chortled gently as Matt coasted to a stop.

'Come on, Mais. Where are you?' he muttered, as he sat on his scooter.

The old market place in the centre of Stowmarket was quiet, even for Monday lunchtime. Had it been a Thursday or Saturday, the streets would have been alive with market stalls. Instead the only inhabitants Matt could see were a handful of semi-tame mallards, their feathers ruffled and lifting in the cold wind. They'd hunkered down near a deserted bench.

Matt, now stationary, put one foot on the ground and steadied the scooter while he sat and waited. He'd arranged to meet Maisie at precisely ten minutes past one. 'Me mornin' shift finishes at one,' she'd said, and he reckoned ten minutes was plenty of time for her to walk the fifty yards from Pipits to the market place. Pipits was a clothes shop with retro appeal and Maisie worked there part time.

He spotted a figure in skinny jeans and padded jacket hurrying towards him from the direction of the old post office building. He pushed up his visor and waved.

'Hiya, Mais. Over here,' he yelled, his voice reverberating against the old stone faced banks and building societies, their premises styled to impress a previous century. A sudden icy blast bowled a discarded water bottle across an empty pavement. It scuttled and clattered towards the mallards.

'I could hardly miss you. There aint no other scooters around,' she said before planting a poorly aimed kiss under his open visor. The wind caught her blonde straggle-effect hair and a pink highlight whipped across his eye.

'Arrgh, Mais,' he muttered as he blinked away the wisp.

'Thanks for givin' me a lift. Hey, you aint forgotten we're off to Bury again this Sunday.' She climbed up behind him on the scooter.

'Sunday?'

'Yeah, the Bury Christmas Fayre.'

'But it's still November, Mais,'

'Yeah but this Sunday, it's like... it's the last weekend before December.' She play-pinched him. He felt the tweak through his denim jacket and sweatshirt.

'Ouch, Mais.'

He flipped his visor down, twisted the accelerator and slowly took off through the centre of Stowmarket. They headed for the Finborough Road and the back route to Bury St Edmunds.

He felt the warmth against his back as she snuggled close, her arms around his waist. It was nice but distracting.

Of course he'd known he'd have to leave the Academy during his lunch hour. He was due to ride to Bury for his Monday afternoon session working at Balcon & Mora. However Maisie's request for a lift meant leaving sooner. His routine had been disrupted and he'd barely had time to grab a bacon butty to munch.

Before he'd logged out of his computer and set off to fetch Maisie, he'd been delving into coursework – explaining the maths behind calculating the ease with which a password could be broken. It meant taking into account the variables of length, along with the mix of numerals, letters and symbols in the password. The fun part was illustrating the work with examples and this was where his thoughts returned now.

'You OK?' he felt the familiar prod in his ribs.

He lifted his hand in a thumbs up sign and pictured the letters in the word *baconbutties*. Yeah, he reckoned, as a password that would be twelve letters, and if all lower case, only take about seven minutes for password-crunching software to crack. So it had taken seven minutes to munch, seven minutes to crunch. Next time he saw Ley he'd run *baconbutties* past him, see if he laughed, see if the wordplay worked as a joke. Leyland, or Ley as he preferred to be called, was another student on the same course.

Feeling more cheerful, he turned his mind to a more pressing conundrum. Chrissie's request for a trawl through Clive's cases. He'd have to ask Damon if he could use some of the firm's apps.

'Hey, we turn here, Matt!' Maisie shrieked.

'What?' He saw road stretching ahead, a junction to the right and now almost behind him.

'Turn here!'

'Oh pixel,' he yelped.

His mind flicked back to scootering mode. He braked. The two-stroke engine spluttered, he regained his bearings.

'Flamin' malware,' he muttered and retraced the yards to their missed turning. Now with his mind solely on the journey, they rode northwest, along roads between flatly rolling fields and clumps of woodland, all trunks and branches, the deciduous leaves already taken by late autumn and the wind.

They rode into Bury St Edmunds, breezed around a busy traffic junction and threaded toward its old heart, the ancient buildings clustering near the cathedral. He couldn't help but see the notices everywhere, warnings of *The Christmas Fayre* and *road closures 23 – 25 Nov. 2012.*

He did the maths. 'Phishin' pixel! The 23rd is this Friday,' he muttered under his helmet.

'You'll 'ave to speak up. I can't hear a word you sayin',' Maisie screeched behind him.

He felt the dig in his ribs and took it as a signal to slow. He dropped her off close to the Arc shopping centre and weaved back to the Buttermarket and the Balcon & Mora office.

'Hi, Matt,' Damon said when he released the catch on the office door for him five minutes later.

'Scamin' hell. There's notices everywhere. The Fayre starts Friday,' Matt moaned, dispensing with the niceties. He stood for a moment and soaked in the blanket of warm office air and the faint ambient whirring, as fans cooled hard drives and motherboards.

'Close the door, will you. I guess if the Fayre's anything like last year, you may have to park further away and walk.'

'Walk?' He turned his back on Damon and flicked the kettle switch. The idea was a nonstarter. 'Can I have a hot chocolate?'

'Yeah, OK. And while you're about it, another coffee for me, thanks.'

'Right.' With his query about the Fayre out of the way, Chrissie's search hijacked his next thought. 'How'd you like the news app you were tryin' last time?'

'It's good. Why?'

'I were wonderin' if I could use it.'

'Oh yeah? Why are you asking before you've seen your first batch of today's names?'

'Cos....' Matt didn't want to lie. He knew he didn't do it well, but he didn't want to say about Chrissie's search request either. Something held him back.

He shrugged. He hoped it was a Gallic shrug, something he'd seen in a comic-strip. The Mighty Cayenne takes on La Grande Pomme.

'And what's that supposed to mean?'

'Nothin'.'

'Let me guess. You've got some project, a commission or something. I'll find out soon enough, so you might as well tell me. Otherwise you can turn around and walk. You're here on Balcon & Mora time, remember?'

Matt felt his face burn. He tried to swallow, but his mouth was too dry and there was nothing to swallow. He certainly wasn't going to try another Gallic shrug.

'Balcon & Mora time? I aint paid by the hour. It's on results, right?' His words came with conviction. It was how it worked. He had to correct Damon.

'Ah – so this is what it's all about. You think if you bring in work for the business you should get paid more than £3 a name.'

'What?'

'Don't think I don't know what you're after. You want to go it alone, break away and start your own business.'

'No, Damon. Honest. I told you before, I don't do billin' and stuff. I just like searchin' and sometimes I get asked to look into things. That's all.'

'Oh yeah?'

'Yeah, Damon. And you don't know Chrissie. When she asks you to look into somethin' it's–'

'Chrissie? Your carpentry friend from Utterly Academy? Now you come to mention her, I've exchanged emails with Chrissie. She lives with that detective, doesn't she?'

'You mean Clive.'

'That's the guy. DI Clive Merry. I've spoken to him a couple of times in the past. He seems OK. Searches sometimes throw up weird stuff and... well it pays to stay on the right side of the law.'

'Has Chrissie said somethin' about the stalking, then? Did she call you as well?'

Damon didn't answer. Matt felt confused. Was his boss testing him? Had Chrissie called both of them, or was Damon just talking history - emails sent months ago when she had a problem on a selling-site?

He had to know.

'Hey Damon, why aint you tellin'?'

'I work on a need-to-know basis. And so should you.' His tone changed. 'I need to know I can trust you and that you aren't skimming my business. If you're using my computers, my apps, my office, then the customer is Balcon & Mora's and there's a charge to the customer. Only I decide if we waive it. Nothing goes on behind my back; nothing goes on without my say-so. Got it?'

'Got it. But it don't, Damon.'

'Good. Have we had this conversation before?'

'Yeah, but–'

'Here's the extra bit. If you bring in new customers, they become Balcon & Mora customers. I bill them and you get a percentage... say 20%.'

'Yeah, but if I'm doin' a mate a favour, then....'

'You don't have to take your percentage. I'll drop it from the overall charge.'

'So can I use the news app?'

'For Chrissie's search? Yes, but get through today's list of names first, OK?'

'OK.' He spooned a further measure of chocolate powder into his mug. 'Brain food,' he muttered as he caught Damon's questioning look, but inside he glowed. A percentage on new customers? It was like... well like being taken on as an associate.

'Thanks, Damon.'

Damon didn't answer, just shrugged. Was that the Gallic shrug, he wondered.

This time when he slumped onto the plastic stacker chair and settled at the computer facing the wall he wasn't just the hired hand, he was a percentage player. When he logged on and opened his first list of names, it felt like a warm-up, the muscle-stretching other people did before serious exercise. He figured it wouldn't take him long. The names to trace for the debt collectors weren't usually professional fraudsters using multiple identities. His warm-up list was more likely to consist of softer targets - people with cash-flow issues, chaotic lives and impulse spenders. They weren't real criminals, didn't cover their tracks so well, and were generally easier to trace. By his reckoning he'd be onto Chrissie's search, aka the serious exercise after muscle-stretching, within a couple of hours or so.

He lifted one name at a time from his list. He began by checking it against the Electoral Register, but more often than not he drew a blank or the address was no longer current. Next he worked methodically through Facebook, Twitter and LinkedIn, and tried to build up a profile matching the gender, date of birth and any other details he had been given alongside the name on his list. If it turned out the name was a car owner, he sometimes pretended to be the name and reporting a lost driving licence. Every so often the Swansea DVLA gave away a surprising amount of information. Next it was a case of calling estate and letting agents, the last known employer or place of work and concocting scenarios to charm or wheedle forwarding addresses from well-meaning, helpful people.

It amazed him to see what an innocently posted photo on Facebook could turn-up. And here he was again, fifteenth name down his list and ready to make a call.

'Yeah, see I just seen the FOR LET sign outside the house,' he said, using the Balcon & Mora office phone.

He was so focussed on steadying his voice and forging ahead with his phone patter, he barely gave the letting agent time to reply.

'No I'm not at the location. I saw the house on a Facebook photo. Well it weren't of the house, it were in the background, but.... Yeah, that's where I got the lettin' agency number. Your FOR LET sign was.... Yeah it looks nice, near a park.... Yeah.'

He'd prepared the ground, now it was time to slow down and ask what he really wanted to know.

'I was wonderin' if the let's still goin'?'

'At Forest Road?' the agent replied, 'I'm afraid it's been taken. I don't know how old the Facebook photo was, but we've had tenants in there for the past month.'

'Yeah, that would fit. The photo was posted in October.'

'We've other properties in the area, if you're interested.'

'Like number... I think it's fifteen?' he said taking another squint at the photo on the Facebook page.

'If it's the rental I think you're talking about, it's thirteen. Was it an upstairs flat you wanted?'

'Yes, like thirteen… B,' he hazarded, 'Forest Road.'

'As I said, I'm afraid it's taken. We've another rental in the same postcode area, if you're interested.'

A few more oblique questions and he'd got the postcode. Matt reckoned DD Smith had taken a photo of herself outside her new rental, and then posted the wide angled selfie on her Facebook page, public access setting. Now he had a current address. All he had to do was cross reference and confirm.

'How's it going?' Damon asked.

It was the usual cue, a prelude to Damon pushing back his office chair and suggesting a coffee break. Matt silently counted. He reckoned, by the time he got to four….

'Time for a coffee, I think. How about you? Another hot chocolate?' Damon murmured as his chair casters sounded over the patch of threadbare carpet.

'Yeah, thanks. This one's just about sorted.'

'I heard.'

'Yeah, it were neat.'

'I tell you what. While we're having a break, I'll show you some of the shortcuts with the news app.'

'Really? Cool.'

Five minutes later the app was open on Matt's screen and Damon was back in his faux leather office chair. This time Matt didn't mind Damon remotely viewing his screen. No matter that he was using the remote access administrator setting; he was going to shepherd him through shortcuts and the slick moves.

'Which search parameters do you want?' Damon asked.

'Well Chrissie reckons it's somethin' to do with one of Clive's cases, so news related to East Anglia.'

'You'll get a cleaner search if you list the counties in the Eastern Region. And the dates?'

'The last five years.'

'Are you sure you don't want to go back further?'

'It'll work out more than five years.'

Matt figured news reported in a newspaper or newsfeed-year covered far more time than the actual year. The crimes might be contemporary, but charging suspects and bringing cases to court could take a while. So a news report covering a court verdict and sentence would have been for a crime committed some time earlier. And using the same logic, reporting on appeals and releases from prison might cover cases first reported years before. He expected a five year search would reveal a lot of older ground.

'So your key words for the search box are?' Damon murmured.

'Clive Merry.'

'How about stalking, as well?'

There were more results than he'd expected.

'Hey, have you seen this, Damon? Seems someone bust Clive's ribs back in 2007. It says *Tyrell Bowfell and Callum Sawry have been arrested and charged with grievous bodily harm. Detective Sergeant Clive Merry....* Detective Sergeant? So, he weren't a DI back in 2007, then.'

He skimmed on, reading out passages, '*Bowfell and Sawry deny setting ladders against the side of the church.* What? They said they were *just passing*? Pull the other one. Course that would fit cos I think Clive used to live in

Lavenham. Might still have a house there, from what Chrissie's said.'

'And they *deny attempting to steal lead from the roof,*' Damon finished for him.

'Sounds like they didn't like bein' asked what they were doing. Swung a few punches and legged it. Left the ladders, accordin' to this.'

'Amateurs. Now look up the case on thelawpages.com and see if it went to court.'

'But I don't know what court, and it don't seem like anythin' to do with stalkin',' Matt breathed, irritated but curious to try out The Law Pages site.

'And… up comes the site. Now, Matt, type one of the defendants in the key word search. Told you, didn't I.'

'Scammin' hell! *Chelmsford Crown Court.* Sawry were the co-defendant but only Bowfell were convicted. He got five years.'

'Right, so back to the news app and see what else you can find.'

The news app threw up plenty to keep Matt busy. Lines like *the police are unable to release the name until the family have been informed* were generally not attributed to a particular policeman. He needed Clive's name.

'Hey,' he'd spotted a name alongside a newsfeed, 'this is more like it, 2009. *Detective Inspector Merry.* I reckon he must've made it to Detective Inspector around then.'

'If he made a statement to the press and they quoted his name, then I bet he was involved in the investigation,' Damon murmured.

'I've been makin' a list.'

The list seemed to be growing: crimes, serious or otherwise; criminals; and now dates when Clive made statements reported in the press.

Another thought popped into his mind.

'D'you reckon I should check out victims as well? I mean, just cos you've been held up at gunpoint in a Post Office heist, don't mean you aint a stalker,' Matt said as he skimmed across a news report from 2009 on his screen.

'True, and as a victim you'd see a softer side to the police.'

'So?'

'Well, take the one you're looking at now. The armed robbery. It names a woman who was in the Post Office in Hitcham and held up at gunpoint. If Clive interviewed her, he'd have been at his most charming, simply because she was a distraught victim.'

'It don't say she were distraught. Anyway, how'd you know he'd be charmin'?'

'It's a fair guess. But my point is what if she misinterpreted his kindness?'

'How'd you mean?' Matt didn't really get it, but put her name on the list anyway. Criminals and victims – at this rate the list would be endless. Scammin' hell! If Damon was right, he'd have to go back over his list and add all the victims as well.

'Look, you're not going to finish this now. It's a lot to check through, Matt. Coffee break is over and there are five more names on the debt collectors' list.'

'OK,' he muttered. Damon might be right, but it didn't mean Matt liked it.

The rest of the afternoon session passed in a blur of multiple pages crowding Matt's screen. He switched between Facebook, LinkedIn and Twitter, phone directories and electoral registers.

All the while, somewhere just behind his conscious thoughts, an algorithm niggled. Something he could work on, something to improve the news app searches, a neat bit of coding designed to cross reference and find links and coincidences within the Clive Merry search and The Law Pages site. The same name cropping up in different contexts wasn't, in his experience, likely to be a simple coincidence. He believed in good luck and bad luck, but coincidence? No.

CHAPTER 7

'Good morning, Mrs Jax,' Ron said as she pushed the heavy wooden door shut and slung her hobo-style leather bag onto a workbench.

It was Wednesday morning and Chrissie felt more cheerful than she had felt in weeks. She couldn't put a finger on why exactly, but Matt's call the previous day might have had something to do with it.

'I been workin' on the stalkin',' he'd said, cutting straight to the point. 'Used one of Damon's news apps, yesterday.'

'Hey thanks, Matt. Did you find anything?'

'Give us a chance. See, there's loads to trawl through. I was just wonderin'... do you reckon I'm lookin' for a bird or a bloke?'

'I suppose....' Her best guess was a woman stalking Clive. It had to be, but something made her say, 'Keep it broad, Matt.' After all, there'd been threats.

'Yeah but that means all the victims as well as them ones arrested and goin' down.'

'And don't forget the bad guys also have families. They probably feel they're victims too. You know, of the system and the police.'

'DOS-in' hell, Chrissie. That's mega loads.'

They'd agreed to talk again on Friday, and said he'd give her an update if there was anything new to tell. He'd mentioned the Bury Christmas Fayre, moaned about the anticipated road closures and rung off.

A couple of things from the call stayed with her. Firstly, she was a victim, but not while she launched a search and took the initiative; and secondly, the reminder of the Christmas Fayre. She'd been too preoccupied to notice Christmas creeping closer, and if there was one thing she'd learnt from two years in the Clegg workshop, it was that Christmas was busy. At least it was busy as far as repairing chairs was concerned.

Now, as she walked through the barn workshop and breathed the scent of mahogany, pine and beeswax on the cold morning air, she felt both at ease and surprisingly upbeat. If someone had asked her to choose one word to describe her frame of mind, she supposed it would be optimistic. 'Yes,' she murmured, 'the only limits are the limits of my imagination,' and she knew she had a bucket load of imagination.

'What's that? I didn't catch–'

'Good morning, Mr Clegg.'

She glanced up at the old rafters. Roof trusses and cross beams, time worn and dusty, spanned the space above and supported the old peg-tiled roof. It was high up, architectural and decrepit, but at the same time inspiring and liberating.

For a moment she saw the old barn workshop with fresh eyes. It was, she reminded herself, the place it had always been - a place to restore furniture, craft wood, and a base from which to expand the business. If there'd been any issues, they were hers; her fear of failure, of being able to attract work, and as a woman, to be taken seriously as a carpenter. She could see that now.

'Only another week and it'll be December,' she said instead.

'I know, and it's already hotting up workwise. I've had a call from Rush Green Golf Club.'

'Don't tell me, they want six of their committee-room chairs repaired. By yesterday.'

'Not quite, but one of their trophies needs attention. Don't look so surprised. It's a hickory club mounted on a wooden board. Apparently there isn't enough space left on the mount board to fix this year's brass plate.'

'Brass plate?'

'Yes, engraved with the winner's name.'

'Ah, so they want it enlarged in some way?'

'Yes, and it's had an accident. The club secretary said it's far too heavy and fell off the wall. You can guess the rest.'

'I knew there'd be a catch. But I'm not surprised - all that brass and a golf club hanging from it. Rush Green? Isn't that where the man was found dead last week?'

'It might be. From Northfield Wood, I'd heard.'

She caught his smile as he turned his attention back to the damaged oak panels in the back of Mr Mawbray's settle. She guessed he knew she'd be curious about the man found dead, and if she was the one going to the golf club, then he must have realised she was bound to ask about the dead man as well as the trophy. So was that a knowing smile she'd just seen, or simply the joy of working with a piece of four hundred year old oak? She could never tell with Ron, he left so much unsaid.

'So how did you leave it with the golf club?'

'I said I thought it sounded just your kind of thing and that you'd drop over there sometime today. You'd need to look at it first but....'

'How'd you know I'd drop in today?'

'Well, aren't you? I didn't think you'd be able to resist a snoop around,' Ron said mildly.

This time Chrissie was the one to smile.

'Am I really so easy to read, Mr Clegg?'

'Sometimes. Now tell me what you think. Which piece of oak is a better match to patch this?'

'Hey, that's neat. You've managed to mend the split panel without taking the settle apart,' she said, stooping to examine where the central back panel fitted into grooves in the frame timber.

'At some point the panel must have got stuck in the frame, along here.' He ran his arthritic fingers along the wood. Years of grime and treacly polish caked the bevelled edges of the frame. 'It couldn't move so when the wood dried and shrank, as you can see, the panel cracked along the grain. I was lucky I managed to free it up and lever the pieces together. I've closed the split without taking the frame apart.'

'Well done. So just some glue to the split. Ah ha – you used an old metal blade from a plane to lever the pieces together.'

'You've spotted the mark it made?'

'Yes, but only because I know where to look. And it's on the back of the panel, so with a bit of polish…. Hey, this is unusual,' she added under her breath, as she scrutinised the hole in the neighbouring panel.

She hadn't really examined the rear of the settle before, at least not closely, but as she crouched and looked more carefully, she touched the old oak. She felt the contour of a shape, as if it had pushed up across the grain. It must have been made by whatever had struck and pierced the panel from the front.

'I'd always imagined someone had thrown a knife at this.'

'Good heavens, Mrs Jax. That's a bit melodramatic. A half inch hole at one end of a sharp one inch long dent? More likely the corner of something heavy, or even a picture frame falling against it, I should say.'

'Well, how about a small axe then? What did Mr Mawbray say?' she murmured.

'I don't remember him saying exactly, but the wardrobe had just fallen onto our dust bag and he implied it was the same kind of accident. He was more concerned about getting it repaired in time for some big family celebration. A houseful of guests the weekend before Christmas.'

She walked slowly around the settle, looking at it from every angle. Basically it was an old panelled chest with a panelled back and wooden arms. A kind of chair. 'Well, as I said, chairs and Christmas, it's a busy time for repairs.'

'You still haven't told me which of these pieces of oak you think matches the grain best.'

Chrissie guessed Ron would have already made up his mind and didn't really need her opinion, but she also sensed it was his way of including her and passing on tips. She, as a fellow carpenter and business partner, was grateful and hoped she didn't make a complete fool of herself.

'Well, that's awkward. The grain's very straight and close, so where you cut across it at the ends of the patch it's going to look very obvious.'

'Yes, it's going to be tricky to disguise.'

'So... yes I think the grain on this piece looks most like the panel. If you cut across, using slightly curved oblique lines, and make an elongated lozenge shape end, it should work like this.' She picked up a scrap of paper and tore it into the shape she imagined, then laid it onto the wood. 'See? Actually, now I come to think about it, it's more the shape of a bullet tip than a lozenge.'

'A very high tech bullet shape, I'd say. Very apt, Mrs Jax,' Ron murmured.

'So the oak was hewn with an axe, cut with saws, damaged with a... hatchet and, repaired with a bullet. I'd say there's a theme there. But seriously, I can't imagine the picture frame, or whatever, came out of it very well.'

'Probably not.'

She waited until after nine o'clock before phoning Rush Green and arranging to drive over and meet the secretary at lunchtime. For the rest of the morning she forgot about hatchets and knives and concentrated on fitting the replacement mirror to the Edwardian satinwood wardrobe door, or what she now thought of as the *dust cloud wardrobe*. It had taken the best part of a week for the replacement mirror glass to be cut to size and delivered.

With the Art Nouveau-style door placed on a workbench, she fitted the mirror into it from behind, like a picture frame. It was held securely in place by a solid section of satinwood spanning most of the door. It was a heavy construction.

'No wonder it swung open,' she murmured. 'And the poor old hinges....' She'd already repaired where they had pulled away from the rest of the structure.

At midday, she checked the time.

'OK, I'm off now, Mr Clegg. Rush Green. I'll take the van.'

'Good luck.'

She swept the Citroen Belingo keys off the hook near the workshop phone, grabbed her bag and still thrusting an arm into her duffle coat, hurried out to the courtyard.

The day was cold and overcast, threatening to rain. A gusty breeze caught at her coat as she sprinted to the van. Wind whipped against the long sidewall of the barn workshop. Seconds later she pulled the door closed and settled behind the steering wheel. Slipping into low gear, she rocked and swayed along the rutted track to the lane skirting the Wattisham Airfield. Her route took her north of the airfield before heading up towards Rush Green.

She realised she must have driven within a stone's throw of the golf club on countless occasions when she'd taken the back routes to avoid the A14. It struck her as odd she'd never noticed before. Perhaps it was the higher ride in the van. The spread of trees shadowing the horizon had always drawn her attention instead. Nice, she thought as she finally swung onto the gravelled car parking area. She didn't pause to take in the architecture of the clubhouse or the beautifully manicured eighteenth green nearby. Fine drops of rain were already spotting her windscreen and instead she focussed on getting inside before the heavens opened and she was soaked.

'Hello, are you from Clegg & Jax?' a voice resonated from somewhere behind her as she stood in the entrance lobby.

She had been wondering where to head. In front and to both sides were doorways, four if she counted, and as she turned to face the large glass one she'd just hurried through, she realised the lobby was the shape of a small pentagon. One door set in each wall.

'Good timing. I've managed to finish my round before the weather turned.' A rain-peppered, middle-aged man closed the glass door and, stood on the mat.

'I'm Paul Cooley, Club Secretary. Sorry, I didn't mean to startle you, but I recognise most of the members and, well I noticed the van in the car park and put two and two together. I guessed you must be from Clegg & Jax. And now I'm,' he brushed the rain from his thinning hair, 'I'm going to leave you for a moment while I pack my clubs and trolley away in my car, and change my shoes. No studs inside the clubhouse, except in the changing rooms and changing room entrance.' He waved vaguely at his feet.

'Yes of course. No studs.' She would have added I'm Chrissie Jax. We spoke on the phone this morning – but he'd already turned to go, and anyway she guessed he had worked it out for himself.

She stood and gazed through the glass door. Well placed trees, lazily curving grass fairways, little coloured flags on six foot poles; it was like a twenty-first century equivalent of a Capability Brown landscape. It soothed her, even as the rain set in. How, she mused, would the club secretary have reacted if her footwear hadn't met club standards, if she'd turned up in stilettos for example. But then he wouldn't have thought she was with the van, she supposed.

No, Paul Cooley, was observant, he likely had a good memory for faces and seemed reasonably affable. If she trod the right balance between nosiness and interest, he might prove a fount of information.

'I've heard great reports about Clegg & Jax.' The voice came from behind her.

She spun round.

'Mr Cooley!'

'Sorry, I've startled you again. I've changed my shoes now, so let's go and have a look at the Northfield Challenge

Trophy. It's in my office. This way.' He turned on his heel and led the way back through a pale sycamore door and into a wide corridor-like room. Along one wall, large boards were mounted. *Winners & Captains* Chrissie read.

'The stairs lead down to the changing rooms,' he said as he indicated an open staircase heading downwards. 'Having it here gives lots of wall space and a great view of the names every time you come up the stairs.'

She followed, unable to resist glancing down at his feet. True to his word, his golf shoes had been changed to a pair of brown leather brogues.

'Right, here we are.' He unlocked his office door, and without glancing back at her, strode in.

'Ah, this must be the trophy,' she murmured.

'Yes, and in a sorry state.' He stood back and let her examine it in silence.

The board, English oak, measured roughly one hundred and twenty by fifty centimetres. There was a central mounting for the hickory club and brass name plates alongside.

'Oh dear,' she said as she looked more closely at the lower edge. 'I can see where the wood has been crushed and split when it fell.' She traced the split up behind the mounting of the hickory club. 'So tell me, why Northfield? Where does the name come from?'

'The wood – Northfield Wood. You probably drove past it. If you look at the names and dates on the brass plates, you'll see the earliest one is in 1967. A lot of new housing was built close to the southern edge of Northfield Wood during the sixties and seventies.'

'But why name the trophy after a wood?'

'Well it was an ancient woodland site and I think at the time there was concern it might be under threat. In the end a lot of it was cleared for Norway spruce and western cedar to be planted as a commercial crop.'

'When of course it should have been oak, ash and hazel.'

'Quite. Well local feelings were running high and I think there was an accident during one of the phases of clearance and planting. Rumour has it someone died.'

'But what happened? And who died?'

'No one knows exactly. And it is only rumour, but I'm guessing a portable sawmill was trailered into the wood and it either malfunctioned, or there was some kind of a dust explosion and an accident. Any tragedy would have brought the whole dispute over the wood's future into the wider public domain and to the notice of conservation groups. Suffice it to say, Northfield Wood is still with us and slowly being returned back into ancient woodland.'

'So this piece of English oak, does it come from an oak felled in Northfield Wood?'

'Yes, I believe so.'

'And is there any other significance? I mean, was it part of the... accident?' She inspected it again, this time alert to possible blood stains, or worse.

'Good heavens, no!'

Now was her moment. She sensed a technical based discussion sprinkled with occasional jargon would impress, win her the work.

'There are two aspects to this restoration. Firstly the design. This oak board is thick and heavy, the engraved brass plates are heavy, and no doubt the hickory club weighs as well.'

'Quite so.'

'That's why it's more common, and weighs less if names are engraved or painted directly onto the wooden board. So perhaps, if we enlarge the board, you might consider breaking with tradition and no longer use brass plates for future winners.' She watched his face, tried to read his expression.

'Secondly, the oak board,' she lifted one end of it, 'is very heavy. I could replace it with something lighter, stronger and less likely to split. If the association with Northfield Wood is important, then I could reduce the weight by sawing slices to use as a veneer on a replacement lighter weight board. Alternatively I could use some of the less damaged oak to make upper mouldings or a cornice for the replacement. I could even explore the possibility of getting another piece of oak or ash from Northfield Wood.'

'The possibilities seem endless.'

'Including, simply repairing the split and replacing the crushed edge.'

'You mentioned design. One of the problems is - well it's one hundred and twenty centimetres wide. Most people simply don't have that kind of stretch of free wall to hang it up at home, so it sits in the garage or somewhere.'

'Are you saying someone drove into it, Mr Cooley?'

'Call me Paul, please.'

'Look, it sounds as if we need to redesign the trophy. Perhaps we could mount the hickory club differently, so it hangs downwards. It might be easier to find that kind of space to put it up at home if you're a winner, don't you think?'

'Quite so.'

She caught his smile, knew she was close to securing the job. 'Would you like me to draw up some designs for you?'

'That sounds like an excellent idea. And obviously we'd need an estimate of the costs.'

They agreed she would take the damaged board back to the workshop, and together they walked out into the rain and her van, she carrying the board while he held up a large golfing umbrella.

'That reminds me, I heard there'd been a walker here, a man from Northfield Wood found dead recently,' she said, as she loaded the oak board into the van while he shielded her from the worst of the rain.

'You must mean the man found collapsed in the rough near the eleventh. Most unfortunate. He wasn't a member, so I don't know anything about him, poor chap.'

'Do you get many non-members wandering around the course then?' The space under the umbrella felt conspiratorial, gossipy.

'It's the footpaths. They were here before some of the fairways. The course has been enlarged over the years, you know.'

'It must be awkward, having people walking through the players.'

'Well no, because most walk the paths regularly. They prefer to walk when no one is playing; early morning, evenings, bad weather – that kind do of thing.'

'So you must get to know some of the walkers, recognise them by their routines. But where do the paths go?'

'Most lead through the wood, I suppose linking Onehouse to Rush Green and ultimately on to Haughley. Right, all loaded up?'

'Yes, thank you for your help. I'll get back to you shortly.' Chrissie flashed a smile.

'I'm generally here on a Wednesday, so I look forward to seeing what you come up with.' He turned to hurry back into the clubhouse as she got into the van.

'Good bye,' she murmured to the retreating figure now almost pixelated by the rain on her window.

This time, as she retraced her journey, she was able to name the wood shadowing the horizon. It felt slightly spooky having a slice of it travelling with her in the van. 'I wonder,' she whispered under her breath.

CHAPTER 8

Nick stood on the slightly raised platform and scanned the audience. He usually tried not to focus on people's faces, but on somewhere slightly beyond. This evening though, was different. Amongst the girls standing with their hands in the air and swaying to the music, blokes nursing pint glasses and grinning, and the resident extrovert drunk bopping to music only he could hear in his head, Nick searched to catch a glimpse of Matt, Chrissie or Maisie. But a pub audience was a pub audience, and live mid-week music venues were tight, noisy and sweaty. The Corner House in Thetford was no exception.

He held his note; a synthetic synced beat emerged from under the melody riff, fused with his voice for a few seconds, and then together they both died away. He glanced sideways at Denton, the new keyboard player, and gave him an almost imperceptible nod to signal the end of the number.

'Thank you,' he honeyed through the microphone and beamed his sunniest smile into the audience. 'We're going to take a break for about fifteen minutes. So don't go away. We've lots more.'

Some of the drinkers hooted and clapped. Someone wolf-whistled. He guessed it was Matt, something he remembered him experimenting with during their lager soaked evening the week before.

He switched off his microphone and turned to Jake who was settling a guitar onto a stand. 'Denton's doing OK, yeah?'

'Yeah, a bit of a mix up with *Rohaneo*, but it was alright in the end. You kinda sang across it when he missed the lead into the repeat chorus.'

'It's a bit cramped back here,' Jason called as he squeezed past the drum kit. He draped an arm over Nick's shoulder and grinned. 'The keyboard fills out our sound, don't you think?'

'Hey, you sound great! You're doing great!'

He looked up to see Chrissie hurrying over. Most of the audience had turned away from the band and were pushing and elbowing towards the bar while she worked her way against the flow. Beer slopped from a bunch of glasses she'd clasped between both hands.

'Oh no!' A large bottle of water rolled from under her arm and hit the floor. 'Shit.'

'*Water hits the deck*,' Nick half sang playfully and ducked down to retrieve the bottle.

'*While we take another rain check*,' Jake chanted, completing the line from one of their numbers.

Nick crouched on the old floorboards and reached out as the water rolled away from him. It wasn't such a bad angle, he thought, down on the black-stained beery wood. It gave him a great view of shapely legs. Most were moving away towards the bar for more lager and refills of vodka and lime, but not all. He squinted up. Girls. A few were lingering. He knew the routine. They wanted a closer look, maybe ask a few questions, maybe more.

As he started to straighten up he saw a woman's face. She wasn't a girl exactly, a little older perhaps, more mature, more confident. She struck him as out of place, not dressed for a live music evening in a pub. No sparkles or glitter, more of a trainers and raincoat outfit. But it was her expression that really grabbed his attention; it was unblinking, intense and unlike the girls around her, wasn't directed at any of the band members. Was she watching Chrissie?

In a flash he made the connection. This wasn't about the band, this was about….

'Hey, Chrissie,' he said, now on his feet, the water bottle in one hand.

He didn't know what was going on, but he wasn't going to wait to find out. He flung an arm around Chrissie. Beer slopped from the glasses as he drew her close.

'What the…?'

He ignored Chrissie talking into his chest. Instead he watched the woman in the rain coat and trainers.

She shifted her gaze from Chrissie and stared at him. The flash of surprise in her eyes was intense, unmistakeable.

'Act like you're my girlfriend,' he breathed from the corner of his mouth.

'What? What are you playing at, Nick?'

'Woman behind you,' he murmured, dropping his head as if to kiss her, but whispering in her ear. 'If we turn, slow dance style, you can get a peep without letting on. Is it your break-in artist?' He didn't want to say stalker, didn't want to frighten her.

He felt a tap on his shoulder and tensed.

'Hey, don't hog all the beers to yourself, mate,' Jason bellowed.

He felt Chrissie pull away a little, sensed the handover of glasses. Around him people moved, jostled. All the while he kept one arm around Chrissie, only a loose hold, but it was an arm between Chrissie and the woman. He caught Chrissie's voice, urgent, somewhere chest level.

'Hey Jason, think you can take a photo? Nick and me... but get all the pub action behind in the shot, OK?' Chrissie hissed.

'But I've got the beers. Hey, Jake, you use your phone.'

'What? OK, then – yeah, one, two, three....'

Nick turned briefly to smile for Jake's phone camera. He felt Chrissie duck.

'Hey,' Jake cried, 'what did you do that for? Just stay still will you?'

'Quick, take some more.'

Nick twisted to see behind, but the woman was already backing away. 'Try and get some of the rain girl back there.' He pointed with the bottle of water as she melted into the hubbub at the bar.

'What the hell was all that about?' Jake asked, half laughing.

'I don't know. I suddenly thought some weird type was....' He felt stupid.

'You are OK, aren't you? You haven't taken speed, have you? We've got the second set to get through, Nick.'

'Course I haven't bombed anything. I'm fine. Really I am.'

'Can I see the photos, then?' Chrissie cut in. 'Listen Jake, Nick isn't off his head; at least I don't think he is. I've been quizzing him about stalkers ever since I disturbed a break-in last week. Trouble is I don't know if I'm looking for a girl or a bloke. So let's see what you've got.'

While Jake thumbed his mobile, Nick sipped from the water bottle and waited. He was torn between hoping

Chrissie recognised the rain girl or her trainers, and wanting it to be nothing. He supposed it was possible he'd over reacted. He could have just misread the rain girl's expression and made a complete arse of himself.

'What do you think?' Jake asked. 'Any good?'

'I don't know,' Chrissie said slowly. 'What do you think, Nick?'

Together they looked through the shots. Jake must have kept his finger on the shoot button because there were countless images – smudgy, poorly lit, the top of Chrissie's head, faces turned away from the camera, eyes closed.

'What about this one?' Nick asked as he studied a blurry shape. The raincoat was obvious. The trainers, or rather one trainer was in focus, but movement artefact merged the nose with mouth and chin. A haze for a face.

'It looks a bit like those grainy pictures you sometimes see on posters taken from CCTV cameras. You know the kind of thing? *Wanted* or *Missing*. Can you send them to my phone, Jake?' Chrissie asked.

'Hmm.'

'Hi, Nick. You were mega!'

He looked round. 'Hey, Matt! Maisie!'

'You've missed all the excitement,' Chrissie murmured.

'Yeah, a girl in a raincoat,' Nick added, still not sure if his mind had flipped off the deep end for a moment or he'd saved Chrissie.

'A raincoat? But that's super cool. You can make 'em look real edgy,' Maisie squealed.

There was no point in dwelling on it, even Chrissie seemed unfazed, but then she wasn't always easy to read.

He gave himself a mental shake. He had the second set to sing and he needed to focus.

'Yeah, if it's a short one and you roll up the sleeves a bit and tie the belt tight....' Maisie's voice merged into the buzz around him.

He turned back to the low stage, swigged more water, parked raincoats and stalkers in the backwaters of his mind and hummed the intro to his next song.

CHAPTER 9

Chrissie kept close to Maisie while Matt lagged behind. It felt safer that way. As Chrissie saw it, Maisie would notice anyone within eighty paces sporting an edgy raincoat, and Matt was watching her back. The gig had finished ten minutes earlier, and it was time to head for home, at least for those who had to be up for work in the morning. They shouldered and jostled their way out of the pub and spilled onto the pavement along with a bunch of the rowdy alcohol fuelled audience.

The Corner House stood on the edge of the station car parking area, sixty yards from the neo-Jacobean style main station building constructed nearly a hundred and seventy years earlier. From where Chrissie was standing, the building looked empty, the windows boarded up. She shivered. The ticket office building next to it seemed more alive, closed at this hour but its old red brick contrasting with its neighbour's grey napped flint and pale brick. The only light was the occasional dim beam cast from tall poles amongst the sea of car park tarmac. She glanced back at the pub. She needed to get home, let all the images and thoughts simmer overnight in her subconscious before even attempting to make any sense of what had, or had not happened in the Corner House pub.

'Bye, Maisie, Matt,' she called as she unlocked the TR7, its yellow paintwork reassuringly visible in the cold dark night. It felt safe, as she got in; a quiet oasis away from the pub.

The engine spluttered into life as the pop-up headlights shone full beam. She eased out of her parking space, briefly caught the stragglers standing outside the Corner House in her lights and then slowly drove along Station Road, checking her rear view mirror for any tailing cars.

Nothing. At least no following car she could identify; it was time to put her foot down and see if anything stuck with her. She gave the four-cylinder engine full throttle. It felt safer as the wedge shaped bonnet cut briskly through the darkness along the straight roads through the forest and away from Thetford.

It wasn't quite midnight when Chrissie crawled into bed. She found Clive fast asleep, turned on his side and dead to the world, drawing slow, almost inaudible breaths. For a moment she contemplated waking him, letting him know she was safely home and that he'd missed a good gig, but common sense told her there was little point. He'd been working late, likely come home exhausted, and waking him was unkind. Let him sleep, she thought when really she wanted to tell him about the raincoat girl she'd only glimpsed, show him the smudgy photos Jake had sent to her phone, and then she wanted him to be able to solve it all.

'Fat chance,' she murmured, exhausted as her head sank into her pillow. It would have to wait until the morning.

When Chrissie next opened her eyes the bedroom was still bathed in darkness but strains of Suffolk Radio issued from her radio alarm. She rolled over and flung an arm in the direction of where Clive was sleeping. The duvet flattened to the mattress. She raised her head and squinted at the empty space beside her. The distant sound of a shower running told her all she needed to know. Clive was already up.

For a moment she basked in the hinterland of wakefulness, her consciousness seeping back. Slowly she became aware of the heaviness behind her eyes and an ache in her forehead. And then it hit her – yesterday, the late night, the raincoat girl, a churning pit in her stomach. Questions, there were so many questions. Would there be time this morning to ask Clive, or even begin to tell him about her stalking fears?

Oh God, she thought, the photos! Where did I put my phone? Hell, I forgot to recharge it.

Groaning, she rolled out of bed and fumbled through the pile of last night's clothes, thrown over the back of a fragile but decorative stripped pine chair. With every empty pocket she patted and squeezed, her angst racked up and her focus shifted from telling Clive about her evening to concentrating on finding her phone.

'Hey, why don't you switch the light on?' Clive's voice blended with the newsreader, as sudden light brutally flooded the room.

'Arrgh!' She blinked against the brightness and turned to squint at him as he stood in the doorway, fresh from the shower, short auburn hair darkened by moisture.

'You look as if you had a good evening. I assume you found the Corner House in Thetford all right?' he said.

'Yes, yes. But my phone, I can't find my phone,' she moaned, turning back to comb through her clothes again.

'Isn't that your phone on the chest of drawers?'

'What? Yes, oh thanks. I thought I'd lost it.'

Relief brought her words tumbling, 'It would have been nicer if you'd been able to come as well. Not a lot of space for the band, of course, but that's a pub for you.' The music, the crush, the raincoat girl were real to her as she spoke.

'How was the keyboard player? Didn't you say they were trying someone new? Dermot or something?' He moved around the small bedroom, taking a clean shirt from a hanger, socks from a drawer, talking as he dressed.

'You mean Denton. He sounded quite good. It worked very well.'

The old floorboards creaked as he balanced on one leg and stepped into his trousers. She watched as he knotted his tie, her thoughts slowing as she began to form the words she'd use to describe what Nick had seen.

'Hmm,' she murmured. 'Actually–'

'Sorry, Chrissie, I can't stop. I've got an early meeting with the press. I should have said. But I'm definitely off this evening. Meal at the White Hart sound OK?'

'Hmm. But I've–'

'Right then, see you this evening. Love you.' With a brief kiss he was gone, leaving behind the faint scent of cedar shower gel and minty toothpaste.

'Good luck with the press meeting,' she called after him and sat on the edge of the bed. She felt cheated. She'd almost found the words to open the subject of stalking, they had been on the tip of her tongue but he hadn't the time.

'A press meeting?' she whispered, as the implications sank in.

He must have made some breakthrough with a case, but which of his cases, and what breakthrough? Normally he would have told her, but this time he hadn't. It made her feel excluded.

She checked the time on the radio's digital clock. 06:45. Wearily she plugged her phone in to recharge and headed for a shower. 'I'll tell him this evening,' she sighed. In the mean time she had a business to run.

•

Chrissie edged her TR7's shovel shaped nose into the space next to the Citroen van outside the barn workshop, switched off the engine and hurried inside.

'Morning, Mr Clegg,' she said as she closed the old door behind her. She felt as if she could have done with another couple of hours sleep. The heaviness hadn't disappeared from behind her eyes and the ache still gripped her forehead.

'Have you had a chance to look at the trophy board yet?' she added, as she dropped her bag on a workbench and paused to watch him sanding the patch of wood in the settle's back panel.

'Morning, Mrs Jax. I haven't yet, and anyway I thought I'd rather look at it with you. You only brought it in yesterday, and it's your project.'

'Yes, I suppose it was only yesterday.' Her Wednesday visit to Rush Green and meeting with Paul Cooley felt ages ago, pushed backwards in her perception of time by the midweek gig. Just realising reminded her.

'Mug of tea?' She murmured. It was easier than talking about the gig.

While she waited for the kettle to boil, she settled her mind into work mode. She needed to design a new layout for the trophy and draw up the plans.

'As I see it, Mr Clegg, there are several fundamental issues with the trophy board. For a start, it's made of oak which grew in its namesake wood - Northfield Wood. I can't just discard it and start with a new piece of wood.'

She placed a mug of tea on the workbench for him.

'Oh thank you, Mrs Jax. Do you think the significance might be more that it was felled there?'

'What? The club secretary said something about an accident, but he didn't say what. You don't think it has a sinister importance, do you?'

'I was thinking more symbolic than sinister.'

She mulled over his words. Was it, she wondered, like the symbolism used in paintings. She remembered reading about the decoration worked onto the dress Queen Elizabeth I wore for her very famous sixteenth century portrait. The symbols meant nothing to a twenty-first century eye, unless you were in the know. However, to a sixteenth century eye and the people under her rule, they would have been obvious.

'So?'

'So nothing, Mrs Jax. As long as some of the oak survives onto the new design, the essence of the message is still there.'

'And you might say the hickory club displayed on it represents the golfing hack. It's a symbolic play on words, the hack and the hacking down of a magnificent oak tree.'

'Now let's not get carried away with symbols, Mrs Jax. It is only a golf trophy board.'

'Yes I know, but do you think I'd be able to take some slices of the board and use them as an oak veneer?'

'Let me have a closer look.'

Together they examined the board; lifting it, tilting it, minutely inspecting its front, back and sides.

'It'll look like a nasty case of death watch beetle attack when you take out all the screws holding the brass plates, Mrs Jax.'

'But how deep do the screws go?'

She answered her question by selecting a suitably sized screwdriver and removing a screw.

'The screws are ten mil – not quite half an inch long. So allowing for the thickness of the brass plate and countersinking the screw head, the holes in the wood will be about six mil deep,' he said.

'And it's a thick oak board, so....'

She spent the next hour thinking and sketching. While she measured and designed, her curiosity fermented. What was the accident? Who had died? What exactly had happened back in the 1960s, she wondered. She supposed a search on the internet could answer her questions, but it would have to wait. The internet speeds at the barn workshop were dire, so slow it was easier and quicker to wait until the evening when she could settle with a mug of tea at her small kitchen table and use her laptop in Woolpit.

By late afternoon, she'd drawn up a series of new designs for the trophy, cleaned, waxed and polished the dust cloud wardrobe and begun work on repairing the base of a drawer in a Queen Anne walnut bureau.

'Tea?' Ron asked as four o'clock passed.

'No thanks, Mr Clegg. Do you know, I think I'll get on home. I'm going out for a meal with Clive this evening. If I leave now, I'll have time to email my designs to Paul Cooley before I have a shower and freshen up.' She could have added it would also give her time to check through Jake's photos taken at the gig, gather her thoughts and possibly surf the net for any reports relating to Northfield Wood in the 1960s.

•

Chrissie sat with her back to the wall in the White Hart pub while Clive waited at the bar and bought the drinks.

She couldn't help recalling Nick's warning that a visit to her local pub was like telling the village she wasn't at home and as good as inviting a break-in. She drew the old salvaged treadle-base table closer, as if it could separate her from threat, and scanned the other drinkers standing near the bar and sitting at similar tables. Coats, anoraks, woolly scarves, winter footwear, but no pale coloured raincoats, or wild crazy eyes. If she was honest, the crazy eyes were her embellishment; Nick had used the word intense, but in her book that was pretty close to crazed.

The air in the bar felt warm and the voices around her sounded muted, almost soothing. She watched Clive's back for a moment and then glanced to one side and into a larger room, an extension with smooth plastered walls and scrubbed pine tables and chairs laid out for dining. It looked uninviting, somewhere to spill into when the popular tables in the main bar area had been taken. More importantly, it looked empty.

She turned her attention to the *Specials Board* hanging by the old brick chimney breast on the far wall. Christmas star lights were strung along the top.

'Have you decided what you'd like?' Clive said, smiling as he set down a glass of white wine and a pint of ale.

'Ah thanks.' She sipped the wine. 'That's nice. I thought partridge roasted with shallots and bacon, sounded tasty.' She noticed the weariness in his face as she caught his profile. He seemed to frown as he read the chalky writing on the board.

'I think it's the steak and ale pie for me. So,' he glanced at her face, 'partridge for you? I'll go and order at the bar.'

She watched him as he ordered. It was easy to watch. Most people seemed unaware of what was behind them, their attention was on what they were doing.

I need to tell Clive, get this stalking business off my chest, she thought, and tried to recall the words she'd formulated when she'd first woken. And then she remembered he'd had a press conference and the memory rocked her plans.

'Hey Clive,' she said as he sat down, food ordered, 'I haven't asked how your meeting with the press went this morning. Was it OK?'

He lifted his pint and drank some beer, as if collecting his thoughts.

'Come on, tell me. How did it go?'

'It went fine.' It was obvious from his face he understood exactly what she was really asking.

She shot him a look.

'OK, OK. You want to know who, what, where and how. There've been some developments in the Rush Green case. I think I may have already told you.'

She shook her head.

'No? Well the post mortem raised more questions than it answered. It seems John Camm died as a result of his head injuries, or rather one in particular.'

'Injuries? You mean he had more than one?'

'Yes. A minor golf ball injury to the temple and a blow from something more like a golf club, to the back of the head.'

'But surely that could fit with being hit by a stray golf ball and falling backwards?'

'Yes, so one would have expected the golf ball strike to come first. There are obvious marks where the ball hit his temple and he should have fallen sideways. But he was found lying on his back and there was nothing on the ground the same shape as the depressed fracture in the back of his skull.'

'Unless he'd been moved after he died. But what's a depressed fracture?'

'Where the skull breaks and instead of just splitting, broken bone gets pushed inwards. The pathologist said it's like leaving a footprint in the sand.'

Chrissie tried to picture it. 'You mean like when you put your foot through the ice formed on a puddle?'

'I suppose so.'

'But what's the significance?' All thoughts of stalkers had flown out the window.

'The pathologist reckons the fracture to the back of the skull came first, and the ball struck him while he was already lying on the ground. And besides, the way he was lying, he was facing the wrong way for a ball to hit him where it did, from the fairway. Wrong temple.'

'Wow, it sounds, well it sounds as if there's more to it. Did you find the ball?'

'There were lots of old golf balls around, but....'

They fell into silence as one of the kitchen staff brought their food over and set it on their table.

'Thank you,' Chrissie said and smiled. She turned her attention back to Clive. 'I was over at Rush Green Golf Club yesterday. Funny, I must've driven past it a hundred times, but I've never really taken any notice before. This time of course I was, well I was all eyes and ears.'

'Whatever were you doing over there?' He sounded preoccupied with cutting into the puff pastry topping his steak and ale pie, but she noticed he looked up as she answered.

'We had a phone call from Paul Cooley.'

'He's the club secretary, isn't he?'

'Yes, they have a trophy board they want repaired. The Northfield Challenge Trophy and they asked us for an estimate. I don't suppose you know its history? The secretary told me some half-baked story about some accident in Northfield Wood back in the 1960s.'

Clive shook his head and the conversation moved on as they ate and drank and talked some more. Chrissie relaxed, happy in Clive's company. 'We should do this more often,' she said between mouthfuls of parsnip and carrot.

'Yes, I wish I'd been able to come to the gig with you last night.'

'I don't think we'd have been able to talk like this, though. It was very loud. But hey, I've some pictures on my phone; they'll give you an idea of what it was like. I don't know what you'll make of them but, here have a look.' She rummaged in her bag and pulled out her mobile.

She watched him frown as he tried to make something out of the photos. He flicked through them twice. 'It looks as if most of these were taken inside someone's pocket. The venue was at a pub, wasn't it?' he said, laughing.

'Well, Jake took the photos in a bit of a rush.'

She took a deep breath and explained about the girl in the raincoat and Nick's theory.

'So what looks like a pocket lining is in fact–'

'An out-of-focus raincoat. Yes.'

She gauged his reaction. Calm, she thought and a little surprised. Thank God he didn't appear irritated, and there'd been no accusations of taking things into her own hands.

'Well, at least Jake got a good shot of one of her trainers. We can put it through the database of trainers and their sole patterns, see if it matches any imprints from the break-in. And we should be able to get some idea of her hair colour, and possibly her size and build from these fuzzy images.' He drained his glass and handed her mobile back to her. 'Can you email those photos to me?' he said.

They stood up, scraping their chairs back on the old floorboards.

'Come on, time to walk home.' He slipped his arm around her waist.

She felt so safe she almost forgot to check over her shoulder as they walked.

'Of course the Corner House will probably have CCTV pictures. We can look to see if there's anyone who might match some of the parameters Jake captured,' he said, his mind clearly running on.

'And of course, Nick got a good look at her.'

'Hmm, it might be worth following up.'

CHAPTER 10

Matt pulled at his scrappy beard. It was something to occupy the frustration in his fingertips as inspiration deserted him on the keys. He stared at the computer screen and mentally retraced the steps through the start of his algorithm.

'Hi, Matt. I don't seem to see you around here much these days. How are things?' Rosie's voice cut through his concentration, dragging him back to the library and his favourite library assistant.

He looked up, squinting at her as she stood facing him across the small computer station. The library lights caught the fine wisps of her hair, as if floating where they had escaped from her loose ponytail. He liked Rosie, sensed her kindness, but he'd never been able to get her to flirt with him. In fact most of his efforts in that direction generally backfired.

'But it were only last Thursday I saw you. That's just over a week ago.' He remembered calling *bye* as he left the library. She'd been loading paper into the photocopier.

'Well I don't remember. So what are you working on these days?'

'I'm tryin' to design an app for searchin' news sites. Somethin' to speed things up if you're after a name or a particular type of story.'

'One of your course projects, is it?'

'Not really, though I s'pose it could count towards one. Nah, I'm workin' part time for Balcon & Mora.' For a moment he basked in her gaze. 'I'm due there later today.

Over in Bury St Edmunds,' he added in case there might be any confusion.

'Cool. Do they make ice creams, or design logos on tee shirts or something?'

'What?'

'I don't know. The name sounds kind of Italian, so I'm guessing creamy gelato or maybe Milano designs?'

'In Bury? Nah, its tracin' missin' people. Internet tracin'.'

'Ah – I should've known. Computers. Sounds... well it sounds kind of cool anyway.'

She smiled. Not the easy to recognise sunny smile. This was a fainter curve of the lips. Something he'd only picked up by concentrating on her face. He'd learnt the sequence, realised she did it just before turning away and leaving to attend to some other library task. It signalled the end of the conversation.

'See ya,' he murmured and tried to mimic her smile.

Funny, he thought, how birds seemed to be drawn to all things Italian – the fashion, the ice cream, even the names. What if he changed his to an Italian equivalent? Matteo? He already rode a Piaggio, admittedly the Zip rather than the Vespa, but it was all he could afford. For a moment he toyed with the idea of further personalising his COMPUTER SMART sweatshirt, so as to pass it off as Italian design, high-end fashion. And then he remembered it was lying in his bedroom in a heap along with his stale socks and boxers, waiting for the wash. The Italian alter ego would have to wait and the earthly tussle with the algorithm resume.

He pulled his mind back to the moment and broke the problem down into sections. Firstly, he asked himself, what was he trying to achieve? The answer was pretty simple. It was a non-paper based directory where he could add names, dates, crimes and locations plus details he'd found on the news app searches or from his own net surfing. Initially it would be time consuming to set up, but then it would make his life easier.

'So it's just a database,' he muttered, and then he thought it through a little further.

'But it aint.' He wanted to be able to search through the data, be able to cross reference the information stored, find similar crimes in similar locations and recover the names of the charged or convicted criminals linked with the crimes. And he wanted dates, repeating patterns, coincidences.

'No, it'll be more than just a database.' He'd need a programme to retrieve the information from it. Another thought dawned. He couldn't just store it on one of the academy computers or some solid state external memory source; he wanted to be able to access it from different computers, different locations.

He decided to talk it through with Damon. He checked the time on the bottom corner of his screen. It wouldn't take him more than a couple of minutes to skim the local news site before logging off and scootering over to Bury.

He moved the cursor across the screen and seconds later he was on the Eastern Anglia Daily Tribune site. *Police Appeal for Help*, the headline read. Matt scanned on. *Police investigating the death of John Camm, a local resident from the Northfield Wood area near Stowmarket, are appealing for help from the public. His body was found last week, Thursday 15th November. The police are trying to piece together his movements between Wednesday evening*

14th and the morning of Thursday 15th and are asking anyone who may have seen him or any person walking on the footpath alongside the Rush Green Golf Course, to contact the police. His death is being treated as suspicious.

'DOS-in' hell,' Matt muttered. 'Nick'll be right pissed off. He were real cut up about findin' him.' It brought back the evening he'd spent with Nick after the terrier woman waved him down and he'd seen the body, the lager infused headache and the sore bones from sleeping on the floor. Probably best not to text him a link to the news site, he decided and logged out.

'Oh scam,' he moaned as the next thought struck, this time nearer his solar plexus. 'The Bury Christmas Fayre.'

Working on the algorithm had made him forget, but now it popped back with the annoyance of a pop up screen advert. 'PUP,' he muttered. He'd have to thread a way through the back routes into Bury if he was going to find anywhere to park his Piaggio and avoid a long walk to the Balcon & Mora office.

With his mind torn between John Camm, and visualising his route through the back ways, he gathered up his backpack and swung it over his shoulder. This time he raised his hand in a half wave and mouthed *bye* to Rosie as he hurried from the library.

•

He sensed the festive excitement as he slowed the scooter to snail pace. He had skirted around Bury to the northwest approach and now weaved a path along narrow side roads with names like Pump Lane, Well Street, Short Brackland, and Cannon. They evoked a picture of the past, but he only had eyes for the festive bunting as he neared the heart of the town. Sounds of a funfair filled the air, and when he raised his visor, the smell of roasting chestnuts, warm cinnamon and ginger tantalised his nose. He found a space to park his scooter, tucked behind the Bury Free Press offices and some large plastic waste bins.

Now on foot, he elbowed and jostled his way past stalls crowding the Buttermarket. All about him people grazed on spicy samosas, burger buns and kebabs. Like flotsam in a current, he stall-gazed as he passed carved wooden animals, colourful scarves, sheepskin gloves and handmade soaps, displayed on covered stands, all tempting the punters.

He worked his way through the bustle, quickening his pace where the crowd thinned. Everyone was on foot, the roads closed to cars. Soon there were only stragglers – lost visitors or locals taking short cuts to the Abbey Gardens, Angel Hill or the Arc shopping centre. A sharp right and left, and at last he puffed his way up the narrow staircase to Damon's office still wearing his helmet.

'Hi, Matt. I see you made it. And earlier than usual for a Friday,' Damon said, opening the office door to let him in.

'I parked me scooter the other end of the Buttermarket,' Matt mumbled.

'Right. So you found somewhere OK. The roads have been closed round here since early morning. And we've got this for two more days. It's mad out there.'

Matt pulled his helmet off. 'It were easier than tryin' to carry it,' he said, finishing his thread of announcements. His mind raced on, fired by everything outside.

'I've been thinkin' about makin' a database, somewhere to store names an' stuff from that news app. But

I got to programme in a search function to retrieve stuff from me database and....'

'Yeah, the news. DI Clive Merry made a press announcement yesterday and John Camm was in the news again today, but I didn't need a news app to find it. Seems he was probably murdered.'

'Yeah, I read that too.' The reminder acted as a damper. He was back down to earth.

'What I'm saying is the news app is like an information filter. You don't want to link your database only to the news app, Matt.'

'So what you sayin'?'

'You'll have to spend a lot of time loading information in yourself. You can't leave it only to the news app. Now come on, you've a list of names to trace, so make yourself a hot drink and let's get on with some work.'

'But I've spent a load of time gettin' names and stuff from the news app. It's how to manage what I've already got,' Matt muttered.

Damon didn't seem to have heard, his eyes were already on his screen and his fingers tapping across his keyboard. Matt gave up explaining where he was coming from and turned his attention to making a mug of hot chocolate. He knew the first batch of names would be waiting for him as soon as he logged on and he needed to focus his mind.

Late afternoon passed into early evening and a first batch of names was replaced by a second batch and new contact details and addresses found. Behind him, Matt picked up on Damon's arm stretch and office chair push-back – the signal for a break.

'Coffee, I think. Hot chocolate?' Damon said as predicted and stood up.

'Thanks.'

'Git!'

'What?'

'Git and GitHub. That's the answer to your problem. You've heard of GitHub haven't you? It's a website. It hosts Git code repositories. It's private access, unless you want to make it public, but my point is you use Git, which is a distri-build control programme. In other words, we can both work on it at the same time and at different locations without blocking each other's access.'

'DOS-in' hell. You'll work on it as well?' Matt had difficulty taking it in. 'But that's mega. And it gets round usin' memory sticks. I, we... could access the database from here, from me laptop, from....'

'Exactly, but you'll need to enter the data - the names, dates, crimes etcetera in a comma-delimited file.'

'That's a csv file, right? With comma separated values?' He spoke, reading from his visual memory, '*A simple format for storing tabular data like... spreadsheets or–*'

'Databases. Yes.'

'Mega DOS-in' scam,' he murmured. Christmas had come early.

•

Two days later Matt found himself riding once again from Stowmarket to Bury St Edmunds, ready to trace the back ways into the heart of the Christmas Fayre. This time he had Maisie behind him on the Piaggio. It was late Sunday morning, and only minutes earlier they'd crept from his bedroom and along the cigarette scented hallway of the modest bungalow he'd called home for all of his twenty years. In the background the sound of daytime television seeped from the living room.

'Come on, it's the last day. There'll be loads of bargains,' Maisie had whispered in his ear, nudging him onwards as he'd opened the front door.

He'd hesitated. Should he check if the TV was on from all night? See if his mum was awake and up? He knew she wouldn't thank him for taking the trouble; more likely give him an earful.

'Yeah, well as long as there's plenty of food left on them food stalls,' he'd said in a low voice to Maisie before calling over his shoulder, 'I'm off now. Bye, Mum.'

Home was simply how and where it was, Tumble Weed Drive on the Flower Estate, a fact he had never thought to change or question, just as the world was round.

Riding the Piaggio away from Stowmarket and feeling Maisie warm against his back quickly blew all thoughts of home and his mother across the fields and into the trees and hedgerows. He had more pressing things on his mind. Brunch.

He knew the biggest cluster of food stalls would be at Angel Hill and in the neighbouring Abbey Gardens, and that's where he planned to head first. This time he threaded his way towards Eastgate and the Abbey Gardens, Maisie whooping and laughing as they passed *Closed Road* signs and slipped along little more than alleyways. He found somewhere to leave the Piaggio amongst the residential parking, stowed their helmets and let their ears and noses lead them from there.

'Can you hear that? It's a funfair, Matt. I love funfairs. We've got to have a go on one of them rides.'

He slid his arm around her, hugged her towards him and took the Abbey Gardens path.

'Hey, but it's that way.'

'Yeah, but the food's this way. Rare Breeds sausages. See, other people are cuttin' through this way. Got to be right.'

'OK then. Didn't you say Nick and...?' They dodged a gaggle of kids with a woman pushing a buggy. 'Hey, did you see that? They've got candy floss.'

'Why's it always pink?' Matt let his question float on the strains of a brass band playing *Rudolph the Red Nosed Reindeer* somewhere in the distance. 'Yeah, Nick, Chrissie, maybe Clive... they said they'd be comin'. Everyone's comin'. Maybe Ley from me course. What about your mates?'

'Most of them came yesterday, but I were working then weren't I. Today's good though, I'll be the one to get them bargains. You know, the last thing on the stall, *better to sell it cheap than load it back on the van*, kinda thing. They'll be right sick about it when I tell 'em.'

'Cool. Hey, that smells good. Pancakes and waffles. Do you fancy one?'

The path took them past the edge of a zone where grassy banks had been manicured to expose flint foundations and low crumbling walls, the ancient ruins of St Edmunds Abbey. Their route cut quickly to the wide path between formal flowerbeds, now hidden behind covered stalls. They paused at the crossing of paths.

'He don't look like he's charging much.' Matt pointed to where a man stood by a large tricycle. A small gas burner and hot plate were attached to the front, with space for what looked like a small barrel of batter. They watched as he poured a spoonful onto a flat griddle pan. Sweet buttery smells filled the air.

'I don't reckon he's official. Bet he's a food busker, tryin' his luck,' Maisie whispered loudly.

'Hey, how much for a pancake?'

Matt moved closer, captivated by the aroma, drawn by the need to watch the yellowy batter cook on the hot surface.

'A couple of quid, mate,' the man said and grinned.

'Then I want toppin'.'

'Chocolate sauce, or cocoa and cinnamon?'

'The second one, cocoa and,' Matt let his voice trail as the man reached for a container of brown powder and pulled at the lid.

'Arrgh!'

The lid flipped into the air, spinning above the pan. The man lunged to catch it. The lid brushed his fingers and launched into a scything flight. The man dived across the pan, eyes on the lid, arm outstretched. Down at hip level he knocked the pan.

'Hey, me pancake,' Matt yelled.

Cocoa and cinnamon powder tipped from the container, flying loose, propelled with the force of the man's movement. It rose above the dislodged pan and exposed burner. A fine dust - a cloud carried upwards on the warm air.

Matt's eyes were on the pan and his pancake, his senses flooded with delicious smells.

Whoosh!

A ball of scorching white erupted from the burner. It blazed a couple of feet into the air above the pan. The man leapt back. Maisie screamed. The white burned yellow, blackened and was gone. It was over. The naked blue burner-flame flickered back to its normal size, calm.

'What the DOS-in' hell?'

'Shit,' the man shouted, 'that were close. Cocoa powder! It aint cheap, you know. Just as well the whole friggin' lot didn't go into the air. Have I still got eyebrows?' he patted his face.

'I thought cocoa were chocolate, OK to eat. But it's bloody dangerous. You sure you should be puttin' it on pancakes?' Maisie said, breathless.

'Awesome! But, I still want me pancake. I reckon a discount's in order after that,' Matt said. 'And I'll settle for just loads of chocolate sauce instead.'

Even as he spoke, the ball of blinding white played back across his retinas. He was fascinated. Had he just witnessed a dust cloud ignite?

'Mega cool. A cocoa dust cloud,' he whispered.

CHAPTER 11

Nick stood and gazed at the specially erected bandstand in front of the Abbey Gate, and beyond it the Abbey Gardens. The medieval stone gatehouse exuded an air of the past. It framed one side of the staging, serving as a baffle and reflecting sound back onto Angel Hill. Around him, the Christmas Fayre crowd stall-gazed and food-grazed, talked and laughed. A few paused to listen, but most walked on, eager to sample hot spiced ale or mulled wine, while the ever present sound of funfair rides competed in the distance.

He was drawn by the all-encompassing timbre of the brass band playing on the temporary platform. *Rudolph the Red Nosed Reindeer* might not have been the best choice to show off their warm rounded sound to full advantage, but it jogged along happily, the band keeping good time and descant riffs on the saxophone weaving above the melody.

He liked the sound, not so much of the band as a whole, but of the soprano saxophone. He concentrated on the player. A girl. Unusual he thought. She looked into the crowd and caught his eye, her festive red hat drawing her hair back from her face.

He gasped, unable to contain the shock. What the hell? He started to turn away, but a second glance told him it wasn't Mel.

Mel was a girlfriend from the past. She'd been special, his first serious affair and doomed to failure. She'd played with his emotions, almost broken him. As sure as hell, he wasn't going to let something like that happen to him again. How could people have such power over you, he wondered.

He forced himself to study the saxophonist's face. She had the same bone structure as Mel, but her hair was a shade darker and her skin less pale. He couldn't tell if she had the same coloured eyes – a pale green. He was too far away. He hadn't thought of her in months. Other girls had come and gone; in fact there was one he'd left only five minutes ago looking at a stall selling pottery mugs. But in the moment he'd thought he'd seen Mel on the platform, it was as if he'd been punched in the guts.

'Are you OK? You look as if you've seen a ghost.'

'What? Hey, Chrissie! Clive!' Nick shouted, noticing them standing next to him in the crowd as he struggled to get his equilibrium. He searched the faces beyond, 'Matt and Maisie with you?'

'Not yet. I should have guessed we'd find you in front of the bandstand,' Clive laughed.

Chrissie flung her arms around him. 'The hug's just in case we're being followed,' she whispered.

'So have you?' Clive asked. 'Have you seen a ghost?'

'More like a blast from the past. I-I thought I'd seen Mel. The girl playing the soprano sax looks a bit like her. I was about to cut and run.'

'Mel? Wasn't she the girlfriend from your Exeter days?' Chrissie said.

'Exeter?'

'Yeah, Clive, that's where I met Mel. I was at uni there. Environmental Sciences, but it didn't work out. That's before I discovered carpentry.'

He turned his attention back to the bandstand. He didn't want to revisit those painful months before he dropped out of the course and came back home to Suffolk. Instead he watched the band shuffling score sheets on music stands in preparation for the next number. He cast a furtive glance at the Mel look-alike.

Chrissie caught his look. 'Right, we'll leave you to it. We haven't had a browse around some of the stalls here yet.'

'No, it's OK. It's not what you think. I've got…. There's a girl I met last night. I left her looking at mugs. I expect she'll show up in a moment.'

'You really are impossible,' Chrissie giggled, 'We'll be back in about fifteen minutes. See you then.' She grabbed Clive's hand, dragging him off towards a stand of colourful knits.

'Oh no,' Nick moaned. Only a few days before, it had been the raincoat girl and now he'd just admitted to thinking he'd seen an old girlfriend from the past. If he had been mistaken about one, he could have been mistaken about the other. Clive must think he was unreliable, seeing things in the shadows, imaging threat where there wasn't any, hysterical.

While strains of *White Christmas* floated around him, his mind replayed some of the phone interview with Clive.

'So you're absolutely sure the woman was following Chrissie,' Clive had asked on Friday. 'And you think you would recognise her if you saw her again?'

He had said yes and after describing what she'd been wearing, agreed to drop in at the police station in Stowmarket and help compile a photo fit. Apparently they would be expecting him. Since then the weekend had arrived and driven all thoughts of the raincoat girl away, until of course seeing Clive and the Mel look-alike.

'Hey, what do you think?'

He felt a hesitant tap on his shoulder and turned to look into the face of Aimée, or was she called Anna? She must have read the doubt in his eyes and frowned.

'What do I think?' he countered quickly, slipping into smooth chat-up patter. 'I'd have to take a look to be able to say.'

'Well I chose the snowman one. I thought it would look kinda cool drinking from it all year. You know, the mug's not just for Christmas?' She smiled at her joke and nodded towards the bandstand. 'Hey, do we have to stay and listen to this?'

He was about to say *not if you don't want to* but changed his mind. Did he really want to spend the next few hours with this girl?

'I said I'd meet some of my friends here,' he said, turning back to look at the brass band.

'Well in that case, a bunch of my mates are having a beer at Wetherspoon's. I think I'll go and join them. We'll probably be there for an hour or so.'

Her meaning was clear, and so he hoped was his.

'OK, then. I think I'll hang around here a bit longer. Bye for now, Anna.' He tried to keep his voice light, but it was difficult with the crowd all around.

'It's Aimée,' she said and turned on her heel.

He reckoned he wouldn't be hearing from her again.

While *Sleigh Bells Ringing* pounded out at a jolly trotting pace, he hoped he hadn't pissed her off too much, and by two numbers later, Chrissie and Clive had returned.

'Have you had enough of this?' Chrissie asked bluntly.

'What, listening to the soprano sax?'

'No, I meant the Fayre. We've seen enough now, all the stalls are starting to look the same. We thought we'd go and have a walk through Northfield Wood. Do you want to come?'

'Northfield Wood? Are you driving all the way to Onehouse now?'

'We've got to go in that direction anyway. It's only a couple of miles on from Woolpit,' Clive said.

'Right, yes I suppose that doesn't make it too far from the White Hart. But there's a walk here, through the Abbey Gardens and alongside the river. It's closer if you want a walk. Why go all the way to Northfield Wood?'

'Because of the Trophy. Something happened there in the 1960s. I've done some reading about the wood. I couldn't find much, but there are some parts of the wood I think might be worth a visit,' Chrissie explained.

'How'd you mean?'

'Well, although they started clearing the old wood in the 60s and planting with commercial conifers, it took some time. The last conifers went in in 1970. A lot has happened since then. The Great Storm of '87 being one of them.'

'So there's not much to see?'

'Well not of the 1961 planting – most of those came down in the storm. But after the storm and in the rest of late 80s there was a change of heart and they started restocking with native broadleaf trees.'

'I don't get it. You're being obtuse again. What are we expecting to see or find?' Clive asked, irritation written across his face.

'My point is - anything to find would have been found in 1990 when they restocked with common ash and oak after the Great Storm. But I reckon there are still a couple of areas with the commercial conifers from the 60s, in fact planted in 1967 and '68. I think we should have a walk around there. Also, somewhere amongst it all there are two large earth mounds.'

'Earth mounds?' Nick found himself drawn into her train of thought.

'Old charcoal mounds. They made charcoal there in the old days,' she explained.

'So what exactly are you saying, Chrissie? I thought we were just going for a walk in the woods. Are you suggesting we bring spades or something?' Clive's voice cut across the jostle of the crowd behind him.

'Oh come on, Clive. There won't be any flowers or much wildlife to see at the moment and there's got to be an objective to a walk. It's only a bit of fun. What do you say? You were all for it earlier.'

'Yes but that's before you started on about–'

'Yeah, I'll come, Chrissie,' Nick butted in as he caught Chrissie's look, 'but no spades.'

He was intrigued, and the prospect of a crazy expedition to explore Northfield Wood was just what he needed. As for chatting-up the Mel look-alike? Fate, in the form of Northfield Wood, had just stepped in. At the age of twenty-three he didn't need to relive an eighteen year old's emotions. Instead he'd leave a note for the soprano sax player saying to give him a ring if she was interested in playing in Jake's band.

'Come on, Clive,' he added. 'You can see Chrissie's determined to go and have a look. And it's better she's walking with us than by herself. Any stalker following either of you will be obvious.'

'Exactly. So is that decided then?' Chrissie asked.

They agreed to meet in the Onehouse community centre car park in about an hour. 'It's where the Northfield Wood website said to park,' Chrissie explained.

•

Nick followed Chrissie and Clive through the kissing-gate. The path was wide and muddy as they entered Northfield Wood. Ahead, conifers fifty yards away blocked out light and cast shades of grey across the cold winter afternoon.

'You can see where the native trees have sprung up on the edge here and where the wood management team have started coppicing again.'

She waved her arm towards the common ash trees. One or two were mature but most were only three or four meters tall, like poles growing up in clumps from ground level tree stumps. Light played between their rod-like trunks and down between their fine leafless branches. Nick felt drawn towards the more open coppiced ash area, while underfoot rotting fallen leaves, mud and dank puddles slowed his pace.

The path soon forked, one track branching off and heading deeper amongst the confers, the other leading on between the coppiced ash. Chrissie stopped and unfolded her printout map of the wood.

'This way,' she said and set out along the narrower muddier path through the conifers.

'Hey, can I see the map,' Nick called and hurried to catch up. He knew how abysmal her sense of direction could be and made sure he'd orientated himself with the map. 'So what's so special about where you've marked?'

'They're the areas which I reckon haven't been disturbed since the conifers were first planted in 1967 and

'68. So Scots pine there.' She pointed to an area circled in pencil, 'And the Norway spruce and western cedar here, where we are now.'

'And the crosses are the mounds, right? In amongst the spruce and cedar?'

'Yes, that's right.'

'Our biggest problem is the mud, Chrissie.' Clive peered down over her shoulder and slipped his arm around her to point at the map. 'We're going to have to leave the footpath and walk into... here.'

Nick read his practicality, sensed his attempt to soften the negativity.

'But come on, we can at least try.' She sounded belligerent.

'Does your phone track your position, like a sat nav, Clive?' Nick knew it was a long shot, but he had to at least ask. He'd already checked his own mobile.

'That'll be the day. No bloody signal!'

'No, I can't get one either,' Nick murmured.

They walked in single file, picking their way as best they could around the worst of the mud and into the gloom cast by the dark trees. The path led them past some tall straight standard oaks stretching up to the coniferous canopy above.

'At least they spared some of the standards when they'd cleared all this to plant commercial trees,' Nick murmured. He felt the sadness of the wilful destruction inflicted in the 1960s. It seeped from the cold damp bark and accused. All around, even the spruce and cedar trunks oozed malevolence, as if to say *don't you like us interlopers? Would you have us cut down?*

'Here!' Chrissie called from a yard or so ahead. She stood to one side of the track staring into the trees.

'Are you sure it isn't an animal track. There'll be deer in the wood,' Clive said.

'No, look. You can see people have walked it. There are boot prints. If you look at the map, the old charcoal burning area is on this side of the path, off over there.' She pointed.

'Is it leading off to the left?' Nick called, picturing the map.

He was bringing up the rear, keeping his ears and eyes peeled for the slightest hint they were being followed. The scent of pine made him wonder if the ground underfoot might be easier if they strayed off the path and onto a smaller track. There would have been less footfall to churn up the ground, and all those dead pine needles and fallen leaves and cones would have matted into the mud, firming it up, binding it together.

'This way, then. Into the unknown,' Clive said, as Nick caught up.

He followed them off the path and onto firmer but still muddy ground. The winter undergrowth was meagre, starved of light from the dense canopy above, but brambles had sprung up where trees had fallen or died back.

They forged on, the mood of an expedition speeding their steps. Nick found it difficult to judge the distance they'd walked, as the track cut across the lines of planted trees, then weaved between them.

'I think I can see something. Is that a charcoal mound?' Chrissie's voice carried on the still air, the direction distorted by the surrounding wood.

It took Nick a moment to catch up, and at first he couldn't make out anything resembling a mound. Instead his eyes were drawn to the disturbed earth. Shovelfuls of dark soil had been tossed across the ground. Rough holes had been gouged out of an area cleared of its natural ground cover. It could have been an archaeological excavation, except for the untidiness and the heavy-handed spadework.

'What the hell?' But he didn't expect an answer.

He stared, slowly identifying where the ground rose barely a foot in height. The earth had been disturbed across what at first glance, could have passed for the remains of a flattened ancient bank. Except there was no accompanying ditch. And it was too wide - about three metres across.

He crouched to examine the exposed soil more clearly. Fragments of charcoal were obvious. Now he recognised it for what it was. Its true contours had been disguised by its sparse ground cover, eroded and altered by time. It was an old charcoal mound.

'Vandals?' Chrissie asked.

'It looks as if someone was searching for something specific. See how the area is peppered with shallow holes and then there's this deeper one? This was recent. And they were in a hurry.' Clive thrust his hand into his pocket and then seemed to hesitate. 'I'd forgotten. No bloody signal,' he muttered.

'Should we get back to the car? We can call from there.' Chrissie's voice sounded thin and strained.

'Do you want me to wait here, by the... evidence?' Nick asked, and immediately wished he'd kept his mouth shut.

'No, Nick. The light will be fading soon. We can't leave you out here. I'll take some photos, but then I'll need to check this out with the warden or woodland manager, and probably have this area of the wood closed to the public. It'll just have to wait until we get back to the cars before I can make the calls.'

Nick stood and gazed at the largest hole while Clive started to take some pictures with his phone.

'You don't need to hang around here for me. Start back with Chrissie. I'll catch you two up in a minute.'

Something made Nick shiver. 'No, let's all walk together. No splitting up, right? We'll wait for you.'

Twenty-five minutes later, back at the community centre car park, Nick was about to unlock his old Ford Fiesta. Something made him pause as a thought struck.

'Weren't our cars the only ones parked here when we set out on our walk?' He stared at a dark metallic grey saloon parked next to Clive's black Mondeo.

'If it's only one car, then I don't mind checking it out,' Clive murmured and took a quick shot of the number plate with his phone.

'Why? Would it make any difference if the car park had been full of cars? If someone's following us they're following us. It doesn't matter how many other walkers or cars are here. Doesn't sound logical to me,' Chrissie said, and Nick recognised her anxious reasoning as she struck a hands-on-hips pose.

'Ah signal!' Clive said triumphantly.

'I think it's time for the White Hart,' Nick muttered as he wondered if there'd been a similar discussion earlier in the day in the Christmas Fayre car park. Something on a vaster scale.

CHAPTER 12

'Where are you, Nick? I've been texting. I thought we were supposed to be meetin' up at the bandstand.' Matt couldn't keep the whinge out of his voice as he answered the call.

He had been annoyed earlier, but by the time Nick eventually phoned, most of the irritation had worn off and he was secretly pleased to hear from his mate. Maisie, on the other hand, was still cross. She'd hung around Angel Hill when she could have been exploring the stalls on Cornhill and Buttermarket. In the end they'd given up waiting.

'Chrissie had some mad idea to take a hike through Northfield Wood, and I had a girl hanging around I didn't really fancy. It got a bit complicated. Sorry, mate. I should have texted you, but I had other things on my mind and then no signal on the walk.'

'What? The stalker bird was chasin' you again?'

'No. At least I don't think so. But there've been vandals in the wood. And now Clive is busy making phone calls.'

'That wood, the Northfield one? It keeps croppin' up. What's so special about it? Is that where you're callin' from?'

'No. I just said no signal. I'm in the White Hart, with Chrissie. Clive will be ages yet, so we'll be here for a while. Why don't you and Maisie drop in for a pint on your way back to Stowmarket? We'll tell you more about it then.'

'Yeah, OK.' He ended the call.

He glanced fondly at Maisie. Her skinny jeans seemed to accentuate her slender legs as she bent to look at a straw and cane antelope. It stood about two foot tall with festive red ribbons tied around its neck.

'See I told you there'd be bargains,' she mouthed, turning back to Matt.

'Yeah, but what you goin' to do with it, Mais?'

He felt weary. Even the light was starting to fade. Two circuits of the Cornhill and Buttermarket part of town had drained his energy, but an invitation to drink lager and the prospect of sitting down were exactly what he needed. Maisie might still have the oomph to dart through the crowd milling in the old narrow streets, but Matt had peaked. He was already flagging, a spent shadow with sore feet.

'Who were you callin', Matt?' She sounded sharp but her eyes were on the antelope.

'No one. Nick just called me. Seems he's been caught up with some vandals. Northfield Wood.'

'But we were meetin' him here at the Fayre, weren't we? What's he doin' in a wood?'

'How'd I know, Mais? But if we drop in at the White Hart on the way home, he'll tell us.'

'Well I aint hangin' around for him if he's not there. Right? Now which of these reindeer, do you reckon?'

'I thought it was an antelope.'

'Nah – the red ribbon. It's got to be a reindeer.'

He watched, disconnected, as she haggled with a burley stallholder. He followed the pointing, the shrugs, the nods and shakes of heads, her pink highlights seemingly electric and hinting of candyfloss.

'But I thought....,' Matt protested. He had read the gestured interplay and drawn a different conclusion.

He helped her carry it, not the two foot tall reindeer, but one the next size up, apparently knocked down to half price. A bargain.

'How are we fittin' it on the scooter, Mais?'

He didn't catch her answer, as they dodged past colourful stalls, buskers and portable chestnut roasters.

They left Bury and took the back routes to Woolpit and the White Hart; Maisie sitting behind him on the Piaggio, the reindeer wedged between them and catching the wind.

'It's DOS-in' spikey, Mais.'

She'd jammed its body across her lap, its legs jutting down on each side to well below her knees. Its belly scratched his lower back - the part where his sweatshirt parted company with his jeans as he sat leaning into the wind. Its head stuck into his arm and shoulder, the antlers poked the side of his helmet.

It wasn't cosy or comfortable as Maisie huddled the reindeer against him, but at least it felt good to get away from the crowd. The constant jostling, the half snatched conversations, the fragments of words, they all buzzed around in his head like an auditory kaleidoscope.

He concentrated on the road, the tarmac merging with the grey of the grass verge as the light quickly faded. The scooter made good time despite the extra load of Maisie plus a passenger with antlers, and within the half hour they rode into sleepy-Sunday Woolpit. It seemed so quiet after the noisy bustle of the Bury Christmas Fayre.

'We aint leaving it out here,' she screeched as he drew up outside the White Hart.

'What you talkin' about? Me Piaggio'll be OK here.'

'Not the scooter. The reindeer.'

He didn't dare turn to watch Maisie dismount, he wasn't going to risk an antler injury. He felt the pressure of straw and cane ease against his back, and then for a moment he was Matteo again, breath smelling of the Italian sausage Maisie had bought him from a stall selling Italian olives and cheeses.

'Come on, Matt. Aint you getting' off that thing?'

He stowed his helmet and sauntered after her, catching up in time to help with the reindeer as they negotiated the door into the main bar. It could never quite have the feel of a second home, like the Nags Head or the Academy library, but just in that instant, it was up there with the Utterly computer lab.

'Hey, over here!'

Nick's voice carried from a corner of the bar where he sat with Chrissie at one of the old salvaged treadle-base tables. No Clive.

Secretly he was pleased Clive was still wherever he was making calls. It meant he could have a word with Chrissie about his project. Not that Clive wasn't an OK kind of bloke, but he couldn't always read him, couldn't work out what he meant when he said something straight but his eyes creased. Chrissie said Clive had smiley eyes. He reckoned it must be what she meant, and waved at Chrissie.

'My round. What are you going to have?' Nick asked as he walked over. 'I see you've brought Rudolph with you.'

'Rudolph? See I told ya.' Maisie raised her voice, 'See, Nick knew it were a reindeer. Yeah I like that, but...

Rudi don't drink. So a Rum an' Coke for me and Matt'll probably have–'

'A lager, I'm guessing,' Nick said and turned to the barman.

'Rudi?' Matt hissed to Maisie. If it had to have a name he wished she'd asked him first. He'd have said Rodolfo. At least it was Italian.

They carried the reindeer over to where Chrissie sat while Nick paid for the drinks.

'Hey, that looks Christmassy.'

'Yeah, hi Chrissie. Rudi were a bargain. A stall on Cornhill. I thought you were goin' to the Fayre,' Maisie chirped.

'I did, but... Rudi? You brought it back on the scooter?'

'Yeah,' Matt muttered. He reckoned *yeah* was enough said about the ride. 'But what the DOS-in' hell have you been up to? Nick said there's vandals in the wood. Is everyone OK? Is Clive around?'

'Yes, Clive's around. He's just making some calls, and we're all fine. But I'm dying to hear what you've found on your news search. I was hoping for an update on Friday, but if you remember you were working late in Bury. I left ages before you ever made it to the Nags Head.'

'Right.' He flopped into a spindle-back pine armchair. It was a relief to focus his thoughts on his project. He closed his eyes and visualised computer code as he retraced the steps – the ones he was making with Damon to build a virtual crime news library. The logic was reassuring, the structure of GitHub calming.

'Here, Matt. You look as if you need this.'

He heard Nick's voice, felt a cold glass of lager pushed into his hand, and opened his eyes.

'Thanks, mate.' He gulped down a mouthful.

Then it struck him. He was so taken up with the process of creating a virtual cross-referencing local crime library that he'd forgotten to concentrate on the names. He had allowed the computing to take him over. Chrissie wanted answers, and that meant names - the people posing a threat, the names of potential stalkers. And here he was, about to tell her about *pip package manager, Git, GitHub*, and *virtualenv environment manager*. What was he thinking?

'Right,' he murmured as he dredged his memory and focussed on what he'd found surfing the net so far. 'Well there was a case of his, five years ago when he were still a DS. Tyrell Bowfell were sent down for theft and grievous bodily. He got five years, but he were let out a couple of years ago and I aint found nothin' he done since. So it aint him or any of his family.'

'Because the threats would have started two years ago, right?'

'Yeah, I reckon so. Or even earlier when he went down, Chrissie.'

He glanced across at Maisie. She seemed to be talking about reindeer with Nick.

'And of course there were that spate of post office raids,' Matt continued, 'and he were part of the investigatin' team. But that were armed robbery and the hoods are still inside.'

'I suppose it would help if you knew exactly when the threatening emails started, wouldn't it?' she murmured.

'Well yeah, Chrissie. It would narrow the search. But there's always arson and shotgun deaths. There's drownin's in reservoirs, dykes and flooded gravel pits. What's an accident and what aint? I figure he were on the team investigatin' those bodies found in that container. Remember, the one stolen from Harwich Docks? And take the gangs constantly nickin' farm equipment and diesel. I don't think they even know what their real names are any more. I mean handles like Bazu Band, Joey Coeur and Riley Roller? They don't sound Suffolk and they aint easy to trace.'

He watched Chrissie nod slowly. Was that a *yes*, or *kind of yes*?

'What's Clive said? He must've told you somethin',' he said.

She looked up and waved. 'Why don't you ask him yourself? But don't mention your search, OK?'

He followed the direction of her smile and spotted Clive standing near the bar. He must have come in a few moments earlier while they were talking. He wore a winter anorak and dark chino-look walking trousers, dried mud splattered the fabric below the knees.

Of course, the walk in the wood! The questions about his internet crime search had driven it from his mind. He let his glance drop. Fine tell-tale spots and smears of dried mud spattered Chrissie's lower trousers. Crumbly earth peppered the boards, shed from Nick's jeans and trainers where he sat, legs outstretched. Not my kind of a walk, Matt thought and relaxed. Thank DOS he hadn't been included. Not his type of thing at all.

'You look happy,' Chrissie said, as Clive walked over with a pint of ale.

'Well yes, I think we've got the stalker.'

'Really? That's fantastic!' Chrissie gave him a kiss as he sat down on one of the spindle-back chairs next to her.

'So come on, tell us. Does she look anything like the smudgy photos Jake took, or my photo fit picture?'

'Yes, Nick. That, and some help from the CCVT footage from the Corner House is partly how we got her. I thought I'd seen her before, thought she looked familiar, but I couldn't place her. And we hadn't found anyone on our files who matched. But that parked car, we–'

'I knew it. I knew that car was going to be something to do with the digging,' Chrissie interrupted.

'Let me finish, Chrissie. I asked someone to check the registration details on the DVLA website. I recognised the name, remembered interviewing her, but hadn't thought anything about it at the time because it was her son we were interested in. And of course now it all falls into place. She must have become obsessed with me. I asked one of our team to stop her when she came back to the car. They're interviewing her now, but this is where I step away from it. Too close to the case.'

'But the digging we found, how does that fit in? What's all that about?' Nick asked.

'I don't think she's anything to do with the digging. I think whoever was looking for something in that charcoal mound was... well I don't think they're connected.'

'What digging? What charcoal mound?' Matt asked, but no one seemed to hear him.

'So this woman was threatening you? But why?' Chrissie asked.

'She wasn't. It was her son. Supposedly some prank or dare after I'd visited the school to give a talk about the police and law enforcement. PR stuff really, but cyber bullying was part of what I covered. Someone from the internet forensics team came with me. After the threats came we traced the emails. I interviewed her son while she was present. It was a few months ago now.'

'You give talks in schools?' Maisie squeaked.

'But why break into our home? And why take your computer?'

'I'm not sure, but I think we're going to find her trainers match Jake' photos, and also match the partial sole-print we found after the break-in.'

'Right,' Nick said.

They sat in silence, sipping their drinks. Matt's auditory kaleidoscope had returned. Sound bites of information whirled into different patterns. He needed something solid to peg them, like names and dates.

'So what's this stalker bird called?' he asked.

'She hasn't been charged yet, so I'm not free to say.'

'And when was the break-in? The date?' Matt persisted, following his focus.

'Monday, 12th of November,' Chrissie said softly.

'But the digging. What about the digging? What did the warden or ranger say? Can you at least tell us that, Clive?' Nick's voice sounded sharp.

'Reindeers? Did you just say reindeers, Nick?'

'No, Maisie, rangers. But Clive, have you managed to contact the warden or whoever knows the wood?'

'Yes, and I'm meeting him first thing in the morning, as soon as it's daylight and I can show him the place. We'll take it from there.'

'But Clive,' Chrissie protested.

'Think of it as an early morning run, and besides, the warden said there shouldn't be any digging there or anywhere else in the wood.' He sipped his ale. 'Look, it's only twelve days since John Camm died. His final walk may have taken him through the wood. Apparently it was on his regular circuit, and I don't know how fresh that digging is. I have to take it seriously, Chrissie.'

'I hadn't realised you think it could be related,' she murmured.

'But...,' Matt's mind still wrestled with something. The identity of the stalker and the author of the threatening emails had been nailed. Cool news, but there was one more thing he needed to know. 'How long ago did the threatenin' emails start, Clive?'

'September. Why, Matt?'

'Just wonderin'.' He wasn't going to say, but his five year search window had been way too large. Now he needed a new project, something more manageable. He reckoned he'd ask Damon if he'd continue to help him build a site, but this time maybe a John Camm and Northfield Wood site.

'Right, does anyone want another drink? Hey, I like the reindeer, Maisie,' Clive said, and smiled.

'Shush, keep your voice down, Clive. I don't think reindeer are allowed in the bar,' Chrissie whispered loudly.

CHAPTER 13

Chrissie lifted her duffle coat from the row of hooks in her narrow hallway, slipped her arms into the sleeves and hugged the blanket-like material close. A blast of cold air cut around her ankles as she pulled the door further open and followed Clive outside. It wasn't yet light, sunrise another twenty minutes away. It might only be seven in the morning, but Clive was about to get into his car and drive over to Northfield Wood to meet the warden. By the time he arrived, the dawn light would be sufficient for them to find their way through the wood.

She would have liked to be going with them, but he'd said, 'This is police business, Chrissie.' She hadn't argued. She knew he was right, but it was difficult to swallow her curiosity and so her restless mind had her up, dressed and ready to leave for work instead.

'Let me know what you find. Bye,' she called and turned to lock her front door.

For the last couple of weeks she'd barely shown her back to the quiet road outside her home without continually glancing over her shoulder. She had imagined the stalker waiting, watching, ready to run at her and bowl her over. However this morning was different. The stalker was held in Ipswich, still being questioned. It felt safe, and for the moment that particular weight had been lifted.

She hurried to her TR7, reining her thoughts in and forcing herself to focus on the work waiting for her in the Clegg workshop. By the time she turned off the Wattisham Airfield boundary lane and rocked along the rough track leading to the courtyard in front of the old barn, she had made the transition from weekend to work.

'Good morning, Mr Clegg,' she said as she closed the heavy wooden door. 'Wow, the oak settle looks amazing. Mr Mawbray should be pleased with that.'

'Good morning. Yes, now it's had a good lick of polish it—'

'Positively glows. Don't forget to take a post-repair photo. It'll make a good *before and after* for our website, if we ever get one up and running.'

'Website, Mrs Jax? I can see the logic of taking photographs of furniture when it comes in, before we start work on it, and I admit it's already proving quite useful. In fact it's been a very good idea of yours. But a website? Let's not go overboard about this shall we?'

'I know, one step at a time, and all that. But a website is hardly going overboard, Mr Clegg, and we've got to join the twenty-first century. One day there'll be better internet access here and we'll be able to move on from purely paper records.'

'A strong mug of tea would be nice, if you're making, Mrs Jax,' Ron said and returned to slow buffing movements as he polished the arms of the settle.

While she filled the kettle and dropped teabags into a couple of mugs, she remembered the tussle over introducing the camera into the workshop. It was difficult to justify buying one for the new partnership, and a computer tablet to take photos was out of the question, too alien for Ron. However when Sarah said she was buying a new camera and didn't know what to do with the old digital one, Chrissie leapt at her free offer. The hand-me-down had a good lens, simple controls, and with automatic flash, focus and zoom options, Ron had taken to using it. She simply kept two memory cards and at intervals swopped them around so that she could download the photos at home and print hard copies to bring back for the files in the workshop. And while Ron worked on a piece, he could always view the photos on the camera screen.

Thank God the stalker didn't take my laptop, she thought and made a mental note to backup the photos.

'The police have caught the person who broke into my house,' she said, as she set a mug of strong tea down next to Ron.

'That's excellent news. So who was it? A youngster?'

'Not exactly. All I know is it's a woman.'

'A woman burglar breaking into houses? Actually breaking in when there might be someone at home? Isn't that a bit unusual, Mrs Jax? I mean for a woman to do that?'

'I think she already knew our movements. I don't think she was expecting a physical confrontation, if that's what you mean by unusual,' Chrissie said, and then went on to explain further and describe her Sunday.

It was the first time she'd mentioned her stalking fears to Ron. Discussing work was good, but personal baggage? Something which might be considered an irrational emotional fear? It would have meant crossing a line, exposing too much to a business partner and risked looking weak. But now she'd been proved right about the stalking it felt safe to tell, and reaffirming to show she'd been correct all along. It was official - her nose for this kind of thing was bang on, as Matt would say.

'You should have told me, Mrs Jax. If I'd known I'd have kept an eye out for anything suspicious around here.'

'Yes, but I didn't want to appear neurotic.'

She could have added that he rarely talked about himself and his reticence sometimes made her hold back in return, although it didn't stop her being curious. The bond between them had begun as trainer and apprentice, the formality persisting despite her joining the business as a partner. She had contented herself with guessing about him and piecing together fragments of his life; she supposed he'd once been married, that there'd been no children and that his wife was no longer around. She also guessed it was a great sadness to him. A lot of guessing, as Clive would have said, but she reckoned she had a nose for this kind of thing.

'Have you heard from the golf club? Do you know which of your designs they've chosen?' he said, changing the subject and throwing her off beam.

'I thought it would be a bit soon to hear. I only emailed the plans to the club secretary after I got home on Thursday. He's at the golf club on a Wednesday, so if I haven't heard by then I'll give him a call.'

'Fair enough. But the trophy? Is that why you went for a walk in Northfield Wood yesterday?'

'Yes, but it was silly really. I mean the "accident" was so long ago. I don't know what I expected to find,' she said and sipped the last of her tea. 'Mind you, the digging was a surprise. Clive reckons it's most likely vandals or even something to do with John Camm.'

'Ah yes, John Camm. The man found dead on the footpath by the golf course.'

'Hmm, but it seems he didn't just drop in his tracks with a heart attack. Something whacked him on the head.

There were golf balls nearby, but apparently it doesn't all add up.'

'Really? But aren't there always golf balls around golf courses, Mrs Jax? Surely there's nothing unusual in that?'

'I suppose not. But....' She remembered Clive's words, *the way he was lying, he was facing the wrong way for a ball to hit him where it did, from the fairway. Wrong temple.*

'But what, Mrs Jax?'

'I don't know. It's just there are so many questions begging for answers. I tend to get drawn into things, don't I? I must be basically nosey, but on this one it's Northfield Wood, not John Camm that really intrigues me.'

'I'd have said curious rather than nosey. But enough of that, it's time to get on with some work.'

He was right of course. She had a Queen Anne walnut bureau to finish restoring before she started work on the trophy. That was assuming Paul Cooley hadn't been put off by her repair designs and still wanted her to work on it.

She inspected her repair of one of the bureau's drawer bottoms. She had found a suitably aged piece of oak amongst the wood stored in the old brick outbuilding, a stone's throw from the main workshop. She'd been careful to make sure the grain of the wood ran from the front to the back of the drawer in keeping with the age of the piece, somewhere around 1710. It was definitely a genuine Queen Anne bureau with a fold down writing surface, walnut veneered onto oak, no fakery, and no botched earlier repairs.

'Right, now for the pull-outs,' she murmured. They had a proper name; Ron called them lopers, but she preferred the term pull-out bearers, the struts which when pulled out, supported the writing surface while folded down. One of these had failed. The block of wood glued to one end and acting as the stop had worn and broken so that when she pulled the loper, it came out of the bureau completely.

The mechanism was relatively straightforward, and as she bent to peer more closely at the bureau she caught the faint smell of old wood and wax polish.

'Just as well I've got small hands,' she sighed as she took the top drawers out and felt upwards to the pull-out's slider channel. She had to get her arm deep into the space vacated by the drawer, knocking her elbow against the drawer rail and front post.

'Lucky the bureau was made in one piece,' Ron said, pausing as he walked past her to the shelf of waxes, polishes and oils on the far wall.

'Yes, I was worried it was constructed using the older technique, you know, in two pieces. A separate bureau top and separate chest base with a sheet of wood in between to obstruct me. But it's an all-in-one. It's the strip of moulding that makes you think there might be a sheet of wood there.'

'Yes, the advances in cabinet making, Mrs Jax. But the new lines were obviously still too plain for the customer of 1710.'

'So, they gave him what he was used to seeing, hey Mr Clegg? They attached a strip of moulding, not as a cover-up, but for decoration. He was made to think there was a join underneath when really there wasn't, and they made the piece more quickly and used less wood. Manipulate and deceive, that was the name of the game.'

'I'd have said it was progress. You're sounding very cynical, Mrs Jax.'

'Not at all. I'm just thankful I can get my arm up inside here.'

It didn't take her long, working on her bench, to cut a fresh stop from a piece of old oak and remove the worn broken one from the loper. She prepared the wooden surfaces and heated granules of animal glue with water, in keeping with the techniques of 1710.

Her work completely absorbed her as she struggled with the restricted access and poor view to reach and glue the replacement stop onto the pull-out. It would have been the work of a few moments out on the workbench, but this had to be done while it was back in position in its slider channel inside the bureau.

'Finally, tea,' she murmured, triumphantly.

The job was done. She had a sore elbow and a stiff neck, but it was time for their mid-morning break. That's when the questions about Northfield Wood rushed back. She figured Clive should have had enough time to find something out by now. She reached for her mobile.

'You're frowning, Mrs Jax.'

'I was just thinking about manipulating and deceiving.'

'In what way?'

'Well, take the digging in the wood. It could have been truffle hunters, but my eye, or rather my brain explained the digging as proof someone had been searching for something much larger and deeper. I was hoping for clues, something to tell me what might have happened there in the past. And so I saw it through biased eyes. I imagined buried secrets, if you see what I mean. But it was my brain doing the manipulating and deceiving.'

'Like the bureau?'

'Kind of, Mr Clegg.'

She pressed Clive's automatic dial and listened to the call tone.

Her last words to him earlier that morning had been *let me know what you find*, so it should have been him making the call. He answered almost immediately.

'Hi, Chrissie.' He sounded pleased to hear from her, as if expecting her call.

'Hi,' she said briskly, 'how did you get on with the warden? Did you discover what the digging was about? You promised you'd let me know, remember?'

'Oh yes....'

She held her breath as he let his voice trail. Was he collecting his thoughts or playing with her? She suspected he was half teasing, and felt irritated. Two could play at this game. She kept her voice even, controlled.

'So do they have a problem with truffle hunters like I said? Was I right, Clive?'

'I don't remember you saying anything about truffle hunters,' he answered, his tone now questioning, alert. Then she caught his quiet laugh before he said, 'But you didn't did you? You're just messing with me, right?'

'Right, but come on, tell me. The suspense is killing.'

'Yes, sorry. The warden was very helpful. He'd been through that part of the wood just three weeks ago and he said he was sure he'd have noticed if there'd been any digging then. But as you know, it's a bit off the beaten track and even then not easy to find, so he could have missed it. For the moment I'm guessing it's likely been dug in the last twenty-one days. I've requested the SOC team to check it out and Stickley's over there now.'

'Stickley? Your poor sergeant, the weather's turning really cold. He seems to get all the rotten jobs. But twenty-one days? John Camm died eleven days ago. Do you still think they could be connected? What were they digging for?'

'I don't know, but it was much easier to see this morning than yesterday. I guess someone was in a hurry or had too much to carry because they'd left a spade. Yes, and something curious. The remains of a small padlock they'd smashed.'

'A padlock?'

'Hmm, an old Squire one, but it needs to be looked at properly by the SOC team. I'll be able to tell you more by this evening. So how about you, everything OK? I kind of thought you were calling about the stalker.'

'Oh yes, the stalker.'

'She's being charged and her solicitor is negotiating bail.'

'Bail? You mean she could be released? But she'll be out there stalking again. What's to stop her?'

'The conditions of the bail will hopefully include tagging. Apparently if a stalker knows they're being tracked, it takes some of the pleasure out of it. They're the one wanting to do the watching, not the other way round.'

'A deterrent? Well let's hope it works, because the thought of looking over my shoulder all the time….'

'But it was me, remember who was the real target. So calm down, Chrissie. It'll be OK. Look, it's busy this end, so I've got to dash. We can talk about it this evening. Bye now.' And he was gone.

The weight of the stalker news pressed into her chest and tightened on her stomach. It caught her breath, surprising her. She slipped her mobile back into her bag and automatically glanced at Ron, a kind of *sorry I was talking on the phone during our tea break* kind of a glance. He could only have heard her half of the conversation with Clive, but she picked up his look, saw his concern.

'I was thinking,' he said slowly, 'as you've more or less finished working on the Queen Anne Bureau, you might have time to help me return the oak settle to James Mawbray.'

She dragged her thoughts back to the workshop and raised her professional front. It was a mode she found natural to assume, a mask behind which she could hide.

'He lives out towards Framlingham, doesn't he?' She remembered entering his address in the paper filing system, and now talking about matter-of-fact things calmed her, restored the normal balance.

'Yes, Earl Soham, so not so far as Framlingham. It's a nice run and a pretty village, it'll clear your head. James said someone will be in around midday, so when you've finished your tea we can load it into the van and get going.'

This time they used a wheeled pallet to help move a large piece of furniture. The memory of the dust cloud wardrobe incident was still painfully fresh, certainly for Chrissie, and she didn't want to risk a repeat with the oak settle. They decided to take the ex-Forestry Commission Citroen van with the yellow stripe down its side announcing *Clegg & Jax* where once *Forestry Commission* had been written.

'You can drive, Mrs Jax,' Ron said and climbed into the passenger seat before Chrissie could protest.

She knew his intent, understood his motives. She guessed he was thinking distract her, keep her busy, make her rational brain take over and the emotional reaction subside. And to an extent he was right.

The journey was relatively straightforward. It was a cold wet miserable November day; no ice on the roads, but standing water still collected on the fields. Unusually for Ron, he seemed happy to talk and Chrissie was content to listen, only making occasional comments as he chatted about the oak dresser and then the Mawbrays. She assumed it was part of his strategy to distract her.

'I haven't seen Benjamin, that's James's father, in years. And of course the family didn't live out at Earl Soham when I was at school. That was forty-five years ago. It's a long time. I'm surprised Benjamin can even remember me. I certainly haven't thought of him in years.'

'It doesn't much sound like you were friends then, Mr Clegg.'

'Well, I suppose we weren't, but we weren't enemies either. We just didn't have a lot in common, that's all.'

'I can't imagine you as a school kid. Where did you go to school?'

'Coombs, near Stowmarket. Of course the school's long since gone, amalgamated and absorbed into something much bigger in Stowmarket. I left for an apprenticeship when I was about sixteen.'

'And James's father?'

'Well that's the thing. He just stopped coming to school, if I remember.'

'You mean, he disappeared?'

'No. People usually look for you if you disappear, but in his case, people just stopped talking about him. It's not the same thing. At the time I thought he must have reached school leaving age and so he'd left. He'd always been a bit of a wild one and a bit older than the rest of the class.'

'And James? What do you know about him?'

'I didn't even know he existed until he rang asking if I could repair his oak settle. It seems Benjamin must have had kids, as people usually do.'

'Not everyone, Mr Clegg,' she murmured, and then wished she hadn't said it. She'd been thinking of her own situation, not Ron's and bit her lip as she drove past flatly rolling winter fields.

'No not everyone has children, Mrs Jax. I think James has the same restlessness as his father. Now what did he say he did? Ah that's right, milling plastic – something to do with recycling. I think he's set up his own company.'

They lapsed into silence for the last few miles. Chrissie found herself thinking about Bill, her much loved, late husband. He'd run a recycling business milling down old car and tractor tyres, but he'd died inhaling the latex fumes. That had been over four years ago. The sudden memory felt intense.

'Are you OK, Mrs Jax? Do you want the heater turned up?' Ron asked.

'I'm fine, thanks. I was just thinking about… these recycling processes. They can be dangerous. Milling plastics, you said? There must be loads of safety issues. I imagine fine plastic particles airborne in a cloud could be quite nasty.'

'Stop fretting about the wardrobe, Mrs Jax. No harm done.'

'No, I suppose not.'

Nevertheless Ron had given her plenty to think about, and for the moment her stalker fears were pushed to one side. He was right, distraction was therapeutic. They had a repaired eighteenth century oak settle to deliver.

CHAPTER 14

Nick stepped up into the passenger seat. It was like old times. Dave was about to drive the Willows van, loaded with the tools and materials to a new job, and Nick was about to sit alongside, bracing himself for Dave's rally-driving techniques. He still felt the slight trepidation he'd always felt, as he fastened his seatbelt and gulped air. Except now he sat with more confidence. He was a fully-fledged carpenter, a junior in the firm and no longer the apprentice. He was expected to have an opinion and surely that meant he could object when Dave hurled the van into corners and attempted handbrake turns. And added to that he'd had a good night's sleep, admittedly somewhat alcohol soaked but he'd had something to celebrate. The stalker had been arrested. All in all he felt positive, at least he reckoned he would just as soon as he'd cleared the six or seven miles to Forward Green.

'So, another Monday morning. Only four more Mondays until Christmas. Did you have a good weekend?' Dave said as if not really expecting an answer. He pressed the ignition before bending to fiddle with the radio.

'Yeah, thanks. I went to the Bury Fayre yesterday and....' Nick gave up, it was obvious Dave's ears were tuned to the radio.

'So the pressure's on to get these kitchen units fitted in time for the big day,' Dave said, 'and I'm glad you're working with me because we've got to build some of them on site.'

'It's an awkward space then, is it?'

Nick hadn't seen the client's kitchen. It was Dave who'd done all the measuring, designing and visits; and it was the foreman who'd assigned Nick to work with Dave on this final stage. He must have guessed Dave would be working under pressure and realised Nick would cope with a few cross words and a stressed Dave. He'd caused enough in his time as an apprentice and they'd never fallen out.

And now for the news brought to you today on BBC Radio Suffolk read by....

'Good, we're tuned-in to Radio Suffolk. What did you say you've been up to?'

'On Sunday? The Bury Christmas Fayre, a walk in Northfield Wood and then a skinful at the White Hart.'

'The White Hart? I thought the Nags Head was your preferred boozer.'

'It is, but I'm lodging in Woolpit, so it's my local now.'

'You've left home? You kept that close to your chest. Good for you! I bet it went down like a lead balloon.'

'Yeah well, my mum still does my laundry, so they see me at least once a week.'

'Best of both worlds, hey?' Dave revved the engine, thrust it into first gear and let the clutch out with a jolt. They were off.

Nick gripped his seat as the tyres burnt rubber and they accelerated towards a T junction.

Specialist police with cutting gear have removed eight women who chained themselves together outside Sizewell Power Station since seven this morning....

'Watch out,' Nick yelped as Dave slammed on the brakes then nipped out behind a delivery truck.

They are protesting about plans to build a third nuclear plant....

'I see your driving hasn't changed,' Nick murmured and closed his eyes.

And finally, some strong reactions to Ipswich's new-look Christmas tree made from 41 aluminium spheres and 40,000 LED lights....

A nuclear cloud conjured in Nick's imagination. He opened his eyes as Dave swung the van onto the roundabout under the A14.

'Shit, Dave. Can't you slow down a bit? You'll make me throw up.' There, he'd said it; he'd crossed a line and asserted himself with his onetime trainer.

Dave accelerated smoothly out of the roundabout and drove on at a steady pace. 'Sorry, Nick, I was forgetting. I've got used to driving the van without a passenger. Force of habit.'

'Yeah, well maybe I should drive the van for a change, sometime.'

'Sure, but we want to get there today, don't we.'

They lapsed into silence as the newsreader's voice faded. Deep opening chords and Adele's voice in mellow tone flowed from the radio. 'Skyfall – this is great. It's from the latest Bond film,' Nick said as he recognised the notes and turned up the volume.

While piano, orchestra, Bond chords and Adele's voice rose in crescendo, Nick let the sound wrap around him. Road, hedges and cars flashed past. For a couple of miles he even wished he'd hung around on Sunday to speak to the soprano sax player. But that was the thing about music, it spoke to you, plumbed emotional depths. He'd left his number for her, but would she call? Yesterday he hadn't been too bothered but today, maybe he'd changed his mind. It was the music.

The van slowed and he was pulled back into the moment. A row of mature horse chestnut and lime trees stood back from the road, bordering the edge of an expanse of grass, small cottages framed a more distant side.

'Forward Green, the village. And that's the green,' Dave said, as he drove on at a respectable 30mph. 'They planted those trees to stop people destroying it. Travellers, gypsies or whatever. It looks great now, doesn't it, but back in 1930 before they were planted....'

'I'd forgotten you were interested in local history, Dave.'

'Yes, if it hadn't been for carpentry–'

'Don't kid me about history. Given the chance you'd have been a professional rally driver.'

'Yeah, but I couldn't find a sponsor, and carpentry brings in the money. Hey, we're here now. It's along this track, further than I remembered.'

'Well remind me to ask later. I've a local history question for you. Something bugging a friend of mine. So, what did you say the client was called?'

The answer was lost to the damp breeze as Dave slowed to a halt and flung the driver's door open. Seconds later and he had jumped down onto a roughly cobbled drive.

Automatically Nick slipped into the usual routine. While Dave talked to the client, he opened the rear doors and started to unload. He'd seen the plans and had an idea of what he was expected to construct. A storage unit built into an alcove. The tricky bit would be lining up the unit panels precisely with the rest of the kitchen counter tops and unit doors, most of which were already in sections in the workshop. He just hoped the floor was dead level, but he knew that would be asking too much. This was a new build extension to an old cottage with a height drop of thirty centimetres between the ground level at the front and the back.

By the time they'd measured and marked the walls and concrete floor with black marker pen, it was time for a quick coffee break.

'So what was this local history question you had for me?' Dave asked as he poured steaming coffee from his thermos.

'Northfield Wood. What do you know about it?'

'It's over towards Onehouse, near Stowmarket, right? I've never walked it, but I'd heard it was planted commercially in the 1960s and now they're trying to return it to ancient woodland. So what about it?'

'Well Chrissie, my mate from the Utterly carpentry course, she's repairing the Northfield Challenge Trophy for the Rush Green Golf Club. The hickory club's really the trophy and she's working on its oak board. The board's supposed to be from an oak felled in the wood.'

'And Northfield applies to the wood near Onehouse?'

'Well the golf club secretary told her it was. Apparently an accident or something happened in the wood during one of the planting phases and soon after someone incorporated the wood's name into a competition. But no one seems to know any details.'

'And you took a walk in the wood yesterday? What's it like?'

'Muddy. A nice walk, apart from the mud. They've thinned out quite a lot of the spruce and cedar, and replanted with native trees so those areas are starting to look natural. But the rest, well it's a bit dark and spooky. Someone's been digging in there. Yeah, I'd say spooky.'

'Well I was born in the late sixties, so most of this will have been before my time. I don't recall hearing anything about the wood. Not as a kid when I was growing up. I only know of it now because of driving past from time to time. But the sixties are well within living memory. Someone is bound to know.' Dave stared at the ground.

'But that's the thing. No one seems to know, Dave. Doesn't that strike you as odd if it's within living memory?'

'Maybe that's the whole point. Local history is full of legends and rumoured sightings - usually to explain something. Of course sometimes they're spread deliberately to keep people away and stop them prying. What if nothing really happened? People always like a mystery or scandal. If there was gossip, but with no hard facts, the meat won't have stuck to the bones.'

'So just vague references to an accident? I suppose that's always plausible. After all, they were felling trees. Is that what you're saying, Dave?'

'Maybe... I don't know, I'll ask around. So how long ago did you say?'

'I reckon about forty-four, forty-five years.'

Nick sipped his coffee and wondered, but then he couldn't even imagine ever being forty-four or even forty-five years old. He reckoned he was better off expending his energy building the alcove unit and leaving the wondering to Chrissie. At least he'd remembered to ask. He'd text her later and let her know.

CHAPTER 15

Matt sat at one of the computer stations in the library and made a list. Nothing as mundane as a handwritten list on actual paper. He'd grown to prefer the keyboard and a computer screen. To his way of thinking, lists were data, and if he could perfect the software project Damon was helping him with, then who knew where his lists of different data could lead. So his Monday morning list comprised of cocoa dust, Northfield Wood and John Camm.

He sat back and stared at the words. They reflected the key bullet points from Sunday, and the things he wanted to research. He checked the time on the edge of his screen. He had an hour, long enough to netsurf before catching a bite to eat and setting off to Bury for his Monday afternoon session with Damon.

'Yeah, and Rodolfo,' he murmured. The reindeer was another thing pricking at his memory from Sunday, but the cane and straw creature was something he'd rather forget.

'Your place, but only temporr...arrry,' Maisie had slurred, after she'd downed her third rum and Coke at the White Hart, and then struggled to pin the reindeer between them on the back of his scooter. Now it was an unwelcome guest in his bedroom in Stowmarket, so much closer than where she still lived with her parents in Stowupland.

He dismissed the spectre of Rodolfo and looked beyond the screen. In the middle distance he saw a back drop of library bookshelves and racks of journals, but closer in his mind's eye he glimpsed a rising pluming flash of burning cocoa powder.

He typed *cocoa dust fire* in the search box and waited. Within seconds he was watching a YouTube video of a man wearing a white lab coat surrounded by students and puffing cocoa powder into the air above a naked Bunsen burner flame. Whoosh, a rising plume flashed as the cocoa powder ignited and burned. It was like a replay of the pancake man at the Bury St Edmunds Christmas Fayre. Wow!

Excited, he typed in more search phrases. Soon he was reading about the flammability of dust clouds and how the composition of the dust, its particle size and shape, and even the surrounding atmosphere lay at the heart of why a dust cloud came to ignite and burn. The ferocity and spread of igniting particles was awesome, and if in a confined space, explosive. The more he read, the greater his amazement. He was hooked. He'd been aware of the danger of electricity, water and gas - but dust? It was a well-kept secret.

'Hi, Matt. That must be hot. What grabs, mate?'

'Sugar.' Matt looked up from his screen to see Ley, one of the students on his course standing close by.

'You only just come in, Ley? Well you aint missed much this mornin'. Smith's tutorial is all on the website, mate.' But he could see Ley wasn't listening. His eyes were scanning the screen.

'Why're you lookin' at weird stuff about sugar dust fires and explosions in sugar refineries in the USA?'

'It were more about what happens if it sets fire. And I mean it aint just sugar, the dust could be from anything - grain, plastics, wood, cork, starch, coal; even metals and... yeah, cocoa,' he said, remembering Sunday again.

'Doh. I thought you were workin' on course work, mate.' Ley tapped his head in what Matt had learnt was meant to be a Homer Simpson manner.

'Yeah, but cocoa powder, Ley? I saw it go up in flames at the Bury Christmas Fayre.'

'Hmm, I've heard of fires and stuff in flour mills and granaries. Hey, are you eatin' yet?'

'Not for a bit. I got more to check out first.'

'OK, then. See you, mate.'

Matt watched Ley wander over to the library assistant's station, and then he was gone, the library door swinging behind him. Matt didn't have much in common with most of the students on his course, but he quite liked Ley. He was the only one who thought cartoons were cool. The problem was that Matt just didn't *get* The Simpsons, and Ley wasn't much into comic-strip superheroes. Ley preferred his imagery in computer game style, whereas Matt's life as a young kid hadn't included access to a computer at home. The absence had shaped his tastes. However there was something Matt had *got*. He understood the danger in dust clouds on a particle size, shape and composition level.

He turned his thoughts back to the rest of his list, Northfield Wood and John Camm. The last time he'd looked up John Camm, he remembered being in the library talking to Rosie. The phrase *all things Italian* floated back to him. That had been only three days ago and Matt guessed there wouldn't have been much printed since. However for completeness a surf across the news sites would pick up where he'd left off and start his search.

'DOS-in' hell, there's birds chainin' themselves to Sizewell this mornin'. And feelin's are runnin' high about the *space-age Christmas tree in Ipswich,*' he muttered as he scanned the headlines, his eye immediately resting on the words *bacon sandwich* and *apple* quoted in differing opinions about the modernistic Christmas *"tree"*. He clicked on the image of the Christmas *"tree"*.

Cool, he thought and read on, but there were no fresh headlines about John Camm.

'Bacon sandwich,' Matt murmured, his stomach groaning as he voiced the words he'd read a few moments earlier. Crispy bacon between soft bread was exactly what he wanted, and if he logged out now he might just have time to hit the canteen and maybe catch up with Ley. John Camm would have to wait.

Twenty minutes later he bit into a sausage pressed between the halves of a long bread roll, and headed outside to his Piaggio. Ley hadn't been in the canteen and bacon wasn't being served, crispy or otherwise. He had settled for a sausage.

The ride to Bury St Edmunds seemed longer than usual as the cold and wind nipped and chilled. His arms and legs felt stiff and clumsy by the time he pushed his scooter onto its parking stand and climbed the narrow staircase to the Balcon & Mora headquarters.

'Hi, Matt,' Damon said as he let him into the office.

'I'm scammin' freezing,' Matt muttered, and narrowly missed elbowing Damon, as he pulled off his helmet.

'Why the hell don't you leave that outside with your scooter?'

'Cos it'll stay warmer in here. Outside, and it'll feel like I've put me head in the freezer when I ride home.'

'Right. So how's it going with building data for the GitHub site?'

'Ah, I need to say somethin' about that.'

Matt pulled off his Alpine Monster gauntlets and opted for directness.

'The stalker,' he launched, 'the person targeting Clive, the people we reckoned would have somethin' to do with one of his past cases - well, she's been caught.'

'What?'

'Yeah, it kinda takes the heart out of me project. And I wanted to build somethin' on the GitHub site with you. So now d'you think we can concentrate on Northfield Wood and John Camm instead?'

'Hey, slow down, Matt. Tell me, who was the stalker, and was she connected with a past case, like we'd thought?'

'I aint got her name.'

'So how do you know about her? How was she caught? I'm not getting this.'

Matt slumped into the plastic stacker chair, the seat reserved for clients if they visited the office. 'Clive said he wouldn't tell us her name before she'd been charged. Look, it were only yesterday.' He explained about the car in the Northfield Wood car park, Chrissie's suspicions and Clive getting his police colleagues to check the registration with the DVLA.

'Right, I see how they got her, but did he say what the original crime was?'

'Threatening emails, but now he tells us the computer forensics team sorted it pretty quick a couple of months ago.'

'So, would we have eventually found her name and a link to a news report about the email threats? Have we set the parameters for our programme right?'

'No… see, I don't think the news sites would have known about the email threats. And it turns out it were her kid who did it. A kinda underage prank, so too young for reportin' names in the press.'

'So the kid is the computer–'

'Geek? Yeah, and targeted Clive cos he'd got his name. That's what Clive said.'

'Got Clive's name?'

'Yeah,' Matt grunted, 'school talks on stayin' safe online.'

'But then you'd expect… I mean we've all been geeky computer kids. You'd expect it to be the kid who goes on to steal Clive's laptop at the break-in, not his crazy deluded mum.'

They sat in silence, the fans on the hard drives whirring softly in the background. Matt hadn't thought about how a geeky computer kid would behave. He couldn't, he hadn't been one. He would have needed plenty of access to a computer, and for him access came late. He was, as Chrissie had once said, a mature onset computer geek, but she'd smiled when she said it and he'd taken it as a compliment.

'Hey, I've got it,' Damon said. 'Maybe the mum stole it for the computer geek son?'

'Nah, that'd be weird.'

'But she is weird. We've already established that.'

He didn't get where Damon was going with this, and pulled the focus back to his main concern. 'But she's been caught now, so how's about we start a new data collection, say for John Camm and Northfield Wood?'

'It sounds a smaller project. Less data, so yes, it's a cool idea, although I don't quite get why you want to link the man with the wood.'

'But you'll still help me with Git and GitHub?'

'Sure. Now we've wasted enough time. You've a job, remember? I'm going to send you the first batch of names, so log onto your computer. Oh, and make yourself a hot chocolate and me a coffee, while you're about it.'

'Yeah OK,' Matt groaned, but inside he felt good. Everything was back on track, back to how he wanted. The subject data he was going to collect for the GitHub programme might have changed, but he was still working with Git. As long as no one asked him to take a hike in Northfield Wood, the rest would be fun.

The next hour and a half passed quickly as he concentrated on tracing names for the debt collecting agency, so when Damon's arm stretch and office chair push-back signalled it was time for a break, he was almost surprised.

'If we're takin' a break, I'll do a quick social media check on John Camm and start his data file,' Matt said.

It didn't take him long. It was the sort of thing he'd been doing for the past hour and a half. Within minutes he had an image of the man smiling on his public access Facebook page. He'd found his address from the Electoral Register and his business from LinkedIn and a local business directory, although it read as if he was recently retired, or about to retire. Matt had enough information to contact him if he'd been alive, but of course he was dead.

'So what have you got?' Damon asked, as he put a mug of pale milky chocolate on Matt's narrow computer table.

'Well he lived on Elter Road. It edges Northfield Wood. He repaired lawn mowers – seems all sorts of mowers. Yeah, an' he had a wife.' Matt pulled up the Facebook page again and clicked on the public album. A picture of John and a woman wearing a wedding ring smiled out of the screen from somewhere sunny and with palm trees in the background.

'Any shots of him in the wood, the one you want to link him to?' Damon asked.

'Now you come to ask, there may be. But unless it's got a notice sayin' *Northfield Wood* on it, I wouldn't know. I mean a tree's a tree, right?'

He clicked his way through the album while Damon gave a commentary and named the trees.

'Palm trees in the background somewhere on holiday; next - he's collecting sloes for sloe gin, so I guess that's a blackthorn bush; next - he's grinning at us and wearing a woolly hat and scarf in front of a Christmas tree; next - he's crouching and feeding a squirrel, there's a tree trunk almost out of shot, probably an oak; next - and we're back to the palm trees again,' Damon finished.

Matt turned to look at Damon. 'So what d'you think?' He gave a palms-up shrug, the Gallic one he'd pinched from *The Mighty Cayenne takes on La Grande Pomme* comic-strip. He hoped it fitted the bill.

'What do I think? I think John Camm is the subject of a murder investigation, right?' Damon's tawny eyes were compelling.

'Yeah I reckon so.'

'Well, everything we do must be above board. Do you understand? I don't want any trouble with the police. They may be able to tell if we've been looking, they may have even set some traps.'

'Yeah, but all this were out in full public view. I aint broken into his friends-only Facebook file or asked to be a friend.'

'Well you could hardly ask to be a friend, could you? He's dead.'

'Yeah, but why aint they closed his Facebook page?'

'It takes time, Matt. But they will, so save screen shots of his public album photos for your data file.'

A sense of urgency crept into the back of Matt's mind. What else might vanish from the internet, he wondered. He knew from his online people tracing work that trails went cold the further back in time you delved. Websites vanished as domain names and hosting fees fell into arrears, and then it became the pre-scanning and pre-computerisation era for record keeping. Finding a current address was the work of minutes, but finding an address from forty-five years ago was nigh impossible.

He clicked on the *John Camm Grass Mower Maintenance & Servicing* business website and saved a series of screen shots. Then he pulled his mobile from his jeans and texted Chrissie the link to John Camm's Facebook page and thumbed a quick message: *Check out his public access photos. Trees or what?*

'Right, break over, Matt. Time for the next batch of names,' Damon said softly.

CHAPTER 16

Chrissie pulled off the road onto a narrow track. 'Are you sure you want to do this Mr Clegg? James said his father was... he said he was changed. Maybe it would be better to remember him as he was?'

She slowed to a halt and turned to watch Ron's face.

'He also said Benjamin wanted our opinion on some furniture he was thinking of selling,' Ron said quietly.

'It could be just an excuse to talk, catch up on old times.'

'But if he wants to talk furniture, now is a good time. We're already out in the van. The oak settle is delivered and we've space on board, so unless you're in a hurry to get back to the workshop, Mrs Jax....'

'No, there's no rush. You're right, if there's any furniture to pick up, we're both here to load the van.'

Ping! A message alert sounded. Now what, she wondered. Could Clive be letting her know the stalker was out on parole? She reached for her mobile.

'Ah, that's OK,' she breathed in relief, as she read Matt's caller ID. She opened the message. It read: *Check out his public access photos. Trees or what?* And there was a link to a Facebook page. What was he on about? It would have to wait.

'Is everything all right, Mrs Jax?'

'Yes, just Matt and something about trees.' She slipped the van into gear and moved off.

So this is Broad Green, she thought. There didn't seem to have been much to it other than rough hedges of hawthorn, hazel and elm, and the occasional house. James

Mawbray had said to turn down a muddy track before the wind pump and to just keep driving, but she wasn't sure if she wanted to be here. Not for this particular visit.

When James talked about his father, she'd picked up a subtext. She wasn't quite sure what it was, but she sensed Benjamin was ill, something self-inflicted but somehow not his fault, if you could describe years of heavy drinking in those terms. It was as if James wanted his father to reconnect with his past, as if meeting someone from his school days would help. She couldn't think how, but if Ron and Benjamin had ever wanted to rekindle their acquaintance or held the slightest interest in contacting each other, then in forty-five years, they'd never made the effort.

She drove slowly. It didn't look as if many cars had passed along the same way, judging by the tyre tracks. She replayed James's instructions in her mind, hoping she hadn't made a mistake.

'We're going to have to keep going. There's nowhere to turn around,' Ron said, echoing her fears.

The hedgerows grew taller and wilder, with brambles stretching up to catch the lower branches of the elm and hazel. With every metre she drove, she imagined James's father as rougher, more desolate, even feral. The trail took a sharp left, the hedges thinned and now she could see ditches edging the track. If she glanced beyond, winter fields stretched to distant hedge-lines while twenty metres ahead, the track widened into an uneven rutted parking area. A sprawling 1980s L-shaped bungalow blocked any further progress. She'd reached the end of the track.

'Not quite what I'd imagined,' Ron murmured and got out of the van.

'Is there something beyond those huge leylandii?' Chrissie asked as she followed him up a short gravelled path to the front door and pulled her duffle coat tight around her.

If he answered, she didn't hear because a dog started barking from somewhere inside the bungalow. Ron stood for a moment and straightened his back before pressing the doorbell. Chrissie was curious, but she sensed the tension in him as the barking racked up to fever pitch. Moments later the front door opened and an elderly man stood and stared at them.

She saw at once he was a smaller, older version of James. He had the same nose, heavy brow and small chin, but there was no fat to his cheeks, and his aging skin drooped in folds from jaw line to neck.

'Hello. You must be Ron Clegg. My son said you'd be calling.' He turned to shout back into the hall, 'Stop barking!' His voice sounded harsh, gravelly.

Instinctively, she glanced at Ron. Time had been kinder to him. His eyes were gentler, more relaxed, and there was flesh filling out his cheeks. It was difficult to believe there was only a couple of years between the two men.

'Hello, Benjamin,' Ron said calmly, 'This is Mrs Jax. She works with me. It's good to see you again. How many years has it been?'

'I'd say about forty-five. So how are you keeping, Ron? You look pretty good.'

'Mustn't grumble. And how about you?'

'I've been told to watch my liver, sugar, and to stop smoking,' he said and led them through the bare hallway to the dining room.

The dog barked, but with less conviction.

'OK, OK,' Benjamin muttered, and opened the kitchen door for a black Labrador. It padded stiffly into the dining room.

'Hey, were you the one I heard barking just now?' Chrissie said and bent to scratch behind the old dog's ear.

'Yeah, that's Dyson. He eats anything. Just swallows it down, doesn't even bother to chew, greedy bugger.'

'You've a quiet place out here,' she said, thinking of the muddy track, and catching the cloying smell of stale cigarette smoke from the grubby carpet.

'It looks out-of-the-way, but my parents built it for their retirement, you know, next to the workshop, or should I say sweatshop. But it's mine now, their legacy - like I needed another bloody millstone round my neck.' He sounded angry and jerked his head towards the window.

'Right,' she said, and opted to leave the talking to Ron.

'You mean your father's business? Didn't he make suitcases, holdalls, golf bags? Wasn't he using some new plasticised material?' Ron enquired mildly.

'Yeah, but the Chinese and Taiwanese flooded the market. And they made their bags and holdalls lighter, and cheaper.'

'So what happened to the business?'

'It couldn't compete. But the stupid bugger didn't want to see it. He expected me to turn it around. It wasn't fair of him to push it onto me. Take the money and run, I said.'

'So did you?'

'What are you saying, Ron?' Benjamin narrowed his eyes and stared at Ron.

'I'm just trying to fill in the years, Benjamin.'

'Oh, you mean that bloody stupid quarrel. No I'd learned my lesson. This time I was better off sticking around. And besides, there wasn't anything worth taking to run with. So I stayed, like the dutiful son and fed off what was here while my wife left and my parents died.'

He stared at Ron, as if daring him not to see him as the victim. The undercurrent of anger chilled. Chrissie bit her tongue, determined not to speak.

'But what about the furniture?' Ron said softly, 'James told us you had some furniture for us to look at.'

'Yeah, and thank God for James. He took over the works site, chopping up waste plastic for recycling. Yeah, my boy's clever. He's made a business out of what other people throw away. But me – it's set me thinking, I could be sitting on a pile of money with this furniture.' He tapped the back of one of the dining chairs.

'Tell us about it,' Ron said.

'Well, for starters I thought I'd sell these dining chairs, the dining table and the display cabinet. There's also a mahogany settee in the living room.'

'Does any of it need repairing?'

'Yes, a couple of the chairs need putting right. But I want your opinion. You see, I remember my dad saying something about Hepplewhite and Chippendale. So I reckon it means this lot could be worth something.'

'But if you're planning on selling them, why not put them straight in the auction rooms? The auctioneer will give you a valuation.'

Chrissie watched the unspoken interplay. Was Ron about to turn away business? Restoration was costly and the value of "brown" furniture had dropped in recent years, but was this purely about profit margins for Benjamin?

'This is mahogany,' she said as she bent to examine the chair, 'but people prefer a lighter coloured wood these days. It's a genuine late eighteenth century chair and the shield-back means it is in the Hepplewhite-style. I'm sorry if I'm disappointing you, but....'

'Hepplewhite-style? So he didn't actually make it himself? Is that what you're saying, Mrs Jax?' His tone cut abrasively.

'Yes. It's old. Over two hundred years old. It would have been worth more twenty years ago, but if you hang onto it, it will eventually go up in value again.'

'Fashions change, Benjamin,' Ron murmured.

'But labour costs go up, so if you repair now and keep this as an investment to sell in the future, you'll maximise your profits, and be able to enjoy it in the meantime.'

'Win, win. I like that, Mrs Jax. But I don't think you were listening. I have a cash flow problem.'

'I may have an answer,' Ron said quietly.

'Oh yeah? What?'

'Your display cabinet, over there. I need to look at it more closely, but I think it's Sheraton-period, made in about 1790. The pale satinwood means it's fashionable at the moment.'

'And it's elegant, restrained and not too large. Very desirable,' Chrissie added.

'What are you suggesting?'

Twenty minutes later they'd hammered out a deal. Benjamin would find a specialist auction or trader and arrange to sell the display cabinet. It would feed his immediate cash flow needs. Ron and Chrissie would concentrate on repairing two of his six Hepplewhite-style dining chairs. In payment, instead of cash they agreed to take the mahogany chair-backed settee from the living room. In its current state, it was a disaster - an Edwardian version of a Hepplewhite / Sheraton shield-back design with a broken cane seat and dog stained cushions.

'You don't have to go back down the track,' Benjamin said after they'd loaded the van with the two chairs and the settee. 'If you follow the gravel driveway to the side of the bungalow, it'll take you beyond those leylandii and then you'll see the old sweatshop and what is now James's waste plastic business. If you drive through the site you'll find you're actually quite close to the A14. All the lorries come in from that direction.'

'Thanks, Mr Mawbray. We'll give you a call and let you know when the chairs are ready,' Chrissie said, pleased to be driving away at last. She'd found the bungalow depressing, and even as she left, Benjamin's resentment and millstone memories sat darkly in the back of the van, clinging to the furniture. They tainted the air with the smell of stale cigarettes and dog. She opened her window a fraction. The bad karma needed to escape.

'Did we really want that settee?' Chrissie asked, wishing they'd left the stained cushions behind.

'He wouldn't have paid us for our work, Mrs Jax. The chairs deserve to be made good to survive another couple of hundred years, and at least this way we get something out of it.'

'I should have followed your lead and told him to send it all to the auction rooms.'

They drove in silence for a few minutes as they passed a shabby warehouse-sized unit and rusting skips filled with discarded plastic chairs, bowls, storage crates – anything and everything made in hard plastics and now broken and no longer wanted.

'So what did you think of him? Has he changed?' She knew at once she'd asked a stupid question. Of course the man had changed. They'd last seen each other longer ago than she'd been alive.

'It reminded me of why I'd never really liked him. And whatever was remotely nice in his character he's destroyed. Bitterness and resentment are corrosive, Mrs Jax.'

'And so is alcohol. Do you think he'd have told us why he'd disappeared all those years ago if we'd shown more interest?'

'Only if it cast him as the victim, and somehow I don't think he was.'

'So do you think he'd have drunk away the family business whatever had happened?'

'Yes, Mrs Jax.'

'So why didn't he sell the furniture years ago?'

'I don't know, maybe he didn't realise it was worth anything. I hadn't thought of him as being sentimental. And if his debts are escalating, he'll shed his last ounce of sentimentality if he needs the cash.'

'Well let's hope poor old Dyson doesn't cost him too much.'

'No, Mrs Jax. Don't even think it. The workshop doesn't need a resident dog.'

The late November light started to fade on the drive back to the workshop, and by four o'clock the sun had set. They unloaded the van in the dark and afterwards Chrissie felt too exhausted to even make a mug of tea.

'You know, I think I'm going home, Mr Clegg. I'll get an early night and make an early start tomorrow morning.'

She felt drained. Physical work never consumed her energy in the same way her restless mind sapped it. She liked to think she was on top of everything, relaxed and in control, but beneath her role as Ron's innovative new business partner, she knew she was a bundle of questions, and visiting Benjamin Mawbray had merely served to throw up a dozen more.

She barely remembered driving home. Only when she'd locked her front door, kicked off her shoes and brewed a mug of strong tea, did she feel she could begin to unwind, and attempt to work her way through everything logically.

Top of her list was the stalker, but she knew she had to leave that one until Clive got home. Second on her list was Matt's text. He could be off-beam and weird, but there was always something triggering the tangents he took. She opened his text message again. *Check out his public access photos. Trees or what?* And there was the link he'd added to a Facebook page.

She carried her laptop from the kitchen through to her living room and the comfort of her sofa. If she stretched out on it with her back against the arm cushions, she could relax and think more efficiently. Quickly settled and cocooned, she typed in Matt's link and waited, idly tracing the geometric patterns on the rug near the sofa. Burgundies neighboured midnight blues and merged with beige, the shapes repeating and inverting. She felt herself sinking, all senses shrouded, her vision blurred. Down she drifted. She couldn't resist. Down she slipped into deep, dense tranquillity.

'Hey, Chrissie. Are you OK? Wake up.'

Something or someone touched her shoulder. A gentle pressure. Persistent.

'Hey, wake up sleepy head.'

The words started to register and consciousness seeped back.

'Clive? Are you back already? I must have....'

'Drifted off. Have you eaten?'

'What? Eaten already? I've only just got back from work.'

Eyes still blurry, she moved her wrist to check the time. Her hand caught the edge of her laptop and the screen flipped down. It started to slide.

'Hey, careful!' Clive breathed and lunged to catch it.

She clutched at empty air.

Clive caught low. 'Owzat!'

'Is it alright?'

'I think so. You'd better check.'

Without thinking, she flipped up the screen, and typed in her password. They both watched as... up came the Facebook page for John Camm, Matt's link live once again, just as it had been before the screen saver cut in almost a couple of hours earlier.

'What the hell are you looking at John Camm for?'

'I'm not. At least I wasn't but Matt texted me a link, something about trees. I must've fallen asleep before it loaded.'

'Well you were certainly out for the count, but Chrissie, it's a murder investigation. Please, we've been through this before. I don't want you poking around in what's nothing to do with you.'

'I know, but it was Matt and it's only the man's public page, and I mean anyone can look at it, can't they?' She opened John Camm's public Facebook album as she spoke.

'Ye-es but....'

'He looks younger than I imagined. Pretty good for sixty-six,' she murmured.

'The photos may date back a few years, Chrissie.'

'But you've seen these before, right? I mean someone must have checked his online activity, Clive.'

'Yes, of course. John Camm kept all his passwords in a folder, and I mean a paper folder, so we've been able to access his emails and his Facebook account. But none of the team singled these photos out as important. Can you spot something in them, then?' His tone seemed mild but she caught the undercurrent.

'No, not yet, and anyway I'm only seeing them for the first time. Is the woman in the photo with palm trees in the background his wife?' She watched his face and added quickly, 'Sorry, I shouldn't have asked. She's still around and the investigation is active, right? Yes, I've got it.'

Clive's expression had answered her question. It was Mrs Camm.

'You are impossible. Sometimes I wonder if you're in the right job.'

'Don't tease. You know I'm too old to join the police. But seriously, can I ask a couple more questions?'

'Go on, but then we need to eat. I'm starving.'

'Do you know why John Camm was murdered?'

'Not yet. According to his bank records he wasn't in debt and he didn't owe any money. His business was healthy and he was in the process of retiring and selling up, and there don't seem to be any other women in his life, either.'

'How very unhelpful of him!'

'Exactly, no motive. We've checked through his client list and his diary - both his visits to clients and the mowers he'd serviced in the last couple of months. I'd hoped the digging in the wood might be connected to him in some way. A lead to follow.'

'And is it?' she asked.

'No, and now I've answered the second of your "couple of questions". Let's eat.'

'But that's not fair. The last one didn't count. Come on, please. Tell me what you discovered in the wood.'

'OK, but after that, food.'

She flipped her laptop closed and made more space for him on the sofa. 'You said someone left a spade behind,' she began, hoping to prompt him into unguarded talking.

'Yes, and a small padlock. A Squire, made in the 1950s.'

'Well that would still kind've fit with something being buried in the 60s, I suppose. And what else did you find?'

'Well, the footprints were difficult to make out on that kind of dead-leafy ground, but there was certainly one clear set and he–'

'Or she.'

'From the size it's more likely to be a man, and he was looking for something specific. That would explain why he dug the small test holes before the large one. And the marks in the bottom of the large hole suggest something had been buried there. Something the size of a suitcase.'

'Really? My God, you don't think there was a body in it, do you?'

'I hope not. But luckily for us, the man must have wanted to check inside the case before he took it away. He prized off the padlock. If he used the spade to do it then Forensics will hopefully find traces of the case on the spade.'

'Can they do that?'

'Well I hope so. The SOC team have taken lots of samples of soil from where the suitcase was buried, and that'll help check out any dead body theory. They said they'd found some flakes of something that could be enamel.'

'Tooth enamel?'

'No, enamel on metal. It's got to be analysed but that strikes me as curious.'

'Wow,' Chrissie breathed, trying to take it all in, 'so the stalker was in the wood because she was following us. You don't think she has anything to do with whatever was buried there, or the digging we found?'

'Ah, the stalker. No I don't think she has anything to do with any of this. But I should have said, she's out on bail and tagged, as of... about now,' Clive said, checking his watch.

'What? Oh no! Couldn't they just lock her up?'

'Her son is too young to be left to fend for himself. And before you say anything, I know he's old enough to send threatening emails. But at fourteen, he's still a kid, and given the choice between him going into care or her being tagged, well it was a no-brainer for the judge. Sorry, Chrissie.'

Clive gave her a hug. 'Come on, let's shake all this off. Let's go for something to eat at the White Hart. You can tell me about your day.'

CHAPTER 17

It was Thursday and Nick sat next to Dave in the Willows van, rain splattering the windscreen. The radio murmured and hummed in the background as he bit into a cheese and pickle sandwich. They were taking their lunch break, and it was a warm comfortable place to sit, much cosier than in the new build kitchen extension. The concrete floor might have under floor heating installed, but nothing was connected yet, so the cold struck up through the ground and chilled the kitchen air.

'The units are going in well,' Dave said between sips of milky coffee.

'Hmm.' Nick chewed and nodded, remembering the struggle with the units to the side of the Butler sink. Best not to remind Dave about it, he thought and bit into the sandwich again.

'I've made some enquiries, at least I've asked down at the pub and also my old mum. Her knees have gone, but her mind's still as sharp as a knife. Remember you asked me at the beginning of the week if I'd ever heard rumours or knew about an accident in Northfield Wood? You said your friend Chrissie wanted to know.'

'Yeah, that's right.' That had been Monday, and it felt a long time ago. There'd even been talk of arranging a work's Christmas do since then.

'Well, no one remembers hearing about any accidents, and some of the regulars have clocked up a good few years. I'm talking about my local, mind. I don't think I've ever had a pint in Onehouse.'

'Right… right, thanks Dave. I'll pass it on to Chrissie.' He chewed in contemplative silence, and then reached for his mobile.

His last text to Chrissie had been a surprised-face emoticon in response to her *The stalker is out on bail. Bloody unbelievable or what?* message. He scrolled past her link to the John Camm Facebook photo album and thumbed in a quick text. It didn't take him long to relay Dave's news of no news, but not before checking for any missed calls or unopened messages.

There were none, at least nothing he reckoned could be from the saxophone player. In his experience, girls tended to postpone making a first call or text for a day or so, not wanting to appear too keen. With that reasoning he'd hoped for something by Tuesday or Wednesday.

'Is there a pub near Onehouse?' Dave asked in the background.

'What?' Nick dragged his attention back to Dave. That was the trouble with girls, they could get between you and your concentration, and he knew this one was starting to get under his skin, just like Mel had.

'A pub near Onehouse?'

'What? For the work's Christmas do?'

'Come on Nick, speed up. That's where you should be asking about the wood. Why don't you go for a pint closer to Onehouse?'

'Right, and ask about the wood. Good idea, Dave. Will you be buying then?'

'Cheeky bugger,' Dave murmured and bit contentedly into a ham sandwich.

Half an hour later and the lunch break over, Nick checked his phone again before slipping it into his pocket.

'Are you expecting a call or something? You've been looking at your mobile all morning.'

'I was hoping to hear back from a sax player for the band.'

'Ah, and there was me thinking it was some girl! Come on; time to get back to work. We're almost ready to start fitting the worktops,' Dave said, as he got out of the van.

The worktops were solid wood, made from lengths of four-inch width oak, bonded and tongue-and-grooved together. For the moment they lay flat, resting on battens and protected in packaging. The solid wood needed more care in fitting than a composite or stone worktop. To Nick it was almost a living material, responsive to damp, still able to warp and bend, shrink and expand.

'So how do you want to do this, Dave? Start over there and work round clock-wise?' Nick asked, pointing to where the American-style double door fridge would be going.

'No, I thought we'd do the length with the sink first.'

'Right,' he said and rested the spirit level along the top of the units nearest the Butler sink. 'I'll go and get the jig and router. They're still in the van.'

He didn't need to explain they were for cutting the recesses on the underside of the wood for the worktop bolts, or that he'd be bringing back a bag of slotted brackets. From here on, just about everything they were going to use or do in fitting the worktop was designed to allow the wood to move with changes in humidity.

He hurried outside, turning his back against the wind driven rain as he flung open the van. He reached for the router and jig.

Ping!

That'll be Chrissie about the *no news*, he thought.

Ping! The message alert repeated.

There was nothing else for it, he'd have to check, otherwise he wouldn't be able to settle into the afternoon. He pulled his phone from his pocket and stared at the screen. An unknown mobile number headed the message. He opened it.

Hi. I was given a note to contact this number. Are you looking for a saxophone player? What kind of band – jazz?

'Yes!' he punched the air. He'd been right all along. The girl was interested. But how should he play it now? He opted for a simple text reply saying yes the band was looking for a sax player and he'd phone after work to tell her more about the band. He finished by adding his name. The real test would be if she answered his call.

The next few hours passed rapidly as he helped Dave position the first section of worktop. The sweep of counter filled the corner and had to be joined at a right-angle to the next section of worktop. There was plenty of measuring, marking, lifting, checking, repositioning, lifting and finally cutting. Nick routed the recesses on the underside, ready to take the worktop bolts which would hold the butt joint together. They were careful to leave a small gap between the oak and the walls so that any expansion and contraction of the wood wouldn't cause damage.

'The finishing strip will cover the expansion gap against the wall,' Dave said.

'Yeah, I know. And we fix it to the wall and not the worktop. Remember you taught me?' Sometimes Nick wondered if Dave had forgotten he wasn't the apprentice anymore.

'OK, we need one more coat of sealer overnight on that end grain before we assemble the joint properly tomorrow.'

'Yeah, and seal the joint again with sealer when we tighten the parts. Yeah I know.'

Soon the light was fading and it was time to finish for the day. It was only as Nick helped to pack up the van that he realised he hadn't thought about the sax player all afternoon. It seemed strange how work had driven it clean from his mind, and yet now when he remembered her, he felt a frisson of anxious anticipation. Was his brain like a series of compartments and he moved between them, like rooms – shutting the door on one as he opened the door to the next?

'You're frowning,' Dave said as he started the van and flicked on the headlights.

'Am I?' He wondered if it meant he was shallow and his face was too easy to read.

'You know, I reckon we deserve a pint.' Dave said cheerfully.

'Yeah, maybe a quick one.'

'We'll try the pub on the road to Onehouse.'

'What? But that's miles out of our way. I've things... calls I want to make.'

'Then make'em now.'

'No, no – it can wait.'

But could it wait? Certainly he'd be more relaxed, more confident if he had a pint on board before he called the sax player. But why was it his luck to have Dave as such an inquisitive workmate, Chrissie as such a questioning friend, and while he was on the subject, such a frankly nosey landlady in Sarah? Why? Please God, a bit of indifference. And then he thought about the sax player. Perhaps not complete indifference, he conceded.

'Careful what you wish for,' he murmured under his breath.

The windscreen wipers swished and clicked and water splashed from puddles as they traced their way from Forward Green to Creeting St Mary and then through the back ways into Needham Market. Dave parked the van in the Willows secure area. From there they decided they'd each drive their own car to the pub. It meant afterwards they could take their separate routes home.

'I think there's one called the Dog & Parrot on the way,' Dave said as he jumped down from the van.

Dave led in his old series 2A Land Rover. It was the vehicle he drove in bad weather, something he swore could tackle flooded roads, swollen fords and thick snow. It was his winter transport of choice, a bit of fun. He drove it like a man possessed. Nick reckoned it was because it reminded him of his rallying days, and he didn't really need the excuse of bad weather. So far the winter had only thrown persistent rain at them.

Nick followed in his aging Ford Fiesta. Ahead the series 2A rocked and tilted with the camber of the lanes, the tail lights barely visible. He pictured Dave at the wheel, juddered about by the fifty year old suspension and deafened in the unlined metal cab, so like a giant sounding box for the engine. He decided to let Dave forge ahead. This wasn't going to turn into a race. He'd never been competitive and he wasn't going to start now.

When Nick pulled into the pub car park, he reckoned Dave would have got there about five minutes before him.

He expected to see the series 2A already parked and find Dave inside at the bar, beer ordered and drawn into glasses.

'What?' Nick moaned, spotting Dave still outside.

Two figures stood next to the Land Rover, bonnet up while they talked and pointed at the 2.5 litre petrol engine. The dull beam from a light on the side of the pub cast shadows.

'Everything OK?' Nick asked, as he got out of the Fiesta, the rain now settled into a fine drizzle.

'Yeah, yeah,' Dave said. 'Ray here has a series 2A as well. He was just telling me about the trouble he's had changing the steering relay.'

Automatically Nick glanced around. So where was Ray's Land Rover?

Ray must have seen him looking, because he smiled and explained, 'Mine's up on blocks. I'm in the Toyota today.' He waved in the direction of a large modern 4x4 parked alongside.

'Well I'm not hanging around out here. See you inside,' Nick mumbled, and hurried into the bar.

There were only a few drinkers inside, regulars by the look of them. Dave had been right. If they wanted to chat with locals, now was a good time to come. The bar had an old fashioned feel, no harsh lighting, no music and no jukebox, but there was a dartboard and bar stools. White and silver concertina paper balls and stars hung from a beam, an early nod to Christmas. He ordered a pint of the on tap Adnams, but before he'd had a chance to get his mobile from his pocket, Dave and Ray came in.

It was obvious they'd connected over the Land Rover, but he doubted they had much else in common. Ray looked as if he was in his late sixties and judging by his weathered face, had spent a good deal of his life outdoors.

'Hi, I'm Nick,' he said and sipped his pint.

Ray smiled a greeting.

'You were saying you've done some rallies and competitive off-roading,' Dave said, as if continuing a conversation, but at the same time catching the barman's eye.

'Yeah, of course the series 2A was a great off-roader. Robust engineering. It was cutting edge in its time. Yeah, more of an off-roading vehicle than a road-runner, I'd say.'

'A pint, no I think a half of… is that Elgoods Black Dog?' Dave asked the barman.

'And I'll have a pint of my usual,' Roy said.

'So where's the off-roading around here? I mean like the competition stuff?' Nick asked.

'Well if it's hills you're after, then you can't beat Wales, but round here I suppose the forest trails, or out towards the coast and the inland sandlings – lots of rough heathland. Yeah, but these days I mostly stick to Thetford Forest.'

'I didn't know you could take vehicles into Thetford Forrest,' Nick said, surprised.

'Well you wouldn't normally see them because they're not on the walking trails. Have you ever seen the off-road extreme cycling trails when you're walking? No, because they're kept separate. Hell, but the forestry people take in some pretty massive vehicles. You can't treat the whole place like it's a bowling green, you know.'

'Right, but how about the woods round here?' Nick asked, an idea starting to crystallise.

'If you mean like Northfield Wood, the conservation people have it now. They're returning it to old-style woodland. You can't off-road in there.'

'Yes, but before that?'

'Well yeah, but that was back in the 60s. I thought you meant now.'

'So what was it like?' Nick tried to sound casual.

'You mean when the landowner decided to sell it for commercial planting, and they ripped out the old stock for conifers? It was bloomin' fantastic for off-roading. Rutted tracks, ditches like half-pipes – you know the sort of thing skate boarders do their tricks on, except of course it was earth, and damned good fun in a Land Rover. And there were plenty of felled trees with their roots part-pulled out of the ground. It was a dream for an off-roader. Of course the chaps felling didn't give a damn about someone like me, just as long as I didn't damage the new planting. I mean whatever tyre ruts I made were nothing compared with what they were doing to the ground.'

'So how long were you able to off-road in there?'

'About ten years, right through the 60s.'

'The golden years before conservation took a hold,' Dave murmured.

'Yeah,' Ray nodded.

'That's awesome. I shouldn't think there are many around who can remember the wood back then,' Nick added, trying to bring Ray back on track. 'Do you know, I've a friend who'd be really interested. She's researching the wood's history around the 60s and 70s, and there isn't a lot on record. Would you mind talking to her?'

'I don't know if I'd call myself... a historian,' Ray said slowly.

'No, but I'm sure anything you can tell her about those days would be really helpful.'

'Well, as long as she's not expecting too much.'

'No, anything would be useful.'

Nick took Ray's number for Chrissie and bought him another pint of his usual to seal the deal. He suspected deep down, Ray was secretly flattered and his reticence was only for show. Nick had met plenty of people like that. They liked attention, liked to win; they were alpha personalities in beta clothing.

The atmosphere in the bar was starting to change as the *on the way home from work* drinkers thinned out and were replaced by the ones out to make an evening of it. With Nick's mission to find out more about Northfield Wood as good as completed, the old restlessness started to return. The sax player would be expecting his call, and he'd said after work. He downed the last of his pint.

'Sorry, Dave, but I really must get going.'

'Yeah, OK. Actually I should be getting home too. See you tomorrow.' He eased down from his bar stool.

Outside the fine drizzle had stopped, but the darkness seemed denser and the air felt damp and colder. Nick sat in his Fiesta and watched as Dave drove the series 2A out of the car park.

Now, he thought, now. He pulled his mobile from his pocket. A moment's hesitation, and then he pressed the sax player's automatic dial number. The ring tone sounded strangely detached. He composed his thoughts and his opening line, and waited.

'Hi.' Her voice sounded mildly squeaky.

'Hiya, I'm Nick. I'm calling about… well my band are looking for a saxophone player and I wondered if you'd be interested.'

'I might be kinda interested.'

'Meaning…?'

'I already play in a sax quartet and well, you heard me in the Colchester Institute's brass band in Bury. You musta guessed I'm studying Music at the Colchester Institute, so I'm kinda busy, but what's your band's style?'

'We're a bit mixed – mainly covers but some of our own stuff. Funk, groove… jazz-folk. We've just got a new keyboard player, so the style is kinda developing,' he said, relaxing and slipping into her turn of phrase.

'So where are you based? Cos Bury's a kinda long way from Colchester.'

'Yeah, I suppose it is… but we play all over. If you're interested, we've got a band practice this Saturday morning. Why don't you come along? Bring your saxophone. It's in Stowmarket, only half an hour from Colchester.'

'And kinda only fifteen minutes from Ipswich.'

'Do you live in Ipswich then?'

'Yeah, so if you text me the place and time, I might come.'

'That'd be great. I hope you do. Hey, what's your name… so I can tell the band?'

'Pearl. Bye, Nick.' She ended the call.

'Phew,' he breathed. So had that gone well? He couldn't be sure. She might look like Mel, but she certainly didn't sound like her.

CHAPTER 18

Matt glanced at Rodolfo. Rodolfo stared back. The straw and cane creature seemed to have become a semi-permanent feature in his bedroom. It was Friday morning, the last day of November and almost five days since the Christmas Fayre, but Maisie seemed to have forgotten Rodolfo was still in transit to his final destination, her bedroom in Stowupland. Maybe it was the layer of grubby tees and discarded sweatshirts thrown across his back, or the whiffy socks tossed at his feet like droppings, but Rodolfo, aka Rod the dirty clotheshorse was in danger of taking root.

'You aint stayin',' Matt muttered, as his mind moved on to the larger and more terrifying subject of presents. Christmas presents.

He'd found a stall at the Fayre selling tees and sweatshirts. Any colour, any design; it was the punter's choice. He'd asked for the outline of Italy with PONTEDERA and a red dot marking the home of Piaggio, or more accurately the museum dedicated to the history of the Vespa.

'Pontedera? Where's that then? I can't do it 'ere now,' the store holder had said.

'It's in the province of Pisa, sort of... near the coast,' Matt had explained, picturing the map.

He'd chosen a light brown to blend with his Piaggio, and cut a two-for-one deal. Hopefully they would arrive through the post any day. He reckoned he might even give one to Maisie, but he knew it wouldn't be enough.

The single bulb in his bedroom cast a dull light on the faded blue walls, more like the extract of Mediterranean smog than a pure colour. He dressed slowly, his thoughts drifting as he pulled on his socks and jeans. It was something Damon had said about maybe the crazy stalker woman breaking in and stealing the computer for her son. Was it supposed to be like a Christmas present for him? An early one?

He reached for the only clean tee-shirt left in his wardrobe. Maisie had bought it for him when the pub had been raising funds for a charity. The white cotton had a small animal, an ape and a woman printed in a line across the front, suggesting evolution. Below the images 2G, 3G and words THE NAGS HEAD were printed in bold, with 2G under the small animal, 3G under the ape and The Nags Head under the woman. He *got* that it was a gift, but mobile internet access and then the name of a pub? It didn't make sense. The pub didn't have its own wi-fi. What's more, tomorrow was the beginning of December and the countdown to Christmas, another thing he didn't quite get.

He scooped yesterday's sweatshirt from the shabby flooring, changed his mind about his old denim jacket and thrust his arms into his latest find in a Stowmarket charity shop - a faux leather flying jacket.

By the time he shuffled through the morning gloom of his mum's narrow hallway and out into the half-light, he felt almost pleased to face the certainty of Tumble Weed Drive and the Flower Estate.

The faux leather charity-find protected him from the worst of the cold as he rode to the Academy car park. A Christmas tree, bedecked with lights and tinsel stood in the entrance hall, the pale marble flooring mimicking snow.

Notice boards were crowded with flyers for Xmas quizzes, parties and the winter ball, and when he logged on in the computer lab, even the department webpage was filled with reminders for last dates to hand in projects and course work. Everything seemed to point towards a countdown, spiralling excitement, and Christmas, but rather than feeling part of it, he sensed he was on the side lines, an observer.

He hoped he'd be shielded from the tide of seasonal reminders when he reached the Balcon & Mora offices in Bury St Edmunds for his afternoon session, but when he arrived the countdown was still in the air.

'We've got a big list today. The debt collectors want the contact details four days earlier than usual. I guess it makes them feel good giving it a rest on Christmas and Boxing Day,' Damon said, barely leaving Matt time to unzip his flying jacket and settle at the computer before sending him the first batch of names to trace.

'But bein' on everyone's backs so soon don't look good either. And anyway, they're national holidays aint they?' It seemed the countdown had started for debt collection as well.

Matt concentrated on his first batch of names. He was looking for a Rona Smith. She had moved from her last known address, had no phone number on record and her trail had gone cold. He signed in to Facebook and pulled up her public page. There wasn't much on it and certainly no recent entries, but a link to a blog site led him to *Trials & Tribulations – all in a pooch walker's day*. It was a blog by someone called *Pooch Walker*. There were no entries since October. It was a long shot, but could Rona Smith be Pooch Walker, and not simply a follower of the site?

'This one might 'ave a handle,' he muttered as he pulled up PeekYou, a free people search engine. It was neat because he could use it to search for monikers and handles rather than names. He typed "Pooch-Walker" in the search box.

A sudden thought struck. John Camm had used the handle *Mower Man* on his business website. Matt remembered seeing it on the website's troubleshooting page where questions about lawn mowers were answered. In itself it was hardly earth-shattering, but he reckoned it was worth following up. He looked over his shoulder. Damon appeared engrossed in his own screen, so if he was quick, he could search before Damon noticed he wasn't working on the batch of names.

He typed "Mower-Man" in PeekYou's search box. He'd be able to go back a page and look at the results for "Pooch-Walker" in a moment.

'Bloggin' hell!' The screen was filled with loads of things Mower Man was doing on the Web. This amount of posting, blogging and reviewing couldn't all be down to John Camm alone could it? Matt reckoned there could be hundreds of mower men out there. Where to begin? He'd have to park it for a while.

He sighed.

'Everything OK?' Damon asked.

'Yeah, just aint into pooch keep fit,' he groaned and flicked back a screen to the Rona Smith search.

'Pooch *keep fit*?'

'Yeah, this bird on me list might 'ave a handle. Pooch Walker.'

'Then see if she's registered on Facebook with her handle as a name.'

'Cool.'

It didn't take him a moment. Pooch Walker's page had full public access and the wallpaper on the title page showed a photo of happy pooches on leads, just to emphasise the point. He scrolled through the most recent posts. *I seem to attract strays even on holiday...* was followed by a photo of a thin scruffy dog sitting next to a woman in sunglasses and a baseball cap smiling into the camera. Matt studied what he could see of her face.

'What you think? Do you reckon she's the same bird?' He displayed the two Facebook pages, Rona Smith and Pooch Walker side by side on his screen. He knew Damon would be looking.

'Yep, that's her all right,' Damon said.

'Then it looks like she aint in Suffolk anymore,' Matt murmured, as he read the comments left by other Facebook visitors to the page. *Great – but don't bring it home with you. We've no more space,* someone had written. He clicked on the small photo of a face at the start of the comment. A new Facebook page opened. Sure enough, the face looked remarkably similar to Rona Smith's, just a little older and with the name Jennie Rona. Too much of a coincidence, Matt reckoned.

'Hey, you've a slippery one there,' Damon said, obviously still following on his admin computer access, 'she's probably the sister and Rona is the family name. I guess your Pooch Walker has a long history of using different names. Trace Jennie the sister and we can pass it on to the debt collectors as a *care of* contact address.'

The afternoon passed quickly as Matt worked his way through the batches of names. First he shed his flying jacket and then his sweatshirt as he warmed up. Daylight faded and the darkness deepened outside, making the office feel like the hub of the world. By the time Damon switched on the kettle for the final coffee and hot chocolate break, Matt felt exhausted. Not physically; he'd barely moved. It was the mental concentration that sapped.

'You're getting faster. You traced a good number of names today,' Damon said as he spooned coffee granules into a mug. 'So what are you doing for Christmas?'

'I dunno. I aint thought 'bout it yet.' But there was a hint of an idea deep in his mind. It had been floating in the backwaters ever since ordering the Pontedera tee-shirts.

He sighed. 'Yeah, me calls went well. It's the time a'year.'

'Well you wouldn't think it was the season for goodwill if you'd heard the news just now. They've found another body.'

'What? Near the Rush Green Golf Course again? Someone dug up in Northfield Wood?' Matt opened the news sites as he spoke.

'I only read it a moment ago. No details yet.'

'Then how'd it get in the news so fast?'

'I don't know, but it's six and all this breaking news suits people getting home from work.'

'Meanin'?'

'It's when you chuck your keys on the table, look in the fridge and switch on the TV.'

'I don't,' Matt mumbled.

He stopped listening, all his attention focussed on his screen. *Dead body found in water-filled ditch on Stowmarket to Framlingham road*, he read. There was nothing else, just the stark bulletin with a *Breaking News* prefix. It was a hook to catch and hold, designed to make the reader want more. And Matt wanted to know more.

'Chrissie'll know,' he blurted, unexpectedly proud of his connection.

'What? Oh yes, I remember. She's the one with the DI.'

'Yeah an' I reckon Clive'll be out investigatin' most of the night, so she'll hang in the Nags Head instead of rushin' home.'

'Meaning?'

'I'll get to hear more. Yeah, and Nick'll be there an' all. It'll be a good evenin'.'

'Right, now I get it. The Nags Head's a pub, isn't it,' Damon said, eyeing up Matt's tee.

'Well yeah. What did you think it were?'

CHAPTER 19

Chrissie heard the ring tone just as she was about to leave the Clegg workshop. It *brrring brrringed* at her insistently from somewhere deep in her bag. The caller ID told her it was Clive. It was Friday and his weekend off. Perhaps he was calling to let her know he'd booked a table for later that evening, somewhere nice to eat in Ipswich and seats to watch the latest Bond movie – Skyfall. She'd dropped enough hints.

'Hi,' she said, 'you've just caught me. It's been a long day repairing some chairs. I was all set to dash to my car from the workshop. It's tipping it down.'

'Yes, bloody awful weather. Just my luck to be out in this while the SOC team put a tent over the scene.'

'What are you talking about? What scene?' She couldn't help the sinking feeling.

'Sorry, I should've said. Another dog walker, another body. Except this time it's half submerged in a ditch. At least it was a ditch before all this bloody rain. It's a small torrent now.'

'How'd a dog walker…? I mean it's dark now.'

'Earlier this afternoon. By the time the ambulance decided she was cold, obviously dead and called the police… and then the SOC team got here with their tent, it's been a couple of hours. Needless to say it's dark now. And there's been another cloudburst.'

'Did you just say she?'

'Yes, this one's a woman.'

'Oh God. That's horrible.'

'No sexism now. It's always horrible. They're setting up arc lamps, so I should get to see a bit more in a moment. Thought I'd better give you a call and let you know I'll be dealing with this for a while.'

'Poor you, it sounds grim. I know you can't say how long you'll be, it'll take you as long as it takes.' She realised there was no point in saying *so you'll be late, what time will you be home?*

'Keep me posted if you're going to be the wrong side of midnight, otherwise I'll be really worrying,' she added, trying to sound upbeat.

'Hey, you don't need to worry about the stalker.'

'I wasn't. I meant in case you'd had an accident driving home. But now you've reminded me, I'll worry about the stalker as well!'

She heard him laugh.

'Actually,' she added, 'I think I'll drop by the Nags Head. Matt texted me. It'll probably be something he's found on one of his searches, and Nick and the usual crowd will be there. So don't worry about me, I'll be fine, Clive.'

'I wasn't worrying, but maybe now I should. Hey let me know what Matt's come up with this time. Got to go. Bye now.' She caught the mix of amusement and distraction in his voice.

'Hey where's this body? You didn't say.' But she was too late. The connection had died.

She imagined the arc lights beaming through the dark, the rain glistening as it sheeted down and everyone stooping against the weather. There'd be a tent over the body and someone wearing an all-in-one and waterproofs waving Clive onto the crime scene.

She slipped her phone into her bag, rummaged for her car keys, and ran to her car. Her Friday evening with Clive had just evaporated and she couldn't help but be disappointed. And to add to it all she felt shallow for her disappointment in the face of someone else's misfortune, if misfortune was quite the right word for death. It was certainly miserable luck for the team to be out in the cold and wet on a dark November evening. She flicked on her headlights and heater, and eased the TR7 along the rutted track away from the Clegg workshop.

By the time she'd driven to the Nags Head, her curiosity had surged like a spring tide. She still felt disappointed, but it was merely a ripple on the water, nothing compared to the questions fighting to reach the surface first. The who, where and why.

She pushed the heavy door into the pub. It swung open and a wall of warm air tinged with the scent of beer and humanity hit her. It was busier than she'd expected, but of course it was a Friday, the festive time of year and groups of people, dressed for a night out, were already clustering near the bar. She stood for a moment and scanned the place. Tinsel and fairy lights were strung along the main beams and above the jukebox.

'Hey Chrissie, over here.'

She recognised Nick's voice as she heard her name through the noise. 'Hi,' she mouthed and headed into the quieter area further from the bar. Nick was sitting on a bench, his back against the wall, his long legs out straight, his ankles crossed and his feet resting on the old floorboards. He looked the very picture of relaxed end of working week, still in his day jeans, clean but not obviously on the pull. An almost empty beer glass stood on the table nearby.

'I see it's still raining,' he said.

'Afraid so.' She took off her rain-splattered duffle coat and draped it over the back of a chair.

'What'll you have? Your usual?'

'Hey you don't need to get up, Nick. I've only just got here. It's my round,' she said, but she had read his glance and guessed he wanted to briefly check out the bar, see if there were any nice girls amongst a new group starting to gather for a work's pre-Christmas jolly.

'I think they may be from the Nails & Hair place,' she added, inclining her head.

While Nick made his way to get the drinks, Chrissie settled in her chair and collected her thoughts. If Clive was going to be busy investigating this latest dead body, it was a fair bet he wouldn't be free to help her put up the Christmas decorations over the weekend or to tramp through Northfield Wood again, even with the added incentive of Ray leading the way. Chrissie was also quite sure she didn't want to risk going into the wood alone with Ray. She'd only spoken to him on the phone once and had no idea what he was like. For all she knew he could be a mass murderer.

'You're looking very serious,' Nick said as he set a couple of brimming glasses on the small scrubbed pine table. 'Everything OK at work?'

She waited while he sat down on the bench seat.

'Yes, it's getting crazy, plenty of work, so that's good. No, I was thinking about Ray, the bloke you discovered in the pub out towards Onehouse. The Northfield Wood off-roader.'

'Oh yeah, have you called him yet?'

'Yes, and I reckon I owe you a drink. So thanks and cheers,' she said raising her glass.

'Great. So what did he tell you? Was he able to answer all your questions, fill in some of the history?'

'I don't know yet. I've arranged to meet him in the Dog & Parrot, Sunday lunchtime. I was going to ask him about it over a pint.'

'That's a good idea. Hey, if Clive's with you, don't let on he's a DI. I got the feeling he's the sort of bloke who'll probably open up more if he doesn't realise there's a policeman breathing down his neck.'

'Hmm, well I don't think Clive's going to be able to make it. He phoned to say there's a dead woman been found in a ditch. And knowing Clive, he'll be investigating it most of the weekend.'

'Oh God, not another murder. Did he say more?'

Chrissie sipped her ginger beer and let the talking and laughter in the bar drift over her. How much should she tell? It was always a problem to know. At least in this case it was easy because there wasn't much to say.

'They were setting up arc lamps when he called. Apart from him moaning about the rain and the ditch being filled with water, he didn't say much. I think he was still waiting to get a decent look. He didn't even say where it was.'

'Shit, who'd be a policeman?'

'I'll drink to that. Hey, I don't suppose you'd want to drop by the Dog & Parrot on Sunday as well, would you?'

She watched his face, saw the slight frown as he reached for his glass.

'Ah, is it complicated? Let me guess. You're meeting a new girl?' she said.

'Well it could be a heavy day on Saturday. Band practice in the morning and a gig over in Framlingham - starts eight thirty, setting up seven, seven thirty.'

'Framlingham?'

'Yeah, it's only a pub. We've played there before.'

'That's great. A return venue. The thing is I was kind of hoping Ray might show me around the wood as well and I don't want to go on my own. I'd said Sunday because I thought Clive'd be around.'

'You could always ask Matt.'

She sipped her drink and considered her options. Nick was avoiding Sunday and she knew he wasn't teasing because if he was he'd have given in by now. She was intrigued.

'In fact you can ask Matt now. He's wearing some kinda leather. It'll be a Harley Davidson next.'

Nick waved and Chrissie turned to look towards the door. Matt had obviously just walked in. He stood, brushing rain off his leather jacket, the droplets forming rivulets on his sleeves.

'I think it'd soak in more if it was real,' she said, blinking as she took in the full effect.

'No, it's really happening. That's Matt.'

She watched as drinkers moved away from his dripping sleeves and stepped back to make way for him at the bar. The rain droplets must have looked contagious; it was the only explanation she could think of.

'So what have you been so busy with?' Nick asked while they waited for Matt to be served by the barman.

'Some chairs. It's funny how one job leads to another. We repaired an oak settle and the customer was so pleased with it he's asked us to repair some furniture for his father.'

She described the visit to Benjamin Mawbray, his depressing home, his bitter time-ravaged face, the recycling works tucked out of sight and the overwhelming weight of hopelessness and failure. 'How can anyone waste their life like that?' she finished.

'Who's wastin' what?' Matt asked, appearing as if from nowhere, lager slopping down the side of his glass.

'Hi,' Nick said cheerfully, 'awesome jacket, mate.'

'Yeah well Maisie says you can't beat Stowmarket charity shops. But you still aint said, Chrissie – who's wastin' what?'

'I was just telling Nick about Benjamin Mawbray. He's a rather weird customer. He's... like it's everyone else's fault he's wasted his life.'

'Mawbray? I've seen the name somewhere, but it weren't Benjamin.' Matt set his glass on the table and slumped onto a chair.

'James? Was is it a James Mawbray?' she asked.

He closed his eyes and she guessed he was leafing through his memory, picturing lists and screens of print.

'No, it weren't a James. But I don't think I ought to say cos Damon'll kill me if 'e ever finds out I'd said.'

'So if it's Damon you're worried about I'm guessing Mawbray was one of the names on your search lists,' she murmured. There was no need to add it was the debt collectors' list. No wonder Ron had settled for furniture in lieu of payment. They already knew Benjamin had a cash flow problem. What if James had a problem too? He could have been playing the old trick of putting more work their way, a psychological game intended to lull them into assuming he had plenty of money to pay his bill. Except the extra work was for his father, and there wasn't any spare cash in that quarter. What was the saying? Like father, like son? She hadn't thought....

'Are you OK, Chrissie? You're frowning again,' Nick said, pulling her from her thoughts.

'What? No, I was worrying James Mawbray might not pay his bill.'

'Hey I already said it weren't James Mawbray I were tracin'. It were a bird and her last name were Mawbray. I traced her to an address in Earl Soham. That's all I'm sayin' otherwise Damon's really gonna kill me.'

'Earl Soham? James lives in Earl Soham. At least that's where we delivered his oak settle.'

'Sounds like there's a load of Mawbrays, probably all related in some way,' Nick said.

The pub door swung open and a girl with pink highlights and wearing skinny black jeans strutted in. She held a helium star-shaped balloon on a string with *HAPPY BIRTHDAY* printed in lurid pink. Conversation stopped as a whoop of excitement filled the bar.

'For a moment I thought that was Maisie,' Chrissie murmured as the commotion died and the girl joined the group from the Nails & Hair place.

'Nah, Maisie's highlights are more kinda pink and anyhow, she's workin' late,' Matt said before gulping more lager.

'Hey if you're free Sunday lunchtime, how'd you fancy helping me out?' She looked at Matt as she spoke, hoping he'd say yes.

'You might need to throw in lunch at the Dog & Parrot, Chrissie,' Nick butted in. 'Oh yeah, and you'll have to take a hike in the wood with her and a bloke called Ray, Matt.'

She closed her eyes in frustration. Her smooth delivery was about to backfire and she couldn't see any chance of Matt volunteering after that line. 'Thanks Nick,' she muttered under her breath.

'A hike? A wood? Ray? It aint my kinda thing, Chrissie. Lunch sounds cool though.'

Before she could explain, her mobile blared out its ring tone. 'Now what,' she groaned, hardly taking in the caller ID.

'Hi, Chrissie.' Clive sounded upbeat.

'Is everything OK, Clive? At least you don't sound like you're out in the rain anymore. So is it going to be an all-nighter?'

'I don't know yet. I just thought I'd share something with you. Set your mind at ease. The dead woman, she's wearing an ankle tag and I recognise her. I figured you'd want to know. She's the stalker.'

'What?'

'Yes, I thought you'd be surprised. I know it's awful, but at least you won't be having any problems from her anymore. And you don't have to stay out in the pub to feel safe.'

'Oh my God. That's... but why? Why her? And her poor son. Can you at least tell me her name?'

'Mandy Rokin.'

'Mandy Rokin,' she repeated softly.

'Look, I can't stop to talk. It's mad this end. I'll call you later, OK? Buy now.' And he was gone.

Chrissie slipped her phone back into her bag. For a moment she was unaware of the pub with its drinkers and noise. She hardly saw Nick and Matt watching her face, they were just shadows, forms.

'Is everything all right? You look kind of weird, Chrissie.'

CHAPTER 20

Nick leaned forward on his bench seat. The noise in the Nags Head seemed to lull for a moment. What had Chrissie just said? Mandy Rokin? The girl he'd spotted at the gig in Thetford wearing a raincoat and trainers was called Mandy Rokin? He'd thought of her as the stalker for so long he'd forgotten she was a real person, might even have an actual name.

'That was Clive you were talking to just now, right Chrissie? And he was telling you something about the stalker, wasn't he? The same girl who we saw at the pub in Thetford. The same one who parked her car in the car park at Northfield Wood, right?' He pressed the words out slowly, deliberately. He needed to be sure he'd heard correctly and there were no misunderstandings.

'Yes,' Chrissie murmured.

'Yes?' he queried. 'That's all? But there must be more.'

'Hey, Chrissie. I were here too. I heard you talkin' to Clive. He were tellin' you 'bout the body they just found, weren't he?' Matt's face seemed almost cherubic, its round contours softened by his beard and the dull lighting, but his voice sounded surprisingly sharp.

'Yeah, Matt's got a point, Chrissie. This stalker's been all that's been going on for weeks. And not just for you.'

'OK, OK, Nick. I get what you're saying. But I'm having trouble getting my head round it too. Hell, you were here. I was only on the phone for a couple of minutes. Clive didn't say much.'

'So if he didn't say anythin', why'd he call?' Matt muttered.

'Because he wanted to set my mind at rest. Stop me worrying she was still out there, still stalking me even though they'd tagged her.'

'And?' Nick coaxed.

'And he knew straight away who they'd found in the ditch because she had an ankle tag and he recognised her face. Now you know as much as me.'

'And her name were Mandy Rokin? It's scammin' freaky,' Matt muttered.

'Weird,' Nick added. It was how he felt.

Friday evening changed for him in a flash. Nothing made sense. It was difficult to take in and almost impossible to process. In a matter of seconds his carefree drink with mates had transformed and the festive tinsel and fairy lights had lost their sparkle. He didn't have the stomach for more beer, and any thoughts of chatting up some of the girls in the bar evaporated. At least he wasn't the only one whose mood had flipped. Chrissie looked obviously shocked, and even Matt seemed distracted. It was time to retreat, make his way back to Woolpit, fill his garage-attic room with loud music, lose himself in the songs and move on.

•

Nick slept better than he'd expected. When he awoke his mind felt clearer. He'd got it at last - learning of the stalker's death was like hearing about the sudden death of a film or pop star. It was unrelated to him, but his initial feelings were still shock and sadness, as if losing someone he actually knew. And why did he think he knew his stars? He reckoned it must be their ability to connect with him, make him feel their performance was solely for him. It was as if he had a relationship with the star. But of course it was all a fantasy. He'd never spoken to his stars, and he only knew what their publicity machine wanted him to know. Sometimes he didn't even know their real names. The star's family would say he didn't know them at all.

It was the same with the stalker. He felt he knew her. He'd pictured her face often enough, even pieced together her features for the police identikit image. But just like his stars, he had never spoken to her, didn't even know her real name until last night in the pub. And just like a star, she'd made Chrissie, Clive and him feel her performance was just for them.

'Get a handle on it,' he muttered to himself.

It was OK to be sad for her and her family, but not for himself.

'I haven't lost someone I know or like. It's spooky, that's all. And I'm... yeah I'm pleased she's off our backs at last.' There, he'd said it. And he wasn't going to feel guilty about it. It wasn't his fault she was a bit crazy. What's more, *Stalking in the shadows* sounded like a great opening line for a new song. Jake would love it.

Bolstered by the musical psycho-babble he'd worked through during his sleep, it felt good to have got his head around Chrissie's shocking news. Now he needed to set his mind on the day ahead. He'd *use* the energy, *feel* the energy – as one of the songs might have said, and if Pearl turned up at band practice, then he needed to look cool and sound great. He flicked on the kettle for a strong mug of tea; he'd hydrate with bottled water after that.

The miserable dribble from the tiny shower unit chilled. It sent a shock of cold down his arm and back.

'Y-ouch,' he squealed as the icy rivulet pained, but he soaped himself down, hoping he'd feel refreshed and invigorated when the water eventually warmed. One day, he swore, he'd brave the main house and have a superior shower, but for the moment it would have to wait. He still hadn't worked out if Sarah was simply a slightly oddball landlady or if she had other designs on him. Until then, there was no way he was venturing in there only partially clothed.

He dressed in faded jeans, a designer gash near one knee, and pulled on a dark blue and brown striped sweatshirt. He didn't want to look as if he'd tried too hard, so he gave up on a shave. The last time Pearl had seen him he'd a day's growth on his face and was standing in the crowd at the Christmas Fayre. In fact it was the only time she'd seen him, so a day's growth seemed a solid bet.

It didn't take him long to gather up his ring folder of words and sheet music, and a notepad and pen. He grabbed his bomber jacket and hurried down the outside wooden stairs from his garage-attic. His feet were too long for each slippery wet step, so he rocked and hopped down the last few rungs, a rhythm set in his head and a song in mind for the saxophone player to try.

Band practice was usually held in Stowmarket, round at Jason's place, a double length garage squeezed down the side of his parent's house. It had become a dumping place to store old bicycles, tools, piles of magazines and eventually a tired discarded sofa. It was the obvious space for a young teenage Jason to set up his first drum kit, and of course eight years later it was still his territory, more of a music den than it had ever been a garage or storeroom. And his dad's car lived on the drive, as it always had.

Nick headed straight there, his car heater on full fan, the roads near Stowmarket dark and glistening. Was it damp tarmac or black ice? He took the bends slowly. He wasn't in the mood to dice with death. He flicked on the radio as he drove. *A woman was found dead yesterday in a flooded ditch near the Stowmarket to Framlingham road. The police haven't released her name yet, and are treating the death as suspicious.* The newsreader's voice blended with the tones of the car heater. Nick had to tune his ears to pick out the words.

It was one thing to hear the news by chance, but to make an effort and strain to listen? Now he was thinking about the stalker. Soon she'd be getting into his head again, just like she had at the pub. It seemed the stalker could take over the radio. She was everywhere. It was sick. He turned it off.

'I hadn't thought you'd get at me through the airwaves,' he muttered, as if she could hear. Shit, he needed to get a grip, toughen up and concentrate on the next line for the song.

'Yeah, how about – *silent messages on the answerphone?*' It rhymed with *alone*. Yeah, he needed to toughen up and *use* the energy.

He drew up outside Jason's parents' home with its double length garage at the end of a residential road of 1950s houses. Cars crowded drives and spilled along kerbsides. It was still a little early at nine thirty on a Saturday morning for the residents to be up and about, and as if to endorse the fact, an illuminated Santa tied to the outside of number 23 was still switched on from the night before. It was Stowmarket suburbia at its best. Nick kept his head down against the cold damp air and hurried to the garage side door.

'Hiya,' he said, as he scanned the makeshift studio and did a headcount. Jake was fussing with the speakers, and Jason was plugging in a kettle for some tea.

'Hi,' Adam the bass guitarist nodded.

'Is Denton coming?' Nick asked. They were one band member missing, and of course Pearl was nowhere to be seen.

'Yeah, he said he was. What about the saxophone player Ruby?' Jake asked.

'Ruby? She said her name was Pearl, Jake. Try to get it right if she turns up.'

'Yeah, yeah.'

Ten minutes later Denton had arrived with his keyboard. There'd been a quick fiddle with speaker settings and then they were straight into their first number. It didn't take Nick long to settle into the vocals. He'd always found breath control and phrasing came naturally with the words and music, so no effort was required. He'd realised it a couple of years ago when he'd been hit by a series of panic attacks. His breath had come faster and faster, rasping in his throat as his world speckled and his head tried to float away. He'd discovered, first by humming and then singing, that his breathing slowed. As soon as he filled his head with the melody and his mouth with the words, the song took over and the panic passed. And of course once he knew he could control the attacks, he no longer feared them. Now it was all past history, apart from the breath control which was part of him. He supposed Chrissie would call it a life skill.

While his band mates played he sank deeper into the song and the moment, singing for once with his eyes closed and his back towards the side door. He didn't even notice when Pearl opened it and crept in during the number. At first he thought the bars of a hauntingly high counter-melody were Denton messing around on keyboard. But when he opened his eyes it was obvious something had changed. His mates were grinning, Adam moving one shoulder in an exaggerated manner to the beat and Jake nodding. Jason spun his drumsticks and whooped to make the point. They were all looking behind him. The song disintegrated. Nick spun on his heel, saw Pearl with her soprano sax and almost died.

His cheeks flamed. Thank God he hadn't shaved. His skin was on fire under the stubble.

'Hi! Pearl? I didn't realise you were here.' He knew he was stating the obvious, but with the others laughing and a face redder than the Santa on number 23, it was difficult to come up with a cool opening line.

'I guessed,' she said quietly.

It struck him she was a quiet kind of person. It was probably why he hadn't heard her come in… well that and the volume blasting from the speakers. While the others introduced themselves he watched. She seemed unfazed by the situation and at home among the amateur musicians, but then it made sense because, if he'd heard her correctly, she was a music student at the Colchester Institute.

'I see you've brought two,' he said.

'Yes, two saxophones – the soprano I played just now and of course the alto sax.'

'Why *of course the alto*?' he asked.

'Well, people are sort of used to hearing the alto. I didn't know if that's what you were after. It might like… suit your music better.'

'Could be,' Jake said.

'But if you remember Kenny G, he was like… a kinda first to hit the charts with the soprano sax. So I also play soprano cos it's a bit different.'

'Very 80s,' Nick added, hoping he'd got it right.

'Yeah, and it was also a kinda novelty for people to hear the soprano sax back then.' She seemed to know her stuff.

'So can you play us something on the alto one?' Jake asked.

For the next eight minutes she took them on a tour of well-known sax solos, starting with Gerry Rafferty's *Baker Street* and ending with Hazel O'Connor's *Will You?* She made the alto saxophone scream its notes, bend them, sound reedy or warmly rounded and even orchestral. It was difficult to believe so many qualities of the same note could come out of the same instrument.

'It's a bit like a human voice,' Nick said.

'I know.' She smiled, and the smile seemed to come from deep behind her eyes. He noticed they were a reassuringly different shade to Mel's. Pearl had hazel flecks amongst the green. It complimented her dark brown hair; a shade darker than Mel's.

'Right, Pearl, that sounded great. Now let's get back to our numbers. We've a gig this evening so we need to run through the set. And we've a couple of new ones we're trying. So just jam along as you like,' Jake said.

'OK.'

'Nick can tell you the keys they're in. They'll be in his lyrics folder,' Jake added, before turning to the rest of the band. 'Count us in, Jason. Right everyone? On the count of four.'

Nick sensed Jake was OK with Pearl because he'd made the effort to get her name right, but it didn't mean Jake was cutting her any slack, in fact it seemed quite the opposite.

Jason tapped his drumsticks together three times and on the next beat Denton played the opening chord while Adam struck up a funky rhythm on bass. Nick hurriedly opened the folder for Pearl while the eight bar intro played. It was the only time he could give her before he had to sing his opening words. The band was being unnecessarily mean, a trial by ordeal. He wanted to say something but instead he settled for an unspoken gesture of *I'm sorry but what can you do* kind of thing, and then the music took over.

By the end of the practice session it was obvious Pearl could hold her own. In fact she added another dimension to the music. This time it was Jake who asked why she chose mostly to play the soprano sax.

'Cos you didn't give me time to get my head round the numbers. It's easier to transpose up to C on it and then I was like... improvising by ear.'

'You did great,' Nick beamed. 'Really you did.'

'Yeah, come along to the gig tonight, if you like. It's at the pub in Framlingham. The Horseshoe,' Jake said.

'Wasn't there a woman found dead somewhere up that way? I heard it like... on the radio on the way here,' she said.

'Yeah, there weren't many details. I expect we'll hear more at the Horseshoe. Hey, talking of pubs, does anyone fancy a pint at the Nags Head? Pearl, how about you? I reckon we owe you a drink, and you can take a proper look at the music in my folder.' Nick flashed his most winning smile.

He read the answering smile in her eyes.

CHAPTER 21

'What's wrong then, Matt?' Maisie asked.

On the face of it, not a difficult question. But how to explain when he wasn't sure himself? Perhaps if he didn't say anything the question would go away and he could concentrate on the more pressing problem of planning the rest of his Saturday.

'It's December the first today. Aint you gettin' how Christmassy it is?' she added, her voice rising to a squeal. He had learned her squeaks and squeals and he was pretty sure he was hearing excitement.

'Yeah, well there's decorations everywhere, Mais.' He jerked his head upwards and stared at the star shaped lights hanging from cables strung across the pedestrianized precinct. They were both standing in the centre of Stowmarket. 'You can't miss 'em, and they aint even on.'

'And there's only three more Saturdays till Christmas,' she murmured in a *we could be missing a bargain* kind of way. She followed it up with playful pinch in his ribs.

'Hackin' scam, Mais. There's still four Saturdays countin' today.'

'But that's what I mean. You're like... there's loads of time, but there aint.' She didn't look at him as she spoke, her attention seemed to be taken by a shop window display.

'But there is loads of time, Mais. All this countin' down. It's like we're bein' squeezed.'

'Bein' squeezed? What you mean? Like you aint got enough cash?'

'No… well yeah, there's always that. I mean me. It's like me head's being squeezed.'

'Your head? Squeezed? It don't look squeezed, Matt.' Her voice softened half a tone as she linked her arm through his, 'It's freakin' cold. You sure you aint goin' down with somethin'? A cold? Hey I know, let's have a Costa. I reckon a hot chocolate with extra marshmallows'll sort your head.' She steered him towards the coffee shop.

He liked it when she fussed over him, and the warm air and smell of coffee hit as she nudged him into the shop and past the counter loaded with muffins, biscotti and panettone.

'It's nice here, aint it,' she whispered.

'Well it's Italian, like me Piaggio, Mais.'

'So what's this thing with your head then?' she asked when they finally sat down with two mugs of frothy topped hot chocolate spilling into saucers.

'I feel… I feel….' But what did he feel?

'Go on,' she said as she scooped some of the marshmallows off her hot chocolate and spooned them into her mouth before they melted.

'I feel like I've got all this stuff goin' round in me head. Questions. Searches. Everyone wantin' answers like yesterday, but then I don't have facts to get them answers. An' all the time there's this countdown cos it's Christmas in four Saturdays.'

'What facts? What questions?'

'Well take yesterday–'

'Friday?'

'Yeah afternoon, an' I'm at work tracin' for Damon, an' I'm lookin for Mower Man and no, he aint a superhero, Mais - he's lots of people and also he's John Camm.'

He ignored what could have been a frown and ploughed on, 'And this stalker bird, the one botherin' Clive an' Chrissie, well I got her name but only cos now she's dead. And Nick's playin' some gig in Framlingham.'

'Weren't Framlingham where the woman were found dead yesterday?'

'Yeah, Mais, somewhere out that way. She's the stalker, an' if I go to the gig I might hear more cos of where it is.'

'She's the stalker? Well I aint goin' with you if all you're doin' is askin' about her. In any case I'm on a late shift, so I'll be well shattered. But why'd you want to know more? It's sick.'

'Cos her son were the one into computin' an' hackin'. An' that aint all, Mais. Chrissie wants me to go to the Dog 'n Parrot and then round Northfield Wood with some bloke called Ray on Sunday.'

'What Dog 'n Parrot? An' what about me?' she squealed.

'What you on about? It's a pub on the way to Onehouse. Hey I know, you could go instead of me. Then I'd be let off walkin' round the wood. Honest, Mais, all this countin' down is doin' me head in.'

'I aint goin' to no Dog 'n Parrot just to get you out of it. You're sickenin' for somethin'. That's what this is.'

She reached across and laid her warm hand on his slightly less warm forehead. 'See – I knew I were right! You're cold. Hey I hope you'll be OK by Christmas!' She gave him a kiss and pushed her chair back. 'No,' she said standing up, 'you stay here in the warm for a bit, I've got to go. Me shift starts in ten minutes. I'll give you a call later to see how you are. OK? I reckon you need an early night, an' all.'

Matt watched her leave. He thought she looked kind of cute in her skinny jeans and padded jacket. Maybe she was right and he was going down with something. He stared at her empty mug. Dried froth coated the sides and cold milky chocolate pooled in the saucer. It summed up how he felt, his head so squeezed it was empty, his shell nothing but a footprint left by hot chocolate. And to top it all, now she'd given him another countdown; to be well by Christmas. He felt more pressured than ever. What was he going to do with the rest of his Saturday? Retreat into his world of computing, or plunge into his realm of comic-strip heroes?

A *two birds with one stone* kind of a compromise dawned on him. If he stoked up with muffins and headed back to the Academy library, he reckoned he could both retreat and plunge. There were so many people using the handle Mower Man it virtually qualified for super-hero status. And tracking Mower Man's online activity meant some computing, so he'd have a comic-strip hero and the World Wide Web to squirrel under. He'd cocoon himself in his tried and tested security blankets. He'd be OK. Getting answers would clear his head.

Forty minutes later he parked his scooter and slipped into the Academy entrance, his backpack stuffed with a couple of Costa muffins and Italian biscotti in a festive cellophane wrapper. He'd thought the little hard-baked almond cookies looked cool and fitted his *all things Italian* phase. If Rosie was around he'd get them out.

The library door swung open when he pushed against it. So who else was here? He scanned the long room with its bookcases, computer stations and racks of journals. It was only midday but the December sky appeared grey and overcast through the large windows, the dusty lights hanging low from the ceiling were already switched on. There was no sign of a library assistant, but then there weren't official library hours for students on a Saturday. Matt counted the others; there were only a handful, most likely working on projects and assignments with course deadlines more pressing than shopping on the fourth Saturday before Christmas. So he wasn't the only one escaping the present-buying countdown. He felt a warm glow. Perhaps he wasn't so unusual after all.

He settled at his favourite computer station away from the others and close to the wall. There'd be a few hours yet before Security did the rounds to lock up, but by then he'd have melted away. In the meantime he was going to make the most of those few hours.

First he revisited the PeekYou site and entered "Mower-Man" in the search box. This time Damon wasn't breathing down his neck and Matt used a logical system. He'd narrowed the field using dates and geographical locations and then started with Mower Man's Facebook activity.

Were there any postings which could possibly be linked to Northfield Wood? Nothing caught his eye. Next he turned his attention to Mower Man's activity on Suffolk members' pages. He scanned through the list, and using his own login to work from inside Facebook, looked up each posting location in alphabetical order. Mostly he found photos of neatly mown lawns with precise edges bordering flowerbeds. The accompanying message generally ran on the lines of, *your annual mower service will give your mower a new lease of life and improved cutting to create a lawn like this. Mower Man.*

'Just promo stuff,' Matt muttered.

A name jumped off the screen. 'Mawbray?' he murmured, 'Benjamin Mawbray? Weren't he the bloke Chrissie was on about last night?'

There'd been another Mawbray of course, a Stella Mawbray; she'd been on the debt collectors' list. But Benjamin Mawbray? He recalled Chrissie saying he was old and bitter.

He didn't know what he expected to find on Benjamin Mawbray's public access pages, but a quick scroll through showed he was an infrequent poster. Matt reckoned it was most likely the age thing and it seemed Benjamin was one of the seniors who'd shied away from becoming a silver surfer. However something struck him as odd. Most of the postings on the old man's Timeline had been posted by someone else.

'Scammin hell, them's the same photos as on John Camm's page.'

He recognised the one with John's hand out to a squirrel near an oak, and then the one of him standing in front of a Christmas tree. He scrolled on down, past John Camm picking sloes and finally the shot with the palm trees in the background.

And the message with each photo? *Good to find you again. It brings back memories of the old times, hey? Mower Man.*

A photo and message had been posted at monthly intervals starting in August and ending with November 1st. Four photos. Four messages. It was the same message each time.

'That's scammin' weird,' Matt breathed, but then a lot of what was posted on Facebook was either weird or uncool. So were John and Benjamin old friends? He decided to take a screen shot and email it to Chrissie. She'd know what to make of it.

Before leaving Facebook, Matt idly typed Mandy Rokin in the search box. 'Scam,' he muttered. Apart from a public access page of photo albums, her security setting was for *friends only*. He'd have to settle for the albums. Usually he liked looking at pictures, but these were plain boring. 'They're all scammin' selfies!'

Matt had never *got* selfies, it was the whole face thing again – too many expressions, so many interpretations. And anyway, why this preoccupation with a face? Maisie had said it was cool to take selfies, but this seemed extreme. Of course she was a stalker, so was it part of the fixation thing? Matt didn't know. He certainly wasn't going to waste time trying to decipher her different looks. It would be too frustrating.

He turned his attention from the foreground face to the backgrounds in her shots. 'Now that's more interestin',' he murmured.

'Watcha, Matt.' The familiar voice made him jump.

'Scammin' hell, Ley. What you doin' creepin' up like that?'

'Doh! I've been here for ages. You just aint noticed me over at the printer. So what's...?' Ley peered at the screen. 'Aint she a bit...?'

'A bit what?'

'I dunno.'

'Like blue screened?' Matt blurted, voicing his thoughts.

'Blue screened? You mean like dead, mate? That's kinda harsh. No I just mean... old?'

'I reckon she's the one on the news found dead yesterday.'

'Ah right, now I'm gettin' you. I thought you fancied her. Unless?'

'Fancied her? She's dead mate.'

'Yeah, I know, that'd be weird even for you. Hey, will you be down the Nags Head later?'

'Tonight? Nah, I thought I'd try the Horseshoe, Framlingham.'

'That's a bit out your way, aint it?'

'Yeah, but there's a gig there. Me mate Nick's band is playin'.'

'Right.'

It only took a few minutes talking about it before Ley said he wanted to come along to the gig as well, have a night out in Framlingham and support the band. Matt reckoned if Maisie cut up rough about him going to the gig without her, he could always say it was Ley who'd twisted his arm because he needed wheels to get to Framlingham. They arranged to meet in the Nags Head a bit before seven o'clock, which would allow plenty of time to get to the Horseshoe by eight for the eight thirty gig.

'And wear somethin' for the wind. You're on the back of me Piaggio, remember,' Matt added, as Ley started to move away.

'Yeah, 'course. Doh!' Ley tapped his forehead with the palm of his hand. It was the Simpsons' thing again. Matt wished he got it.

He watched Ley meander across the library to the door, and then he was gone. Ley was OK, but he wasn't into the searching and finding in the same way that it fascinated Matt. In fact Matt reckoned Ley thought it strange, and so he always held back from talking to him about his delving, hunches and impossible missions. Perhaps it was the difference between the Simpsons and comic-strip heroes. So he decided he'd keep his curiosity about Mandy Rokin under wraps, at least as far as Ley was concerned. Time for a lemon poppy seed muffin, he decided and delved into his backpack.

He refreshed the Facebook page and looked at the backgrounds in Mandy's selfie shots. As he bit and munched, crumbs of lemon sponge dropped onto the desk, landing dangerously close to the keyboard, but he barely noticed, his attention was focussed on the minutiae of blurry images. He'd need to ask Damon if there was any way of sharpening up the backgrounds.

Around three o'clock the daylight filtering through the library windows began to fade. Within a matter of forty minutes it had changed through shades of grey into darkness. 'Time to split,' Matt muttered. He wanted to slip away before Security made their rounds. He logged off, mopped up the lemony muffin fragments with his fingers, licked them clean and followed a straggling student out of the library.

•

A Christmas tree with coloured lights had been erected in the small square in the centre of Framlingham. Old stucco fronted timber frame shops and houses surrounded Matt. It might be called a square, but strictly speaking it was more of a loose triangular shape. He eyed its gentle slope with distaste. Framlingham and its castle had been built on the highest point for miles around, and although barely fifty metres above sea level, it counted as a hill. The scooter's two-stroke engine had complained and whined all the way up, loaded with the added weight of Ley on the back.

The Horseshoe was away from the square, and it was heaving with young people by the time Matt and Ley slipped in through the side door to the bar. It didn't appear particularly old with its stuccoed front, but once inside, its age was obvious. Low ceilings, thick oak beams and dark flagstones stretched through a series of rooms, with an eating area tucked away at one end of the building. The band had set up in an alcove mid-distance between the bar and dining tables. The excitement in the air was obvious. The smell of steak and ale pies mingled with beer and the smoky fumes from a token log fire in an old open-hearth brick chimney breast.

'Nice, aint it,' Matt shouted above the noise, and followed Ley to the crush at the bar.

He knew he'd find Nick easily enough. If he wasn't sitting quietly and sipping his bottled water near the band's instruments in the alcove, he'd catch sight of his head above the rest of the crowding drinkers. At six feet three inches tall, Nick wouldn't be difficult to spot. However Matt wanted a pint of lager first. He needed to dull the chill of the journey, and Ley was buying.

'Sorry I'm late,' someone called over his head, 'but they've closed Earl Soham Lane and I had to take a detour.'

'Yeah, well they found that dead woman somewhere along there, didn't they,' a bloke said across him.

'Really? I assumed it was flooded again, but that explains why there weren't any flood signs,' the voice boomed back.

Matt stood his ground. This was getting interesting.

'Do they know how she got there? I mean, there aren't any houses along that way, at least none I've noticed. Was she from round here?' someone else asked.

'Don't know, but I heard she was from Stowupland,' a girl to one side of him said. He caught the obvious smile she radiated to the bloke close to his shoulder.

'That's Stowmarket, isn't it?' the voice boomed from behind.

'Yeah, near enough,' Matt muttered under his breath, but no one seemed to hear.

'Hey, your drink,' Ley said, startling Matt and pushing a pint of lager into his hand.

Reluctantly he found himself shepherded away from the thick of the throng and the Mandy Rokin chatter, except her name hadn't been released and no one in the bar seemed to be talking as if they knew it. Without a name he reckoned folks were guessing. So had he been listening to nothing but rumour and speculation? The bit about the Earl Soham Lane sounded solid. Perhaps he should come back another day when people had learnt who she was.

'If Mais were here,' he murmured. But would she have got nattering with the bird at the bar? Would the mention of Stowupland have tweaked her curiosity? A fellow *St'uplander* dead? Of course a promise of a rum and Coke might have helped.

'What about Mais? What were you 'bout to say?' Ley asked.

'She... were goin' to call, see how I am.'

'Are you sickenin' with summut then?'

'Nah, I feel OK. Let's go an' find me mate Nick.'

They gravitated to a place opposite the alcove. Ley wanted to stand far enough back so he could lean against the wall during the gig, but Matt spotted Nick and waved. He liked to be up at the front close to the action, and worked his way towards the six inch high dais for the band. Nick seemed to be talking to a girl and didn't notice him at first. Normally Matt would have walked straight up, said hi, and taken a closer look at the girl. Something made him hang back.

Chrissie had once said he should try pausing sometimes and take a stab at reading people's faces and body language before butting in. It had been part of a big sister type of conversation after he'd got them all thrown out of the only department store in Bury. That was last Christmas when she'd been helping Nick choose a perfume for his mum. Matt had taken in the words, dismissed her stridently rising tone as just a girl thing, and later looked up *how to read body language* on the internet.

Now as he hesitated before interrupting Nick, he started to get the body language thing. Nick was leaning in towards the girl, while she for her part wasn't stepping away. They both seemed to be studying an A4 sheet from a ring folder, their heads only inches apart. Cool, Matt thought. Is this one of Nick's birds he's so secretive about? It could be, after all she was holding a saxophone.

Without warning Nick looked up, as if he knew he was being watched and glanced directly at Matt. Matt grinned and did the *Doh!* he'd seen Ley do so many times, complete with a palm smack to his forehead and then accidently slopping lager onto his sweatshirt. Nick smiled, a half shake of his head, and then his attention seemed to return to the girl.

'Mega cool,' Matt breathed. Had he cracked the body language thing? He had no idea what the *Doh!* had meant, but Nick seemed happy enough with it. Yeah it was mates' language; blokes' stuff. Glowing with being accepted and part of the scene, he hooked a piece of Christmas tinsel off a wall light and wound the short strand around his glass. Yeah, maybe he could get the Christmas thing too, he decided as he made his way back to Ley who was propping up the wall.

CHAPTER 22

Was she out of her mind, Chrissie wondered. Apprehension pressed at her stomach and she pushed her half-eaten Sunday morning toast and boiled egg to one side.

'I mean meeting some bloke I know nothing about?' she said, half hoping Clive would urge her to forget the whole mad idea.

'You'll be OK,' he soothed. 'Internet dating means people are pretty much doing this kind of thing all the time, and the statistics are in your favour,' he murmured as he put the milk back in the fridge.

'What? That he's not some mad chainsaw killer?' It was just like him to reassure her with statistics when really what she wanted was an excuse to wriggle out of the meeting.

He turned to face her. 'Sarah is still going with you, isn't she?'

'Well, ye-e-s.'

'There you are then, you'll be fine, Chrissie. Oh and make sure you've both got tracking enabled on your mobiles.'

'But the signal's hopeless in the wood.'

'I meant in case he bundles you both into his 4x4 and abducts you to Thetford Forest or somewhere. You did say he was an old man, didn't you?'

'Now I know you're winding me up,' she said, starting to laugh. But he was right. She didn't imagine there were many mad chainsaw killers out there who'd be willing to take on both Sarah and her.

'I wish you were coming with me instead,' she added, caught his frown and countered, 'Yes I know, no one could have guessed there'd be this latest body or that it would be the stalker's. And yes, I know you're up to your eyes.'

'Come on now, it's only another six weeks until we're on holiday. Hey, aren't you going to eat the rest of that?' He bent across, gave her a kiss and whisked the toast off her plate.

'I thought I'd take the van. If there's any driving to the wood, then we don't have to have the *come and sit in my lovely 4x4* nonsense from him. It is ex-Forestry Commission, after all. Off-road capability, and all that.'

'Ah right, the sump guard and increased ride-height.' He bit into her half-eaten toast. He looked serious, but she guessed he was teasing.

'OK I know there's no driving allowed in the actual wood, but....'

'If Sarah's going with you, why don't you both go in her car? The van's only got front seats, and if you've got the old man with you,' and he emphasised the old man bit, 'then, there'll be more room for you all in her car.'

'Hmm, and avoid a tight squeeze in the front seats.' He was right of course. She wasn't thinking straight. The Citroen Berlingo and her TR7 were both essentially two-seaters.

'Sorry, Chrissie, but I better get going. At this rate I'm going to be late. Give me a call and let me know how you're getting on. Bye.' Seconds later the front door slammed.

She sat for a moment longer at her narrow kitchen table and let the sudden stillness in the house wash over her. Sometimes she felt she was living with a tornado. She supposed it made up for the long hours when he was out of the house working overtime and weekends. Occasionally she even wondered if he had room for anything but work in his life. At least she was interested in it as well as him, otherwise it could have got between them and slowly prized them apart. She gazed wistfully at the small kitchen window, her eye passing back over the porcelain Butler sink and wooden drainer with his mug and breakfast plate standing on the rack. It was like a reminder, trace evidence.

Her dirty breakfast plate could wait. She pulled her laptop closer, flipped up the screen and keyed in her password. She checked through her emails. There was something from Paul, the secretary at the golf club, saying he'd researched back through the records and had a little more information about the Northfield Challenge Trophy, if she was still interested. *Please feel free to drop by Wednesday. I should be in the clubhouse (bar or office) around lunch time or about 4:30 if you're passing this way.*

'I wonder what he's found,' she murmured, her curiosity immediately tickled as she marked it on her calendar. And Matt had sent something as an attachment.

She opened his email, the tightness in her stomach relaxing as her inquisitiveness took hold. 'How strange,' she breathed as she recognised the photos posted on the screen shot of Benjamin Mawbray's Facebook page. They were the same ones she'd seen posted by John Camm on his own Facebook pages.

How did Matt find this stuff? And more to the point, how did he come to think of even looking? 'He must spend half his life glued to a computer screen,' she muttered.

But the message attached to each posting was even weirder. *Good to find you again. It brings back memories of the old times, hey? Mower Man.*

This was definitely something Clive needed to see. Hell, if she was Clive she'd either ask Benjamin, or send DS Stickley to ask Benjamin about the connection between the two men, given John was the victim of a seemingly motiveless and as yet unsolved murder. She pulled a scrap of paper towards her and jotted down their current ages, sixty and sixty-six. By her calculations she reckoned Benjamin would have been aged fifteen and John about twenty-one if she worked it right back to 1967, the year of the presumed incident in Northfield Wood. A six year difference in age? It felt too large a gap for them to have been mates at fifteen and twenty-one. But later in life? It wouldn't have been an obstacle.

An hour or so flew as she puzzled over the photos and posting message.

'Hell, is that the time?' she yelped as she caught sight of 10:15 displayed above the date on her screen toolbar. Sarah would be calling round in another fifteen minutes and here she was, sitting in the kitchen, still in her dressing gown and with a cold mug of tea and a half-eaten boiled egg on the table. She'd better get moving if she wanted a quick shower before throwing on some clothes.

Forty minutes later Chrissie had showered, dressed and was drinking freshly brewed coffee with Sarah. They sat in her snug living room with its patterned rug and comfortable two-seater sofa while Chrissie brought her friend up to speed on the Northfield Wood mystery.

'OK, I'll drive. Do you really think he could be a bit of a lech?' Sarah's voice carried a hint of excitement as well as outrage.

'No, but there's no point in being stupid about this. If he offers to show us where he saw something unusual, or knows where something happened all those years ago in the wood, I'd like to say yes and feel safe if we go and explore. That's all.'

'Of course.' Sarah sipped her coffee. 'Hey, this is quite exciting, isn't it?'

Chrissie looked at her friend. She came across as neat and stylish, the expensive feathered haircut sporting subtle red-coloured highlights in her dark hair. Charcoal jeans and tailored wax jacket had a slimming effect. Ready for anything, Chrissie reckoned.

'How are you finding Nick as a lodger?' she asked, as a thought struck.

'He's no trouble, in fact most of the time I hardly know he's there. He doesn't say much but I'm hoping I can persuade him to come along with me to the fencing club. I know it's in Ipswich, but I could give him a lift and….' She winked.

Chrissie got the picture and laughed. 'Yes, well let's hope we won't need your fencing skills today.'

'Hmm, maybe he'd be more likely to come along if you started coming again.'

'That was nearly five years ago, Sarah.'

A lot had happened since then and Chrissie didn't want to be distracted by her memories from the time when Bill was still alive. Not today. Not now when she needed all her playacting skills and a sharp mind. 'Come on let's get moving. I think we should aim to be at the Dog & Parrot before Ray arrives.'

It was cold, but at least not raining. She hooked an anorak off the wall peg in the hallway and followed her friend outside. Sarah's car was still warm from the drive through Woolpit and it didn't take them long to thread their way along the lanes towards Onehouse.

'Hey, can we just keep going and have a quick peep at the wood? I mean, I've never noticed it before and it might help if I'd seen what you're both talking about. We're still early, right?' Sarah drove, not appearing to wait for a nod from Chrissie.

'Yes, OK,' Chrissie said, catching her enthusiasm. They sped on. 'You should just about see the trees in the distance now. Over there.'

She directed Sarah to some unofficial parking behind the community centre building. They hopped out of the car, excitement nipping at their heels and hurried on foot past a small playing field before cutting onto Woodland Close and the main entrance into the wood.

'Now that's odd,' Chrissie said as she spotted a Toyota 4x4 ahead. It had stopped in front of a closed five bar gate blocking the track into the wood. The driver, a man in his late sixties, had left the engine running, his driver's door open, and appeared intent on rattling a chain and padlock securing the gate.

'Is everything all right?' she asked as they approached.

He looked up, startled frustration creasing his weathered face. 'I didn't think they'd lock the bloody gates. Close them, yeah. But why bloody lock them?'

'I think there's a warden, if it's important you drive in. Otherwise it's the kissing gate there and you're on foot.'

'But I wanted to drive in to get my bearings. I'm… I'm meeting….' His voice drifted as he turned his attention back to the padlock.

'Come on, we're wasting time,' Sarah hissed in her ear.

Something made Chrissie hesitate before walking on. The man was just too much of a coincidence not to be a piece in the puzzle.

'Excuse me for asking and I don't want to sound rude, but… are you Ray by any chance?' she enquired rather primly.

He spun round to face her, suspicion tightening his features. 'What if I am? Who's asking?'

'I'm Chrissie. We've spoken on the phone. I thought I recognised your voice. But aren't we meant to be meeting in the pub?' She checked her watch. 'In half an hour?'

'You're Chrissie?'

'Yes, and this is Sarah. She's interested in the history of the wood as well, so she's come along to help me. We were early so we thought we'd have a quick look here first.' She smiled reassuringly as she tried to picture him wielding a chainsaw.

'Well I'd hoped to have a quick spin round myself, refresh my memory before I met up with you in the pub. These main tracks are meant to take 4x4s, so I didn't imagine anyone would mind or even notice if I drove in. There's no one around.'

'Don't you carry bolt cutters?' She would have mentioned a chainsaw as well, but she didn't want to signal her mistrust.

'What about a hammer?' Sarah said brightly.

'A hammer?' he echoed. He looked nervous.

'Yes. Surely your Toyota comes with tools if you need to change the wheel?'

'Or do they only provide a spray can to fill the tyre with foam if you get a puncture?' Chrissie added. She wondered if it was obvious the questions were a test. Sarah was clearly on the same wavelength, but what about Ray? Had he guessed they were *onto* him?

'If I was in my Series 2A–'

'Old Land Rover,' Chrissie chipped in as an aside for Sarah.

'I'd carry loads of tools, but not with this. It's bloody reliable. Why'd I need bolt cutters or a hammer?'

'They'd come in useful now for the padlock,' Sarah said brightly.

There was a moment's silence. He seemed to tense, then flung back his head and laughed. It was a kind of relaxed sound, rumbling on as he caught the humour. It sounded genuine to Chrissie. He was either all right or a bloody good actor.

'You could use two spanners to wrench the padlock open,' Sarah persisted, as if still trying to break through his guard with a foil. 'Most wheel-changing kits have spanners.'

'But I don't want to break in or damage the padlock. I just assumed it'd be open. I suppose it's back to the Dog & Parrot. We can talk over a pint.'

Sarah shrugged. 'If you say so. But as we're here it seems a pity not to see if it wasn't open all along. Chrissie, can I have another look at your map?'

Chrissie rummaged in her shoulder bag and pulled out a sheaf of papers.

'Thanks,' Sarah said and removed the paperclip holding the sheaf together.

'What are you doing, Sarah?'

'Just a little trick I learnt from a locksmith. We got quite friendly for a while. He used to be a member of the fencing club. Now I need to concentrate – if I straighten the paperclip out and break it... like so, then I've got a torsion wrench and a pick.'

She flashed Ray a smile, grasped the padlock in her left hand, turned her back to them both and hunched over her prey. 'Hell, I haven't done this in a while.'

'Can I have a look at the map, Chrissie?' A hint of nervousness threaded through Ray's voice.

She handed him the map and watched as he orientated it with the track ahead.

'I don't know where the paths and tracks would have been before they started taking out the old stock and replanting with conifers, but this is pretty much how I remember the layout when I was off-roading here. I used to drive along this one, then cut off to the left, here.' His face told he was reliving old memories as he traced the route with his finger.

'OK,' Sarah called, her back still to them, 'it seems the padlock was open all along!'

'Great. So Ray – do you need to drive in, or shall we walk?' Chrissie asked.

'I've never walked it. I only ever drove. I think driving will bring back the memories better.'

'Well I guess that answers my question,' Chrissie said and helped Sarah swing the gate open. 'You never told me you could pick padlocks,' she muttered.

'It never came up before but it's just as well I can,' Sarah murmured as Ray drove through.

It was wet underfoot, the ground as muddy as when she'd walked it with Clive and Nick. Had it been only a week ago? Tyre treads imprinted the soft leafy mulch covering the track close to the gate. She didn't remember seeing so many marks last week, but of course she was forgetting the warden, the police and the SOC team must have driven along this way since then. She needed to concentrate, stay on the ball.

'Last time we walked along a path much too narrow for a vehicle,' she whispered to Sarah.

'We're safer on the wider track. It'll be too exposed if he wants to try anything,' Sarah hissed back, and pushed the gate closed.

'But I think he's OK,' she said before climbing up into the Toyota. Sarah slipped in beside her.

Ray drove slowly. A steady five mph. He seemed to be in his own world, reliving the past as he glanced and peered through the side windows and the windscreen ahead. They trundled along the track, the trees closing in as Chrissie followed their route on the map. She imagined back in 1967 it would have been covered in short young spruce and cedar on one side, and on the other side acres of roughly cleared ground ready for the next wave of new planting. Everywhere there would have been felled ash, oak, elm, hornbeam and field maple - top and tailed, piled up and ready to be transported to the sawmills. All over the place heaps of leafy branches and cleared undergrowth would have smouldered. Smokey air would have blown across the track from make the shift bonfires. Was it possible to equate how it looked then with what it had become now?

'I used to turn left here,' Ray said and slowed to a halt at a crossing of tracks.

'Are you sure?' Chrissie murmured, gazing up at the trees.

'The distances won't have changed. Yeah, it has to be here.' He swung the 4x4 onto a more rutted trail with standing water to one side. 'Yeah, I remember, it was always pretty muddy round here, what with all the digging and planting. Hey what's that?' he slowed to a standstill.

Chrissie spotted blue and white coloured *police keep out* tape stretching across a narrow path. It wove into some densely spaced conifers. There could only be one reason for the police tape. The old charcoal mound. She didn't immediately recognise the path, but Northfield Wood was beginning to all look the same. It confused and disorientated her. Had she walked that particular trail only last week? But of course, there must be a number of tracks and trails leading to the old charcoal mound. The police would have closed them all, and this could be any one of them. It had to be the explanation.

Should she tell Ray about the digging? She opened her mouth to speak.

Crash! Out of nowhere twigs and dead leaves smashed down against the windscreen. Ray slumped over the steering wheel, his hands to his face. She heard the moan. It rose, then broke.

'What the hell?' Sarah breathed.

'Oh, my God! Has he had a heart attack?'

'He's still breathing. Hey, Ray! Ray! Are you all right?' Sarah yelled.

'I'm OK,' he groaned. 'God, that gave me a fright.'

'It was only a bunch of twigs, Ray. It blew down from one of the trees. What did you think happened?' Chrissie said quietly, as she tried to steady her nerves.

'I don't know. It was like a face flashed against the windscreen.'

'Something flashed? Can you see OK? Have you got pain in your chest?' Sarah shot at him.

'No, no. It's nothing like that. It... it startled me, that's all.'

'Well you startled us,' Sarah countered.

'Did it bring back a memory of an accident? Like something hitting your windscreen?' Chrissie asked softly, now curious.

'Maybe.'

'In the wood? Was it here, when you used to off-road? Did a tree hit you... or a deer run across your path?' She nearly added *or did you hit one of the workmen?* But something held her back. She didn't want to rush this. It needed a sympathetic touch. She cast Sarah a *we need to tread lightly* look.

'The pub!' Sarah blurted. 'We all need a drink. Let's go back to the Dog & Parrot and relive the memories over a beer or a G & T. What do you say?'

'If you like,' Chrissie murmured, hoping they hadn't lost the moment with Ray.

'Well I can't turn round here. We'll have to drive on and I'll turn left at the next intersection. We can circuit round to the entrance gate. OK?'

'Yes,' they both said in unison.

Sarah silently signalled a shrug and heavenward glance to Chrissie.

The rest of the tour passed without event. Chrissie spent most of her time furtively watching Ray. He appeared to regain his composure, but he couldn't be drawn into talking. She guessed he was back in his old world of memories. He drove, his eyes darting left and right.

The circuit complete, Ray dropped them off on Woodland Close. Chrissie's head was a blur of Northfield Wood tracks and questions, but underneath it all on some primeval level she was just relieved to have escaped a chainsaw dismembering.

'See you at the pub,' they called, 'we owe you a pint.'

The chill in the air felt more intense and the sky had closed to an unbroken grey. There'd been reports that snow was on the way, and Chrissie shivered. 'Do you think he'll join us for a drink? He was a bit shaken up. He might just nip away,' Chrissie said as they walked the shortcut to Sarah's car.

'I don't know, but either way I need a drink. So come on, to the Dog & Parrot!' she mock-cried.

'Hmm, I hope he shows. You can tell something must have happened to him. I want to get to the bottom of it.'

'You and your nose,' Sarah muttered and unlocked her car.

Barely five minutes later they pulled into the pub car park.

'He's here,' she said, spotting the familiar 4x4, 'Now don't frighten him off, Sarah. We need to coax him into telling us what he meant by "a face flashed against the windscreen".'

'I thought we were fending him off not egging him on. Make up your mind, Chrissie.'

Inside the Dog & Parrot Chrissie hoped their combined charm would finally loosen Ray's tongue, but secretly she suspected it was more likely to be the warm soothing atmosphere in the bar with its familiar beery scent and background babble of drinkers. The second pint of ale also played its part. Clearly he liked the sound of his own voice and it was obvious he wanted to impress them both as he described the wood when he used to off-road there. She watched his reticence wane as the level in his glass dropped.

'So tell us, Ray. Why were you so upset today when something hit your windscreen?' she asked quietly.

'You were obviously one hell of a driver, back in the day,' Sarah purred. 'So if there was a crash or something, we know it couldn't have been your fault.'

'No it wasn't my fault.' He stared into his glass.

'Go on, you can tell us. We were there with you this morning. We saw how it affected you. It must have been terrible,' Chrissie murmured.

'It... he ran out of nowhere.' Ray looked up and fixed her with aging watery eyes. 'It was a boy with a case. I swerved, jammed on my breaks... nearly rolled the Land Rover. I think I must've clipped the case, because it flew at me, bounced on the bonnet, smashed into my windscreen and....'

'And what?' Chrissie was on the edge of her seat.

'I thought I'd hit him as well. He couldn't have been more than about fourteen or fifteen. A skinny lad, but my God he had a mouth on him.'

'So had you hit him?'

'No, thank God. But I almost wished I had. I got out of the Land Rover. Ran over to check he was OK. And there he was yelling and cursing me. He jumped up, grabbed the case... or maybe it was a holdall, and swung it at me. I couldn't believe it; he was up on his feet attacking me. I swear he was going to kill me. He tried to knock me out. He shouted I'd broken everything, ruined everything. It was horrible. He was so angry, and his face....'

'And this happened in the wood, where those twigs hit your windscreen this morning?' Chrissie asked.

'Yeah.'

'And was it a holdall or a suitcase?'

'It was... I suppose it could have been either. I was concentrating on the boy. I remember thinking it looked quite modern. Not an old leather one... some kind of plasticised material. This was back in the 60s, remember. Why, does it matter?'

'It might,' she said slowly. 'So then what happened?'

'He ran off and disappeared amongst the trees. He took his case, or whatever you'd call it with him. I had nightmares for weeks, but there was nothing reported in the local papers and I never head another word about it.'

'And when was all this? When did it happen?'

'I don't know exactly. It'll have been... sometime in '67. Why?'

'No reason really.' She knew what he'd told them was important in some way, but for the life of her she couldn't see how it had anything to do with the Northfield Challenge Trophy. More likely it was connected to the recent digging in the old charcoal mound. This was spooky. She'd put Clive onto him.

'Would you like another drink, Ray?' Sarah asked.

'No, no I'm driving and I best get off home now. It's been nice meeting you two girls. Any time you think of

228

more questions about the old wood... you've got my number. Give me a call.' He smiled, but it was strained.

Chrissie guessed he was embarrassed, or regretted opening-up to them like that. He looked uncomfortable as he shook their hands. They watched, lost for words as he hurried out of the pub.

'Well!' Sarah said on a long breath.

'He's not the only one who feels drained,' Chrissie added, finding her voice as she tried to digest what Ray had just told them.

'There's only one thing for it, Sarah. Let's go back to Woolpit. There's some Beaujolais in my kitchen. You can teach me how you did that thing with paperclips and a padlock.'

•

When Clive got home, the Sunday afternoon had stretched through fading light into five o'clock darkness.

'Hi,' Chrissie said happily. 'Get a glass, and pour yourself some Beaujolais. There's still some left in the bottle.' She patted the space beside her on the sofa.

'Hiya, Clive,' Sarah slurred from the small armchair.

'Sarah?' He bent down to kiss Chrissie. 'You said it went OK with Ray when I rang. That's great. Are you having a party or something? What's with all the broken paperclips on the table?'

Chrissie focussed on the coffee table for a moment and composed her thoughts. 'Ah yes, the paperclips and padlock. We've lots to tell you, Clive.'

'Oh God, what have you two been up to?'

She made a mental note to show him Matt's email with the screen shot of Benjamin Mawbray's Facebook page later. But first they needed to tell him about Ray.

CHAPTER 23

Nick walked slowly, taking care to keep his pace in step with Pearl. She had spent Sunday afternoon with her saxophone quartet entertaining Christmas shoppers with festive music in the Tower Ramparts shopping centre in the heart of Ipswich, and he had spent the afternoon listening to her. Strictly speaking, it had only been part of the afternoon because he had felt shattered after the gig in Framlingham the night before, crashed out when he'd got to bed, woken after midday, and once he'd showered, dressed and driven to Ipswich, time was already eating into the afternoon and the quartet's performance. He'd parked his car on a side road near Christchurch Park and hurried down the gentle hill into the town centre with its new-look Christmas tree made from 41 aluminium spheres and 40,000 LED lights. He was late, but then he didn't want to appear too keen. Maybe late would seem cool if he played it right.

'Great sound,' he said afterwards as they threaded their way across Crown Street and back up towards the park. 'Are you sure you don't want a coffee or anything?'

'No thanks, but thanks for asking. You know I can kinda find my way home perfectly well. This must be like... way out of your way,' she said.

He didn't catch any hint of irritation in her voice, and relaxed. 'I always park my car on the side-roads around here, and I'm done with Christmas shopping for today, so I've got to head this way.' He pulled a face and hoped she got the humour in his purposely unchivalrous answer.

She laughed. 'Thanks for coming to hear the quartet. You didn't have to. You must have like... plenty of other stuff to do.'

Was she testing him? Should he say no he didn't have other stuff to do and risk sounding sad. If he told her he could have been talking to an old man and checking out Northfield Wood with Chrissie but he'd passed it up to come to the quartet, then he'd risk uncool or sound as if he was coming on too strong and frighten her off.

He settled for, 'Yeah... and no.'

'Yes and no? How's that?' She sounded interested.

'Yeah, I've got other stuff I probably should've been doing, like walking around a cold wet wood. But I overslept and amazingly, the prospect of spending Sunday afternoon somewhere dry and festive was more appealing. So the Tower Ramparts won. Oh yeah, and I had some shopping and you just happened to be playing your saxophone.'

'A cold wet wood?'

'Yeah, Northfield Wood. It's near Stowmarket.'

He was tempted to explain about Chrissie and Ray, but he knew it would sound complicated, and in his experience mysterious usually worked better than complicated in the early chat-up stakes.

'And the shopping?'

'Something for the work's Christmas lucky dip,' he murmured. He reckoned she could be fishing for evidence of girlfriends. He smiled. It was a positive sign if she was bothered enough to fish.

It was his turn now. He didn't want her to really think he wasn't interested. No matter that he'd driven to Ipswich specifically to listen to her play in the quartet and hopefully have a coffee or drink with her afterwards. Or that he'd parked near Christchurch Park because she'd let slip on Saturday that she lived nearby. It had given him both an excuse to walk with her, and a face-saver in case she'd given him the brush-off. Of course he was interested.

'So how about you? What sort of presents are you looking to buy?' he asked.

'Well my dad's kinda into old clocks. I've heard there's loads in Norwich so I was hoping to like... go and have a look around. See what I could find.'

'That sounds fun. I don't know much about old clocks.'

'Well I only know what I've picked up from my dad. Why, are you interested?'

'Yeah, anything mechanical.'

'So were you one of those kids like... into train sets? I think I must've disappointed my dad when I preferred making the whistle noise more than playing with the train.'

'I'm afraid I was pretty much into wooden bricks and then Lego. So why are there so many old clocks in Norwich?'

'There were some famous clock makers based there. Thomas Church, for one. You must've heard of Norfolk clocks. Wall clocks with wood casing and a kinda encased pendulum?'

'Wall clocks?'

'Yes, with a painted dial face and like... a so-called trunk attached below to house the pendulum.'

'You're making them sounds like some kind of weird elephants.'

She laughed and he knew she wasn't going to be anything like Mel.

They walked and talked, the conversation ebbing and flowing as she told him more about clocks and he explained his enthusiasm for carpentry.

'This is where I kinda live,' she said slowing her pace to a halt.

They stood outside one of the late-Victorian houses backing onto the park. 'I'm in a room on the top floor.' A string of outdoor LED lights had been threaded between the branches of a cherry-plum tree close by, and her face glowed a mix of red and blue.

'Haven't we just walked the long way round Christchurch Park?' he asked, amused.

'Well we could have kinda taken a shortcut through the park but its dark and....'

'And it was nice to just keep walking,' he finished for her.

She didn't invite him in, but suggested they meet up again for coffee or a drink.

'That'd be great. I'll text you. Bye, Pearl.' He smiled and hesitated, awkwardly building up to kiss her, but then she turned away and the moment had passed. It didn't matter; he could tell she liked him.

His mood lifted and he felt buoyed up. It lasted the whole drive back to Woolpit and even through to Monday morning.

•

'You're cheerful,' Dave remarked. 'Good weekend was it?'

'Yeah, I reckon so.'

They were in the Willows van and Dave was driving. It was ten past eight, Monday morning. The lanes twisted and turned, and any let-up from the churning in Nick's stomach lasted only seconds, before a faster section of road hurled them into another sharp corner. He sat braced, his legs stretched into the footwell and his body held secure by his seatbelt. It was either that or head down, crouched sitting, the so called aeroplane crash position. He prayed they'd reach Forward Green without a smash.

'Did your mate Chrissie learn anything useful from the Series 2A Land Rover bloke?'

Nick glanced at Dave. It looked as if his eyes were fixed on the road ahead and both his hands were gripping the steering wheel. It was probably safe to talk to him.

'You mean Ray? Yeah, she met up with him yesterday. She texted me last night. Said she'd found out loads of stuff. She didn't say what, but I guess she'll tell me sometime.' He swallowed back the taste of acidy tea rising to his mouth.

'So, what else? You're grinning like a Cheshire cat.'

Nick relaxed his jaw. 'No, I'm trying to hold onto my breakfast. For God's sake, Dave, this is like being on one of those whirling teacup rides at a fair.'

'Sounds like you had a good weekend, then.'

They drove in silence while Nick tried to gauge Dave's mood. He was a nosey bugger in the nicest kind of a way, another one to add to his list of inquisitive friends and colleagues. Nick reckoned he'd have to feed Dave some crumbs if he was to get him off his back. He certainly wasn't ready to talk about Pearl yet.

'The gig in Framlingham went great, yeah and I learnt a whole lot about clocks.'

'Clocks?

'Yeah, Norfolk clocks, or rather, Norfolk wall clocks. I didn't know there were such things.'

'Ah yes... they're like a smaller version of a Tavern clock.'

'A Tavern clock? Is that like one of those big old fashioned round-faced things you see on stations and in schools? Yeah, and with Roman numerals?' Nick knew from experience that it only needed a few genuine questions asked with real interest, and Dave wouldn't be able to resist answering. He'd be talking for hours.

'Kind of, but Tavern clocks date from an earlier century and have an older working mechanism. There was an act of parliament in something like 1797 to impose a tax on watches. But they weren't taxing clocks so there was a demand for cheap clocks, particularly in the taverns for your common drinker and working man.'

'It sounds like a kind of window tax.'

'Exactly, and like windows, you need'em. So some bright spark took the big expensive standing clock design, the so-called grandfather clock, shortened the hanging weights and pendulum, boxed them into a wooden case and hung the cheaper, smaller clock on the wall in taverns.'

'Ah... creating the so called trunk beneath the face,' Nick murmured, remembering Pearl's description of the housing for the pendulum.

'That's right. Sometimes they're called Parliament clocks, or Act of Parliament clocks. So your Norfolk wall clock is really a smaller version of its bigger cousins. And small is desirable, these days.'

'So are they valuable, these Norfolk wall clocks? Or even hard to come-by?'

'I've heard you have to be careful what you buy, and it helps if you know a bit about clocks. You can be fooled. Genuine parts from one clock can be harvested and incorporated into another, to make it appear what it's not. I mean we're probably talking about dial faces rather than a moving cog or wheel – that would count as a repair. It's the world of fakery and deception again.'

'Yeah, like antique furniture. So where would you look to buy one?'

'I don't know. I can ask around if you're serious.'

'If you're asking in pubs, they'd be Norfolk pubs, right?'

'Hmm, find another Ray, but in Norfolk and a horologist,' Dave laughed. 'I hadn't thought it through.'

The conversation broke naturally as they turned off the main road running through Forward Green. The van lurched as Dave drove along the track they'd followed every day the previous week. He swung with a final flourish onto a roughly cobbled drive.

'Right, Nick, we're here. Let's start unloading the unit doors and drawers. Are you OK? You're looking a touch green.'

CHAPTER 24

Matt stood in front of the service counter in the Utterly Academy canteen and considered his options. Jam doughnut or festive mince pie? Spaghetti Bolognaise or a plate of chips? How much time did he have and how much cash was in his pocket? He eyed up a stainless steel pan heaped with pale spaghetti nestling against its neighbour, a Vesuvius of brown. He gazed at the tray of chips. Options - was it to be Stowmarket's take on Bologna or Suffolk's garlic French fries? And following it, a jam doughnut or mince pie? Except he'd never got his head around mince pies. All those currants and raisins. So not the mince pie, but he knew where he was with a jam doughnut.

'Spag Bol an' a doughnut,' he muttered. He watched as a woman in a tunic overall spooned and scooped and dolloped.

'Doughnuts're down the end, luv. Next!'

He shuffled in line to the end of the counter, paid at the till and scanned around for somewhere to sit. More options – next to the window or cosy-up close to the tinsel Christmas tree? He pictured the choice in algorithm computer speak and headed for the window table, pushed a flyer for the Xmas quiz to one side to make room for his tray, and flopped onto a chair.

The canteen was quickly filling with the lunch-hour rush of students, and Matt sat facing the window. Snow was forecast, but then it had been forecast overnight and nothing had happened. Monday morning had dawned on Tumble Weed Drive and the Flower Estate just as it had for the past month, cold and wet; no sprinkling of crispy snow. He'd hoped to leave tyre tracks, instead it had been dirty wet spray from his back wheel.

'So is it gonna snow?' he asked himself and squinted at the sky through the canteen window. Grey.

'Hiya,' Ley said appearing at his table from across the canteen and dumping a tray down. 'Are you stayin'?'

'What?' Matt considered Ley's arrival, 'Nah, it's me Balcon & Mora afternoon.'

'Doh! I meant are you still eatin'?'

'Well, yeah. I only just sat down.' He indicated his over-large serving.

'You still doin' that Italian thing? I asked her to put the Bolognaisey stuff on me chips. It's safer, mate.'

They ate in silence, Matt concentrating on digging into the heap on his plate and transferring it to his mouth without flicking it everywhere. He'd read up about pasta – pasta meals before marathons, the different shapes, regions and traditions. It was the *all things Italian* again, and he relished the knowledge as he sucked in a strand of spaghetti, yeah - Spaghetti *Bolognese* dude.

'You ever been to Italy, Ley?' he mumbled between mouthfuls.

'No, mate.'

His thoughts moved to the future as he spooned, sucked, chomped and swallowed; the journey to Bury, his afternoon people tracing, Christmas, Italy, and Mandy Rokin.

'I gotta get movin'. The weather'll be turnin',' he said, more to his plate than to Ley.

'Yeah, reckon so. Ciao, mate.'

'Chah-ow? Aint that Italian?'

'Doh!' Ley laughed and palm-tapped his forehead.

'See you tomorrow,' Matt muttered and hurried to stack his tray on the dirty crockery trolley.

Funny, he thought, how Mandy Rokin kept popping up on his to-do list. Those fuzzy, just out of focus backgrounds on her selfie shots were still a secret waiting to be unlocked, and secrets intrigued him. He'd looked at them again on his laptop on Sunday. Really he needn't have. His photographic memory should have held the images, but somehow he couldn't recall the blur in a pixelated form; the sharp focus of Mandy's face – yes, but not the fuzzy backgrounds. And then earlier that morning in the library he'd asked Rosie to log him in to the Photoshop programme.

'I'm busy right now, but I'll be back in a moment,' she'd said, but she'd never come back and he'd had to leave for a tutorial. Fate was nudging him further towards Damon for help.

He lumbered down the main staircase and out through a side door, his mind still wrestling with Mandy's fuzzy backgrounds and why he couldn't see them in his visual memory. He hustled past some lawn and spent flowerbeds as he skirted the building and cut to where he'd parked his scooter. The sudden drop in temperature bit into his forehead and shocked his nose. He zipped up his faux leather flying jacket, donned his helmet and pulled on his gauntlets.

'Alpine Monsters,' he breathed as he read the lettering across the knuckles, and then wished he hadn't as condensation threatened to bead on the inside of his visor. He flipped it up, rocked the Piaggio off its parking stand, started the engine and rode out of the Academy car park.

Damon's office felt warm when Matt finally pushed the door open and flopped onto one of the plastic chairs.

'What's it like out there? Any sign of snow yet?' Damon asked.

'Nah, but it's fraggin' freezin'.'

'There's a pile of names to trace, so you'd better get started in case you have to leave early.'

'Leave early?'

'There's snow on the way. I'm not risking you getting stranded and spending the night here.'

'But I've got some computin' questions, Damon.'

'Then ask them while I put the kettle on. You've got four minutes, then you start your first batch of names, deal?'

'And if it don't snow?'

'It will.'

Matt weighed up his options. He reckoned being holed up in an office with computers wouldn't be so bad.

'And remember the heating is on a timer. It goes off at night,' Damon added as he flicked the kettle on.

'Ah....' No heating altered things. Write that into his algorithm and he'd come up with a different first choice.

'How'd you make out what's in a blurry area on a photo?' he blurted.

'I'd use Photoshop, why?'

'Yeah, I get that, but how'd you do it on Photoshop?'

'You can use the Sharpen tool, or the Smart Sharpen Filter, or... the Unsharp Mask Filter. Yes, I know the last one sounds crazy but the Unsharp Mask Filter elevates the contrast along the edges of the image.'

'You're losin' me,' Matt mumbled.

'Look, I'd have to play with it a bit, see what worked.'

'Play with it?'

'Hmm.' He nodded. 'I tell you what. If you send it to me, I'll play with it, see what works and then I'll show you what I've done, and how I did it. How's that sound?'

'Cool. Thanks Damon.' Matt reckoned he had a couple of minutes to send a selection of Mandy's selfies without her name tagged to them. Any longer and Damon would be back at his desk and able to see both computer screens and the Facebook tags.

He shed his Alpine Monsters, unzipped his faux leather, turned the chair to face his own computer and logged on. By the time Damon set a mug of milky hot chocolate down by him he was out of Mandy's public Facebook page and album. Instead the screen was filled with Matt's email page. Now it all depended on whether Damon chose to look at Matt's internet browsing history or not, and if he didn't he was in the clear. He wasn't going to think about how Damon might react if he knew he was working on a murder victim's fuzzy areas.

'Your first batch of ten… coming now,' Damon said a few seconds later.

Matt settled on the first name on his list. He was too busy focussing on his searches to register that Damon hadn't made a comment about Mandy's selfies he'd just sent.

'Did you catch the news today about that woman found dead on Friday? Seems they think she was murdered,' Damon's voice cut into Matt's consciousness.

'Nah,' he lied, and turned his attention back to his hunt through an electoral register.

'I think they've released her name. Mandy… yes, Mandy Rokin. That was the name,' Damon persisted.

'Yeah, most likely,' Matt mumbled with his brain wholly engaged in matching first and second name initials against surnames on the register and failing to pick up the trap in Damon's words.

'Weren't you rushing off to the Nags Head or somewhere, last time you were here? Something about Chrissie knowing about the dead woman?' Damon's voice seemed to float on the office air somewhere high above the whirring of the computer fans.

'Hey, answer me, Matt.' His tone had turned sharp, cutting. 'Am I,' he continued, 'doing some kind of unofficial police work here on the quiet and cheap? You know – DI Merry asks his girlfriend to find out if there are leads in fuzzy backgrounds. And if there are, what then? He asks his own forensic computing team to do the same thing, but he's directed them to what to search for? He's cut the time and costs to get a result? Is that it, Matt? Am I some kind of a cheap-arse stooge?'

'What?'

'And what if there is a lead and I miss it? What then? Am I responsible if a killer isn't caught?'

'What you on about, Damon?'

'These are Mandy Rokin selfies, right?'

He caught the rising pitch. Matt knew he was on the precipice of trouble. 'Yeah, but....' Cheeks on fire, he turned to face Damon.

He hesitated. Should he own up or let Damon think it was down to Clive and Chrissie? This algorithm of choices was tricky.

'Well, Matt?'

'It were my idea, Damon. Chrissie don't know anythin' about them Mandy Rokin selfies. I checked her Facebook page on Saturday and….'

'Go on.'

'And I were curious. See, she were the one stalkin' Chrissie and she were the one breaking in and stealin' Clive's laptop. An' when I saw all them selfies, well the fuzzy bits seemed important.'

'Why? Why should the fuzzy bits seem so important, Matt? I just don't get it.'

'Cos I can't see it in me head. It's like just not there, but when I look at the screen with me eyes open, on some of them I see another face.'

'Another face?'

'Yeah.'

'Well that's weird because I've got a face in the background on some of them when I use the Unsharp Mask and then a touch of brush and blending mode on the Sharpen tool.'

'Can I see?' Matt got up, eased around the trestle desk and squeezed behind Damon.

Something which could have been a splodge of bread dough on the screen morphed into a pale face and stared at the camera lens from somewhere behind Mandy's left shoulder. It was still fuzzy, but the proportions of nose to chin to eyes and forehead were clear enough.

'Scammin' spear phishin'!' Matt whispered.

'What've you seen?'

'That's… well it looks like it could be Stella Mawbray. She were one of the names on me list from last week's debt collectors.'

'Are you sure, Matt?' Damon's voice softened.

'Yeah. I know it don't make sense but do a Google facial recognition search or use you facial recognition app if you don't believe me.'

'Right, I will. Now get on with your list of names while I think about this.'

The air in the cramped office felt hot. Matt shuffled back to his plastic chair, a bead of sweat breaking on his temple. Scam Almighty! What had he done? Had he blown it with Damon? His thoughts fragmented, flicking between the Electoral Register search, Photoshop, Mandy, Stella Mawbray, stalking, a killer escaping through Damon's fingers....

He hunched forwards, his head in his hands, closed his eyes and tried to shut it all out, but the thoughts kept flying towards him, glancing off his face and head. Behind him he heard Damon pick up the office landline.

'Hello. Please would you put me through to Detective Inspector Merry...? Yes it is important.... I have some information for him.... No it can't wait.... It's Damon Mora.... Thank you.'

While Damon waited on hold Matt struggled to clear his head. He forced himself to concentrate on algorithms, the images started to fade and he began to think straighter. He realised his options were simple – run, or stay and face the consequences. His stomach twisted and a shot of acidy Bolognaise sauce refluxed into his mouth.

'Clive Merry? Hello, it's Damon here from Balcon & Mora.... Yes that's right, the on-line tracing agency.... Yes that's right, I have a possible connection for you.... We stumbled on it by chance. A bit of a co-incidence really....'

Matt stopped listening. He was distracted by his stomach and the foul acid taste. He focussed on swallowing it down and refreshing his mouth with hot chocolate. He knew Damon would be telling Clive about Stella Mawbray, but why was it all right for Damon to tell people outside the office about the names on their lists? How could it be one rule for Damon but Matt was bound by a code of total silence? It didn't seem fair or consistent.

'OK, Clive. I'll email you the photos.... No problem, goodbye now.' The phone call ended and apart from the whirring of the computer fans, silence filled the office.

'Are you all right, Matt? You don't seem to be doing much.' Damon asked.

'I don't get it, Damon. How come you can give Stella's name to the police?' The words just burst from his mouth.

'Well, strictly speaking, she wasn't on our debtors list. It turned out there was a dispute with the credit card company. Apparently Stella maintains her son stole her credit card and the card company should pay. The debt collectors have refused to pay us for tracing her name, even though it was on their list. They say until they've sorted it out with the credit card company, it's a stale mate. I only found out about it this morning.'

'We won't get paid? 'An I don't get me percentage? But that aint fair. How old's the son? DOS-in' hell! Were Clive interested?'

'Hmm, he was particularly interested when I mentioned the son. I got the feeling he thinks the connection between the two women may be related to a friendship between their sons. They're both still at school.'

'But he don't think the sons are killers do he?'

'No, no, but I wouldn't be surprised to learn Stella Mawbray gets a routine visit from the police asking questions about Mandy.'

'Right – so are we OK, Damon? You'll teach me them tricks on Photoshop, right?'

'Later. Now get on with your list.'

CHAPTER 25

Chrissie swung into the entrance to the Rush Green Golf Club. Icy snow crackled and crunched under her tyres as she drove slowly across what had been until recently a large gravelled parking area. Now it was transformed into a thin wind slab of white. The Citroen van cut steadily across old tyre tracks as she headed for the huddle of cars near the clubhouse.

It had made sense to leave her TR7 at the Clegg workshop and drive the van while snow still clogged the lanes, but even so she had been tempted to ring and cancel her Wednesday meeting with Paul, the club secretary. In the end she'd settled on lunchtime, rather than the 4:30 he'd also suggested. He'd mentioned he'd selected one of her designs for the trophy repair as well as wanting to tell her more about its history. She was intrigued to learn more.

She stamped the snow off her walking boots on the large mat in the lobby. Should she head for the clubhouse bar or Paul's office? 'I've probably got the wrong footwear for the bar,' she muttered and headed in the direction of his office. The pale sycamore door leading into the wide corridor-like room was ajar. She craned her neck to squint up at the names as she walked past the *Winners & Captains* wallboards.

'Hello, Chrissie.'

'Ah, Paul... Mr Cooley.' She turned to see the middle-aged secretary climbing the last few steps to stand next to her. She smiled. 'Thank you for looking into the history of the Northfield Challenge Trophy.'

A thought struck as she took in his sleeveless goose-down jacket worn over a fine-knit sweater. 'You haven't been playing golf have you?'

'No, no. Not with the course covered in snow. I saw your van and thought you might come in through the players' entrance, so I went down to meet you. But it seems you came straight in through the main entrance.'

They both looked down at her walking boots.

'Are socks acceptable footwear in the bar?' she asked slowly.

'I'm sure yours would be, but we needn't worry. I thought my office would suit better. I've a box of old papers and ledgers to show you, and there's plenty of space to spread the papers. You haven't got studs on those boots have you?'

'No, but what a good idea. Thank you for suggesting it.'

Paul laughed. 'Very good, I like that.'

She smiled and tried to tread quietly as he led the way to his office.

A cardboard storage box sat on his desk, its presence the focus of the room. Instinctively she moved closer.

'Are these the old records?' she asked.

'Yes. I've never looked through the archives before, there's not usually much call for a historical trawl. But you set me thinking, and it seemed pretty poor for the club to have a challenge trophy and none of the golfers who'd won it know how it came into being. So I decided it was about time I had a check through the records.'

'And was it difficult?'

'Not really. They're locked away downstairs: membership records; minutes from committee meetings;

annual accounts; ground plans and building records - they're all stored in sections and filed in year order. There are even separate books for all the competitions, cups and trophies.' He took the lid off the box as he spoke. 'This seemed the obvious place to start.'

He lifted a bound ledger from the box and handed it to her.

'The Northfield Challenge Trophy,' she said, reading out the title written in bold italic capitals.

'And these,' he added, passing her the minutes from club committee meetings for the years 1967, '68 and '69.

'I've marked the relevant pages with bookmarks. I suggest you start here.' He helped her open the file at the first marker, September 1967.

A letter has been received from a Mr Sampson Mawbray, a local businessman manufacturing cases and golf bags. He proposes making a gift of two hundred pounds to the club. He would like the money to be put towards creating a golf challenge trophy. Mr Runnings suggested that a trophy named after a golf bag would be inappropriate and asked what strings were attached. He wondered if Mr Sampson Mawbray was trying to curry favour and strengthen his application to become a member of the club. The membership secretary assured the committee that no such application had been received.

There followed a lively discussion relating to motive behind the gift. The prevailing opinion that Mr Sampson Mawbray was attempting a public relations manoeuvre to dissipate the recent scandal surrounding his son was dismissed as mere speculation. Mr Runnings reminded the committee that two hundred pounds was a considerable gift and not to be rejected lightly.

'So what happened?' Chrissie asked as she turned the page and the minutes moved on to record the next item on the agenda.

'Well, to cut a long story short it seems the committee accepted the donation of two hundred pounds but refused to spend it on a silver cup. Instead they procured a hickory club and some recently felled oak from Northfield Wood.'

'What? And as a final snub to poor Mr Sampson Mawbray, named a challenge trophy after the wood and not him or his golf bag business?' Chrissie cried, guessing the rest of the scenario. 'But I thought you said there'd been some terrible accident. A portable sawmill or something? Somebody injured or died, right?'

'I know. That's always been the story, but do you know, Chrissie, I think it was just something made up to cover the committee's behaviour. I've looked through pages of minutes and it pains me to say it, but it's the only logical conclusion. They needed the money but they didn't want to be bought.'

They sat in silence as Chrissie leafed through more of the ledgers, finding more of the bookmarked minutes.

'I'll ask the bar to send through some coffee and sandwiches. I don't know about you, but I'm starving. This cold weather is bad for the waistline.' He patted his stomach.

'Yes, just the sight of snow makes you feel hungry,' she laughed. 'But tell me, what was the scandal surrounding the son? I can't see anything referred to directly.'

'Well that's just it. I can't find anything either. I don't know if there'll be anything in the local newspaper archives....'

'Hmm,' she murmured, as a teenage girl knocked before carrying in coffee and a plate of thick-cut sandwiches. 'And do we even know the son's name?'

Chrissie, of course was fishing. She pictured Benjamin Mawbray. It had to have been him. Hadn't he said his father made suitcases and golf bags with some newly designed plasticised material? Ron had told her Benjamin disappeared and no one seemed worried about what had happened to him. Of course there could have been more than one son.... Her thoughts went round and round as she bit into a ham and mustard sandwich.

'Are you all right, Chrissie? You've gone very quiet.'

'You disappear after a scandal? Lie low and wait for it to settle down, don't you?'

'If you're talking about Sampson Mawbray, he didn't disappear. He supplied golf bags and holdalls to the pro shop for years.'

'The pro shop?'

'Yes, it's part of the golf club.'

She thought for a moment. 'I suppose the good thing to come out of all this is discovering there's no terrible significance to any particular piece of oak in the trophy board. As long as it comes from Northfield Wood is all that matters.'

'Quite,' Paul concluded.

She sipped her coffee and collected her thoughts. For weeks she'd been living with the certainty something terrible must have happened in Northfield Wood and the trophy was some kind of memorial. Now it turned out her instinct had been completely skewed. Learning there hadn't been a disaster was a good thing, but it was still a surprise and she felt wrong-footed. So, what about the digging they'd found, and all Ray had told them? How did it fit in? Maybe it didn't.

'Pieces of a different puzzle,' she murmured.

'You seem a bit... almost disappointed, Chrissie.'

'Not at all. Surprised, more like. So what will you tell your golfing trophy winners in the future?'

He frowned. 'I'll need to give it some thought. But, in the meantime, are you happy to get started on the repairs now you know you're not working on a piece of oak from a tree that might have fallen and killed someone?'

'Or was splashed with blood from a sawmill blade. Much happier. So which design did you choose?'

'The one with the hickory club mounted hanging downwards, and oak from the old board veneered onto some lightweight multi-ply board.'

'And the oak edging to frame the board?'

'Ideally to be sourced, old or new from Northfield Wood.'

'So not a nice length of French oak, then?'

They both laughed. 'I'll let you have the hickory club. You'll need it to mount on the board.'

She finished her coffee and they walked back past the *Winners & Captains* wallboards and into the main entrance lobby. She eyed up the dark patches on the mat. Any snow she'd brought in earlier on her walking boots must have melted into the bristles.

'You could always stick a label on the back saying the trophy was donated by Sampson Mawbray in 1967,' she said.

'And repaired by Chrissie Jax, 2012,' he added.

'Nice Christmas tree.' She nodded towards the entrance to the bar, 'And many thanks for the coffee. I'll get it back to you in a couple of weeks, OK?'

The sky had dulled and the air was still. A kind of eerie silence gripped the golf course as she hurried to her van. 'Please no more snow,' she breathed. It wasn't that she didn't like the snow; it was just that it got in the way of deliveries and clients. Everything seemed to slow down, and now she'd spent longer at the golf club than she'd intended. She was behind schedule and her mind was buzzing with the Northfield Wood riddle.

'At least it explains why Matt couldn't find any reports of an accident or death,' she murmured as she drove out of the car park.

She opted for the back roads. The A14 would be salted, gritted and fast, but she knew there'd be fewer cars on the narrow lanes. So, as long as she didn't meet a car coming in the opposite direction, she figured the back roads would be just as quick. After all, driving to the golf club had been easy enough. Somewhere deep in the recesses of her mind she wanted to enjoy her ex-Forestry Commission Citroen van with its limited slip differential traction control option. And that was before even considering its extra ground clearance. A few inches of snow was exactly what she sought.

It set her thinking about the holiday she'd planned with Clive for a week in January, barely six weeks away. It was he who was the skier and the one wanting to go skiing; she was the complete novice. He'd promised to book her lessons on the dry ski slope in Ipswich before they went, and back before it had snowed it seemed like a great idea. Now as she drove the tyre-tracked snowy lanes the holiday felt chancier. What if she smashed a wrist or ankle? In a worst case scenario, she supposed she could still spend the rest of the holiday on a snowmobile, a kind of jet-ski for snow.

'I'm sure I could drive one in an ankle plaster,' she muttered. But her wrist? That would really mess up the business once she'd got home. Maybe she needed to talk to Clive.

When she turned onto the track to the old barn workshop it felt less rutted with its blanket of snow. The potholes and puddles were filled and frozen, and she smoothed her way along it in the Citroen van. Perhaps accidently straying off-piste wouldn't be such a risk. The thought helped to sooth her mood as she parked.

'Hi, Mr Clegg,' she said as she opened the sturdy wooden door to the barn and hurried inside. The smell of wood, beeswax and linseed oil enveloped her.

'I see you've come back with a hickory golf club, Mrs Jax. Does that mean, you're taking up golf, or is it something to do with the trophy board you're going to repair?'

She walked over to where Ron had lifted one of Benjamin Mawbray's chairs onto a workbench.

'You might well laugh, but I was actually asked if I'd ever thought of taking up golf,' she said, adopting a mock superior tone and handing him the hickory club to inspect.

'So, an invitation to join?'

'No, but do you remember if Benjamin Mawbray had any brothers?' She caught the surprised look. 'Perhaps I'd better explain.'

It didn't take her long to recount all she'd been told by Paul Cooley.

'The secretary let you look through the old records?'

'Well only selected sections in a few ledgers. He was amazingly frank about everything.'

'Hmm, Benjamin... I don't remember him having any brothers at the school. And I don't remember any scandal or whisperings about his mother or father, either. Mind you it doesn't mean there weren't brothers or scandals.'

'But you think the disgrace Sampson Mawbray felt he had to make amends for was Benjamin's?'

'I don't know, Mrs Jax. You're forgetting it was 1967. Times were different. A son's wrongdoing would have reflected badly on the family, especially his father. So yes, Benjamin's shame would have become the father's, and I might add, vice versa.'

'So what are you saying, Mr Clegg?'

'I suppose I'm saying I don't know of any scandals, but it was Benjamin who disappeared. Now let's not waste any more time speculating on what the Mawbrays may or may not have done, Mrs Jax.'

A thought gripped her. 'Do you think Benjamin could have been sent away to prison? I mean that would have been a scandal worth hiding.'

'Yes, but as I said, you're just speculating now. This is how rumours begin.'

Ron was right. Wanting to know more about the scandal had nothing to do with repairing the Challenge Trophy, at least not any more. She needed to rein in her overactive imagination.

'How's the work on his chairs coming along?' she asked, changing the subject. Except of course being Benjamin's chairs, it was merely a shift in direction on the topic of Benjamin.

She gazed at the dark mahogany dining chair standing on the workbench. It had elegant but sturdy square tapering legs with spade feet at the front. She saw the obvious damage. A side and front stretcher looked cracked and broken. There was a small split where one of the elbow arms joined the top rail of the seat frame. Chrissie took it all in and made a snap conclusion.

'It looks as if the chair took a heavy fall on that front corner,' she murmured.

'But there's no sign of damage to the front corner of the seat. I think the impact was centred lower down, Mrs Jax.'

'Of course, the stretchers and lower leg.' She took hold of the leg and gently rocked it. 'I can feel it's loosened at the top as well, where it's joined to the rail. I suppose it's better it was loosened than the leg break off. Do you think Dyson the black Labrador careered into it?'

'Careful, you're starting rumours. The old dog can hardly move.'

'Hmm, well just so our feet stay firmly planted in reality, don't forget to take some photos before you start, Mr Clegg. We don't want Benjamin cutting up rough with us. I'm going to put the kettle on. Do you want a mug of tea?'

She left Ron to the chair leg and stretchers. It was time she ordered the multi-ply wood for the trophy board. She also needed to figure out how she was going to best work the old oak to harvest the veneer. In its current state it was a single board of oak, peppered with screw and nail holes and far too wide for the size of their band saw to slice into veneer. She would have to cut it into several widths first. She would also need to make a height extension to fix to the fence used for guiding the oak boards through the band saw. She searched out her tape measure and a piece of paper to jot down her calculations.

By late afternoon the band saw blade and fence were set, and the old trophy board oak had been sawn up and passed through the drum sander. She was ready to start cutting the first slice of veneer.

'An eighth of an inch OK?' she shouted across the workshop to Ron, 'then I can sand it back without risking the plywood showing through.'

'Well don't forget to wax the band saw table and fence before you start. The oak'll pass through more smoothly. It'll make it easier, believe me,' he called back.

It was close on six o'clock by the time she'd sawed the boards into eighth of an inch thick veneer slices. Despite a long afternoon and concentrating fiercely, she felt surprisingly good. Even as she walked out to her van in the darkness, the cold striking her face and the crisp snowy crust crunching under her walking boots, she knew she was back on track, focussed on work and looking forward to Christmas. Clive hadn't phoned to say he'd be late, so she had the whole evening ahead with him as well. She felt at peace with her life.

'Good night,' she called to Ron as he emerged from the brick outhouse close to the barn workshop, a piece of old mahogany in his hands.

She started the van and eased slowly over the snow, headlights on low beam. She took in the soft light from the open barn door bathing Ron as he turned, not yet inside.

He waved; she saw him slip.

He launched, an arm outstretched, the other cradling the mahogany. *Wham!* He was spread-eagled on the snow, one hand straight into the side of the barn.

'Oh my God!' she breathed.

CHAPTER 26

Thursday dawned cold, icy and white. There hadn't been any more snow since Wednesday but it still blanketed the ground. Nick couldn't believe his good fortune. The foreman was sending him to a house in Ipswich to make and fit some built-in wardrobes. It was another rush job to be completed before families descended on their relatives' homes for Christmas. Secretly he wondered if half of Suffolk hadn't gone just a little bit mad setting completion deadlines for Christmas Eve.

'Dave can spare you from the job in Forward Green,' Alfred Walsh had said in a matter-of-fact way twenty minutes earlier that morning.

'You do realise there's at least one kitchen wall unit to come down again?' Nick had queried.

'Yes, Dave said about the electrician needing to run a spur to the cooker hood. He has to get at the electric cable behind the wall units. But you've already drilled the wall fixings so it'll be straightforward for Dave to put them up again on his own.'

'OK then, if you're sure.' Nick hadn't wanted to get half way out of the Willows & Son workshop only to be called back and sent to Forward Green.

He plucked a set of keys from the hooks by the door in the office-cum-restroom and hurried out to the secure parking area. It resembled a snowy patchwork where vans had shielded the underlying tarmac and gravel from the worst of the snow. Yesterday's tyre tracks crisscrossed the area, linking the patches like a spreading winter tartan. He loaded his toolbox into the van and started the engine.

'St Williams Road,' he murmured, repeating the address. Hadn't he parked somewhere near there only last Sunday when he'd driven up to Ipswich to listen to Pearl playing in the Tower Ramparts shopping centre? She lived near Christchurch Park and probably within half a mile of St Williams Road. It would seem natural to text her and let her know he was working in the area. He could casually suggest meeting up for a coffee without it appearing a big deal. Fortune had dealt him a lucky card.

Buoyed with anticipation he drove the Willows van along the icy lanes and joined the A14, only to leave the salted and gritted dual carriageway after ten minutes. He headed through the northwest approaches to Ipswich and towards Christchurch Park.

The residential roads were narrowed by parked cars and mounds of snow, shovelled and brushed from driveways and pavements. No attempt had been made to clear St Williams Road and dirty compacted snow tracks had been left by cars driving in single file down the middle of it. He scrutinised each house as he passed, counting down the numbers.

'This must be the one,' he murmured and drew to a halt. He spotted the small partly cleared driveway and pulled into it.

The house had a wide frontage with a double height bay window and a single garage. Nick guessed it must have been built in the early 1930s. Nice, he thought, but the daylight seemed filtered and dulled by the neighbouring houses, and dark foliage of mature conifers overshadowed it from the rear garden. He got out of the van and walked the short cleared pathway to the front door, a tape measure, pencil and pad of paper in one hand.

'Mr Stukeley? I'm Nick, from Willows & Son,' he said when a man in his forties with thick mousey hair opened the heavy white-painted door.

'Ah yes. I've been expecting you. Come on in.'

He stepped onto a large mat, took off his walking trainers and followed the man into a large square hallway dwarfed by a wide staircase leading to a first floor landing. White glossy bannisters dominated the feel of the hall, like overly white enamelled teeth. He stood at the foot of the stairs, taking in his surroundings as the man talked.

'We had no idea my sister and her family were coming. I mean they must have booked their flight months ago. You'd think they'd have realised we'd need some warning they'd be visiting us for Christmas. I mean did they even consider we could have been away ourselves?' He stood, hands on hips and his back ramrod straight with the unreasonableness of it all.

'I suppose that's families for you,' Nick murmured.

'She said she wanted it to be a surprise for Mum. But that's no reason to spring it on me. She should have said weeks ago. I expect you've probably known for months where you're spending Christmas,' the man muttered.

Nick nodded, but in all honesty he hadn't given it a thought. At twenty-three, Christmas was something you rolled up to on the day. Families were pleased to see you; mothers over-fed you, someone kept filling your glass. But sparing it a thought three weeks in advance? No way.

He picked up the faint aroma of coffee and wax polish, and gazed around. An open framed clock rested on a stand at the head of the staircase, two weights hanging down on long cords and almost touching the ground floor. Several rooms led from the hallway. He guessed a dining room as he caught sight of a long table and set of chairs with a window beyond and views onto a snowy garden.

'You'll be working in the flat at the top of the house,' the man said, breaking into his thoughts. He led Nick through the hall, past a downstairs cloakroom, and to a back staircase.

'You've two sets of stairs?'

'Yes, these link to the first floor but were originally to serve the flat up in the eaves. Come on, it's up this way. Follow me.'

'Your mother lives up here?'

'No, she's got a flat near the waterfront, overlooking the marina. In fact she could probably get a view over Portman Road and watch the football from her bathroom window if she wanted.'

'Sounds nice.' Nick sensed he was in the presence of money and climbed the stairs.

'OK, we're up the top now, Nick. This is where I'd like the wardrobe built.' Mr Stukeley indicated a chimney breast standing proud of a bedroom wall. 'Out to about here. I'll leave you to measure up and sketch out some plans. I'll be downstairs working in my office. You can't miss it - it's more or less opposite the cloakroom, just off the hall.' He nodded and left.

Nick stared up at the ceiling. From the outside, the roof had appeared a standard A-frame shape, but on the inside it felt like a mansard with dormer windows jutting from the walls. Quaint, roomy and light. He might be standing in an attic flat, but this was far more spacious than his room above Sarah's double garage. For a start there was a room on either side of the chimney, and if he counted the toilet and shower, it came to a total of three. And his brief?

It appeared pretty straightforward. He was to construct a wardrobe in one of the rooms incorporating the space around the chimney breast.

He sat in a boudoir-style armchair and began to sketch. This of course was where Chrissie had the advantage. She had an automatic sense of style. He knew he could do modern and old beamy, but did this warrant Art Nouveau? Something to fit the 1920s, or Art Deco to suit the 1930s? He pulled his mobile from his jeans. Yes, he had signal. He didn't need to call Chrissie, he could look up Art Deco wardrobes on the internet.

It would have been easier if he'd been able to get more of a handle on Mr Stukeley's taste. With the memory of the main staircase and tooth-like bannisters fresh in his mind, he settled on a 1930s *skyscraper* style - stepped vertically to reflect the mansard shape of the ceiling and walls. A couple of panels with *rising sun* motifs in stained glass added the finishing 30s touch. He experimented with drawing lattice end doors as added options and then scribbled some suggestions for colour and finish. 'Bet he'll go for white gloss paint,' Nick murmured and drew a floor plan, and shelf and hanger options for inside.

The measuring and calculating was less of a challenge. It was closer to his comfort zone, and forty minutes later he hurried back down the stairs to Mr Stukeley's office.

The door was open and Nick knocked gently on the doorframe.

'Oh hi, Nick. How are you getting on?' Mr Stukeley asked, looking up from his computer screen.

'You said to keep it sympathetic to the age of the house, so this is a preliminary sketch for a 1930s feel. You don't have to go with the *rising suns*, but I've included the skyscraper shape.' He smiled nervously and waited for a reaction.

'I like the stained glass. But will you be able to get it in time for Christmas?'

'I hope so. It's a pretty standard design but it would have to be in the *style of* rather than actual eighty year old glass,' Nick explained.

'Hmm… if you give me an hour, I may be able to source the genuine article.'

'How's that?' He watched the man frown.

'I suppose you could call me a dealer.' His tone suggested he was choosing his words, 'I source things for people. It's what I do for a living. I get asked to look for the most obscure things, so a pair of *rising sun* stained glass panels should be easy enough.'

'So do you like the design?' Nick held his breath.

'Yes.'

'Great! And the wood – do you want solid oak throughout? Or veneer on ply for the wood panels, or…?' He hesitated as he glanced at the office door, 'or painted?'

Mr Stukeley held up a hand. 'Stop. Give me an hour with these sketches. Why don't you walk into the town centre or something? I know you want to get on with ordering the wood and picking up what you need from Frosticks, but put it on hold and come back in an hour.' It was a statement, not a request.

'Right, an hour then.'

It seemed strange. Was Mr Stukeley happy with the design and dimensions, or was it just the *rising sun* he liked? Nick had never been asked to leave a client's home for an hour and then come back for a decision, but then he'd only been a fully trained carpenter since the summer.

Working with clients at this early stage of a job was new to him. He tried to imagine how Dave would have handled it, as he retraced his steps through the hall. Slightly unsure of himself, he pushed his feet into his walking trainers and left quietly through the front door.

Now what, Nick wondered. Sit in the van and listen to music? Of course, what was he thinking? It was only an hour but it was still a Pearl opportunity. He pulled his mobile from his jeans and fired off a text. *I'm in Ipswich, near Christchurch Park. I've an hour before I have to meet the client. Coffee?*

Ping! The text alert almost made him drop his phone.

'That was quick,' he murmured and opened her reply. *See you in 20 mins. Coffee house on St George's St. It's off Henley Road. Not far from where we walked on Sunday.*

Great! he texted back, all thoughts of Mr Stukeley driven from his mind.

He locked the van and strode along St Williams Road to the Henley Road. The air was cold, but at least there was no wind. He zipped up his bomber jacket and hurried across gritted pavements, dodging muddy puddles and un-trodden snow. He made good time as the road took him downhill past the park, with its white blanket of snow, and onto St George's Street with its tall, pale brick Georgian townhouses, terraced against Victorian and Edwardian equivalents.

The coffee house, when he reached it, looked warm and welcoming, the windows steamy on the inside. A damp fibre mat lay in the entrance and dirty moist boot prints fanned across the boarded floor inside. The smell of coffee caressed and soothed. He scanned the tables. No Pearl. He checked the time on his mobile. He was still a little early.

He turned to find a free table, just as the door opened and a girl in a faded green parker with faux-fur trimmed hood stole in. He recognised her immediately.

'Hiya, Pearl. You nearly did it again, like band practice. I almost missed you coming in.' He beamed his most charming smile. 'What can I get you?'

'Hi, Nick. A flat white if you're buying, thanks.' She pushed back her hood and shook her dark brown hair free.

He queued at the counter, running through chat-up lines in his head before carrying two regular sized cups of coffee over to where she'd settled at a corner table.

'Great to see you,' he murmured, chat-up lines flying out the window, as he set down the cups.

'Yeah well, it's kinda my morning for practising, so your text was like... permission for a break. So where are you working?'

Around him the coffee house hummed with customers, and the espresso machine hissed and gurgled behind the counter. He launched into a description of his morning.

'Rising suns? Isn't that like... dated? A kinda cliché?' she said, smiling.

'Yes, but that's the whole point.'

'So did he have Clarice Cliff vases all over the place as well?'

'No, but he had a strange clock with its cogs and wheels showing and its weights hanging down the side of the staircase.'

'That'll be a Turret clock, I reckon. That's kinda unusual. Much older than 1930s.'

The conversation seemed to falter for a moment and he sipped his coffee. 'So are you still going to Norwich,

Christmas clock buying?' he asked, remembering her interest in clocks.

'You bet. My dad says there's a glut of old clocks suddenly out there for sale. I don't want to like... miss out on an opportunity. He reckons either a collector's decided to sell a collection, or there's a stash of dodgy stuff flooding the market. Christmas is a good time to sell dirty goods, less likely to be noticed in the rush.'

'Dodgy stuff? Dirty goods?'

'Yeah, stolen antique clocks. Why?'

'I guess I've never thought about it before, but if they're valuable, I suppose it follows. So how can you tell? I mean, you could be buying a stolen clock.'

'That's the problem. And some will have been like... used for parts.'

'So is there a register of stolen antique clocks? Do clocks even have serial numbers?'

'Not that I know of, but then like... it's my dad's hobby. Insurance companies might keep some kinda record I suppose, but nothing I could access. And serial numbers are a relatively modern idea, and we're going back several hundred years.'

'Right,' he murmured and noticed how she folded her paper serviette into ever smaller squares as she flattened it on the table. Busy hands, he thought.

'And if you discovered you'd bought a stolen clock by mistake, how would you feel?' he asked mildly.

'Sick. Yeah, definitely kinda sick. It means someone's had their house burgled. And besides, you buy a clock because you kinda like it. You want to enjoy it, not look at its face and be reminded it's a crime sitting on your mantelpiece. And that's before the police come knocking on your door to like… take it away.'

'But there'd have been a chain of people involved. No one could blame you.'

'No, but I'd be the one at the end losing both the clock and my money.'

Her words brought Mr Stukeley spinning back. How had he described himself? Sourcing articles for buyers. 'I bet Stukeley would know if collections or stolen clocks were flooding the market,' he said under his breath.

'Sorry, I didn't get that, Nick.'

'I said I was thinking it was Wickham Market, but it's Woodbridge we're playing on Saturday. Will you be able to play as well? The Oak & Oyster's a great venue.' He hoped she hadn't picked up on Stukeley. It was a stupid thing to say, and anyway, he wanted to know if she'd be there on Saturday.

'Yes, if the band want me. But I, like… won't be able to make it to band practice on Saturday morning. I'm rehearsing with the saxophone quartet for a concert we're playing on Sunday, Hadleigh Guildhall.' She checked her watch and stood up.

'That's a pretty cool reason,' he said, following her lead and also standing up. 'I'll email you the set, music sheets and keys we've settled on after band practice, OK?'

'Great. And… thanks for the coffee.' He was sure he caught her cheeks flush as she turned away to thread between the tables and head for the door.

Outside, the cold air bit as they walked back up the gentle hill to the Henley Road. He hoped they'd take the long way, circuiting Christchurch Park just as they had on

Sunday, but he knew he'd be cutting it fine. He had to get back to Mr Stukeley and the *rising suns*.

She slowed her pace as they neared an entrance gate to the park. 'Are you taking a shortcut across?' he asked.

'Yes, and St Williams Road is up that way. Clarice Cliff and the *rising suns* will be kinda calling. You can't be late, Nick.'

'I'd sort of forgotten about Mr Stukeley,' he lied.

'No you hadn't. Now go and like… I hope you get the contract. See you on Saturday.' She pulled her parker hood up around her head.

'Do you want a lift to Woodbridge on Saturday?'

'Thanks, if you're offering. And thanks for the coffee. Bye, Nick.' She smiled and headed through the gate.

Wow, had that really happened? Frissons of excitement ignited the double shot of caffeine. He quickened his pace. Pearl was right. He couldn't be late getting back to Mr Stukeley, even if it was just to hear him say he'd changed his mind. The man could have spent the last hour sourcing a free-standing clothes rail for his sister and her family. Something like the 1930s lines running across cinema curtains. Alfred Marsh would kill him if he messed up on this job.

A sudden surge of anxiety powered him up the rest of the hill. He broke into a run, slipping and skidding across pavements and kerb stones to St Williams Road. Panting, he tried to catch his breath as he rang Mr Stukeley's door bell.

'Nick? Are you all right?'

He read the surprise in Mr Stukeley's eyebrows, toyed with the idea of saying he'd taken a jog around the park, and blurted, 'I was worried I might be late.'

'Well you're not. You're dead on time. I've managed to find a pair of genuine stained glass panels. Come on through to my office. I've got the exact measurements written down.'

'That's amazing. But how? Where from?'

'It's what I do, Nick. They'll be delivered here by Monday.'

'So you'd know if....' He stopped. What are he thinking? This was a potential client, a rushed assignment to measure up and give a quote. He needed to win the contract, not antagonise the man by asking if the stained glass panels were stolen goods.

'So I'd know what, Nick?'

'I-I simply wondered if you knew the size of the frames they're mounted in. I assume they are set in some kind of a frame?' He was conscious of Mr Stukeley's gaze.

'Yes, and as I just said, I've got the dimensions and details for you. Now, about a plain wood or painted finish – I think oak would be too dark and imposing.'

'So you'd like a lighter wood or have it painted?'

'I think... up in the eves I'd go for painted. Yes white–'

'Matt or gloss?' Nick couldn't help himself.

They sat in Mr Stukeley's office, Nick using the calculator on his mobile phone to work out rough cost estimates for different types of finish. 'It'll be labour and VAT on top, plus I don't know if you've got any fancy handles or drawer and hanger sliders you have in mind. We've allowed for full and shirt length hanging space. There's a place for shoes, a bank of shelves and some shallow sliding drawers for ties, socks and other stuff.' He couldn't quite bring himself to mention underwear.

'That all sounds good.' Mr Stukeley nodded his approval.

Twenty minutes later Nick was ready to leave and drive back to Needham Market. They'd agreed he would email the plans along with a breakdown of the estimated costs of labour and material; and Mr Stukeley for his part would get back to Willows to give a yes or no so they could order the wood before the end of the working day.

If he got the job, which Nick was pretty sure he would, then he'd ask about the glut of clocks flooding the market. There was no point in upsetting Mr Stukeley yet.

CHAPTER 27

Beep-itty-beep! Beep-itty-beep beep! Matt pulled his mobile from his faux leather flying jacket. What could Chrissie want, he wondered as he read the caller ID.

'Hi Chrissie,' he mumbled, conscious of the spanking-new glossy Vespa scooters propped on their parking stands down one side of the motorcycle shop. 'You kinda caught me–'

'Matt, something awful's happened.'

'What? You OK?'

'Yes, yes, I'm OK. It's Ron. He smashed up his hand yesterday. Slipped in the snow.'

'Smashed up his hand?' Matt echoed, half his mind on a custard coloured Vespa, the other half trying to take in a smashed hand.

'Well, it's mainly his fingers. Fracture dislocations.'

'Scammin' hell! What's that?'

'I'm not sure. They've put wires down two of his fingers for internal fixing. It looks kind of mediaeval. He'll be OK, but he can't work for the moment. Are you in the library? You usually are on Thursday afternoons.'

'Nah. I'm in the Bury scooter shop, but I'll be back in Stowmarket later.'

'Is your scooter OK?'

'Yeah, but I were thinkin' about part exchangin' it. See I reckon with all this snow about, they won't be sellin' many scooters. Could be me best chance to nail a megadeal for a 125cc.'

'Hey, good for you. Look I don't want to hold you up but I'm going to need help lifting some of this furniture

272

around and… well you've got two hands and when the Academy breaks for Christmas….'

'Yeah, but I'll be doin' some extra hours at Damon's. I'll know which days after me session tomorrow and then….' He pictured the old barn workshop. Internet access was a joke there, and besides, he generally avoided physical work. He fought his conscience. It hurt. He closed his eyes and imagined a comic-strip superhero.

'I'll see you in the Nag's Head tomorrow evenin'. Tell me what you need, an' I'll tell you what I can do,' his superhero said.

'Thanks, Matt. I knew you'd help,' Chrissie's voice purred through his phone.

'What, Chrissie?'

'Thanks for saying yes, Matt. See you tomorrow in the Nags Head.'

Epibotics! What had he just agreed to do? He guessed he'd find out on Friday over a pint of lager, but for the next half hour he'd take a reality check and look at the price of the scooters. He slipped his mobile back into his jacket.

'Can I 'ave a look at your second hand Vespas?' he asked a young-looking sales assistant.

When Matt rode back to Stowmarket he had a list of deals and prices in his pocket and a head spinning with excitement. Snow covered the verges and fields, peppered the hedgerows, and collected in drifts along the sides of the minor roads, but it didn't worry him. He was too taken up with the vision of a 125cc Vespa.

Even when he lumbered up the wide Academy staircase, slipped into the library and slouched at his favourite computer station, his mind still whirled with the

Italian dream – pasta, a trip to Pontedera, locals calling him Matteo....

'Hi Matt. Are you OK?'

He hadn't noticed Rosie with her trolley of books easing past the shelves to one side of him.

'What?' he said startled. 'Hey Rosie, I aint seen you in a while.'

A silver star-shaped helium balloon floated close to her. For a moment he wondered if it was a vision, then he spotted the thread tying it to a book on her trolley-rack.

'Cool,' he murmured eyeing the inflatable.

'It'll probably have lost all its helium by Christmas, but it's a bit of fun; you know, spreads a little cheer.' She smiled. It was her faint-curve-of-her-lips smile, the signal he recognised when she was about to move on and leave him.

'Hey, Rosie, are you goin' anywhere exotic this Christmas?' he asked, trying to hold her attention a little longer.

'I don't think I'd count Bungay as exotic, Matt.' She started to push the trolley away.

'No, reckon not. But Italy?' he said to her back. She didn't seem to hear him.

He turned his attention to his computer screen.

A holiday in Italy? A 125cc Vespa scooter? He hadn't considered the cost beyond part-exchange and a monthly repayment scheme for the scooter. He'd paid for the tee-shirts, the hound dog brown ones with an outline of Italy on the front and a red dot denoting Pontedera, but that's as far as current funds had stretched.

Inspiration struck. If he couldn't pay for the holiday, how about just buying a suitcase instead? It could double as a Christmas present for Maisie. He pictured her on the back of a Vespa with a retro style 1960s case. Yeah, megabit! How cool was that?

He typed *1960s cases* in the search box and sifted through the selling platforms. Soon he was looking through a selection of genuine 1960s cases. A name caught his eye.

'Mawbray? *Cases made in the 60s by Sampson Mawbray of Stowmarket,*' he breathed as he read the description.

Could this be one of the Mawbrays Chrissie was talking about a week or so back? He knew Stella Mawbray from his debt collecting search lived out at Earl Soham, not far from Framlingham. And James Mawbray? Chrissie said she'd helped Ron return a repaired oak settle to him, and then James had sent them to his dad, Benjamin Mawbray.

Didn't Chrissie also say James had turned the failing family business into a plastic recycling unit, milling down used plastic into pellets and granules? And Benjamin lived in a rundown bungalow next to the recycling unit in Broad Green, Stowmarket? So *Sampson Mawbray of Stowmarket* could be the father of Benjamin, grandfather of James, and once ran a business making suitcases which had now changed to a business milling-down used plastic. The original unit was still in Broad Green. Wow!

Matt expanded the picture of three matching cases of different sizes; one stacked on another, the smallest a travelling vanity case. A plastic label *Stowmarket Mawbray*, was tacked to the plasticised exterior, just beneath the carrying handle of two of them but was missing from the middle-sized third one. He scrolled to the next pictures and looked more closely at each of the three cases displayed individually.

The middle-sized one seemed grubby and to have lost its nametag. He could see the tack holes left by the missing name label. The other two cases looked altogether smarter and all three were covered in a blue-taupe plastic material bonded to a dense but lightweight type of cardboard, in keeping with the 60s. The cases were lined in a geometric patterned grey satin, bonded to the suitcase interiors. Hard plastic carrying handles and nickel-plated lock catches completed the look.

He peered more closely at the grubby case. It was minging. Definitely minging. The blue-taupe material had lost its blueness. Blotches and watermarks disfigured every surface except where the lid had overlapped the rim. There were even what could have been rust stains from something metal lying against it in its past. The lock catches were pitted and corroded, the lining stained and damaged. *Needs some love and attention / would make a good stage prop* was the comment attached to the picture.

'Why'd anyone wanta buy that?' Matt murmured, but of course Chrissie had said the man was tight. 'Yeah, I reckon it could be old Benjamin tryin' to sell. Well I aint buyin' that one.'

He clicked idly on another 60s suitcase. His eyes took in the image while out of nowhere his mind zinged a warning. It was as if he had a robot file, a so called *crawler* sorting through his mind data.

In a flash of clarity he realised his potted summary of the Mawbray family line was all well and good, but where did Stella Mawbray fit in? And now, as his brain made the conscious connection, was it too much of a coincidence that Mandy Rokin was found dead somewhere along Earl Soham Lane? Didn't Stella live in Earl Soham? Damon had

276

implied Clive seemed to think the link was through their kids. Was it why her body was found out that way?

The horribleness of the implication pressed down on him like wet cloying clay. He didn't want to think about dead bodies and killers. He wanted to think about holidays in Italy and Maisie. On impulse he pulled his phone from his jacket and pressed Maisie's automatic dial number.

'What you doin' this evening, Mais?' he asked when she picked up his call.

'I told you ages ago. It's a girls' night out. Christmas drinks eight o'clock down the Coachman with me mates from work.'

'Oh yeah, you did say. It's a bit previous, aint it? I mean it's–'

'Less than three weeks till Christmas. Your head aint still all of a spin is it?'

'Nah, but I'd kinda....' There was no point. He couldn't find the words, he couldn't explain. How could he say he felt something terrible was going to happen, but he didn't know what or where.

'See you down the Nags Head tomorrow then, OK, Mais?' he said instead.

'Yeah, if I aint too wasted.'

CHAPTER 28

Chrissie rolled the words around her mouth, 'Fracture dislocation. Internal fixation. Kirschner Wires.'

Who'd have thought such words could ever storm through the workshop and hail down like devil dust. She'd spent most of Thursday fearing the worst, planning for the chaotic inevitable and trying to maintain a professional exterior. Inside she was a mess. She sat, her working day officially ended, and talked to Ron. She knew Clive would be dropping by on his way home so he could help her move any furniture around or load the van ready for the morning. It was good to talk to Ron while she waited.

Ron had insisted on returning to the workshop late that afternoon, even though it was only for a mug of tea. She guessed it was an act of defiance on his part, his way of spitting in the eye of fate. He sat on his work stool, left arm in a sling and his right hand nursing his warm mug still resting on the bench. He looked calm and accepting, his face a little pasty and gaunt.

'So are those K-wires a bit like our wooden dowels?' she asked, trying to keep the horror out of her voice.

'Except they're stainless steel. You know those surgeons didn't miss a trick? The K-wires must have spiral markings on them, because they used a battery powered drill to insert them.'

'Really? Like a screw? And you were awake while they did it?' She felt her world pale a little and tried to concentrate on the mechanics of what he was saying.

'Hmm, yes – a tourniquet and injections. I was lucky they thought I'd be able to cope. I had to be awake so I

278

could move my fingers when they asked me to, so they could check my range of movement once they'd popped the joints back and lined up the broken bone. They explained they used the K-wires to stabilise the breaks but it still allows me to move my fingers a bit while it's all healing. This way I'll get a better result. They don't do this for everyone, only if you're willing.'

'Your hands are your job.'

'Exactly. And carpentry is my life. I don't want to end up with stiff useless fingers, Chrissie. The arthritis is bad enough.'

He rarely called her Chrissie, and she'd never heard him talk about his arthritis before. It was an ailment they both acknowledged, but worked around. The fact he'd mentioned it and called her Chrissie spoke fathoms.

'So you see I have to keep moving my fingers a little. I figure I can work using my right hand and just use this one a bit.' He lifted his left hand a fraction in his sling.

'But, Mr Clegg, shouldn't you take time out? Give your fingers a chance to start healing first?'

Deep down she wanted him to be back in the workshop and around to give advice. He'd always been there for her from the first day she'd started as an apprentice, and it was going to feel very strange without him now. It was as if she was standing on the edge of a cliff, the point where the land fell away. She hoped none of her neediness showed through in her voice.

He smiled. 'But you know me, Mrs Jax. I'll get bored if I stay at home. And besides, I won't be using my broken fingers, I'll just use the heel of my hand to steady or guide things. Now, what have you organised so far?'

'I've thrown a bagful of salted grit around outside. I've asked Matt to help out when Utterly Academy breaks for Christmas. Clive is dropping by shortly on his way home to help move anything around and....' She let her voice drift.

'They had a tinsel Christmas tree at the hospital. Perhaps a few decorations might raise the spirit?' Ron murmured.

'I could put some outdoor Christmas lights above the workshop door. How does that sound, Mr Clegg?'

Forty minutes later she followed Clive's black Ford Mondeo tail lights to her end-of-terrace cottage in Woolpit and parked the van behind his car. He held her hand as they walked across the trodden snow to her front door.

'Perhaps we should put up some outdoor Christmas lights here as well, Chrissie,' he said.

'That would be nice,' she murmured as he unlocked the door and reached inside to flick on the hallway light. She stood for a moment.

'Ron will be OK, Chrissie.' The concern was obvious in his voice.

'I know, but it's set me worrying about our skiing holiday. What if I smash up my hands? What happens then? The business can't take it.'

'You're more likely to break your leg and ankle, or twist a knee, Chrissie.'

'Well that's all right then. Knowing it'll be a leg makes me feel a damn sight better.' It was just like him to reassure her with the greater likelihood of a different limb being injured. She smiled despite her inner panic.

'Hey, come on, it's going to work out fine.' He put his arm round her, gave her a brief hug and guided her ahead of him through the doorway.

'Well cheer me up then. At least tell me your day went well, that you've solved a case and caught a murderer.'

'I don't know about catching a murderer yet, but we're building up more of a picture. A week ago it seemed hopeless, now I'm pretty sure we're going to be able to nail it.'

'Really? How's that?'

Her mind had been largely functioning on autopilot while in the background it focussed on the muddle of half-finished repairs and restorations, deliveries, collections, broken deadlines and promises of completion by Christmas. A generalised feeling of anxiety overlaid it all. She needed something totally different to absorb her mental energies.

She turned to face Clive. He must have read the worry in her eyes, recognised the tension in her face, and known she wouldn't settle until her mind was filled with puzzles and riddles, brainteasers to distract from her own problems.

'It's a long story, Chrissie. So first things first - is there any beer in the fridge?'

'Let's see.' She led the way into the small kitchen and filled the kettle as he checked the fridge.

'We're in luck. Are you having a beer as well?'

'No thanks, I'm going to stick with tea. Now sit down and you can talk to me while I make us some supper.'

She moved around the kitchen gathering an avocado, tomatoes, a red onion, coriander, olive oil and a lime, while Clive took the cap off his beer and settled at her narrow table. He took a long slow drink straight from the bottle.

'That's better. Right, now the game changer in this investigation is Mandy Rokin's death.'

'How's that?' she asked as she diced the onion.

'Well it turns out John Camm and Mandy Rokin have very similar head wounds. The pathologist thinks they were inflicted by the same object.'

'I thought Mandy Rokin was found in a water-filled ditch. I assumed she'd drowned.'

'But there was no water in her lungs and nothing on her toxicology tests, not even alcohol in her blood. The pathologist says the head injury killed her. She was dead by the time she hit the water.'

'And you say she had a head injury like the one which killed John Camm?'

'Precisely.'

She knew he was making her work it out for herself, forcing her to engage her over-active mind and distract her from her own troubles. 'So the two deaths must be connected, right?'

'Yes, Chrissie. So you see we've been looking for connections, anything which links the two of them,' he pressed on.

'And have you found anything?' She set about de-seeding and dicing the tomatoes.

'Well we've found connections in common, but nothing to link the two of them yet.'

'So you're saying the connection may be the common factor, like….' She waved her knife as if drawing inspiration from her chopping board. 'Like two people with food poisoning could have eaten at the same restaurant but wouldn't have necessarily known each other?'

'Precisely, Chrissie. Just like two people eating at the same restaurant.'

She caught his look as he eyed up the tomatoes.

'It's OK, Clive. The spicy wine vinegar and chilli paste will kill any bugs.'

'I'm not sure if that makes me feel more reassured or more anxious, Chrissie.'

His grin said it all – she knew he'd clocked her playful return for his *break your leg skiing* reassurance earlier.

'Come on, let's not get side-tracked by my chilli paste,' she laughed.

'Right, back to the connections. Firstly let's think about the photos on John Camm's Facebook page.'

'If you remember, Clive, I was as puzzled as you about them.'

'Except they all featured trees and then they turned up, posted by John Camm on Benjamin Mawbray's Facebook page with the title: *Good to find you again. It brings back memories of the old times, hey?* So what does that tell you, Chrissie?'

She thought for a moment, knife suspended mid-cut. Clive was obviously determined to keep her brain working on the puzzles.

'Well it has to mean the subject of the photos was relevant and part of the message to Benjamin Mawbray.'

'Yes, and it also tells me the two men are connected in some way from the past. We started looking for recent connections first, the *finding you again* bit of the message. The only recent thing we could discover was that John Camm serviced Benjamin's mower at the beginning of the summer.'

'But if they knew each other and John wanted to send a message, why not just ring Benjamin so they could speak to each other?'

'Hmm, exactly.' Clive swigged another mouthful of beer, 'So we looked at John's appointment book more closely and it seems the appointment was actually made for James Mawbray, not Benjamin Mawbray. James was a regular customer.'

'And I bet James asked him to service his father's mower, just as he was leaving. Just like he sent us off to his father's bungalow after we delivered the repaired oak settle.'

'Exactly.'

'I expect James has a habit of springing things on people. So you think it's possible John might not have met Benjamin on the day, he could have been out when he serviced the mower?'

'It's possible, but what it tells us is there's definitely a recent connection. The postings only started after Benjamin's mower was serviced at the beginning of this summer. I don't think they'd met up for years.'

'Wow. But someone must've interviewed Benjamin? What did he say?'

'Well he wasn't very lucid. He'd been drinking. He basically denied knowing John Camm or ever having met him before.'

'Or paying him for servicing his mower, I bet! So have you just left it at that, a dead end?'

'No, but you won't be surprised to learn Benjamin has proved unhelpful, drunk and evasive. However we've discovered he has a juvenile record. We're still delving into that. And, my DS has spent a good few hours sitting with

Mrs Camm listening to a potted life history of her husband. He apparently serviced golf trolleys for a short time many years ago before concentrating on mowers. And earlier, before his wife even met him, he was in some kind of an apprenticeship for a year.'

'Well, if you sent DS Stickley, he's....' She searched for the right words. 'He is rather abrasive, at least his voice is. He's probably well suited for Benjamin, but Mrs Camm? Have you interviewed Mrs Camm yourself?'

'Yes, but not this last time round. And unless I went bearing a bottle of vodka, I don't think I'd get any further with Benjamin either.'

Chrissie started to peel the avocado, her mind grappling with Clive's information.

'And of course there is another connection,' Clive said, as if tipping out the last sweet hiding in the sweetie bag.

He already had her full attention, but now she gave up on the avocado and turned from the chopping board. 'Go on.'

'Mandy Rokin posted selfies on her Facebook page. There is a face in the background which we've identified as Stella Mawbray.'

'Who is Stella Mawbray?'

'Stella is James Mawbray's wife. Mandy's and Stella's sons are friends, and I think Stella is holding something back about Mandy. She knows more than she's letting on to us.'

'So,' Chrissie said slowly, 'is the connection to both Mandy Rokin and John Camm the whole Mawbray family, or one Mawbray in particular?'

'Well, returning to your food poisoning example. I think the Mawbrays are the restaurant, but we don't know which of the many dishes on the menu are....'

'Contaminated?' she finished for him.

'That seems a bit harsh, Chrissie. But you get my drift?'

'Yes, I think so.' She leaned across the table and kissed him. 'Thanks, Clive. I think your puzzles are already working as distraction therapy.'

'Well, in that case I guess another beer might be in order.'

'And brace yourself. I thought I'd make spicy Mexican poached eggs on toasted sourdough bread. They'll look amazingly cheerful, even Christmassy, and they'll put hairs on your chest. Or rather the salsa might!'

She felt as if a curtain had been raised, as if now she could see all the players on a stage. It was time to lose her own problems for a few hours.

CHAPTER 29

'It's good news about Mr Stukeley, Nick.' The foreman beamed over his early morning mug of tea, as he looked through the work schedules for the day.

'I know. He really seemed to like my Art Deco ideas yesterday.'

It was Friday morning and the atmosphere in the carpenters' office-cum-restroom already felt humid. The snow was beginning to melt, and the added fine drizzle from an overcast sky had ensured footwear, anoraks and all-weather parkers were damp.

'Dave's taught you well,' the foreman continued.

Nick was about to respond that Dave had shown him plenty of carpentry tricks and refined his work but Dave wasn't interested in design. He could have also added they'd talked cars, engines, and local history; they'd never had conversations about modern British designers or things like how to achieve a Scandinavian look with pale or bleached wood. However Dave had always shown him loyalty and kindness.

'Yeah, Dave's taught me loads. He's a good guy,' Nick replied.

'You two work well together, so I may send him over to Ipswich to give you a hand next week. Mr Stukeley could be an important customer in the future, so best we get the job done quickly for him.'

'Thanks, Mr Walsh. Any idea when the wood will be delivered?'

After a brief discussion and quick phone call, it was decided, now that Nick had won the contract for Willows, he'd drive over to Ipswich, peel the attic bedroom carpet back right down to the floorboards and re-measure. It was really an excuse to discuss a few more design points with Mr Stukeley, possibly manage a quick coffee with Pearl, and be back in the Willows & Son workshop by lunchtime when the wood was due to be delivered.

Nick grabbed the van keys off the hook and hurried out to the secure parking area. The melting snow had widened the tyre tracks so that plenty of concrete and gravel showed through. The patterns were reversing with only the scattered smudges and streaks of snow persisting, and yesterday's winter tartans had become today's sixties wall paper. He guessed Mr Stukeley would see it as design and Dave as a skidpan.

Happy and excited, he followed the same roads as the day before, but made faster time as he drove into Ipswich. The main residential routes had been salted and gritted and it didn't take Nick long before he turned into St Williams Road and drew up in Mr Stukeley's driveway.

He rang the doorbell and stamped the melting snow off his walking trainers while he waited, toolbox by his feet and some paperwork in one hand.

'Good morning, Nick. Do you want to go straight up? You know the way,' Mr Stukeley said as he opened the white-painted front door.

'Thanks. I hadn't wanted to take up part of your carpet yesterday, but now we're going ahead with the design, I thought I'd best get on with it and do a final measure-up for the height of the plinth board. I'm hoping there won't be any surprises with your old floorboards. The wardrobe has to rest on them.'

Mr Stukeley stood aside for Nick. 'You'll put the old carpet back?'

'Yeah, once the wardrobe's done, unless you're having new carpet laid. I've also brought along some paint colour cards for you to choose from.'

'A myriad of whites in different finishes?'

'Something like that, Mr Stukeley. I must admit I didn't think there could be so many shades of white, but when the *rising sun* panels arrive, you might want to decide on a slightly different shade?'

'Possibly.'

He heard the inflection in Mr Stukeley's voice and guessed a sense of humour lurked somewhere behind the straight façade. Nick hurried on through the room-like hallway with its imposing dental bannisters and climbed the back stairs, two steps at a time. It didn't take him long to pull the carpet back and prize up the gripper strips. He was lucky – there wasn't a layer of old linoleum and the floorboards looked flat enough. He checked with a spirit level to be sure. Dave had taught him it was easier to lay chipboard right at the start, in order to get a dead flat surface, than struggle with uneven floorboards.

Satisfied with the old boards, he rechecked his measurements and made small adjustments. Work completed, he pulled his mobile from his jeans and was about to shoot off a *how about a coffee?* text to Pearl, when a thought struck. How needy and pushy would he sound? He'd left it with her only yesterday that he'd give her a lift to the Saturday gig in Woodbridge. He needed to come up with something more interesting and original as an excuse to text.

Deep in thought, he retraced his steps down the back staircase. Mr Stukeley's office was open and Nick paused by the doorway, not sure whether to knock or speak to catch his client's attention.

Dong! A single chime resounded from somewhere in the hall.

'That'll be my Turret clock striking the half hour,' Mr Stukeley said mildly as he looked up from his computer screen.

'I don't remember hearing it yesterday.' Nick was intrigued. Pearl had been right when she'd guessed he'd seen a Turret clock.

'No you couldn't have heard it, Nick. I've only just engaged the striking mechanism. I thought it might be fun to have it running over Christmas. Of course my sister and her family might not think it's fun.'

Nick put down his toolbox, hiding a grin as he bent.

'Do you know much about clocks, then?' he mumbled, swallowing back his laughter.

'I've developed a bit of an interest over the years. How about you?'

'To be honest I haven't given them much thought before, but I've met a new girl and she's into clocks, at least her dad is.' He let his voice drift. What the hell was he doing talking like this to a client? He felt his cheeks flush and glanced at Mr Stukeley.

'I can direct you to a good website about clocks, if that would help?'

'Well thanks, that would be useful, but it was more a question she'd raised.'

Mr Stukeley looked interested. 'I don't know if I'm following what you mean, Nick.'

'Well, she said there were a lot of old clocks flooding the market at the moment, probably because it's Christmas. She wants to buy something for her dad but... well, as she put it - how can she tell if the glut is because a collector is selling up a large collection, or if there's a load of dodgy stuff suddenly out there? You know, stolen clocks?'

'That's an interesting question. I haven't any clients looking for clocks at the moment, so I can't answer without doing a little research first. Leave it with me. I'll get back to you.'

'Hey thanks, Mr Stukeley.'

'Are you sure this isn't really about you and you're the one looking for a clock?'

'What me? No. Too expensive. Mind you, an old metronome would be more,' he was going to say more Pearl's style but instead murmured, 'my style.'

'Antique or vintage?' Mr Stukeley asked, his eyes back on the screen and his voice business-like as he worked his keyboard. 'I can see several here - vintage Seth Thomas metronomes, Maelzel types ranging from the 1920s, to the 60s and 70s. And there's a choice - either fully restored or serviced, with or without the bell option. Something like forty to a couple of hundred quid more in your range?'

'But how? Have you just gone onto eBay or something?'

'You're forgetting, Nick. I source things for people. I know where to look, which selling platforms to search and for what. It's about who you know, and keeping an ear to the ground. Now you don't expect me to give away all my secrets do you? I have to be discrete as well.'

'No but....'

'Right, I'll let you know the exact shade of white and the type of paint finish once the *rising suns* have arrived. And I'll also let you know that other stuff when I know something, OK?'

'Thanks, Mr Stukeley.'

'Oh, and tell me if you need any help getting a metronome, Nick.'

Nick let himself out through the white front door and loaded his toolbox into the van. So how did that happen, he wondered as he started the engine. Wasn't it Mr Stukeley who was meant to be the client? How had it just changed around and now he was almost the client and it was his money going to Mr Stukeley? At least it had given him an idea.

What do you know about vintage metronomes? he texted to Pearl. Yeah, that would do as an interesting and unusual message. He reckoned she was bound to reply. He slipped the van into gear and pulled carefully out of the driveway.

The traffic was heavy as he drove through Ipswich. It was as if all the drivers who had left their cars parked on residential side roads and front drives throughout the worst of the snow had finally ventured out. Mid-morning, unable to put off their journeys and business any longer, the melting snow had lured them onto the roads where they drove at barely ten miles an hour, wheels straddling the centre road makings and choking the routes.

He switched on the van's radio and settled into the journey. *The Salvation Army's Christmas tree this year is decorated with hand-written messages of hope*, the radio presenter's voice soothed gently, *and of course at this time of the year they have been particularly busy. Their Anglia*

Emergency Response Team assisted the Suffolk Fire and Rescue service when.... Nick flicked the radio channel to a purely music station and concentrated on the road.

Forty minutes later he drove into the Willows secure parking area. He jumped down from the van and checked his mobile. A new unopened text message signalled on the message tab. He felt a beat of excitement. Was it from Pearl? No. He swallowed his disappointment and opened Chrissie's message.

Hi Nick. Are you able to help Ron with some Hepplewhite chairs on Sunday? We've some deadlines to make and... I think he'll be OK with you. Matt said he'd help out... but the chairs are special. I'll be there too and I'll lay on some food etc. Please say yes. Chrissie.

'Shit!'

He'd been too taken up with his work and Pearl to think it through when Chrissie had first called after Ron's accident. He should have been figuring out ways to help, but instead he'd been focussing on Pearl. In a flash of guilt he made a decision. He'd have to share out his time. It looked like he wasn't going to be able to make it to Pearl's Christmas concert and listen to her saxophone quartet on Sunday, after all. He couldn't let a girl completely take over his life. He'd done that once years ago with Mel and look how that ended.

How about I come to your workshop on Friday instead of Nags Head? Also Saturday afternoon for a few hours? Sunday – count me in, but I'll want some decent grub! Last time I looked on a colour chart Hepplewhite was a shade of white!! N.

CHAPTER 30

Matt opened the text message as he ambled from the Utterly computer lab, cut past the storerooms and delivery areas, and joined the long corridor to the front of the old mansion building.

'What's Chrissie on about?' he muttered, trying to make sense of the text message as he walked.

It was no good. He couldn't walk and read and think properly all at the same time. He stopped and leaned against the noticeboard wall. Someone had draped silver and gold tinsel garlands along the top of the information boards, and an end hung down, brushing his ear.

Not going to Nags Head tonight, he read. *Staying late at workshop. Nick coming over to help Ron. Drop by workshop as well if you like! C x*

'Right,' he breathed. So how was he going to square this with Maisie?

He was due to work his Friday afternoon session in Bury, then ride back to meet her in the Nags Head. The Clegg workshop was way off his route back to Stowmarket. Was the text a Chrissie-type prompt saying she needed his help this evening, or was she reminding him to get his holiday work schedule at Balcon & Mora while he was up there today? Why couldn't she just say what she meant?

He'd tried calling Maisie earlier, before the practical computing session in the lab, but her phone was switched off. He'd wanted to dispel the vague feeling something bad was going to happen. He'd got it – the Mandy Rokin and Stella Mawbray connection, but somewhere in the backwaters of his mind he'd started searching for other connections. How about both Mandy and Maisie living in Stowupland? It was tenuous, but it wormed away at him. Was it enough to put Maisie in danger? Is that why she wasn't answering?

He'd wanted to ask how her pre-Christmas drinks had gone and reckoned a dead phone was code for too many Buck's Fizz and added shots of vodka with the girls from work. But was he right? It was time to try again. He pressed her automatic dial number and waited.

'Hey, crazy tinsel, mate,' Ley said, walking past with a couple of students from the computing session.

'What?' Matt grunted, looking up from his phone and snagging his beard on the notice board garland.

'Hi!' a croaky voice squeaked from his mobile.

'Crazy what? Oh hiya, Mais. You OK?'

'Yeah,' she rasped. 'A bit flakey, but it were wild. The karaoke were wicked. What you on about crazy?'

'Nothin', Mais.' He swiped at the tinsel and rubbed flecks of glitter from his beard. 'Just a danglin' streamer. Look, about the Nags Head….'

'A screamer? Wild! Yeah, Nags Head?'

'You're soundin' rough, Mais. You sure you're OK?'

'Yeah, but I aint doing no more singin' and don't you go callin' it screamin'. So what you saying about the Nags Head?'

'It aint the usual crowd tonight, Mais. They're meetin' at Chrissie's workshop cos Ron's messed up his hand and….' He let his voice drift.

'His hand? So?'

'It's a kinda workin' session.' He listened to the silence from his phone.

'Well you aint no good at that kind of thing, Matt,' she finally rasped. 'Let's just have a quiet drink and forget the workshop. It aint your style.'

It was what he'd wanted to hear.

CHAPTER 31

Chrissie felt exhausted, both in mind and body. Ever since the push into Friday evening, a full-on working Saturday and Sunday, and late finishes Monday and Tuesday, her muscles ached, her back felt stiff and she longed to flop onto her comfortable sofa and never have to move again. Nick had been brilliant over the weekend. He'd worked, whenever he was free, on the Hepplewhite chairs with Ron while she'd concentrated on the Challenge Trophy so that now it was finished. Her bandsaw-cut oak veneer had been glued onto the new multi-ply board, sanded and smoothed to a beautiful finish, edged in an oak frame, and the wood sealed and varnished.

On Monday and Tuesday, she'd worked with Ron, taking over where Nick had left off and juggling her time so that the two Hepplewhite chairs were now fully restored, and the trophy's engraved brass name plates and the hickory club re-mounted.

She blinked away the tiredness. It was Wednesday and another early start. She drew up outside a shabby bungalow on Tumble Weed Drive on the Flower Estate. At 7:45 in the morning, daylight was still pushing back night, and in the half-light she hoped she'd got the right front door. Battery powered Christmas candles flickered in a window somewhere further down the road.

'Come on, Matt,' she muttered, willing him to appear, bright and ready for his first day as Mr Muscle and Left Hand assistant in the workshop. She knew if it was left up to him, he wouldn't appear on his scooter until mid-morning, far too late for the start of the workshop day. It was why she was sitting, cocooned in her TR7 and waiting for him outside his home, or what she hoped was his home.

'Oh hurry up, Matt,' she muttered again, this time exasperated as well as impatient.

She pulled her mobile from her leather bag and pressed his automatic dial number. He answered on the second ring tone.

'Yeah, I'm up,' he mumbled, 'I were just puttin' me laptop in me backpack. Is there somewhere I can grab a bite?'

'Just get yourself out here, Matt. There's coffee and tea in the workshop. And a bag of muffins,' she added for extra incentive. 'We've got to get the van loaded. You're helping me deliver furniture this morning, remember? Now move!'

She ignored his almost inaudible reply and slipped her phone into her pocket. She knew the bungalow was devoid of comfort. His mother, judging from whatever he'd let slip about her, sounded uncommunicative, and if she was any reflection of how Matt referred to the inside of their fridge, then stark and empty sprang to mind. Home was a subject he didn't talk about. She guessed he'd separated it off in his mind, so that it only existed when he saw it, and to be honest, in the half-light she wasn't entirely sure if she could see it clearly herself.

A sudden movement in the play of dark on grey told her the front door had opened. Electric light outlined a figure in the doorway for a moment, then the light was gone and Matt ambled towards her car, backpack slung over one shoulder.

'Good morning,' she said, releasing the passenger door lock, her irritation evaporating.

'Hi,' he grunted and slumped into the passenger seat.

'At least all the snow's melted now,' she murmured.

'Yeah, but there's more forecast in Scotland.'

'It shouldn't be a problem where we're going, Matt.'

She started the engine, drew out of Tumble Weed Drive and headed south from Stowmarket to Wattisham and the airfield boundary lane. She glanced at Matt as she drove. His head bobbed forwards and his arms relaxed as he hugged his backpack on his lap. He looked close to dozing off.

'Thanks for offering to help out in the workshop, Matt. Ron couldn't have chosen a worse moment to smash up his fingers, just when we're trying to get furniture back to clients in time for Christmas.' She hoped by speaking she'd keep him awake.

'So where we deliverin' today?' he mumbled, the sleep obvious in his voice.

'The Rush Green Golf Club and then Benjamin Mawbray's place in Broad Green. We've also got an oak table to pick up from a farm out at Somersham on the way back.'

He didn't answer. She guessed he was already drifting, his mind sinking into dream mode. She gave up on conversation and focussed on the road. Matt finally stirred and lifted his head when she rocked along the rutted track to the workshop. Muddy meltwater had filled the potholes the previous day, but now they'd iced over and her car tyres cracked and crunched through the frozen skim as the TR7 lurched from rut to hollow.

'Scammin' hell,' Matt groaned and clutched his backpack tight.

'We're here,' she said, stating the obvious as she parked alongside the Citroen van. She reached for the plastic food box behind her seat. 'Sandwiches and muffins,' she added, and got out. She guessed the mention of food would work where cajoling might fail, and sure enough the Pied Piper effect drew Matt out of the passenger seat and into the old barn workshop.

Ron was already sitting at his workbench. She thought he looked brighter, with less of a hunch to his shoulders than when he'd first come back from the hospital, his fingers wired and his arm in a sling. For the moment he'd shed the sling, and his left hand, swathed in a crepe bandage, rested on the workbench.

'Morning,' he said softly, 'and thanks for helping out, Matt. I haven't seen you in a few months. How are you doing? Computing still suiting?'

Mornin' Mr Clegg,' Matt mumbled. 'Yeah, I brought me laptop. Sorry 'bout your hand. Did you say somthin' 'bout muffins, Chrissie?'

'Yes, in the container.' She pointed to the heap of leather bag and her discarded duffle coat on the worktop close by. 'I'll put the kettle on. Tea, coffee everyone?'

She made tea for Ron but reckoned on a double dose of coffee for both Matt and herself. Twenty minutes later they were ready to load the van.

'Why aint you droppin' the Challenge Trophy at the golf club on your way home, Chrissie? It'd save havin' to do it now,' Matt said, a frown creasing his normally smooth forehead.

'Because it won't fit in my TR7 and at the moment I just want to get it delivered and another job off the list. Anyway, I could do with some help carrying it in.'

'Hey, try slowing down a little, Mrs Jax. You're in such a spin you're going to drive yourself into the ground. There's plenty of time,' Ron's kindly voice soothed. 'We're getting through the work nicely, and you're a week ahead of schedule with the trophy board.'

'I guess so,' she replied, but she was on a treadmill and couldn't slow her pace. If she'd had the time to reflect, she'd have seen Ron was right but she was a worrier; her thoughts ran fast, action was how she coped.

'Come on, Matt, let's get the van loaded,' she murmured.

It didn't take them long to carry the two Hepplewhite chairs to the van and wrap blankets and dustsheets around the Challenge Trophy board before securing the load. They left Ron with another mug of tea, an opened tin of wax polish and a corner cupboard to buff into a warm patina.

'Did I tell you I got to the bottom of how the Northfield Challenge Trophy came about?' Chrissie asked Matt, as they swayed along the rutted track, the Citroen's raised road clearance and suspension making smooth work of the bumpy surface. She took his grunt as a no and outlined the tale as told by the club secretary the week before.

'So old man Sampson were the one makin' cases and golf bags, yeah? He were the *Sampson Mawbray of Stowmarket*, the *Sampson Mawbray* case of 1960?'

'Yes, have your heard of them, then?'

'Not till I did some reseachin' for retro stuff.'

'Well his son Benjamin didn't make a success of taking over the family business and now James–'

'The old man's grandson?'

'Yes, James has turned the failed family business into a unit milling down old plastic ready for recycling.'

'I've scootered past a scammin' big unit with a tall chimney,' Matt muttered.

'That'll be the new power plant to be run on recycled rubbish they're building out Great Blakenham way. I don't think it's anything to do with James. In fact I reckon he'd more likely see it as competition, if he's anything like his dad, Benjamin.'

'How's that, Chrissie?'

'James's plastic milling unit looked pretty tatty when we took the short cut past it a couple of weeks ago, and I didn't see much activity there. I guess when he first started he was the only recycler round here. Now he's a small player in a crowded field. It didn't look to me like it was thriving.'

'You're soundin' like an accountant.'

Chrissie didn't answer as she took the fork past Onehouse and drove on towards Rush Green and the A14. Matt was right. She hadn't stopped thinking in terms of balance sheets, assets and returns just because she'd changed her life around and trained as a carpenter. She couldn't cast aside her previous career as an accountant. It was part of her. But the reality was she'd visited enough clients in her previous life to instinctively recognise the signs of a failing business.

'Here we are, this is the golf club,' she said as she slowed and turned into the entrance, Wednesday's steely winter daylight fully dawned and bathing the first tee and fairway. She parked the van near the clubhouse.

'I aint ever been in a golf club before,' Matt muttered taking one end of the trophy board and trailing awkwardly behind her as he helped carry it through the wide door.

'Mind the Christmas tree,' she hissed as they walked past the entrance to the bar and took the open doorway into the corridor-like room, hung with the names of previous captains and winners and with its staircase leading down to the changing rooms.

'Are we hangin' it up here?' Matt asked as they passed the wall-mounted boards.

'No, the secretary said to leave it in his office if he wasn't around when we dropped it off.'

They left the Northfield Challenge Trophy, complete with its mounted hickory club, propped against Paul Cooley's office wall. She took a last look at it before they hurried back to the van. Should she have stuck a label on the back, as the secretary had joked, *Repaired by Chrissie Jax, 2012*.

'I wish I'd stuck one on saying *Donated by Sampson Mawbray 1967*,' she said under her breath.

'What you sayin', Chrissie?'

'We're making good time. Next stop is Benjamin Mawbray's place.'

CHAPTER 32

Nick carried the portable workbench and led the way up the back stairs to the attic bedroom. Behind him Dave brought a toolbox and rechargeable drill. The Willows van was parked outside, loaded with the wood for the wardrobe frame and cut to length, along with the side, top, back and base panels already made by Nick in the workshop. There was a lot to carry in and the foreman had assigned Dave to help, as promised.

It was Wednesday and the first time Nick had returned to St Williams Road since his final measure-up on Friday morning. It seemed like weeks ago, but in reality it had barely been five days. He supposed working late in the workshop on the Art Deco wardrobe on Monday and Tuesday had somehow stretched his perception of time.

'Busy weekend?' Dave asked as he trailed back down the stairs to collect more from the van.

'You bet,' Nick replied. He could have added it was more like a rollercoaster, a blur of Hepplewhite chairs, band practice and the gig in Woodbridge.

'How's that girl shaping up, the one you said was joining your band? A saxophone player, didn't you say?'

'She's great,' Nick replied. He could have added she was more than great, but it wasn't the moment. Dave would only want to know details and some things were better kept private. Suffice it to say she was on his mind, not as a confusing negative influence but in an exciting way.

'I heard the body count was rising – you know, the local murders, first that John Camm bloke and now a woman in a ditch,' Dave said, letting his voice drift and obviously trying a different tack.

'Not now, Dave,' Nick said.

He knew Dave was fishing, something to chew over during the day, but Nick had already heard plenty enough supposition and theory mooted by Chrissie while he'd worked on the Hepplewhite-style chairs. He didn't need to visit the subject again.

'Mind you,' he said relenting as he watched Dave's face, 'they think the two deaths are linked, John Camm and Mandy Rokin. She was the woman in the ditch.'

The talk died for a moment as they walked past Mr Stukeley's open office door.

'Ah Nick, I'm glad I've caught you,' Mr Stukeley called.

They both stopped, Nick turning and looking through the doorway, Dave hovering near his shoulder.

Now what, he wondered. 'I haven't forgotten, Mr Stukeley. I was going to bring the wardrobe doors and fit the *rising sun* panels here. I thought they'd be less likely to get damaged. You said they were fragile when we spoke on the phone about the measurements.'

'No, it wasn't about that. I wanted to tell you something before I forgot. That business you were talking about last Friday.'

Nick felt Dave edging closer.

'Well, I asked around, made a few enquiries and it seems there are some interesting clocks suddenly appearing on the market. The word is they were stolen about forty-five years ago from a clock restorer in Norwich. Part of the haul was never recovered at the time.'

'Are you talking about Norfolk wall clocks?' Dave butted in.

'Oh hello, I didn't realise you were there as well. Are you interested in clocks too?'

'More the history around clocks, right Dave?' Nick answered for him.

'Well yes, I suppose. But,' Dave added, 'how can you tell they were stolen?'

'The clock restorer is still alive. He's old but his memory is still intact. Apparently he alerted the police after he spotted one on a selling site. It seems there's been damage, at least to the one he spotted. He thinks it was stored badly and handled roughly.'

'Stored badly? How'd you mean?' Nick asked, intrigued.

'From its casing it looked as if it had lain on its side in the damp. Also there was damage to some of its enamel work.'

'Enamel? It doesn't sound like a typical Norfolk wall clock,' Dave murmured.

'No, but I didn't say it was. It's a small Dutch mantel clock. Originally it came all the way over from Amsterdam.'

'Wow, so?'

'Be careful, that's all.'

A thought struck with a sudden flash of clarity.

'Could they have been buried? I mean buried inside something in the ground?' Nick asked, but there was no answer. Mr Stukeley's eyes were back on his computer screen, seemingly deaf to the world.

Dave grabbed Nick's arm and guided him away from the office and out past the white-gloss bannisters.

'What are you on about, Nick? *Could they have been buried in the ground?* Are you off your head? What will Mr Stukeley read into that? Now come on, we've a wardrobe to build, a job to complete.'

'No seriously, Dave. That digging in Northfield Wood and the story the off-roader bloke told Chrissie. Something, I don't quite see it yet, but something's connecting in my head – and I don't know if it's even possible or how it fits in with anything.'

'Sounds like you took something at that gig you played. Now straighten you head out and let's concentrate on the wardrobe, hey?'

'No, Dave. Chrissie was on about Northfield Wood at the weekend while I was helping out with a pair of Hepplewhite chairs. You weren't there. If you'd heard you'd understand. I-I'm going to let Clive know about the stolen clocks. Then I can let it go. OK?'

'Hepplewhite chairs? You must've had a skinful. Are you sure anything you remember is real?'

'Sorry, Dave. I'm going to make a call.' He pulled his mobile from his jeans.

CHAPTER 33

Matt slumped into the passenger seat as Chrissie reversed the Citroen van out of the parking space at the Rush Green Golf Club.

'Are we takin' the road through Stowupland to Broad Green?' he asked, wondering if he'd spot Maisie. He reckoned she'd likely be waiting to catch a bus into Stowmarket at about this time.

'I think I'll take the long route. There's a shortcut but I don't think I'll find it from this side of the A 14.'

'So is that a yeah we're goin' through Stowupland?'

Usually she was one of the few people he could always understand, but recently he reckoned she'd taken to talking and texting in half sentences, like riddles. 'You OK, Chrissie?' he asked.

'Yes, apart from being stressed out. Why do you ask?'

'Nothin'. No reason.' He relaxed as the van swayed over the potholes. More were appearing in the road since the snow and ice, a death trap on a scooter. His mind drifted as he imagined riding the road on a 125cc Vespa. The man in the scooter shop had said it would be an investment; Matt thought it more of a statement, being on trend, Italian and liberating fun.

'Are you buyin' yourself somethin' for Christmas?' he asked.

'What? For me? No.'

'How about Clive? You buyin' him somethin'?'

'Well yes, of course. I thought I'd get him something for the skiing holiday.'

They lapsed into silence as Chrissie threaded her way through Combs and onto the Stowupland Road. Matt gazed at front doors with holly wreaths, inflatable Santas pegged to handkerchief-sized patches of front turf, outdoor lights slung like icicles along roof eaves, and of course, model reindeer dotted everywhere. He decided it was a sign, time to free Rodolfo. The reindeer couldn't double as a clotheshorse in his bedroom forever. Christmas was in the air.

While Chrissie drove, Matt wrestled with the practicalities. How to strap Rodolfo to the back of his scooter? Would the cane and straw creature fit inside a suitcase? Could he persuade Maisie to agree to wedge the reindeer between them and ride to Stowupland? 'I should've loaded it in the van,' he muttered.

'What?'

'Nothin'.'

Chrissie swung the van off the main road and onto a narrow lane heading towards Broad Green. 'Watch out for a wind pump. If we pass it, we've gone too far. Last time we took a muddy track... ah, this must be it.'

Matt stared at the wild hedge ensnaring the track. It blocked the light and held the dampness. He shivered as they passed giant brambles, the woody stems reaching out from the hedge and brushing the van door. The trail meandered on, narrow and rutted, then turning hard left it opened up to a vista of winter fields. Twenty metres ahead a 1980s L-shaped bungalow blocked the trail, and beyond it a row of huge untamed leylandii cast dark shades of green and held the eye.

'It looks...,' Matt searched for the right word.

'Bleak,' Chrissie finished for him. 'Inside isn't any better either.'

While Chrissie hurried along a short gravelled path to the front door Matt took his time getting out of the van. He thrust a hand into his denim jacket. It was all right, four ten pound notes still nestled in his pocket. He'd reckoned it would be enough, but actually being here and seeing the place was unnerving.

He hadn't been inside many houses, not even Maisie's parents' semi. He'd imagined the Mawbray bungalow would be grander, something more on the lines of the golf clubhouse. This reminded him of his mum's sad bungalow, just larger, more sprawling, but with the same flaking paintwork, rotten windowsills, and dirty expanses of window glass.

He heard voices at the front door and a dog bark from somewhere deep inside the bungalow. He opened the back of the van and started to untie the chairs, all the time going over in his head what he was going to say. Moments later Chrissie appeared by his side.

'OK, let's get these inside for Mr Mawbray,' she said cheerily.

She led the way. They each carried a Hepplewhite-style chair, but Chrissie seemed to make light work of hers, talking to Benjamin as she walked through the hallway to the dining room.

'You've done a good job,' Benjamin said and then coughed, as if talking had loosened the catarrh in his chest.

'It weren't me, I'm just helpin' carryin' stuff today,' Matt puffed. He paused while he caught his breath and sized up the old man. Was it the moment to blurt out his prepared words? If he was right and the man really was selling the retro suitcases, Chrissie's van was outside and freed up for transport. It was a sign.

His confidence surged. 'Are you sellin' *Sampson Mawbray* cases from the 60s?' he asked, cutting straight to the point. He heard Chrissie gasp.

'Matt, you can't–'

'But I've seen 'em for sale on the net.' He turned his attention back to Benjamin. He noticed how the old man's skin seemed to droop from his jaw, but his mouth – was that a scowl he was seeing?

'Are we talking cash?'

'Look, Matt, I don't think this is a good idea,' Chrissie hissed.

'Leave him, Mrs Jax. If he wants to buy an old case and he's got cash on him, I've plenty if he's interested.'

'That's cool, Mr Mawbray. Look, Chrissie. It's a Christmas present for Maisie. It'll be wicked with me Vespa.'

'What? OK, I'll wait in the van, Matt. You've twenty minutes max, and then I'm leaving. And for God's sake don't let him fleece you,' she added under her breath.

'Well, this is turning out to be a very good day,' Benjamin muttered. 'Right then, Matt. It is Matt, isn't it? Now if you'd like to follow me.'

Matt trailed behind the old man into a tired galley kitchen. A black Labrador stood blocking their path.

'Out of my way, Dyson. Come on, Matt. This way,' Benjamin grunted and headed outside through a back door. He let it swing behind him.

'What about the dog? Shouldn't we…?' Matt asked, but Benjamin seemed intent on leading him to the suitcases.

'Dyson'll be fine. Do him good to be outside for a change.'

The black Labrador walked stiffly behind Matt for a few paces, sniffing at his legs and pockets. 'There aint no muffin left,' he whispered to the dog. If there had been a rogue fragment of early morning muffin loose in the folds of his denim jacket, then Matt was pretty sure he'd have fought the dog for it. A muffin was a muffin, after all.

It was further than Matt expected. The dog fell behind as they scrunched along a damp gravel path to join a gritty track cutting between the leylandii. The cold air caught at his throat, and ahead, Benjamin coughed again.

'Hey this is neat,' Matt said when he saw a shabby warehouse-sized unit. 'Is this where you mill down old plastic?' A black Land Rover Defender with a metal cab on the back was parked near a rusting skip.

'Seems we're not alone,' Benjamin murmured, and walked on past it to a factory-style door. 'Come on inside, I keep the cases and memorabilia here.'

Matt felt excitement churn in his stomach. It was colder and danker than outside, but it was the end of his journey. Their footsteps echoed on the concrete floor, and light filtered down through small high windows, almost like ventilation shafts at roof level. The large conveyor belts were stationary, but he could see where they fed into what he guessed were housings for coil-like spinning blades, akin to gigantic metal paper shredders.

'Those are the milling units. First the plastic gets sorted, then shredded and cleaned before being melted into pellets,' Benjamin explained tersely.

'But it aint runnin' at the moment. There aint any workers here. Why's that?'

'You'd have to ask James. He's my son. He's the one in charge. Now, if you're interested in the suitcases, this way.'

It struck Matt as odd. Why all this equipment and yet the place was deserted? An electric motor started in the distance, a kind of churning noise at the far end of the unit. The sound reassured him, it seemed right for the place. He relaxed and followed Benjamin into a storage area with metal stacker shelving lining the walls and metal racks laid out in rows. Boxes, bags of coloured pellets, and tubs of chemicals were loaded high. In the corner and out of the way, the unmistakable outline of suitcases, holdalls, and even a golf bag protruded from the shelves. A faint hint of sewage in the air caught his nose. He reckoned the door at the end of the storage area must lead to a toilet.

'Here they are. Which size were you after?' Benjamin asked, reaching to pull down the suitcases.

'Not that largest one, mate. It's too big for me scooter. I kinda like the blue-grey colour.' He watched as Benjamin laid out a selection of suitcases, his attention riveted.

'Blue-taupe. We called it taupe, not grey. Remember we were in the fancy trade back in those days. What a bloody joke!'

'That one aint weathered well,' Matt said, recognising the stained case with the pitted nickel-plated lock catches and the missing Mawbray nametag. He'd thought it looked pretty minging and depressing on the site photo, but in the dim storeroom light it merely bore a fatigued patina. 'Kinda used and abused,' Matt mumbled.

'What the hell's going on?' a harsh voice boomed.

Benjamin Mawbray spun and jolted in a single electrified movement. Matt's thoughts jumped but his body moved more slowly. In an instant he saw a man three yards away. For a moment he thought it was Benjamin; a younger, larger and un-stooping Benjamin.

'James!' the old man breathed.

'Got it!' Matt yelped. The man was barely forty but he had Benjamin's large nose, heavy brow and small lower jaw.

'Got what? What exactly have you got and who the hell are you?' the man bellowed.

'I got you aint Benjamin. I'm guessin' you're his son, James Mawbray. I-I'm Matt. Hi,' he stammered, the *Hi* coming out like a squeak.

'Did you bring Matt in here, Dad?'

Matt flinched. The cold squeezed his bladder, and the faint whiff of toilets centred his mind. He shouldn't have had that mug of coffee at Chrissie's workshop.

'Sorry - I gotta pee!' he yelped and hurried for the door at the end of the storage unit.

'What the hell are you doing, Dad? I told you to get rid of that suitcase.' James's raging voice carried between the racks. 'This whole bloody mess only started because of you. Can't you just leave it to me? I'm the one who sorts things out. Remember?'

•

Chrissie sat in the Citroen van. What was Matt playing at, she wondered. She hoped to God Clive hadn't taken it into his head to buy her an old Mawbray suitcase for Christmas. It was more likely he'd get her some skiing socks or warm ski under-layers. Of course, silk would be sexy to wear as leggings. Poor Maisie though – why was it that men assumed their girlfriends automatically shared their dreams and hobbies? A retro Italian look? What was Matt thinking?

Something caught her eye. It moved, stopped, moved again.

'Hey, Dyson,' she murmured, recognising the square solid body. She'd forgotten about the Labrador. What was he doing? Had he been shut out?

Without really thinking, Chrissie slipped out of the van and pulled her duffle coat tight around her. 'Hey Dyson,' she called. He moved stiffly back and forth, sniffing the ground, but when he heard her voice he lifted his head. She walked over and gave him a pat and scratched behind his ear. He leaned against her leg.

'So where is everyone, Dyson old fella? Did you think you were included in the suitcase viewing party and now you've been left behind?'

The dog gazed at her with sad brown eyes. She took a few steps along the gravel path towards the backdoor, willing him to follow. He stared at her for a moment, then walked in the opposite direction. 'Hey Dyson,' she called, but he was deaf to his name.

She couldn't just abandon him. Unhurriedly they made their way, he like a slow moving tanker and she impatient as they followed the shingle track between the leylandii to the warehouse-sized unit. She recognised the Land Rover immediately.

'James,' she breathed. 'Now what's he up to?'

The one and only time she'd driven through the site, there'd been little sign of activity. She remembered the rusty skips filled with discarded plastic chairs, bowls and storage crates, but today they were heaped with a load of different plastics. She peered down the side of the unit and spotted a tipper chamber with a conveyor belt feeding a mix of what she guessed must be recent plastic waste into the factory.

Curious, she followed Dyson to the wide factory-style door. She pushed, the door opened silently and they both entered. The air felt noticeably cold and in the distance, an electric engine churned and hummed. She scanned around. Where was everyone? The unit couldn't be running itself. Mildly uneasy, she followed Dyson as he padded across the concrete floor.

Raised voices sprang from somewhere to her left. Dyson must have heard them too and quickened his pace.

'What are you thinking, Dad? You know I went to the wood and dug up the case with the clocks. At least I had the sense to pass them on to a contact to shift. But you? I told you to get rid of the case. Destroy the evidence, not put it on a selling site for the entire world to see.' Something slammed onto the concrete. She froze.

'I was trying to raise cash. Remember? Cash? The thing we don't bloody have.' The tone spiralled into a shriek.

'Oh God,' she breathed, 'James and Benjamin.'

Dyson's head dropped, his tail sank.

'Dyson, stay,' she hissed.

Crash! A suitcase smashed through an open doorway. It bounced onto the concrete; spun into the air. *Wham!* It landed and skidded. Chrissie leaped back. It slid to a halt a yard from her feet.

'What the…?' she breathed.

The case lay open. Exposed lining, a geometric grey pattered-satin almost the colour of the concrete, stared at her, daring her to step closer. Stains disfigured the inside. Rusty watermarks formed strange designs.

'Oh my God. If this is the suitcase, what the hell's happened to Matt?'

•

Matt shivered. It was OK. It was a flushing toilet, small, cramped, no window but not one of those chemical contraptions with a huge reservoir of waste beneath. The smell of sewage was distinct but not overwhelming. He'd been in far worse. He relaxed and for the next few moments he blanked out the shouting and peed.

Crash! The world careered back into his consciousness. For a second it was difficult to locate the sound. *Smash!* There it went again, close by but at the same time faintly distant. For a heartbeat, silence filled the space. Raised voices followed, ricocheting off the other side of the toilet door. He stiffened, his hand paralysed on the flush, and listened.

'It's all because you stole those bloody clocks. The other guy had the sense to lay low, but not you. You were too impatient and where did it get you? I'll tell you Dad, it destroyed your bloody life and ruined ours on the way,' James yelled.

'How'd I know a Land Rover would drive into me, smash my half share? The bloody driver must've set the word about. And that snitch Camm probably planned it all, planned I'd be the scapegoat right from the word go. None of it's my fault!' The voice whined and twisted up half an octave.

'No Dad, but I fixed it for you when he resurfaced and posted his ugly mug, hinting about the stash still buried in the wood. I paid him back, silenced him for good, didn't I?'

'Yeah, but I'm not the only one who's made mistakes, right?'

'And what the hell's that supposed to mean?' Menace oozed from the words.

A knot tightened in Matt's stomach. Silently he checked the toilet lock. It was secure enough, but the door panels looked flimsy. The flush could wait. There was no point in drawing attention to himself. The men might turn on him. He put the lid down on the toilet seat and sat, pulse racing. He always thought more clearly when he was sitting.

CHAPTER 34

Chrissie didn't need to walk deeper into the unit. She'd heard enough. *Get out, get out*, her instinct screamed. She turned, and focussed on the factory door. Outside was safety and sanity. Behind her, James's voice surged abruptly.

Panic kick-started her brain. 'Shite, he's coming out after the suitcase,' she breathed.

One step, two steps, but she'd left it too late. James's voice seemed right behind. A group of plastic barrels were stacked near the door. She dived behind. Oh God, the dog was following her.

'Bloody dog! Go on, get out, Dyson,' James yelled.

She watched through a crack between the barrels. James stood, hands on hips. Dyson slunk to the factory door and nosed it open.

'So now what, James? You run away the moment I mention your mistakes?' Benjamin shouted. He coughed harshly as he followed his son from the store area into the main factory space.

The door and her escape were only a few yards away. So very close. She was pretty sure father and son were too taken with quarrelling to have caught the flash of her camel duffle coat when she'd run for cover a moment earlier. Something held her back now. Did she have time for this? She slipped her mobile from her pocket, flicked off the ringtone and pressed the record option.

'Shut it, Dad. That woman was never part of the plan. She was a mad mum of one of Zak's friends. Nosey cow followed some Sunday afternoon walkers into the wood and found a label from your bloody suitcases. And surprise, surprise - it said Mawbray on it. So what do you think she did? Of course I had to get rid of her.'

'Yeah, but you could have planned it better. You didn't have to choose a ditch only a couple of miles from your own bloody home.'

'That's the whole point, Dad. It wasn't planned. She just appeared, threatening and demanding money. But I've had time to think this one through. I'm going to fix it. Turn our lives around.'

'Fix what? Turn what around?'

'This millstone. So just for once, Dad, do what I tell you, and help, OK?'

'Oh yeah, James? And how's your next bloody master plan going to work?'

'What can you hear?' James said softly, his whole tone and manner changing.

Chrissie froze and held her breath.

'What do you mean, James?'

'Just listen. The shredding machine. I've got one of the belts going. I've been collecting the fine plastic dust from around the shredding and milling units for weeks. We're going to set off a dust explosion and one hell of a fire. We're going to blow the roof off this mausoleum and burn the lot. And then we'll collect the insurance. How's that for a plan, Dad?'

'Bloody brilliant, son. What's a dust explosion?' Benjamin asked as he coughed.

'Oh for God's sake, Dad. But I'll tell you one thing. Those suitcases are going up in the blaze.'

The sea change from combatants to co-conspirators was palpable. It chilled Chrissie as she let her breath go slowly, her head spinning with what she'd heard. The quarrel was over. Their two brains working together were likely to remember Matt had been delivering the Hepplewhite chairs with her and that she might still be out there waiting for him. If discovered, where did she and Matt fit into this master plan? And where the hell was Matt, anyway? Had he wandered back to the van? She fired off a text message to him, *Where are you?* Then to Clive, *Something's going down at Mawbray Plastic Recycling, Broad Green. Send a car.*

She slipped her mobile back in her pocket and considered her options.

'Right Dad, we tip a heap of plastic dust on all the milling and shredding units which are inactive at the moment. We chuck some waste plastic on the conveyor belts so when we switch them on it looks as if we were running normally. Then we're almost ready.'

'To do what?'

'We tip plastic dust on and around the running unit you can hear now. The motors are hot. The dust will billow up and when I throw in a lighted flare, boom - up it goes. A great ball of fire. Then we leave fast, switching on the other conveyor belts and shredders as we go so they shoot dust into the air. The first fireball will ignite them. Boom, boom, boom!'

'And it'll look like the factory was running and it was just an accident waiting to happen?'

'Exactly, Dad.' The excitement in James's voice was scary.

'So where's the plastic dust you've been collecting?'

'In those barrels by the door.'

Chrissie's stomach twisted.

'I'll use the forklift. It'll be easier to move them around and it'll give me some height when I tip the dust out. Whoosh – it'll be nicely airborne. I've got it all worked out.'

'Oh God,' Chrissie murmured. She had to get out. He was about to start the forklift. *Culump!* Barrels rocked. A pair of metal fork-tips invaded her refuge. They inched across the concrete, positioning to catch the bottom rim of the nearest barrel. Instinctively she moved back, ducking sideways, elbowing her shelter. Something tottered above her. *Crash!* The barrel stack fell. Down she went. She was pinned, half under a barrel and tight against the wall

'Who the hell?' James yelled from high above her on the forklift.

She watched through her eyelashes, heart pounding. Benjamin stooped over, his hard angry eyes unblinking, jowls sagging.

'It's Mrs Jax. That lad came with her. They were bringing back my Hepplewhite chairs.'

'My God, I'd forgotten about him. He must still be in the toilet. No leave her Dad, she looks out cold. Go pull some stacking down across the loo door. Block him in. I'll take care of Mrs Jax.'

She heard James laugh. 'After all, it was Mrs Jax who introduced me to dust clouds,' he muttered.

•

Matt closed his eyes and counted as he sat on the toilet lid and waited for the shouting to stop. His ears told him the voices were moving away. He reckoned Benjamin and James were leaving the store area, returning to the body of the factory. If he was right, he'd be safe to come out of the toilet, if he was wrong and it was a trap, then it was curtains for him. He stopped counting and fingered the toilet lock. It moved silently. He held his breath and opened the door a crack.

Ping! A text alert sounded from his pocket.

He clamped his phone close to muffle the sound, then yanked it from his jacket. It was a message from Chrissie. *Where are you?*

But where's she, he wondered. Why couldn't she text something like, *I'm in the van, where are you?* Always half sentences. He weighed it up for a moment, then texted back *Don't leave without me, I'm in the loo* and flicked his phone into silent mode.

Half messages – they were as much use as being only part of a comic-strip hero.

'Mezzo Super Ero.' He rolled the Italian words quietly around his tongue. He liked the Italian inflection. MSE was mega cool. He let his mind drift for a moment. Still in MSE mode he stood up and eased the toilet door gently open. All clear. He slipped out and closed it silently behind him. No flush for an MSE.

Benjamin's and James's voices drifted through the doorway from the main factory space. Excitement more than anger floated on the air. He relaxed, his attention now fully engaged with the Sampson Mawbray suitcases from the 60s. It had, after all been his mission. He bent to catch hold of the long strap-handle encircling the curve of a D-shaped vanity / overnight case.

Culump! Crash! Sudden impacts sounded from the main factory space. What the fraggin' hell was going on out there? Fear punched his abdomen, brought him back to Earth.

'OK, OK. I'm going as fast as I can,' Benjamin rasped, then coughed, as his voice neared the entrance to the store area.

Matt grabbed the vanity case and dodged behind the rows of freestanding racking. He clasped the blue-taupe case to his chest, worst case scenario - it was a shield.

He watched as Benjamin hurried through the store area and pushed and strained at racking near the toilet door. Heavy plastic tubs toppled, boxes of extractor fan filters shed their contents. The racking rocked, groaned and finally tipped. Down it clattered over toilet rolls, suitcases and plastic pellets. It landed, wedged across the toilet door. Benjamin bent, hands on knees and breathed hard.

'Hurry up, Dad. We need to get on with this,' James shouted from out in the main factory.

'Yeah, yeah, I'm coming,' Benjamin wheezed.

What the bloggin' hell was that about, Matt wondered. And then he understood. Benjamin thought he was still in the loo. He shrank against the wall and down onto the floor, the vanity case open and covering him.

•

Chrissie lay still, held her breath and played dead. She was gambling James didn't have enough time to waste on her and that he'd decide he had more pressing work. The sooner the recycling plant went up in a dust cloud fire the better for him. That way she'd still be unconscious or dead and Matt still trapped in the loo, both appearing to perish as collateral damage in the explosive inferno.

She lay motionless, one ear pressed against the cold floor, one arm pinned under her. The forklift truck moved away. She heard it through the concrete. Thank God. Her gamble was paying off.

While Benjamin and James worked to set the scene, Chrissie worked to free her legs from under the barrel. It was heavier than she'd imagined, and she couldn't risk drawing attention to the struggle. She forced herself to concentrate on the moment; no point agonising about what might happen in five or ten minutes. Her future depended on now. As always, action helped. Panic eased as she squirmed and wriggled and shifted the barrel across her legs.

Benjamin coughed and wheezed as flurries of fine plastic dust shot into the air each time the barrels were emptied onto the inactive machines.

'OK, Dad. We're set,' James yelled. 'Now position yourself with your hand on the power switches on the machine next to this one. I've only this last load of dust to tip on the moving belt and working shredder. When I throw the flare into my dust cloud here, flick your switches on and set your belt and shredder going. I'll grab you and we'll work our way out of here, turning on the machines in sequence as we go. Do you understand?'

'Are you sure this is going to work, James? I need to catch my breath, and a second or two to steady my nerves.'

'Oh my God,' Chrissie breathed as she lifted her head a fraction.

Direct in her eye line Benjamin thrust his hand into his pocket, pulled out a cigarette stub, put it between his lips and flicked a lighter.

'No, Dad,' James shrieked.

'Take fraggin' cover,' a voice screamed. As if out of nowhere, Matt hurtled from the store area. A bearded force barrelled across the factory floor, a Mawbray vanity case slung round his neck and bouncing on his back. For an instant he seemed to drop as he grabbed the plastic handle of the stained Mawbray case left spread-eagled across the floor. He rose again and ran towards the factory door.

Chrissie seized the moment. She freed her arm and pushed the barrel the last few inches off her legs. Up she hobbled. A whirlwind of blue-taupe spun past. She reached out, her hand catching the lid of the flapping case. She was jerked into a sprint. Five leaping paces and she crashed out though the factory door behind Matt.

They landed in a heap outside. 'Oh my God, has it gone up?' Chrissie yelled.

'What, cos of that cigarette? Nah, the cloud weren't dense enough where the old man were standin',' Matt puffed. 'You know I done loads of readin' 'bout dust clouds?'

'Cocoa dust, right? Are you OK?' The relief and banality of the words cracked her poise. Tears coursed her face. She rubbed her nose, hiding her eyes behind her sleeve.

She never heard Matt's answer. A police car swerved across the forecourt.

'Come on,' she muttered, 'we've some explaining to do. No don't go inside,' she called to the policeman getting out of the car. 'There's a dust cloud in there.'

Boom! She felt the shock of the explosion. She closed her eyes and put her hands to her ears.

'Blog Almighty! He really done it. James threw the flare into his dust cloud after all,' Matts screamed, shaking her shoulder to get her full attention. 'He must've got the dust density spot-on over the shreddin' machine.'

'Good God,' a policeman yelled. 'Hey, there's some people in there.'

She turned to see James stagger out though the factory door, an arm supporting Benjamin, a cigarette butt still between his lips. The flames of the dust fireball were visible metres behind.

Boom! Another explosion ripped through the air.

'Is anyone still in there?' the policeman shouted.

'No, all accounted for,' Chrissie bawled as corrugated metal flew into the air and glass shattered. Yellow flames licked through the high broken windows. The smell of burning plastic soured the air while black smoke mushroomed high above them.

'Get back, get back,' a policeman shouted, while a siren wailed as a second police car arrived.

'You know we wouldn't have stood a chance,' Chrissie whispered. 'The fumes would have choked us if the exploding fireball hadn't got us first.' Rather shakily she pulled her phone from her pocket and pressed Clive's automatic dial number. Then she held her hand against her eyes.

'At least I got a couple of Mawbray cases,' Matt muttered next to her. 'Mais'll be right pleased with these. It were sick the way the old man pushed the rackin' over. It fell on all the best ones.'

'I think the stained one might just turn out to be the best one,' she murmured, and gave him a hug. Something brushed against her knee. 'Hey Dyson, you're OK!'

CHAPTER 35

Nick stood on the stepladder and stretched to reach the dead light just below the top of the Christmas tree.

'I should have noticed it sooner, but I've been so busy getting everything ready. It was working OK yesterday,' Sarah purred.

'No problem. The string of lights came with some spare bulbs,' Nick said, glancing down at her.

'You're so sweet, offering to help like this.' She looked up at him and batted her eyelids.

Strictly speaking, he hadn't offered to change the bulb. She'd asked him. He'd been filling his time before the party, listening to some easy jazz in his attic room above the double garage and trying out the fully serviced Seth Thomas Metronome de Maelzel. It had been restored and calibrated, and he was having fun checking if it ran as "great" as the seller had assured him. Its vintage wood and solid brass trim virtually glowed. It seemed a pity to have to wrap it up. And then ten minutes ago Sarah had knocked on his door and asked for his help.

'It's exciting, isn't it? Christmas only a couple of days away,' she said, the tree lights casting reds, greens and gold across her cheeks and dark hair.

'Best switch them off now I know which bulb I'm changing,' he said, ignoring any innuendo and trying to keep her hands from brushing against his legs. He felt a bit vulnerable being up on the ladder with Sarah on the loose, circling below in party mode with a glass or two already on board. He changed the bulb in double quick time. 'OK, try switching them on again.'

He fixed the light back in position, checked the fairy and robin were safely secured at the very top of the tree, and hurried down from the steps.

'You're looking very festive. I love the red shirt. Have I said already?' she asked, a frown flickering for a moment.

He knew she was angling for a return compliment, but he wasn't in the mood to flirt. Pearl would be arriving shortly. 'Thanks, Sarah. Is there anything else I can do to help?'

'Yes, can you check the balloons are tied to the gate, so people know where to come?'

He was pleased to escape outside into the cold dark of the evening. It had been a crazy ten days, so much going on, so many different emotions. Chrissie and Matt had almost been blown up. He was still getting his head around it. And to think Benjamin had a juvenile record for stealing and selling a load of clocks, and John Camm, had once been apprenticed to a clockmaker. It wasn't a coincidence. Weird how connections forged all those years ago could change your whole life... and death.

Of course Clive had been great. Just seeing how he handled a traumatised Chrissie – well one had to respect him. And Matt? He'd focussed on the side issues. They'd all realised years ago it was how he coped. But imagining a world without Matt? He shivered, then remembered Pearl. Just thinking about her set off a flutter of excitement. He hoped she'd like the metronome. He better get it wrapped.

'Hey, Nick. What are you doing skulking out here?' He recognised Jake's voice immediately.

'Hi! And Jason and Adam, good to see you, mates. Great you made it.' He gave Jake a friendly thump on the shoulder and walked with his musician friends to the main house. The wrapping would have to wait.

Sarah's neighbours and friends arrived in dribs and drabs and quickly tucked into her mince pies and smoked salmon in the large kitchen. Music blared in the dining room and an elderly couple tried to dance the foxtrot to an acid house rhythm. Nick heard someone whisper they were Sarah's parents.

'She must have put something in the Christmas punch,' a couple from the fencing club said, as they passed.

Nick settled in the living room, the wide French windows thrown open onto a conservatory. Sarah had strung Christmas lights under the glass roof, and it could have passed for a magical starry night.

'You must be pleased, Clive. Your big case finished and tied up by Christmas,' Nick said, a beer in one hand and an arm around Pearl. He couldn't help noticing how much younger Clive looked now the case was as good as wound up.

'We haven't found the murder weapon yet. It always helps to have your suspect's DNA all over the weapon,' Clive murmured, his voice barely audible above the music drifting from the dining room.

'I read the first victim was found kinda near a golf course. Was it a ball or club?' Pearl asked.

'Sorry, I should have introduced... this is Pearl. She plays the saxophone, and this is Clive he's–'

'Oh God!' Chrissie moaned, 'How stupid can I be? I've just... it's all just hit me.'

'It's OK, Chrissie,' Clive murmured.

'No, the photos. It'll be on the photo records we keep in the workshop. The oak settle we repaired for James. The damage... well it looked pretty much like how you described the pathologist's findings, only this was something striking wood rather than bone. He must have been practising at home, or it gave him the idea.'

'Really?'

Nick watched as Clive guided Chrissie into the conservatory. Now why did he have a feeling Chrissie was about to provide some more key evidence for the prosecution?

'What's that kinda smile for, Nick?' Pearl asked.

'Nothing, nothing important. Hey, Matt and Maisie are over there. What the hell is he wearing now?'

Matt approached, *M S E* emblazoned in bold letters across his sweatshirt.

'What the hell does MSE stand for? Maintenance Scheduling Effectiveness? Or are you changing course, an MS in Education or Economics, Matt?'

'Nah, it's obvious aint it? Mezzo Super Ero.'

'Yeah, but it's still economics aint it, Matt?' Maisie squealed, and turned to face Nick, 'It's about Super Euros. They're big coins, right? And you know he's got a real big heart on him? He got me some cool cases. Real retro. To go with a Vespa.'

'Yeah but scammin' hell, Mais, the police've taken them as evidence.'

'But it won't half be special when you get'em back,' Maisie yelped.

Nick laughed. 'Matt likes all things Italian,' he whispered to Pearl. 'He even works for an Italian firm, don't you, Matt? Balcon and Mora.'

'The name kinda sounds more Spanish than Italian,' Pearl whispered.

'What's that?' The words echoed from the hallway, a Sarah-type bellow as Matt also mouthed the words *what, Spanish?*

They turned and hurried into the hall. Sarah stood staring and pointing up at the Christmas tree. What was all the fuss about? Then he spotted it. He'd seen it before in the White Hart when Matt came back from the Bury St Edmunds Christmas Fayre. A substantial straw and cane reindeer with festive red ribbons around its neck was wedged across the rudimentary top branches, bending and distorting the willowy upper trunk.

'Oh no, I should have put the stepladder away,' Nick breathed.

The end.

Made in the USA
Columbia, SC
25 October 2017